THE FIX

By
Robert White

First published in the UK 24/12/13 by Robert White
Copyright @ Robert White 2014
Robert White has asserted his rights under the Copyright and Patents Act 1988 to
be identified as the author of this work.

Acknowledgements

I spent fifteen years of my life as a police officer, five as a member of a tactical firearms team. After leaving the Service I spent four years working in the Middle East and during that time I had the pleasure of meeting and working with several retired members of Her Majesty's Special Forces.

One evening, sitting in an Abu Dhabi bar, I was having a quiet beer with two such ex-servicemen I had grown to know quite well. Casually, one broached the subject of a job offer. They needed a third man to complete a team who were to collect a guy from Afghanistan and deliver him across the border to Pakistan. The job was worth several thousand pounds each and would last three days. I was extremely flattered to be asked.

I knew my two friends would be soldiers until they took their last breath. Even then, in their mid-forties, they missed the adrenalin rush only that level of danger could bring.

Personally, I didn't feel qualified enough to join them and turned down the offer, something incidentally, I have regretted ever since.

I would like to say a big thank-you to those two men, who, with their many late night tales of war and adventure, inspired me to write this work.

"Oh yeah, life goes on, long after the thrill of living is gone."
John Cougar

Also by Robert White

Dirty
Unrest
The Fire
Shoot Don't Shoot
It's Grim Up North

Rick Fuller's Story:

<u>Hereford 1996</u>

To a small-time street dealer, an ounce of cocaine costs around seven hundred pounds. That's twenty-eight grams of relatively pure Bolivian marching powder. He then cuts it with anything ranging from bicarbonate to aspirin. This leaves him with around fifty single-gram wraps to sell at fifty-plus pounds a pop.

If he survives long enough, he repeats this process every week and ends up with a business venture to rival most corner shops.

And you wonder why the kids of today sell drugs?

Barry McGovern born, New Year's Day 1975, and BMW 5 Series owner, was such a small time dealer.

His family had moved from the religiously bigoted west of Scotland to the almost psychotic sectarianism that was Northern Ireland in 1991. They had done so, to get away from the violence and drug culture of Paisley. Unfortunately for them it hadn't worked. Barry had already learned the value of dealing cannabis resin and Ecstasy as a fourteen year-old, running for bigger lads around his shit-hole estate in Scotland. Once he'd moved to Ireland he was introduced to the relatively high class world of cocaine and heroin.

Designer clothes and fast cars replaced the catalogue shop and the local bus service. Barry was heading for the big time.

Until he fucked up, of course.

Unfortunately for Barry, he had been caught selling a wrap of coke to an undercover RUC officer. He'd been roughed up somewhat and had his grubby flat in The Falls turned over.

There, the cops found an ounce block of coke, twenty other cut wraps, scales and a brand spanking new, American police issue Taser gun.

Things didn't look good for Barry. Two to five years in a nasty adult prison beckoned, where a nice, young, smooth-skinned youth would be overly popular with the temporarily homosexually inclined prison community.

A further twelve hours of punishment from the local drug squad had Barry squealing like the proverbial.

Naming your supplier is a common way to get yourself out of trouble, but when the young Mr. McGovern dropped the name of a high ranking PIRA man, the shit really hit the fan.

It had been common knowledge that terrorist organisations were funded by crime for many years. You didn't buy much Semtex with what was stuffed in the collection boxes in the local Catholic clubs on a Saturday night. Prostitution, protection and drugs were the way of the modern terrorist.

I'd always thought it a direct result of young Barry's fair impression of a canary that I was rudely awoken from a very pleasant sleep by my insistent telephone.

How wrong could I be?

I gently removed my arm from around my wife Cathy and held the receiver to my ear. It was the Head Shed.

The fact that I had just returned from a three-month stint in Bosnia was of no consequence.

It was what I did.

I showered and changed into clean Levis and a sweatshirt. I didn't shave and I'd not yet visited the barber since my stint in the former Yugoslavia, and still sported collar-length hair which I hated. The hair and the scruffy beard were standard operating procedure for people in my game on foreign soil. It helped me to blend in with the locals. I'd also perfected the Northern Irish accent over the years. My own South London English would have got me kneecapped where I was headed.

I kissed a very sleepy Cathy goodbye, picked up my carry-on bag and closed the door quietly behind me.

It took me twenty-five minutes of steady driving to get me to my base where I was briefed by the CO in the presence of a very quiet suit. I wasn't introduced. He didn't speak, simply sat behind his Ray-Ban sunglasses and toyed with the zipper on his equally expensive attaché case. He had blond hair and reminded me of a Jehovah's Witness.

If I were a betting man I would have guessed at CIA.

Like I say, I wasn't introduced and it wasn't my problem. Within an hour I had boarded a Hercules and was being bounced around in some very nasty weather over the Irish Sea. I was collected from the airfield by a pair of DET guys driving a seemingly knackered Vauxhall. They knew better than to make small-talk, and within twenty minutes we were waved through security at a secure RUC Station within spitting distance of the Falls Road.

My chosen CTR (Close Target Reconnaissance) team were already there, with the exception of my surveillance man who was already on plot and sending information via secure comms. The CO wanted a covert entry to the house of an unnamed IRA operative. The contents of a particular safe were to be removed and said contents delivered to a DLB (Dead Letter Box). We were to enter and leave without any sign of force.

This wasn't an unusual request. We had done several CTR's on suspected addresses over the years. Normally we would have received information that a timing device or some such piece of kit was hidden in a PIRA safe house. We would complete a covert entry and either steal it, or better still, booby-trap it so when the brave boys set the thing, it didn't work, or blew the fuckers up.

The latter being the best case scenario.

The most important part was the suspect could never know his house had been entered.

The only unusual part of this particular job was the DLB. Why, in this case, we had to drop the booty and leave it to be collected by some other faces, we didn't know. We didn't ask either.

As the officer in charge I was to be the MOE (Method of Entry) man. I had been trained to open just about any lock or safe on the planet, by the best in the world. Her Majesty's Special Air Service. Des, my trusted mate, had been dug in for the last twelve hrs some three hundred meters from the target premises. He was probably piss wet through and freezing, as Ireland was not the warmest, or driest mid-February, but his information was invaluable to the team. His covert comms had been typed into a briefing note and together with some low level aerial shots provided by some brave, or crazy, DET guy hanging out of a helicopter, I had a pretty good picture of the target premises. A board behind me displayed all the info.

This was a four-man op. Des, me, Jimmy 'Two Times' Smith and Dave 'The Butcher' Stanley. Jimmy was named after the character in the film *Goodfellows*, as he repeated himself whenever he spoke, although that was a rare event with Jimmy as he felt at a disadvantage. The thing about Jimmy was, he didn't like to talk, he just liked to get the job done, nice and quiet, which was just fine by me.

Dave 'The Butcher' Stanley's nickname came as a result of the Falklands War. He'd been one of the Paras found with Argentinean ears in his mess tin after the battle for Goose Green. The Paras had cut them off the dead bodies and saved them as war trophies. Good blokes.

Jimmy would get us to and from the plot and Dave would watch my back. Believe me, I couldn't wish for a better team.

Des's orders were to collect his gear and disappear into the night the second we were clear of the building. We would never meet. No one ever saw Des come and go. He liked it that way and I liked Des. His anonymity kept him alive.

The briefing was pretty simple. The house was an end-terraced property with a car-port and a couple of outbuildings at the back, probably a coal bunker and a shithouse. It was backed by the open land that formed Falls Park. Des was somewhere out in those fields.

The DET boys said the target, some undisclosed IRA face, was a creature of habit, and visited his mother in Andersonstown every Wednesday evening. After which he went for a few pints of Guinness, before returning to base.

It was 1110hrs on Wednesday.

The briefing done, we had a brew, took the piss out of each other for half an hour and set about sorting all the equipment and weapons we would need for the job.

By 1815hrs Des had confirmed that the target, and his wife, had left the property and the coast was clear.

We were loaded into an inconspicuous ten-year-old Sierra. Jimmy Two Times drove to the speed limit and I checked my kit even though I knew it was all there. It was gear that any self-respecting burglar would have been proud of.

Most domestic locks were easy to defeat; the safe would be a bigger issue, but all in all, with the kit I had, I would expect to be in and out within two hours. The contents would then be dropped in the DLB for collection by whoever. Just like whose house it was, it wasn't my business to know.

Butch snored loudly in the front passenger seat and gave out the occasional fart. He hated travelling to jobs and found it boring.

I gave him a nudge twenty minutes away from the target.

He stretched and farted again.

"You fuckin' stink, fuckin' stink, Butch," spat Jimmy, in a rare burst.

"Better out than in," he countered.

Jimmy opened his mouth to speak but thought better of it. His speech impediment prevented him from winning a verbal battle with most men.

I figured Butch wouldn't win so easily if it came to a physical contest. Jimmy was one hard bastard. He came from a large family of Yorkshire farmers; they breed them tough up there. He had hands like granite and an unbelievable pain tolerance level. Some people in the Regiment didn't want to work with Jimmy, because he found communication difficult except, bizarrely, when talking into a radio. Once he hit the pretzel, he could talk as good as the rest of us. He just wasn't too clever face to face. He made up for all of it in my book. He was as brave as a lion.

There was an uneasy silence until it was time to kit up. We parked up a safe distance from the target and set about sticking covert comms to each other with gaffer tape.

Jimmy was going to park up within sight of the front of the house. He would keep watch and give us the nod, via radio of course, if any unwelcome visitors turned up. Des had the back covered and would know if O'Donnell's car returned unexpectedly.

Butch and I planned to enter through the back door. According to the intelligence, the safe was against the wall in the back kitchen. The only info on the safe had come from young Jimmy, the unfortunate street dealer. All he knew was that it was green-coloured and had a single keyhole rather than a combination lock.

Piece of piss.

Once we had removed the contents. Jimmy would drive us to the DLB.

A dead letter box was basically a safe place to drop off the documents or whatever, where they could be collected anonymously by whoever.

At exactly 2000hrs, Butch and I were leaning against the target premises back wall in total shadow. Butch had cleared both outbuildings, to ensure there were no nasty surprises behind us as we worked.

I had a quick look at the mortice lock on the back door with a mini Maglite and nearly burst into laughter. The fucking door was unlocked and on the latch.

These PIRA guys never ceased to amaze.

Before we opened the door, we checked the whole frame for any wires or fine string. It wouldn't have been the first time an open Irish door was a booby-trap.

It was clear.

In total silence I lifted the latch and we were in. I found we could work with just the ambient light from a very clear and crisp February moon, so I pushed my Maglite into my overalls pocket. The small parlour-cum-kitchen was cluttered with all manner of pots and crockery. Piles of old newspapers were stacked on every kitchen chair. The place smelled of boiled ham.

Butch was in a crouch by the back door; his Beretta pointed outward into the night, ready to give any nosey Paddy the good news.

Exactly as described, the ancient safe sat under a pile of washing in the corner of the room. It must have hailed from the 1930s. The type of lock used was simple to defeat, but before I removed any kit from my satchel, I did a quick scan of the room. It was important not to disturb a single item in any search.

If I had to lift the washing from the safe, it had to go back in exactly the same order. The CO was insistent, this was covert.

I looked left and right, making mental notes of the position of every item in the room, and then, I saw it.

It couldn't be.

A single large brass key dangled from a hook over the top of the Aga.

Butch had seen it too and made a circular motion with his forefinger pointed to his temple. As soon as I picked up the key I knew what it was for. I gently moved the clean-smelling washing from the top of the safe, placing it on the floor next to me.

I pushed the key into its slot and held my breath. The lock was well oiled and the mechanism turned with ease. The door opened with a creak and several pounds of pure, uncut cocaine greeted me.

Even I couldn't prevent myself from letting out a low whistle.

Probably more important than the charlie, was a pale blue school exercise book with a Biro clipped neatly to the front cover, which sat on top of the drug.

I loaded the whole of the safe's contents into a black plastic bag and stuffed it all inside my satchel.

Then I gently closed the safe door and returned the key to its hook over the ancient fireplace with my gloved hand.

Next I carefully rested the pile of ironing back on top of the old green safe and checked I hadn't left any kit behind. As I backed out of the small kitchen I swept the floor with my Maglite.

No footprints, no drama.

I tapped my covert comms pretzel twice to signal Jimmy Two Times and Des that we were good to go. The night was so still I heard the old Ford Sierra kick into life at the far end of the terrace. Des was out there somewhere. I knew that to be the case, but didn't hear or see any movement.

Moments later Jimmy was driving Butch and me to the DLB. The atmosphere in the car was just short of euphoric.

"Fuckin' hell, boss," chirped Butch. "I've seen it all now. Someone will be in the shit when they find out all that gear has been nicked without any effort at all."

It was weird, but what the fuck did we care? We had about another fifteen miles to the DLB. Once the drop was done, we were on our way home, all safe.

I could see Jimmy's eyes in the rear view mirror, flashing on and off as each streetlamp we passed illuminated his gaze. He fought with his demons. Finally he spoke.

"Funny job this one, boss, this one, funny like."

"True, Jimmy, but it isn't our worry now."

The streetlamps disappeared as we entered country again. His large round face was illuminated by the Sierra's instruments, his eyes screwed up, each word agony.

"True, but I don't like nicking drugs, boss, nicking drugs. Bad news that is, and dropping 'em."

I had the same feelings, but I couldn't let the lads see my disquiet. This was a Regiment operation, sanctioned by the Head Shed.

"None of our business, Jimmy; 'H' gives the orders; we just do the job, mate."

Jimmy fell silent and Butch nodded in agreement. I had to admit, I didn't like this one. I didn't like quiet men in designer suits in on my briefing, and I really didn't like moving tens of thousands of pounds' worth of cocaine across Ireland, just to drop it in the lap of an unseen recipient.

My unease got worse the closer we got to the DLB.

The site that had been selected was a Ford Transit van, parked at the rear of a small industrial park.

I had memorised the registration number. I needn't have bothered.

There was one road in and out. All the units were lock-up premises. Each had roller shutters plastered with UVF graffiti. The transit was the only vehicle there. No one with any sense at all would leave their car out in this area, so I guessed our baggage handler would be on plot watching the drop.

One slack piece of security was enough for one night.

We pulled alongside the van. I got out and scanned the street for life. Butch jumped out with me, Beretta at the ready. He wasn't a big guy. He had the build of a terrier, wire framed, maybe twelve stone. He had a scar along the right of his face that had taken a hundred and twenty stitches, inflicted by a machete-wielding Sudanese freedom fighter.

Despite the horrific injury he took the weapon from the guy and gutted him like a fish.

I was glad Butch was on my side.

The street was silent. I pulled on latex gloves, leaned into the car and picked out the black plastic bag containing the charlie and the book.

I took the six strides to the Transit, lifted the tailgate and dropped the lot inside.

I nodded to Butch.

"Let's fuck off, mate."

Jimmy spun the motor around and we both jumped in. We were about to reach the T-junction and turn right toward home. I felt the bile rise in my gut. This just didn't sit right. Jimmy knew it, Butch knew it.

I tapped Jimmy on the shoulder.

"Drop me here. Do a drive by in twenty and every twenty for the next hour. If I don't show, get yourselves back to the RV, I'll see you there."

Jimmy just nodded, Butch went for his door handle, but I gave him the look.

"I'll do this bit myself, Butch."

He shrugged his shoulders, resigned to driving up and down for the next hour. He was pissed off, I could tell.

"No worries, boss."

I lifted a pair of NV (night vision) binos from my satchel and pulled my balaclava down over my face.

I stepped out, gave the guys a quick 'thumbs up' and closed the door.

As the Sierra sped away I dropped to a crouch and hugged the wall of the first building that formed the industrial estate.

To my left there was a small wooded area that seemed to run all the way around the units. There had been no time to plan but I figured that I would be able to get good eyes on the Transit from the edge of the wood. I ensured that none of my kit was loose or going to fall out of any pockets of my overalls. Silence was the order of the day.

Just for good measure I checked that my Smith and Wesson SLP was cocked with the safety on. Happy, I trod my way in the general direction of the DLB. It had, of course, entered my mind that the collectors would have viewed the drop from the very woodland I was about to enter, so I had my best eyes and ears on. The hundred meters took me fifteen minutes.

I could feel sweat drop from my neck and dribble down my spine. Eventually I saw the streetlights that shone a pool of sodium over the DLB. I wouldn't need the NVs, I could see everything I needed to see with my naked eye.

Why I had returned to see the collectors? I will never know. I had been trained all my life to follow orders without question. Was it the ease with which we stole the contents of that old green safe? Was it the fact that we stole drugs rather than explosive devices? Did I think that somehow we were being set up?

Probably all of the above.

How it would change my life, I could never have imagined. I should have just driven off with Jimmy and Butch.

But as I lay on my belly feeling the cold wet Irish rain seep into my black coveralls, a blond suited man carrying an expensive attaché case stood illuminated in the yellow light. In his other hand he held the plastic bag we had dropped minutes earlier. He then handed the bag to a man I knew very well indeed.

Bootle Street Police Station, Manchester 2006.

The big blonde behind the counter was starting to get right up my nose. She sat, bulging out of her grey uniform, safely tucked away behind two inches of bulletproof glass.

Her make-up was caked onto her flabby lined face and looked like it might crack and fall to the floor every time she put on the false smile she saved for each customer in turn. Some of it was ingrained, orange, into the collar of her cheap, white blouse that was straining to contain her more than ample frame and a packet of Dunhill.

I finally made it to the front of the no-hope queue. I'd been surrounded by a mixture of people, some decent souls who had given up precious time to report a car broken into or produce documents, mixed with tagged louts signing for bail and various other miscreants.

Then, of course, there was me. Where did I fit into this smorgasbord of humanity? I'll let you decide.

The orange-faced woman spoke the way she looked. She had a flat northern drawl, common as coal.

"What can I do for you?" She reached to her top pocket and fished for her Dunhill. It was obviously time for her cigarette break. I was an inconvenience and it showed.

I had grown to actually physically dislike people who smoked. To me they are weak with no willpower. They smell.

"I've come to collect my client's car," I said, my attempt at politeness seeming to work on the Civilian Enquiry Assistant.

Police stations are full of people like her these days. I mean a copper once dealt with you, even a sergeant sometimes; someone with a smart uniform and an equally smart haircut, someone with experience of life, who cared for his profession and the public.

Now, I was faced with an overweight, useless blonde who couldn't wait to get away from her post so she could indulge in her habit. What was the country coming to?

The assistant picked up the phone, smiled, and dialled. She looked me up and down and I'm sure she arched her back to accentuate her huge breasts just for my benefit. She made me feel like having a shower.

"What name is it?"

I slid my business card under the glass. She took it, looked me in the face briefly and then, the light came on in her head. I found the process mildly amusing, a mixture of discomfort, fear and loathing etched across her face.

I managed a smile and kept up the polite manner.

"I've written the registration number of the vehicle on the back of the card. I take it that is all the information you need for now?"

She shot me a look that I've recognised often since my change of employment and I knew it would take time. It always did. The authorities liked to inconvenience people in my line of work, even if it was just a little thing like taking an hour to produce the impounded car. Then they would insist I produce the insurance certificate to show that I had the right to drive it legally. I always carried this together with a letter and the registration document from the owner. It was unusual for me to be collecting cars these days. I mean, any of my client's employees could have done this minor task. It was the unfortunate driver of the said vehicle that was my real duty for the evening. Jimmy, currently in the cells, wouldn't be driving any of my client's cars again. He'd been caught with ten grams of my client's cocaine after being stopped by a traffic copper. No one steals from Joel Davies, especially his bugle.

I found a vacant plastic seat and checked for recent chewing-gum deposits before sitting on it. I did my best to relax but police stations made my teeth itch.

A young woman with two small children was sitting opposite me. She'd be no more than twenty years old. Some people have no fucking idea, do they?

I looked at her. She'd probably been told that if she got pregnant there'd be a council house or extra cash off the old King Cole. Either that or she had the misconception that some scally would stick by her if she had a kid by him. Calm him down, make him get a job and stop thieving.

She'd get more joy from the council, that was for sure.

The woman smiled at me. She had a pink mini skirt half way up her backside showing horrible, mottled legs. Her shoes looked like she had played a full Premiership season in them. One of her kids, a little boy in full Manchester United kit walked over to me. He stood and stared. He'd be about three or four. Worse still, he had an inch long strand of green mucus dangling from his left nostril. The mother let out a stupid giggle.

"Come 'ere, Wayne! Leave the man alone."

This has always got my goat. Parents seem unable to understand why childless adults don't fawn at the sight of a toddler or new-born. Just because they themselves have chosen to procreate doesn't mean we all have to oblige, does it?

The boy ignored his mother. She leaned forward and grabbed the kid by the shoulder. Her movement revealed a tattoo on her left breast. It was some kind of flower or butterfly, the kind that every teenage girl seemed to have. It wouldn't have surprised me if she had her navel pierced either. I mean, what is piercing all about? Why does a sensible human being have a lump of tacky jewellery poked through every available flap of skin? I'll laugh my bollocks off when I start to see the first grannies queuing for their pension with a stupid brass ring through their tongue.

The kid was pulled backwards and the girl's voice raised an octave. "Fuckin' sit down when ya told!"

Classy.

She looked over again and resumed her inane posed smile. She had a canine tooth missing which completed the picture. Then, of course, she realised that half her left breast was exposed and pulled at the grubby sleeveless sweater that barely held them in place. I didn't think the embarrassment was faked.

"We're here to see his dad." She nodded at the even grubbier Wayne.

Why should I be interested? What possible need did I have for this information? I wanted my client's car. The recovery of his property was my main concern, that, and to speak to Jimmy one last time. I had already devised my plan of action regarding Jimmy. I'd spent years of my life watching men like him but that's another story. Jimmy would be shitting himself down in the cells. The elation of the coke would have worn off and he would be on a massive downer. He could choose to run, of course. If he did, I'd find him. I always find them. I'd always hated the Jimmys of this world. Useless individuals placed on earth solely to irritate the law-abiding public by being a fat bully. If you were going to be a criminal, at least have some class.

"They locked him up last night." The young woman was still intent on making conversation and I snapped back from thinking how nice it would be to see Jimmy shake.

"He weren't doin' nothing. They're always pickin' on him."

She gaped at me intently. I suppose a good scrub, a trip to a decent dentist, and she wouldn't look too bad. Born on the wrong side of the tracks, she had only one way to go.

"I seen your picture in the paper."

Recent publicity had caused me some problems. Accusations of bribery and jury tampering by some meddling journalist, coupled with some long distance mug shots, had raised my public image slightly in the Manchester area. I didn't care for any publicity. I liked to go about my business quietly.

"You're mistaken, love." My tone was less of a correction, more a statement, more 'mind your own business'. She looked like she'd got the message.

Looking very nervous, she stood and brushed greasy bleached hair from her face. She held out a shaky hand.

"Karen, I'm Karen Wilkinson."

I leaned forward and reluctantly took it. I value my personal space highly. Why do people insist on touching you? I know how that sounds. You're thinking I'm psychotic. What about friendship? Family?

I haven't any family. I never will have, and my one friend left alive by the PIRA is a miserable-faced jock, so why the fuck should I allow anyone to encroach into my personal space? It makes perfect sense to me.

I do, of course, have physical contact, but it is mainly an unpleasant experience for all concerned.

Her hand was clammy. She gave me the impression that it had taken a lot of guts to approach me and she shook slightly. As I held it I noticed track marks on her forearm.

Another Manchester bag head. This particular Karen was probably one of the many skinny prostitutes walking around Piccadilly each night, blowing businessmen between jacking up.

Still, some of the people I've associated with this last ten years probably sold her the smack. It would make me a man of double standards if I were to lambaste the drugs trade. The trade in narcotics has been around as long as Man himself and morals were not my strong point anymore. Wealth was. I made my living collecting debts and settling scores for the drug-dealing elite so I suppose Karen's habit had helped pay for the new D & G overcoat I was wearing. I had to remember that.

"Hello, Karen." I let go of her hand as quickly as possible and pointed to the kid. "How old is Wayne then?"

She seemed to relax a little. "Four, five in March," a pause, "his dad is Stuart Wilkinson. Do you know him?"

This is it, you see? When you're noted for assisting the odd person of dubious character, every two-bit thief thinks or says he knows you. Worse, they expect you to know them.

"No, sweetheart. I've never met him."

"Oh."

She looked disappointed and lapsed into a very welcome silence. I became so bored that I began to read the old wanted posters dotted around the waiting room. Despite their curled up edges and cigarette smoke stained pictures, I still recognised some faces. Some of the guys were inside. The law had done their bit, probably with the help of *Crimewatch UK*, or some super-grass.

Grasses.

I've seen many of those. In my previous employment I used them to my advantage. These days, one of my tasks is to deal with people who may inform on my clients. Informers have a short lifespan in the higher echelons of the drug trade.

My eyes settled on one particular poster. It was a plea for information, a picture of a fresh-faced young woman stared out at me. She was missing and her family had not seen her for two years. She looked like Cathy might have done when seventeen or so.

Finally a young-looking uniform appeared from behind the counter and broke the spell, and I was grateful.

I knew he wouldn't be the last copper I would have to deal with. He would be the document reader, another inconvenience. The 'Jack' or detective would be next. Probably a DI or above, make me feel important, put on a face, fake friendliness maybe.

The uniform must have been a probationer, I mean brand new. He was bricking it more than Karen the bag head.

"May I see the insurance and registration d...documents for the v...vehicle, sir?"

Again, some people in my profession and position enjoy making life difficult for all law enforcement, it's completely counter-productive. One day when I'm out driving in my car I could come across this spotty kid, so I always try to be nice, very nice.

"Certainly, officer, I think you will find everything in order." I handed over the documents from a plastic folder and tried the pleasant approach again.

"Officer, I have been waiting quite some time now. Is there a possibility..?"

"Well, well, well..."

The new voice was the Jack, the detective, the one I knew would come. I had no intention of being nice to this guy though. He wore a dark blue suit, probably Burton's, off the peg special, eighty-nine quid in the sale, all set off with a pair of cheap unpolished shoes. He needed a haircut. When he spoke he needed the same dentist as Karen.

"You still doing Joel Davies's dirty work, pal?" His accent was pure Salford and he tossed his head back as he spoke, the way some men do when they are trying to get one over on you. He was trying the hard case routine. Not a nice way to be greeted, was it?

I raised my voice just enough for the spotty uniform and civilian counter assistant, who had returned from her legal addiction break, to hear. I felt like a broken record.

"I'm here to collect a client's car and speak to the driver. Is that going to happen today? Or do I get to speak to someone with authority and dress sense?"

The Jack was not perturbed by my show; he put me in the same box as any other common criminal. That was a fair one as far as I was concerned. I'll let you decide for yourself too. He continued his hard knock approach.

"Don't think you can speak to our Jimmy 'till we've finished with him. You have no pull in here, mate."

I shrugged and turned away from the bad suit. I was losing patience. Time was money; in my case, a lot of money.

"Just get me the Porsche and be quick about it."

I could feel his hatred behind my back. He muttered something, but coppers can't slag you off these days. Not in public anyhow. It was enough to get my goat and I felt my fists clench. Then he stood very close. I turned and our noses were barely a foot apart. I lowered my voice so only he could hear.

"You think you hate me, don't you? Standing there in your cheap suit and dirty shoes? But you don't understand hate, detective. Not real hate or pain or sorrow. I could teach you, detective, teach you all about it."

I leaned even closer and my voice became a whisper. "How long would it take me to get to your nice cosy home, detective? Do you drive to work? Wife? Kids?"

The Jack was about to snap and punch me.

I took a step away and brought my tone back to normal.

"Just as I thought, detective, you don't understand those things. I could show you all about them but you wouldn't care for the experience." I turned away again, my tone sharp and demanding. "Get me the car."

A full hour later, I stood in the cool, dim, underground police garage. Nestled like a rose between two thorns, was my client's Porsche 911 Carrera. It had Guard's red paint and white leather interior with red pipe. It was eighty thousand pounds of pure unadulterated Joel Davies penis extension. Either side of the German flagship were knackered white police Astras.

The Porsche's private plate was a mistake. I would have mentioned it to my client but he wouldn't listen. He had no taste. The white leather was a big giveaway; the white leather and that stupid number. Anyone with any taste would know a Guard's red 911 has to have black leather trim with cream pipe. Otherwise, it looks like a pimp's car. Well, I suppose that's how he partly bought it. Maybe it did make my client feel bigger downstairs when he drove it.

The shaky copper with the skin problem from earlier handed me the keys. "I'll open the garage doors, sir."

I pulled out a fifty-pound note and pushed it into his uniform shirt pocket. "Thank you, constable."

He knew he should complain; he didn't want the money. It was against his principles. It was wrong, illegal, but he was far too scared to say so. I had him. He was on the payroll. I made a note of his collar number in my head. Mine forever.

"What's your name, son?"

'Shaky' was staring at the fifty sticking up from his shirt pocket, at nineteen years old, a full day's pay.

He spoke absently. "Geoff."

I pressed my hand on his shoulder and did a quick scan around the garage. Still alone. I dropped my thumb behind his collarbone and applied pressure. It hurts like hell. I know.

"Geoff. I need to speak to Jimmy Albright." I nodded toward the Porsche. "He was arrested in this car last night. You need to help me speak to Jimmy."

The kid's face contorted with pain. I added a little more pressure. It's not that I enjoy inflicting pain, you understand? It is part of the job. Business, that's all.

"You are going to help me, Geoff, aren't you?"

Geoff nodded at me. He looked very worried.

"He's being released now," he gasped. "He'll be going out the front door in a few minutes."

Pressure released another fifty in the pocket, pain and reward, like training an animal.

"Thanks, Geoff. We will be friends for a long time, me and you."

Geoff stepped away from me. I looked in his eyes. The fear had turned to distaste. He knew he had been taken. It wouldn't be the last time. He wouldn't be a copper long, not enough bottle. You need a certain amount of that to be a copper in Manchester. So, maybe we wouldn't be friends for years to come, he had slipped through the net. Either Greater Manchester needed to tighten its recruitment process or no one wanted the shit job any more.

He hit the 'open' button on the garage door and I fired up the Porsche. They don't make a satisfying noise, do they? I prefer the low growl of a real muscle car and they don't make many these days. British TVRs or Aston Martin, that's me.

I blipped the accelerator and watched the response of the rev counter. The interior smelled like the inside of a whore's handbag. The only thing missing was the fluffy dice. You can't buy taste, eh? A brief squeal of tyres and I was out in the open just in time to see my man Jimmy dropping down the nick steps two at a time. There was a God after all, see?

Jimmy spotted the car straight away. For a moment, he didn't know what to do. I could see it in his face. That most basic of emotions in us all. Fight or flight. The adrenalin hits the bloodstream and there is nothing most people can do to control it. He set himself to run and then relaxed the pose. Relax? Well, it's the wrong word. He sort of, deflated. Have you ever seen a rabbit in a snare? They kick like mad for a while until the snare tightens, then they simply resign themselves to their fate. Lie down and die. Well that was Jimmy. He must have known the minute he came down from the coke he was in the shit. You see, Jimmy had been on an errand for my client. It's fuckin' obvious to anyone Jimmy wasn't a choirboy. He'd been dropping off my client's current girlfriend, (unknown to the relatively new wife), hence the Porsche. If Jimmy had tried to get inside the girl's knickers due to his heightened state he would have been in a lot less shit. Even if the numb nut had told my client's wife about his boss's adultery, he may have survived.

No. Jimmy had been sampling my client's produce without paying for it and that is not recommended.

You see I've worked for the higher end of the criminal fraternity. Not your stupid muscle boys, driving around in their Shoguns, pushing their way to the font of the queue at the local nightclub with a big bag of 'E's' in their pocket.

My clients were, to all intents and purposes, bona fide businessmen. The Porsche was registered to a leasing company. The letter I produced to recover it was from a well-respected legal firm in the City. You were not going to see my client's name anywhere in that business transaction.

Don't get me wrong, the big guys are just as stupid as the Shogun brigade, which is why they needed me. The trouble was they didn't like my fees. I come expensive; so they employed people like big daft Jimmy for the day-to-day muscle stuff and ended up getting fucked over. After a while they finally discovered they had a problem that was costing them serious money and called me.

I pulled the Porsche up alongside matey-boy. He was a big lad, well over six foot two and built with it. He looked a hard man. You know the type, all skinhead and tattoos. Look outside any nightclub on a Friday night in Manchester and you'll see a Jimmy. He held his arms slightly away from his bulky frame and sucked in his gut. He probably thought he looked good, a final attempt at intimidating his pursuer. He looked a proper twat.

"Get in, Jimmy. We're going for a ride."

I was being polite again. I didn't want to have to chase the son of a bitch around town and have to wrestle with him in the public eye. He stalled.

"You know it's for the best, Jimmy."

I was still polite, even if I was losing patience with the halfwit.

He spoke for the first time and nodded toward the nick. "I didn't tell them anything, boss. I'm no grass, like. You know I wouldn't. Mr. Davies knows that too, eh?"

I stepped from the 911 and walked to him. The night air was chilled. There was rain in the air and I wished I'd left my overcoat on. Somewhere in the distance a band was playing and the drums reverberated around the hard surfaces of the street. We stood face to face. Jimmy's eyes were watering.

I checked the street for emerging coppers or the odd civilian, but it was all quiet. Any hope Jimmy had was fading fast.

So the scene was set. Me, in my Paul Smith suit, which I was not going to get dirty, and Dopey in his copy Reebok tracksuit. He must have been a good two inches taller and a good two stone heavier than me.

So why was he so fuckin' scared?

Remember the rabbit?

I looked him straight in the eye. "Get in the fuckin' car, Jimmy."

I saw the look. He was thinking of doing one. He hadn't noticed the syringe concealed in my right palm. With one swift movement I punched it into his groin. The reaction was instantaneous. I'd rehearsed the move repeatedly on a life-size dummy. A doctor friend helped with the medical questions and mapped the exact area I needed to hit. The last thing I wanted was the needle to break and get sonny-boy's blood mixed with mine. That would never do.

The move was text-book and his legs gave way. I had to guide him to the car. By the time I got his frame in the seat, he was unconscious.

I kept a secure lock-up just off Oldham Street that held several cars, a couple of vans, and a big old safe for anything confidential. I left the Porsche in a spare bay and heaved Jimmy into the back of an Escort van. He mumbled something in his drugged haze and farted loudly as I dropped him onto his back.

I drove all the way to Salford with the bastard rolling around and stinking the van out.

Finally we got to his building. Jimmy lived on the sixteenth floor of a council high-rise. It was one of three towers that had been built mid-sixties and then recently renovated at a massive cost to the taxpayer. Unfortunately most of the inhabitants didn't give a monkey's about the place and it was rapidly declining again. The grassed areas around the blocks were patrolled by local boys on BMX bikes wearing the standard uniform of hoodies and Stone Island coats. They did tricks and watched the van pull up, suspicious of anyone they didn't know. There was probably enough firepower hidden under those clothes to start a small war. I just wanted to get in and out. Jimmy himself was coming round. The concoction of opiates was beginning to wear off enough for him to stagger from the van, but he was still stoned enough to be a pussycat. The hoodies took a second glance at him and figured I was giving the fat bastard a lift home. He giggled as we stood in the evil-smelling elevator. The lads had been using it as a toilet since Adam was a lad. I read the graffiti to take my mind off the stench. Apparently Susan from 1202 sucked cocks for a fiver.

Once at his door, I had the unenviable task of rooting in Jimmy's rather nasty tracksuit for his door key. Directly inside the outer door was a second metal gate. This was a security measure popular with drug dealers and designed to prevent unwelcome visitors, namely hairy detectives with warrants. It made me smile. Obviously Jimmy liked the feeling of being behind bars even when he wasn't in prison. I pushed him onto the grubby settee and checked the rest of the flat. We were alone. I was happy. The flat itself was sparse and, like Jimmy, in need of a good scrub. The only items of value appeared to be the absurdly large television with the all singing all dancing satellite receiver, DVD recorder, and a fuck-off sound system.

I noticed Jimmy had only three CDs.

I walked back to the poor sap on the sofa and slapped him around the face hard enough to get his attention.

"You buy this gear with Mr Davies's money, Jimmy?"

Jimmy was still out of the game when it came to answering questions. He blubbered a little and let out another rasping effort. I already knew all the answers anyway so why prolong the agony? Jimmy had a small balcony just off the lounge. A uPVC sliding door led to it. Most tenants let their washing dry on the small outside areas. Some, more house-proud people had flowerboxes filled with seasonal plants. Jimmy's just had a green plastic-coated washing line filled with grotty socks and skids.

I ushered Jimmy to the balcony rail, pulled the syringe from my pocket, and showed it to him. He giggled stupidly.

"Good shit, man."

I wiped the item clean of my prints and gave it to the clown. He took it and attempted to remove the needle guard.

Slowly, he looked up from the needle and straight at me. There, in that moment was the grim realisation of who I was. Where he was, and what was about to happen.

I pushed my right hand between his legs, my left under his chin and the balcony rail hit him in the small of his back. His heavy upper body pivoted him over.

The poor useless sod grabbed at the washing line. I watched him drop. The line and its pegged coalition fluttered above him like the tail of a kite. I followed him all the way down.

It was a mess.

Jimmy was a bad boy but he probably didn't deserve to go flying from sixteen floors up. Maybe he should have been given a second chance by Joel Davies. The trouble is, the drug business is one of 'eat or be eaten'. These people have to be seen to be ruthless. One chink in their armour is seen as weakness. Before they knew it, some other meaner, more ruthless guy would turn up and take the business away from them. Fear was their greatest weapon.

Jimmy stole drugs from his boss, simple as.

Me, I've never used the stuff. It's a mug's game.

Joel Davies was forty-four years old. He started out with a second-hand goods stall on Stockport market when he was sixteen. His three older brothers assisted him by actively burgling various quality homes in and around the city. The stall became an antiques shop. The shop, in turn, became a warehouse exporting artefacts to the USA by the container load.

Five years ago, Joel discovered his older brothers were on the take, creaming off the best quality gear before it hit the company. They met with an unfortunate boating accident in the North Sea, courtesy of yours truly.

His seemingly bona fide antique business made Joel over a million quid a year. That would have been enough for most men. Not Joel. He supplied cocaine, Ecstasy, and cannabis in massive amounts to scally crooks who thought they were 'big time' dealers, and recently opened a lab that manufactured enough amphetamine sulphate to speed up the whole of Greater fuckin' Manchester. The drug business made him three times more than his antiques.

His ruthlessness was matched with great business sense. His big weakness, as I told you earlier, is he paid peanuts and ended up with monkeys, for instance, Jimmy the skydiver.

I sat in his lounge. It was a shrine to overindulgence and bad taste. Joel could tell you the story and value of every quality antique in the place, but nothing fitted. Some huge sideboard that looked every inch of Far Eastern origin dwarfed a splendid Victorian child's chair. It's as if he couldn't decide where to put anything. Having said that, any man who was willing to have all three surviving members of his family topped for stealing from him had to be considered decisive and driven.

Totally fuckin' evil, actually.

I sat in a green wingback leather chair. It was very comfortable but cold to the touch, sort of gentleman's club chic.

He smiled at me as I counted my fee the way a shark looks at a seal cub.

"It's all there I take it?"

"It is."

"Fifteen 'K' is steep for a little shit like Jimmy."

"The risk to me is the same no matter who it is. Besides, he was putting two hundred quid a day up his nose. In a couple of months you'll have broke even."

Joel was a small man, maybe only five foot five or so. He was well-muscled and treated his fitness seriously. His body was almost completely covered with thick black hair. A tuft of it protruded from the neck of his shirt. He swallowed a large shot of Blue Label and the tuft was momentarily dislodged by an equally prominent Adam's apple.

"Why don't you work for me full time?"

I wanted to say that I'd prefer not to spend more than passing moments in the company of a psychopath, but instead I was straight to the point.

"I like being self-employed."

I closed up the holdall with the fifteen in it. It had been delivered in twenties, used, like I asked.

"I have to be going. I'll drop the Porsche in a day or two."

I was about to leave when he gripped me by the forearm. I don't like anyone to touch me. When will these tactile idiots realise not everyone likes to play pat-a-cake? I let it show. He shrugged and released his grip.

"Before you leave I want to show you something."

I have to say I wasn't keen. I had things to do.

We strolled the length of the lounge, a walk in itself, and exited through patio doors big enough to drive a bus through. Joel looked crisp and clean with his fresh white cotton shirt tucked neatly into Diesel chinos. He swaggered like a king into the sunshine. The perfectly landscaped garden was totally ruined by God-awful pot figures and privet hedges cut into animal shapes. Topiary, they call it. Shite I say.

He pointed at a large green bird.

"Works of art, aren't they?"

"Different."

He eyed me suspiciously so I added, "I've never seen a bush like it," and issued a practised laugh.

He got the pun and cracked a smile but I could tell he was unsure if I was taking the piss.

A cobbled path lined with beautiful bedding plants took us to his garage complex. I counted no less than twelve newly painted doors. Joel pulled a remote from his pocket and made a show of pushing button 6 and smiling as a motorised door kicked into life. The expression 'big fuckin' deal' came to mind.

The door open, I was faced with an insult to the sensory gift. Joel puffed out his hairy chest and strained the buttons on his shirt. "Beautiful, isn't she?"

The car was a Lamborghini Diablo. One gull-wing door was open. An elderly man was hoovering the interior, the fuckin' white leather interior. Now why a car manufacturer with the prestige of Lamborghini makes a purple car is baffling to me. Why an individual with all the cash in the world would want to choose that colour is unbelievable. I had the greatest difficulty in hiding my disappointment. In fact I almost burst into fits of laughter when I saw the private reg. LAM 130. Joel had ensured the plate was made with the 1 and the 3 almost touching so it read LAMBO. I wanted to tell him what a proper arse he would look driving the thing, but as I had just taken the sap for a quick fifteen, with more to come, I kept my mouth shut.

"Come and sit in her," Joel said, and stepped forward waving at the old boy to stop his cleaning duties. The cleaner shot me a look that told me he was pissed off with being interrupted.

I slid into the driver's seat and smelled the new car smell, something I have never tired of.

"Go on, fire her up."

I looked at Joel; he was like a kid with a new toy. Who was I to say no? The engine roared into life and I had to say it made a fairly satisfying noise for an Italian car. I turned it off almost immediately and stepped from the car with a little difficulty. I had to lift myself from the seat using my right hand on the roof of the car. The old boy scuttled straight over and wiped my finger-marks from the paintwork. Joel gave him a satisfied look and me a derisory one.

I had just about overloaded on the Diablo when I heard the tell-tale bubble of a V8. A big bore exhaust was attached to it. It was designed to produce that delightful sound that should be bottled and sold as stress relief. I turned toward the noise and saw the Mustang. It was a '67 Shelby GT500 Fastback; rare as rocking horse shit; a pure muscle car. A 428 V8 delivered 355bhp at 5400 rpm and 0 to 60mph in just over six seconds. Imagine that in a car just about to have its fortieth birthday bash. Sadly Shelby fell out with Ford after that model and the car was never the same again for me.

When I was a young soldier I had dreamed of just this car.

It was black, the only colour to have, with two fat white stripes running from bonnet to boot. The black interior had a matching white pipe. She was immaculate, someone had loved this car all its life. Massive white walls surrounded gleaming, non-standard chrome spokes which had replaced the old rostyles. If the car was beautiful the driver was stunning. This girl made Julia Roberts look average. She killed the motor and leaned into the big heavy door. The old car creaked slightly as she alighted. The steady *plink-plink* of the cooling engine announced it had been driven hard.

Her legs appeared first. Bare legs, her feet encased in dark blue leather Gucci sandals. A pure white pleated tennis skirt, trimmed in the same blue as the sandals, briefly revealed a little more thigh than she'd planned and there was the merest hint of white cotton. She wore a figure-hugging white Rock and Republic T-shirt which showed her ample assets, and the change in temperature from car to garden was obvious to see.

Her hair was cropped short. Small spikes of auburn brushed her pale cheeks. Her eyes were the most brilliant blue.

I suddenly realised I was staring. She glanced at me. I sensed no emotion whatsoever, maybe mild displeasure at there being a visitor. Joel hardly noticed her. He was embroiled with the purple mess in the garage. He shouted, without turning to face her.

"Susan! Get us two beers."

Her look of mild displeasure turned to defiant anger. Her accent was European, German? Swiss? It didn't matter. She was understood perfectly.

"Get them yourself, Joel; I have important things to do."

Susan strode purposefully down the gravel path toward the house, turned briefly for what I considered maximum effect, and disappeared behind a green lion.

Joel was riled. His pride hurt. To a man like him, life was cheap, well fifteen grand actually. He curled his lip and pointed at me, an action I had no liking for.

"She knows exactly which side her bread is buttered." He thumbed over his shoulder in her general direction. "Just a little Dutch temperament, that's all, my friend. We'll get our beer."

Dutch, eh? Well I was close. So, this was the elusive wife of Joel Davies. You see it was unusual for me to actually meet my clients. Normally a middleman did the business. I had done several 'contracts' for Joel over the years. We now had an understanding. Both of us liked living so we adhered to the rules. This was only my second invitation to the home. I knew Joel had married some two years earlier. I also knew that his wife had got heavily involved in his international dealings. Exactly how involved I didn't know, but I would make it my business to find out.

I heard the sound of Gucci on gravel and saw Susan walking toward us, two bottles of Heineken in hand. Her breasts jiggled under her T-shirt as she approached. Joel was right. She'd obviously had second thoughts. Davies beamed. His authority was restored.

I took the beer. "Thanks."

No reply. She just stood with the second beer outstretched to Joel. He took it. "You haven't met Susan, have you?"

"No."

"Well you have now." He placed a hairy arm around her shoulders. He had to stretch to do so, he was a good three inches shorter than her. Susan tensed visibly. "Pretty, but petulant isn't she?"

We made eye contact for the first time. I gestured toward the Mustang. "How long have you had the car?"

Her face softened slightly as she addressed me. She smiled, but it didn't reach her eyes. "It was a gift for my birthday, so, just three months."

Joel squeezed her shoulder. This time Susan reciprocated with an arm around Joel's waist but I got the impression it was just for show and she was really as tactile as I was.

"Classic car, eh? Cost me a packet," bragged Davies.

His mobile bleeped in his breast pocket. He was still smiling as he answered it.

We've all witnessed it, now we have the mobile phone revolution; we get to see many more people receive bad news than we used to. Not only that, but we are often forced to hear personal conversations that are of no interest. Joel fitted both scenarios perfectly. His face quickly became a picture of seriousness. He screamed at the messenger, "You have to be fucking joking!" He quickly remembered his position, placed his hand over the mouthpiece and spat, "You two go back to the house. I'll be with you in a minute."

We dutifully obeyed and I walked behind Susan, who remained impassive at Joel's barked command. We reached the massive patio where we were surrounded by the immobile green zoo. I sat on a huge cast-iron painted chair and took a sip of my beer. Susan seemed preoccupied with trying to overhear Joel's telephone call.

I could hear him shouting from where I sat, so it wasn't hard. It seemed something had gone seriously wrong with a boat purchase.

I checked my watch. I had things to do, places to go, and people to see, but I could cope with five minutes of small talk with someone as beautiful as Susan Davies.

"Did you design the garden?"

She broke off from eavesdropping for a moment and smiled knowingly.

"Unusual, isn't it?"

"Not to my taste, I have to say."

"Joel loves it, that's all that matters."

"Are you always so diplomatic?"

She folded herself in the next chair to me and crossed her legs. She looked at me intently, seemingly far more relaxed when not being fondled by Joel. She changed the subject.

"So how long have you worked for my husband?"

"I'm freelance," I corrected.

She leaned forward and I could smell her perfume.

"I see. It's strange we haven't met before. I deal with many of his overseas affairs. Does he pay you well …erm…?" She fished for my name.

"Colletti, Stephen Colletti, and yes, I suppose he does."

She seemed to mull over the information I had given her. "Are you of Italian descent, Mr Colletti?"

I balanced my half empty bottle of lager on the matching cast-iron table, which was the size of a small country.

"You ask a lot of questions, Mrs Davies. I find, in my line of work, anonymity is the best policy. And, if you'll excuse me, now I must be going."

Susan stood. "Of course, you must be a very busy man. Joel speaks very highly of your skills."

I nodded, but thought it a lie. Joel was as secretive as I.

"Thanks for the beer. Please tell Joel I have a pressing engagement."

Susan collected my discarded bottle.

"Have a nice day, Mr Colletti."

"I will. Take care of the Mustang, Mrs Davies."

As I walked down Joel's pale pink gravel drive I mused over what I'd seen of Susan Davies, and if I'd known why she was so keen to collect my empties, I could have saved a lot of people a great deal of grief.

Not many men are keen on shopping with anyone else. That does not mean that men don't enjoy some retail therapy just like our female counterparts. Partners, wives and girlfriends tend to slow down the process, that's all. I feared my obsessive behaviour was slowly isolating me from normal society, although I didn't feel sufficiently in control to stop the process. Although I had become somewhat reclusive, shopping remained one of life's normal pleasures that remained. These days, my idea of a good time is shopping alone, and with someone else's money.

There I was driving along the road with fifteen grand in used twenties and Susan's perfume still in my nostrils.

I hadn't had any sort of serious relationship with a woman for over ten years. Past events had seen to that. Susan Davies didn't make me want to rush into another one either. Beautiful as she was, I got the impression she was a cold fish.

There was also a nagging doubt about her that I couldn't quite fathom.

I put it to the back of my mind. Nothing was going to spoil my fun today.

I was really going to enjoy spending Joel's money.

Another of my newfound obsessions was cars, as you have probably gathered by now, they were very important to me. Cars, clothes, risk and making money were all I craved; that and my own personal space. I liked to be a little different but I wasn't into flash for the sake of it.

I was in my daytime car. A near new Range Rover Sport. It was the supercharged 4.2litre V8 Jaguar powered model, nearly 400bhp of grunt. The latest computer-controlled anti-roll system made the car more suitable for on-road. Brembo four-piston front discs stopped it on a sixpence and I liked it. Good sounds inside too. I'd had a six-speaker Bose system fitted that I could connect an iPod to. Snow Patrol played as I drove. The motor was just under fifty-five grand. The bullet-proofing was another eight. You have to be careful in my job.

I pulled up at Thomas Cook's, where I bought ten grand of U.S. dollars in draft form. The girl in the exchange posed the usual twenty questions and asked for two sets of ID. I had no problem with the new money-laundering legislation. I smiled and filled in the form. I used D.H.L. to post Mr. Colletti's banker's draft for $19,800 to a numbered account in the Cayman Islands. I could then move that by mobile phone later and it would be virtually untraceable.

Now, that left me five grand to play with. Where do you start when you have that kind of money to blow on whatever you want?

After all the years of wearing uniform, I had developed a liking for expensive clothes, so, first to Ralph Lauren. I spotted a nice navy two-piece suit for a meagre nine hundred and fifty quid. When you're six foot tall you need a good tailor, and it fitted like the proverbial glove so I took it. A pair of formal plain toe Oxford shoes by Oliver Sweeney came next a snip at two nine five.

Shirts, I love shirts. As I skipped around town I found classic white cotton by Ermenegildo Zegna at a hundred and twenty quid. A blue gingham check by Alfred Dunhill, eighty-five, a couple of casual shirts at Duck and Cover for under a ton and four ties at Thomas Pink for just two hundred dabs.

That's under two grand! I needed to look at boys toys.

Now I nearly lost my fine mood in the first store. I wanted a new mobile. The little shit in the shop was so full of bollocks about, 'you need this, sir, and you need that, sir, you get more free minutes with this model, sir…" I could gleefully have cut his fuckin' ears off and posted them to his unlucky parents. Did I look like I needed free bloody minutes?

Anyway, a few deep breaths and a quick squeeze of the little fella's arm were enough to return me to my pleasant self. I think the manager was close to calling the cops, until I bought the new BlackBerry phone by Motorola at three hundred quid. I liked it. It didn't spoil the line of my suit.

I knew I had a couple of jobs on the horizon that needed a small video camera so I picked up the new Panasonic DS 33 digital camcorder, incidentally the smallest in the world, from a little camera place just off St Peter's Square.

With just over a grand left to spend, I stopped for coffee in Nero's on Oxford Road and pondered dinner arrangements.

I prefer Nero's to Starbucks, even though they allowed smoking at the rear of the shop. The coffee is better, and it feels like a coffee shop rather than McDonalds.

I was served my skinny latte by an overly camp lad with green hair. He almost hissed like snake when he pronounced his S's delivering the company spiel of, "Any cakes or pastries, sir?"

I gave a, "No thank you."

He added a cheeky, "Sweet enough?" as I handed over my money, which I politely ignored.

I found a comfy, if slightly worn leather armchair by the front window and sat to sip my coffee and read the paper. It was a lovely early summer day, and Nero's windows were folded open. I people watched for a few moments. The mixture of human beings wending their way along Oxford Road on a sunny afternoon was enough to keep most people entertained.

I was jolted back to earth by a well-known voice.

"Stephen? Stephen Colletti?"

I turned to see a thirty-something, rather rotund and balding Greek guy, dressed in a dirty green polo shirt, cheap black trousers and Asda training shoes. He reminded me of Jack Nicholson. He had gas flame blue eyes that sparkled when he spoke. I would wager he was popular with the ladies, despite his lack of hair and growing pot belly.

It wasn't as if Spiros Makris couldn't afford the best, I knew full well he could, he was just a tight bastard.

He didn't wait to be invited to sit opposite me, but simply flopped into the chair. He held out his hand and I took it but quickly returned it to my coffee cup.

"Hello, Spiros."

He looked me up and down.

"You look like a bloody tourist," he said and laughed. As he did so his shoulders heaved up and down in the most comical fashion.

"And you look like a cheapskate forger," I retorted, quiet enough for secrecy.

The reason Mr. Makris knew me by name was he invented it, together with my passport, driving licence, National Insurance and medical card. I even had a medical history and a work record. It was one of four separate identities he had formulated for me over the last eight years or so. I also knew he was relatively wealthy as the four ID's cost me ten grand each and I was not Spiros's only customer by any means.

He had a double espresso in front of him and he grimaced as he took a sip.

"Why do you bother drinking in these bloody Italian shops? Greek coffee is so much better."

He put down the tiny cup and patted me on the knee. I sat back slightly so I'd be out of reach should he try it again. He didn't notice.

"I saw your picture in the paper, Stephen. You need to be more careful, my friend."

I nodded. I had amassed a small fortune over the last few years. Spiros was right; the time was fast approaching for another visit to my Greek forger and a change of scenery.

"Nosey reporters, Spiros, it only made the Manchester paper, nothing to worry about."

I could see he wasn't convinced.

"I saw it. Those Irish bastards have long memories, Stephen, and you know they are still active. They might have changed their name. What? They add 'Real' to the front. They are still bloody IRA, my friend."

Spiros's father had fought in the British Army in WWII. He was decorated with the George Cross for bravery in 1944. He saved the lives of three British sailors off the coast of Corfu after their boat was torpedoed. He entered the water three times under machine gun fire to pull them to safety. He had a wife and four sons, and brought them to England in the early sixties. Spiros opened a small Greek restaurant in Manchester. One son, Kostas, still ran the family business, the other two brothers' imported olive oil. Well, it said 'Olive Oil' on the tin. Of course Spiros had his little side-line in identity theft and manufacture.

I drained my latte and stood.

"I know where you are, Spiros. If the shit hits the fan, I'll come and see you."

"Okay, Stephen, but you be careful, eh?"

I shook his hand briefly. "I will, I will."

I lived on the Docklands in the city of Salford by choice. It was a strange place, full of business types with the odd celeb and a television studio smack in the middle. Yet on its surrounding edges was a Manchester gangland hell-hole. The oldest reported gangland battles were reported in Salford. They started knocking hell out of each other before the Mafia or the Triads were even thought of. Bet you didn't know that one, eh?

Still, I liked it because I got good secure parking for my night-time car, and a gymnasium on the top floor meant I didn't have to pay to sweat with a mixture of steroid-popping bouncers and bimbos with a full face of make-up in some local country club.

My apartment was sparsely furnished. I have always disliked clutter of any kind, but in more recent times it had become just another element of my obsessions. The minimalist look therefore suited my taste. I was lucky enough to obtain my floorboards from a two-hundred-year-old mill that had been demolished to make way for further development. I'd had them professionally sanded and laid throughout the apartment.

Once finished with clear varnish, they were a beautiful honey colour and gave the otherwise characterless rooms a feeling of warmth and history. All the furniture, pictures and electrical appliances were provided by Selfridges' in-house interior designer. It worked for me. So it should, not including a Persian panel rug imported from Turkey for close on eight grand, or two La-Z-Boy armchairs I wanted for my den at a grand each, the interior decoration and furnishings cost me sixty thousand pounds.

There were three bedrooms. One I slept in, one was an office-cum-den for my business (the money had to appear to come from somewhere!) and the last I used as one large walk-in wardrobe. I removed all my purchases from their packaging, folded it all neatly and threw it in the compactor before any traces of paper plastic or pins could fall on the floor and force me to vacuum the whole apartment. I then ironed the shirts and ties, polished the shoes and put them all in the correct place.

After a long shower and a shave, it was time to dress for dinner. I had a date with the rest of that five grand. I sipped my second glass of Chablis. It was refreshing and suited my mood as I wandered around my wardrobe.

When people buy something new most like to wear it that day, I was no different. Therefore, I laid out the Ralf Lauren suit I had bought that afternoon.

I changed my mind twice about the shirt and plumped for a Valentino, powder blue with a button-down collar. A dark red tie from Burberry completed the picture.

I stuck my old SIM card in my new Motorola and I was ready.

On the stroke of eight my security phone buzzed. I drained the last of my wine and killed off the Libertines from the stereo. As I lifted the receiver, a small black and white image appeared on a screen on the phone. I pressed the button to allow my guest entry. She strode straight to the underground parking area, without coming to the flat. I took the lift and arrived to find her leaning against the white paintwork of my prized night car. I'll tell you all about the Aston when we have more time.

Her seemingly endless legs protruded from the briefest red mini dress. I hadn't seen it before but to me it looked like a DKNY. Her black skin shone with the Tisserand oils she always applied. Her shoes were as red as the dress, delicate straps and a four-inch spike, definitely Jimmy Choo. Terribly uncomfortable, but she knew I loved them. She dressed the whole thing up with a very chic charcoal wrap from Giorgio Armani I had bought her for her birthday last year.

"Hello, Tanya." I took her hand. She gently pulled me toward her and kissed me briefly on the mouth.

Without a word, she pulled me closer still and kissed me harder. There seemed urgency to her actions and I had the feeling that, should she want sex there and then, I may not have a choice in the matter.

When it came to Tanya, I was all for going with the flow. After all, she was one of the few people on the planet that I could allow to touch me without feeling physically sick. Fuck the new suit, or the risk of scratching the classic motor. If Tanya wanted to romp over the bonnet, there and then, it was going to happen, and bollocks to the security cameras.

Tanya had other ideas and drew away quickly, teasing me. She was of Jamaican origin. Very tall and slender with fantastic muscle definition. She worked hard at her body. It showed. Her voice was deep, with the thick 'Yardie' street accent when she pleased. "Slow, man, you too eager. It be a long night, you take it easy, baby."

Her natural drawl was never hidden when we were alone. Only once in public did her accent become mid-Surrey and businesslike. She slid her long fingers down the centre of my spine and displayed perfect white teeth.

"I got a surprise for you, sweetie."

I was definitely all ears. I always liked Tanya's surprises. Small round Yoji Yamamoto glasses appeared from a Chloe clutch bag. She slipped them on and virtually purred.

"We goin' in style tonight, man. I got new wheels. I'm driving."

She strode away and I followed. I watched the shimmer of her muscular legs in the half-light. With the movement, I caught a glimpse of a slip under her red dress. She was wearing something underneath. It aroused my curiosity.

Later, when we were alone, I knew I would find out exactly what it was. Patience always was a virtue.

Within a minute we were out of the underground garage and in the cool evening Manchester air. The late sunshine had turned the city crimson. It was my favourite time of day.

Jaguars have the nickname 'The Big Cat'. Recent publicity involving Spice girl types and Manchester United footballers have raised the profile of Jaguar's newer models.

They make good motors, for sure, but the new models just couldn't hold a candle to what was in front of me. Pure unadulterated world class.

The 1962 Series 1 E-Type drop-head sports car in British Racing Green paint gleamed in the fading sun. Top down, black leather interior with cream trim by Connolly, what more could a guy want? I slid into the passenger seat and smelled the Wilton and walnut mixed with summer evening air. Everything was original, even the valve radio. Perfect. As Tanya slipped in next to me and fired her up, I was no longer sure if I was in Salford or heaven.

That sound. Nothing sounds like a Jag.

The drive to Solo's, my favourite restaurant in the city, was a sheer pleasure. Who needs drugs? This was better than coke, speed or 'E'. We parked. Tanya didn't even bother to lock the Jag. She'd left the top down too. No chance of rain. No chance of anyone stealing it either.

Tanya and her two brothers ran all the coke and grass into Moss Side. If you don't already know the area, let me advise you. Don't get caught there after dark. In the late nineties, Manchester got the nickname 'Gunchester', simply due to the level of gun crime in Moss Side. Tanya Richards and her family played no small part in that problem.

No one with any sense at all steals anything from the Yardies. The Jag would be there when we came out.

Solo's had a reputation for fine European cuisine. Situated off Deansgate Lock, it was nestled between Manchester's trendiest bars. Fortunately it was avoided by the local paparazzi, and therefore Manchester's soap stars. A double blessing, if you asked me.

I approved of the service and the fact it was small and personal. They knew me and what I liked. The tables were sufficiently far apart as to observe privacy. Bach filtered through the air.

Each place setting was exquisite and boasted nineteenth-century silverware in a cardinal pattern, the makers mark stamped in the spoon bowl. Cream linen napkins with a damask rose to one corner lay to the left of each diner. Riedel crystal wine glasses completed the classic setting.

Tanya was a vegetarian, so the chef cooked a special entrée and main course for her. She was finishing her pumpkin with red curry as she spoke.

"I have a problem." She wiped her full lips with the linen napkin, "I need you to sort it for me, baby. I can't do it myself; a black girl would stand out too much and cause major drama."

I listened intently. This story sounded profitable and if I was to do as Spiros had suggested earlier, and relocate, I was going to need all the money I could get. She continued, "Our boys sent a courier to the other side of the tracks to collect some very special produce. Not a great deal, five grand's worth, a sample. We never received the gear." Her accent slipped and her tone turned menacing. "The *bombaclat* steal our cash too. Our boy was found yesterday by the law, with his head caved in. He was my cousin." She reached across the table and took my hand. It actually felt good. "Stephen, this has got to be put right."

I felt myself nodding slowly. You see, what Tanya meant by 'the other side of the tracks', was Salford. Not the part where I lived, but the estates where those ancient gangs began their brutal trade. If Moss Side was the black ghetto of Manchester, then Salford was the white. Being black, her chances of recovering her brother's investment and revenging the untimely demise of her cousin, quietly and without fuss, would be near impossible.

Tanya and I were in the same business. The collection and delivery business; she hadn't trained in the military, but I could vouch from experience, she was a very fine operator. We had met several years earlier when we were providing security for two high-flying dealers of different skin colours. Hers was buying, mine selling. When the deal was done they celebrated, we talked and the rest was history as they say. Anyone who has underestimated Tanya due to her sex is probably dead.

Don't get me wrong. We were far from lovers. Like I said, I had been unable to hold down any kind of relationship for a long time. I was married once and that was enough for me. This was fun sex and money. We had the same taste. Neither of us asked questions, it wouldn't have been professional, and for some reason my head had allowed this one woman to become close. The mind is a strange thing, eh? No, I wasn't in love but it was probably as near as I could ever get. Knowing Tanya, it wouldn't do wonders for your life span if you messed with her head. Maybe that was the reason I allowed her to get physically close to me. Maybe I'd just got addicted to danger and dangerous women.

Her eyes took on a cold look as she spoke, "You know if my brothers had their way it would be a bloodbath. They want revenge for our cousin." She softened for a second and stroked my face with a red talon that matched her dress perfectly.

"You know me, I'm into subtlety, baby."

Her expression changed again. "The shit that is responsible thinks he is protected in his little pork chop kingdom. I want you to show him he isn't and that he can't fuck with us."

She picked up a brandy balloon and warmed the liquid with her large hand.

"But I want it so just his boys know we have taken action, not the whole fuckin' world."

A drop of the Rémy dangled from her lip. She recovered it with her tongue, which looked unusually pink against her beautiful coffee skin.

The mixture of her beauty and dangerous persona made her incredibly attractive to me. I felt a stirring sensation in my groin. Still business came first. "It'll cost you fifteen, plus half of what I recover," I said without any emotion.

She took on a look that I knew only too well.

"Do it for ten and I'll let you drive the E-Type to my place."

It was time to go.

I'm not going to tell you the bedroom antics. What I will tell you is, I drove the car and I got my fifteen plus.

Oh, the slip, remember I mentioned the slip under her dress? It was a deep burgundy crochet and lace by Janet Reger. If you wanted one for your wife they're two hundred and twenty-five quid.

Worth every penny.

Hereford 1996

Jimmy Two Times and Butch had collected me on their second pass at the DLB. Neither asked what I'd seen and I didn't mention it. We drove in silence for over two hours and headed straight for the airfield, boarded the already waiting Hercules, and were back in 'H' in time for breakfast and debrief. I'd figured the guy in the suit must have been DEA rather than CIA. The other man was Major Charles Williamson. He ran the whole army ground operation in East Belfast. He had the reputation of getting the job done, but not always by the book. I'd met him on several occasions and didn't care for him. Why he needed to collect the bag personally was beyond me. I put it from my mind. When you are part of any operation, it isn't always necessary to see the big picture. I was also delicate enough not to mention any of it in my briefing notes.

I took the debriefing, Des was still over the water and not present. He was probably digging himself another hole in the freezing Irish countryside, whilst Butch, Jimmy and I drank tea and ate bacon sarnies. Once the Head Shed were happy that the operation had gone off as planned, I took a walk to the office and dropped in a leave request to start with immediate effect.

There was nothing left for me to do other than get home to Cathy and catch up on some much needed kip.

As I pulled into the drive Cathy was in the garden digging out borders. She loved gardening and as we hadn't been in the house long, she was keen to make her mark on it. We had decided to buy, rather than rent. It was an old house and was in need of some major decorative work but was basically sound and within twenty-five minutes' drive of the camp. The old lady who had been the previous owner had let the garden grow wild and the paintwork peel. Cathy and I looked forward to turning it into a family home to be proud of. She wore faded jeans and Wellingtons with a thick Aran knit sweater to keep out the chill of the February wind. As she saw the car, she pushed the spade into the damp earth and left it upright. She strode over, and by the time I got the car door open, she was standing in front of me smiling and beautiful.

Cathy was twenty-four, petite framed, and just over five foot three. She had long raven-coloured hair that was as unruly as her persona and I loved her more than life itself.

"Took your time, didn't you?" She had her hands on her hips and a broad smile on her face. Her usually pale complexion was flushed pink from the mix of her exertions in the garden and the cold wind. I never mentioned work, but she had obviously checked with 'H' that the Herc had landed three hours earlier.

"Well, you have my undivided attention for the next two weeks, I've got some leave."

Cathy let out a little shriek of delight and gripped me around the neck. She looked up into my face; her eyes were like the darkest chocolate. One disobedient strand of hair blew across her face in the breeze and she tried to blow it away with her mouth and failed miserably. I assisted and tucked it behind her ear.

"Kiss me," she said.

I did and we both walked inside. The garden could wait a while. We spent the whole day and the following night in bed. We made love to exhaustion, ate pizza and drank wine.

The following morning I left her to go to the local DIY store and buy paint. It was the last time I saw her alive.

The job for Tanya and the boys was proving far from easy. I'd spent three days sitting on and around the plot; a three-bedroom maisonette built in the 1970s, smack in the heart of shit land. Jimmy the skydiver's flat was a palace compared to this gaff. The makers of *Shameless* would have run a mile.

It took me the first two days to ID the target. I was beginning to think he'd done a runner.

I'd bought a 1987 Golf GTi for the job. It stood me at five hundred quid from a local auction. I paid cash and gave false details. It was disposable at that money. I cleaned it and only ever went near it wearing surgical gloves. Flesh-coloured were the best, they didn't attract any attention. At first glance they were invisible.

The reason this job was difficult was Tanya's specific instruction. She insisted the guy knew why he was getting the good news, but she wanted it done quiet. It had to look like an accident but his mates had to know why he was being taxed and who was collecting. It was all about face and reputation.

This was a dress down job and fed my obsessive compulsive disorder to excess. The car was fine, one of many hot hatches floating around the estate and I had a soft spot for V-dubs as they reminded me of my youth.

I looked younger than my forty-five years, but not young enough to wear baggy fuckin' pants and a hoodie from poxy Top Man.

Still, I looked and felt like a reject from Oasis. I bought cheap jeans that were once black but I boil-washed them with a little bleach to give them that, 'I've had these for too long,' look. A dark blue V-neck sweater from Famous Army Stores with a hole in the elbow covered a plain white T-shirt. The only decent things I had were the latest K Swiss trainers. I could get away with those. Every little shit on the estate seemed to have expensive runners.

I must say though, if I had to wear the Polaroid shades for any longer than the four days I'd allowed for the job, I was sure I'd go blind.

I decided to blag my way into the plot on the pretext of a small buy. There were enough customers using the place. One more wouldn't be unusual. I watched maybe twenty or so sad fucks knock on the door each day. Tanya had given me a brief and I knew the target by name and several of his associates. With that knowledge and a wave of a wad, I had a good chance of getting in the gaff and sorting out the boy.

The target was Alfie Summers. He was just twenty-two. He would not see twenty-three. Remember the Shogun brigade I told you about? This boy was typical. A big daft lad from the heart of Salford with his father in Strangeways for blagging and his mother shoplifting more razor blades than Wilkinson Sword could produce, he hadn't much to lose. He thought he was on the up and up. The best thing that ever happened to him was selling his first bag of grass. Drugs were his escape route. Not frightened to get his hands dirty in the process, he'd done eighteen months in a young offenders' institution for tying a seventy-two-year-old women to her wheelchair while he robbed her of her pension and her TV. Once out, he thought he was a bad lad and went from minor deals in grass to moving five grand's worth of charlie around town each and every night. He was making five hundred quid a day and all the coke he could shake a stick at. He, like all dealers, eventually got greedy. You see this whole job was about a designer drug. Alfie boy had stumbled upon a line of gear, probably an E/amphet mix. He and his cronies had put it on the street and it had been selling like the proverbial hot cakes.

Alfie was making a fortune. By his standards he was king of the hill. He'd even given himself the nickname, The Lieutenant.

Tanya's crew had been told by their runners and muscle that a new product was available on the street and wanted part of the action, so they set up a buy. If the gear was as good as they were told, then they had the capability to obtain the chemical formula and manufacture it themselves. They sent their youngest cousin Vivien, a seventeen-year-old kid with no form, to do the business so Alfie wouldn't suss it was Yardie cash. Worst case scenario for Tanya's crew was that they moved the pills and made a profit.

Problem was, Alfie thought he was fuckin' Al Pacino. He'd convinced himself he was big time. Now anyone with an ounce of sense knows, before you go taking five grand of anyone's cash and smashing their runner's brains out with a house brick, you find out who you're going to upset. It's a dangerous game and Alfie was probably using too much of his own product to know better.

From what I'd seen, there hadn't been a delivery to the house in three days. That would be my cue. Then all this shit would be worth it and I would be on an earner.

In the late afternoon of day four I followed matey boy to his local. It was typical of the area, all spit, sawdust, Prada and Burberry. I sat on a filthy stool, just as I had the day before, and listened to Alfie's inane macho conversation. He was describing his third teenage conquest of the week and I was just about to burst when the dick-spring announced to half the boozer that his new batch of super kick-ass whiz was on its way. It was happy days. I'd started to spend my fifteen before I left the boozer.

I'd been forced to ditch the motor for the final night's observations as it was starting to get attention from the local TWOC boys. I was reduced to lying in the mud on a piece of waste ground where I could see the front door of Alfie's pad undetected. I wasn't my idea of fun, but it wasn't like I hadn't done it all before.

I lay in constant drizzle, obscured by two overgrown bushes of doubtful origin, his whole place was in darkness and my spirits started to sag.

I started to think about Susan. Joel's wife, if you could believe that. There was something about her that made me itch. She played the gangster's moll all too well for my liking.

I checked my watch, half one in the morning.

Finally two very nervous-looking faces arrived on plot with a holdall. At last there was some action and lights appeared on in the house. The boys knocked on the front door and dropped the holdall in the doorway, and our Alfie took it from them. No cash was exchanged, which was a shame, I might have considered rolling the delivery boys too. The two faces fucked off quick sharp into the pissing rain.

So it was time for the dodgy bit. The reason I can make five grand a day.

From what I'd seen the past days, I reckoned Alfie, plus two maybe three others were on the plot. Alfie was a big lad and could be a handful. The others I'd seen enter earlier would be no worry. The only problem could be if people were coming and going out the back door unseen and I ended up with six meat-heads to contend with. I could only watch the front.

I strolled up to the door as cool as you like. My only extra was a black woollen hat that turned nicely into a balaclava.

Knock, knock.

I heard activity. Someone looked through the front door spy-hole. "What d'ya want, mate?"

It was a stoned voice.

I'd heard Alfie call the tabs 'green bombers', so I used the same term. I told the kid I wanted twenty tabs. A hundred quid deal. I showed the cash at the spy and hey presto, he opened the door first time. Not noted for their educational qualifications, speed freaks. The small hallway stank of fags, sweaty feet and hash, no carpet, and two pairs of foul trainers, kicked off and left to fester, were a less than fragrant greeting. The door opener told me to close it behind me and turned his back. He was a kid, seventeen maybe; scrawny with a glue sniffer's mouth. I pulled down the mask, grabbed the kid by the hair and punched a .45 Magnum handgun into the back of his head. I had the youth's undivided attention.

"How many guys are in the house, son?"

He whispered and I could feel him shake.

"Just me an' Alfie, an' Alfie's mate, boss."

I was feeling lucky, this was gonna be just fine.

As I walked into the room, Alfie and Alfie's mate were counting tabs on a coffee table. A perfect little pair they were too.

Alfie was there stripped to the waist showing off some big Celtic tattoo, no shoes or socks, just trackies and a big open gob. His mate looked about the same age. He had the compulsory Burberry baseball cap, an absurdly large gold chain around his neck and the worst case of acne I had ever seen.

Once over the initial shock of my entrance, Alfie wanted to be brave and show his minions what he was made of, but when he saw the Magnum he thought better of it. He was still gobbing it though; his kind couldn't help it.

"You're a fuckin' dead man!" he screamed every ten seconds or so. That and, "Do you know who I am?"

I handed Alfie a bunch of cable ties and, after some gentle persuasion he set about fastening his bezzie mates to two dining chairs whilst telling me how many different ways he was going to kill me. I seated Alfie on a third chair but didn't tie him. I couldn't have marks on his wrists.

Alfie was mouthing off even more about what he was going to do to me. Mainly it involved shooting me in the mouth. The other two were gaining in bottle and made the odd remark.

I felt the need to reassert my authority, pushed the revolver into my left hand and kept it pointed at Alfie. I then removed a knuckleduster from my pocket.

It's an old fashioned item, the knuckleduster, not popular with modern thuggery. I'd had it made for me on holiday in Hong Kong. I thought it an item of beauty.

I punched 17 and Stupid repeatedly and heavily to the head. Each blow with the duster caused severe damage. Alfie was silenced and his mate was sick over his Rockports.

The kid's face looked like a burst sausage. He lolled forward, bleeding badly and unconscious. Only the ties kept him in his seat. I had made my point. Even Alfie was looking worried.

I hit Alfie's mate just once. All fifteen stone of me connected with the bridge of his nose. It exploded and I got blood on my sweater. He was screaming and little sick bubbles had formed at the corners of his mouth. I checked that there was no blood on my K Swiss trainers. I liked them and thought to wear them again.

"You owe the Richards brothers from the Moss five grand," I said. Then I noticed the merest speck of claret on one shoe. I inwardly cursed as I realised I would have to burn them with my other clothes. Alfie had lost the bravery contest. He blubbered about not having the cash. He'd spent it on gear. He could get it by the end of the week.

"I want it now."

I did a quick search of the room with a little verbal help from Alfie and found nearly three grand in cash. I reckoned that there were two-thousand-plus tabs, which fitted neatly into a plastic freezer bag I'd brought with me.

I lifted Alfie's mate's face upward. I looked at his terrified eyes and spoke deliberately.

"I'm going to let you, and your young friend here, go now. Don't come back."

The hand-made duster went in one pocket and I removed a beautiful butterfly knife from my breast. It was a fantastic item with a solid silver casing. I cut them both free. 17 and Stupid fell to the floor. Alfie's mate picked him up. "Sorry, boss, we won't come back, he spluttered," and they staggered toward the front door, shitting themselves.

As they fell toward the front door, I ushered Alfie out of the back door. The three K in cash and ten grand's worth of tabs sat nicely in my pockets. I rolled up my balaclava and started the Golf with Alfie looking very worried in the passenger seat. After all, he wasn't going to ID me.

Manchester's Saddleworth Moor is infamous. The murderers Ian Brady and Myra Hindley buried their child victims there.

The Golf drove quite well for an old shed and I'd enjoyed throwing it around a bit on the country stretches, the Magnum in the door pocket mainly there as a deterrent should my prisoner decide to do something silly. Finally Alfie and I parked in a quiet little spot I'd selected five days ago. I then took my time forcing five of his own green bomber tabs into him. Within twenty minutes his command of the Queen's best was unimpressive.

Alfie was of the opinion, in his tiny brainless head, that he'd been due a kicking and that was that. His big brave face kept up for a while but once we got to tab three, I think he got the message and the pleading started. After the pleading, came the tears.

So there I was again, the point of no return, a mercenary with no war to fight, no uniform to wear and no cause, only victims, designer clothes and piles of cash. This is what I'd become and some days I couldn't bear to look at myself in the mirror.

Fuck it.

I shook myself out of my brief malaise, fished two more tabs out of my pocket and stuffed them into Alfie's mouth. OD level was close. The last one, I just popped in his gob like a sweet. The Magnum was redundant. I manoeuvred him onto the back seat. He muttered quiet gibberish. At least the tears had stopped. I nearly spoiled the whole plan at one point by shooting him in the face, he was blubbering that much.

I stepped out into the cool air and stretched my back. Alfie was incapable of any movement. I lifted the tailgate of the Golf and removed a canvas sack which contained everything I would need to conclude the grisly business. I rigged a hose I'd bought from B&Q to the Golf's exhaust using some gaffer tape, and pushed the business end through an inch of open window. By the time I strolled the ten minutes to my van Alfie Summers was dead.

Now I could point out that Alfie was the type who gets young children hooked on drugs. Moreover, of course, he did beat Tanya's seventeen-year-old cousin to death with a house-brick. Did that excuse my line of work? Did it validate my actions? All I can say to you is I'd lost many hours of sleep over the last ten years, but I wouldn't lose any for Alfie or his kind.

No one would shed a tear for me either.

I pushed the van hard, all the way to my lock-up on Oldham Street. Once I'd parked it in a bay, I lit the gas burner on the internal furnace which heated the unit and destroyed anything incriminating in the process. I pushed all the clothing I had on, including the trainers I liked and latex gloves, into the flames. I dressed in a pair of Levis and a Lacoste polo shirt, dropped the cash and pills into my small safe, locked up and hailed a cab back to my flat. Twenty minutes later I sat on my designer sofa and surfed through meaningless TV channels.

Not for the first time I felt a pang of loneliness.

Around one a.m. I gave up and went to bed. Sleep brought the usual mix of nightmares. Alfie Summers didn't figure.

I'm an early riser. I usually wake at seven-thirty a.m. and have breakfast at eight. Once I have consumed my grapefruit, forty grams of bran cereal, low fat milk and two cups of black coffee, Brazilian fresh ground, not instant rubbish, I am ready to start my day.

I took the lift in my apartment block to the gym which was my first task at ten .am. I ran ten kilometers on the treadmill to warm up. Then weights, chest and triceps alternated with back and biceps exercises. Twenty minutes of abdominal work and two thousand meters on the rower to finish. A shower, shit and a shave (not necessarily in that order) and the day was mine.

The bad dreams of the previous night behind me, I read the daily papers in peace. Apparently there were two unfortunate souls, who due to drug abuse had taken their own lives, the first by throwing himself from a sixteenth floor balcony, the second, by a mixture of carbon-monoxide poisoning and a drug overdose.

A picture of Jimmy's body covered with a tarpaulin and a shot of the GTi, with the hose still attached, sat at the top of the articles. The headline, DRUGS PUSH PUSHERS TO SUICIDE, slapped you in the face. I wonder who'd thought that little gem up?

Of course, every two-bit grass in Salford would be telling the law how these two deaths were really underworld hits. The Jacks, in turn, would be telling their snouts to stop using so much bugle.

The people that mattered knew the truth.

Tanya had already been on the phone. My fee had been deposited by code number direct to an account in the Isle of Man. I'd move it later. She laughed at the suggestion that she should sell me the Jag. She'd come around.

Now don't go thinking that I went around knocking off people every week. This had just been a busy, and I might add, very profitable time. By the time I'd collected what was in my lock-up, I'd have banked thirty-five thousand pounds in just under six days. Not bad work.

With that in mind, it had been some time since I had a break. You know, even people in my job needed a holiday.

I flicked through the usual holiday web pages on my laptop, unable to decide where to go, but knowing I wanted to go somewhere, recharge my batteries and feel some sun on my back.

I gave up and clicked on the British Airways site. Within a couple of minutes I had booked a first class ticket to Barcelona, leaving in four hours.

I needed to pack.

I didn't go overboard on expensive luggage. Spend a grand on cases and every airport thief this side of Ringway, will be nicking your best Hawaiian number. Therefore, basic serviceable Samsonite was the order of the day. The contents, however, were a different matter. I was going through my lightweights and casuals, Diesel and Ralph Lauren's Polo Sport collection mainly. Although I did select a little formal stuff, just in case, so I packed a classic black dinner suit by Hugo Boss, a Versace dress shirt and a pair of formal black shoes by John Lobb. Barcelona had some fine dining establishments, and one may have called for formal dress. I wasn't one to break a dress code.

I held three separate passports at the time, courtesy of Mr Makris. Other documentation; driving licences, birth certificates, National Insurance numbers, all matched and were genuine.

None related to my true identity.

For my little trip I had decided to stay Stephen Colletti.

Going on holiday made me feel normal, just to engage in ordinary pursuits, playing a little tennis or golf, eating out and lying by a pool, where no one knew me, made me feel human. I'd also decided to take a closer look at some property, as Spiros's idea of relocation was starting to look much more likely.

I had booked my ticket to Spain using a Platinum American Express card as Mr. Colletti's credit was very good.

I only ever travelled first class. I'd been bumped around in enough Hercs and Hueys in my time and jumped out of too many to count. Now the thought of being squeezed together with a motley assortment of beer-swilling louts and screaming kids, was enough to drive a man to murder.

In first, you do get to sit in a nice comfortable seat, eat with real cutlery and enjoy a reasonable wine with your meal. Small things, but when, like me, you find flying so very tedious, every little helps. I closed the last case and stuffed some emergency cash into my carry-on bag. I was unsure of my return date, so I'd emptied my fridge and cancelled the papers. Normal things, done by normal people.

When I was in such a happy frame of mind, it would be a very brave, or a very stupid man to spoil my day. My phone bleeped and I eyed the number on the display suspiciously. It was Joel Davies.

"Yes?" I had no time for pleasantries.

Neither, it would seem had Davies.

"Get yourself over here now."

"I'm busy. I'm on my way to Barcelona, now, this minute. It will have to wait. You can hang around to get the Porsche back for a few days surely?"

"This can't wait and it's got fuck all to do with that little German number."

"What are we talking?"

"A week's work, maybe two. A big payday, Colletti; sort this for me and you can retire to fuckin' Barcelona."

Now the one thing Davies never joked about was money. I wanted to go on holiday, but, I was intrigued. There was only one thing for it, I would just have to put my plans on hold for a day or two and go to see what the psycho wanted.

I reluctantly cancelled Mr. Colletti's flight and started to unpack. Even if Davies's call to arms meant travel, the Spanish wardrobe was bound to be inappropriate.

I was off within half an hour. The Range Rover was a delight to drive in the Manchester traffic. It was a beast of a motor, but so light and responsive. The high seating position gave great visibility. My mechanic had tweaked the engine whilst I was sorting out Alfred the unlucky. He'd fitted a non-standard exhaust system too. It gave the car a little more edge and made it sound delicious. I felt like the king of the road.

The sprawling city gave way to leafy suburban Cheadle. I pulled the four-by-four up to the gates of Joel Davies's walled estate. Some has-been gorilla checked my face and I was waved through. I crawled the final five hundred yards to the front of the main house, the Rover burbling away and raising my spirits.

I dropped down onto the pale pink gravel path and I was met at the door by Susan Davies. She eyed me suspiciously, I thought. It appeared she'd had a long night.

"Morning, Susan," I smiled.

She smiled weakly. "Mr Colletti."

Despite her obvious troubles, she was absolutely stunning. Her hair was gelled, which had changed the auburn to a deep red. It was scraped back behind her ears, revealing the most exquisite sapphire droplet rings. Even their sparkle struggled to meet the blue in her eyes.

She wore no make-up that I could detect, probably some mascara. I smelled the faintest trace of perfume as she turned. She cleared her throat of a trace of nervousness.

"This way please, Stephen."

She wore D & G jeans and her hips swayed from side to side in front of me as she walked. She sported a ribbed T-shirt advertising FCUK. Once again, she considered a bra unnecessary.

I couldn't lose the tingling sense that something just wasn't right about the lady who seemed to make a career out of simply hanging around and looking good.

As far as I could detect, Susan had been with Joel for two years or so. It was a whirlwind romance so to speak. I didn't know how they had met but I did know that they had married within three months of meeting. She was all too perfect for a short hairy guy who sold drugs for a living. I made a mental note to find out more about Susan. I also convinced myself that it was purely for business reasons.

Susan walked me through to a study. It was a room in the cavernous house I had never had cause to visit. A monstrous desk, befitting the ego of Joel Davies, was centre stage. A computer monitor made the whole structure tall enough to hide Joel's black curly head from view. Susan left without a sound. I found myself in the greenest room I had ever seen.

I mean green too. Everything was fucking green. The leather Chesterfields, the desk tops, the flock wallpaper and every single book in the massive floor-to-ceiling cases. This man had a serious taste problem.

Joel pulled himself from the monitor. He was deathly pale. It wasn't illness. It was anger. I had only ever seen this mood once before and that had resulted in the untimely demise of Joel's larcenist brothers. He signalled me to sit and rooted in his desk drawer. After some cursing he bawled for Susan to bring him a cigar. Within seconds Susan appeared carrying a box of Cuban panatellas. Davies was brusque and businesslike as he selected a cigar from the open de-humidifier box and nipped off the end with a silver cutter. He waved her away with a flick of the wrist and Susan left immediately.

I didn't give a shit if they were the best cigars in the world, they still stank. They made him stink and worse still, made my Versace blazer stink.

I was busy trying to recall if I'd worn the jacket before, when Joel spun around the computer monitor. The image on the screen was encrypted. State of the art encryption was about to be made available to the masses. The CIA, FBI and MI5 were horrified. They thought that criminals would misuse the system. MI5 and 6 had been misusing it for years. I knew.

Joel bragged that he'd had access to the program for over a year. He hit a sixteen-character code and the screen turned from gibberish to text and pictures. I memorised the first eight numbers in his sequence. I also made a note to get the next eight as soon as possible. A very nice picture of an oceangoing cruiser, 'The Landmark,' had pride of place on the screen. Joel talked as he worked the keyboard. "I bought this baby from St Tropez, via the Net. It set me back two hundred and seventy-five thousand pounds."

I recalled his heated mobile phone conversation on my previous visit was about a boat purchase. He took a long pull on the dreadful cigar and filled the area with smoke.

He pointed at the screen.

"Here are the details of the buy completed six days ago. This here," he tapped, "is the previous owner's details."

Joel scrolled through. "The cruiser was delivered from the south of France to Amsterdam under its own steam by a crew, provided by the previous owner. This part of the deal is straight up. The guy has been paid his money and neither he, nor his crew are aware of any other reasons for the purchase. You understand?"

I nodded and tried not to hold my nose.

Joel flicked ash into a large cut glass tray.

"Once in Holland, the cruiser was loaded with one hundred kilograms of pure, uncut cocaine;" he pointed the horrible cigar in my direction and I resisted shoving it back into his mouth hot end first. He continued, not noticing my distaste. "The street value is ten million pounds, Colletti."

Joel then scrolled through more pictures and biographies.

Three men and one woman, all Dutch, were shown. It could have been a police file. Maybe even MI5.

I had to hand it to Joel, he was organised.

Joel spoke in short clipped tones, interrupted by shorter pulls on the cigar. He was really pissed off.

"Susan brokered the coke deal in Amsterdam six weeks ago. These four guys are the runners. We have no pictures of her main contact."

I nearly fell off my fucking chair.

Joel noticed.

"What, you thought she was just a pretty face?"

Well, I knew she had been getting involved with Joel's overseas dealings, but I presumed it was the antiques side.

He blew smoke in my direction again.

"I met Susan in Holland. She was living with some low life skunk grower. I first saw her at a party thrown by some of the country's biggest dealers. She knew nearly everyone in the room, Stephen. You should have seen her work that room.

"A real pro.

"I stole her from the dumb dope smuggler. The rest, as they say, is history. She has worked on a new contact for the supply of cocaine for the last eighteen months. This is the third deal. The other two went like clockwork."

I tried not to gawp at the revelation. I knew there was something but this was a real shock.

Joel went back to the story and the computer screen.

"Now, the boat and cargo was to be taken from Amsterdam to Zebrugge by two of this Dutch crew you see here. The big guy and the woman. As I said, they are not my employees, they work for the supplier. Only Susan has seen the main man. He never meets me either. It was a perfect solution."

"Providing you trust your wife," I muttered.

Joel glared at me, his eyes and tone fierce.

"As I said, she has done this for me before. The supplier has always been a hundred per cent. I have never had a problem. My guys should have collected the boat and cargo from the Dutch players at a pre-arranged point just north of Zebrugge and were to deliver it to me here in the UK.

"My cutters would then work their magic on it and turn it into lots of money for me. Understand?"

I certainly did.

He tapped the screen again. "I always have a customer for the boat too."

The man knew how to make money, no question.

"The boat never made Zebrugge. Susan has been in touch with the Dutch coke supplier. He's telling her that they had delivered to Zebrugge as agreed and waved my boys off into the sunset as promised."

"So where is it?" I asked straight out.

"They say the boat must have sunk en route and that my two boys must be at the bottom of the channel with it."

"Together with the coke of course," I added.

Joel stood and leaned closer to me, both hands on the desk, cigar in the corner of his mouth.

"As I always pay up front for my cargo, I'm nearly two million quid out of pocket and I don't believe a fuckin' word the Dutch bastards are saying."

Joel inspected his cigar to allow the information to sink in and hit a button on the keyboard. The word 'purging' appeared on the screen and the information and pictures relating to the Dutch players disappeared. He let out a large plume of smoke. He'd read my mind.

"I'm not as stupid as you think, Stephen. That information was direct from the Dutch Secret Service files. It's hacked for me by an inside source, sent encrypted and then destroyed. Another of Susan's contacts, she leaves nothing to chance, my friend."

My legs were suitably slapped, but I knew computers, they were the most insecure devices we've ever invented. And, if Susan left nothing to chance, where was Joel's bugle?

He handed me an envelope. It contained the pictures of all four Dutch runners including the two that were supposed to do the final drop.

"I want you to collect my boat, find my cocaine and bring it to me. I'll pay half a million for the boat and goods and I'll double it if you give me the motherfucker who stole from me and lied to my wife."

He stubbed the cigar, "I don't care which pieces."

Now Joel was talking serious coin. However, what he had to realise was this was not a one-man job. There were big expenses, big risks too. You mess with people heavy enough to do a job on Joel Davies and you could end up very dead.

I pressed for a little more.

"Other than the fact you can't trust anyone these days, what makes you think the boat didn't sink?"

Joel talked and tapped at his keyboard again, "First, no distress call to the coastguard."

Understandable, I thought. The guys wouldn't want the coastguard boarding a boat with several hundred pounds of pure cocaine stuffed in the hold.

Joel went on. "Second, there were perfect weather conditions and it is a near new vessel. And third," he spun the monitor again, "this."

On the screen was a nautical map with grid reference lines superimposed over the coastline. It glowed green, which wasn't a surprise to me. A red dot flashed. He tapped it with perfectly manicured finger. He was cold and dangerous.

"They think I won't take them on. The guy thinks he's too big and I'll lie down. He's made good money from me this last year. Now he, or someone on the Dutch side, has got too big for his boots. You know me, Stephen, I'm a careful man, a belt and braces sort of guy. So even though all has been well before, I still had a satellite beacon fitted to The Landmark by my boy in France." He tapped the red flashing dot.

"The fuckin' boat is still in Amsterdam."

I began to count the cost. I would need bodies and weapons. I didn't like the Dutch connection. Susan was a loose cannon. So soon after her marriage to Joel she had got herself involved in a major drug deal. It wasn't just Joel's cigar that stank.

"I'll want a hundred thousand up front. It'll take me a day or so to get a team together."

Joel wrinkled his brow. "I only want professionals on this, Colletti. You can use some of my guys."

I was about to decline the job altogether. There was no way I would be doing any operation with his bozos.

"I'll use my own people, thanks."

He seemed mildly irritated by my answer. Then, casually as fuck, he added, "No matter, do what you want. Susan will be going with you anyway."

I stood to leave. It was my turn to say my piece.

"Listen, Davies, sending your wife on this thing is the worst idea you've ever had."

Davies leaned further over his desk and spoke through his teeth. "She's set up all the deals with the Dutch crew last year. She knows the couriers and she is the only one who can ID the main man by sight. Don't let the pretty girl exterior put you off, son. She's as hard as fuckin nails."

Coming from Joel that was some statement.

The plot really thickened. I didn't argue about Susan. If she was in the game and had done this level of deal before then she might be an asset. I just didn't like the idea of telling Joel she'd been slotted if the job went tits up. So she was a bad girl after all? I still didn't like it. A guy of Joel's standing meets a bird and within the blink of an eye, not only does he marry her but she's doing his major deals for him? I could appreciate the idea of a broker, or middle-man. I myself used them regularly. But having your wife as the only person who can even ID the dealer?

One thing I knew for certain. The next few days were going to get naughty.

Joel detected the disquiet on my face, not that I cared what he thought. I smoothed my woollen trousers as I stood.

"So, who's the guy then?"

Davies paused for a moment, looked me in the face and I thought I detected the merest hint of fear.

"David Stern."

So, we were really playing hard ball on this one. I shrugged my shoulders. The bigger the fish, the bigger the payday.

"You're the boss, Davies. Have someone bring her to my place in the morning and tell her to travel light."

As I made to leave, Joel did the inexcusable again and grabbed my arm.

"Bring her back in one piece, Colletti."

Within minutes I was on the road. My drive back to Salford Quays was spoiled by the smell of cigars on my blazer, and the stench of a conspiracy in my nostrils.

Des Cogan's Story:

<u>Glasgow Airport 2006.</u>

I sat in Glasgow Airport's infamous departure lounge waiting for the last call for my flight to Manchester. I could see from the crowd queuing to hand in their boarding passes, the flight would be full and noisy. This Friday afternoon trip was often crammed with young clubber types, visiting Manchester for its highly charged music and club scene, and I wasn't looking forward to it.

Whatever the occasion, it seemed my fellow weegies were intent to mix it with copious amounts of Blue Wicked, amphetamine sulphate and cocaine. A visit to the gents prior to clearing security revealed more sniffing than shitting.

I hadn't seen Rick in seventeen months. I could've told you the weeks and days too if you'd wanted. Despite our lack of contact, we were the best of friends and I wouldn't hear a bad word about him even though he was a twat, and more recently, mad as a box of frogs. We'd served together in Ireland, Bosnia, Africa and Columbia and he'd got me out of more shit than you could ever imagine, so there you go, there was nothing more to say.

I'd got the call three hours previous. I was just getting ready for a few days fishing in the Highlands and had planned to drive from my home in Loch Lomond along the road to Inverness. Known as the whisky trail, the peaceful but fast driving road that split the country west to east was the gateway to all the major Scottish malt whisky distillers. They, in turn, needed clean Highland spring water to ply their trade. The rivers that wandered along the trail provided the ideal source and great fishing. What could have been total peace and quiet had just given way to almost certain mayhem. Fuck it. It's what I did best and still is.

From Rick's brief telephone conversation, there was a rush job going off in Holland. The money was too good to turn down, but more than the money was the chance to work with Rick again. The job would take about three days to a week. I could fish the trail another time, no bother.

Rick, of course, was using one of his many identities, Stephen Colletti, but I knew him as Rick.

I had known him for twenty-six years. He joined the Special Air Service via the Parachute Regiment. I had served with him my entire regiment career until his life went tits up.

He'd come from a poor background like most of us. He had no family that I knew of, having been in the care of the local authority from being a young nipper. I'd always thought the lack of parents made his life hard especially after Cathy died. At times of terrible grief, you need family no matter how distant they may be. Rick, though, appeared to have no one. Nonetheless he was a good bloke and as tough as they come. He had saved my sorry backside on more than one occasion.

I'd known Rick was freelancing for anyone with big money. When you finally leave a job like ours, it's hard to settle. Most guys had never kept a relationship in one piece, so they lived alone, me included. Some would have a casual affair that kept them home for a while, but all missed the action and the camaraderie. Many ended up fighting alongside some foreign army as mercenaries. I had already done two stints in Africa and I knew Rick had worked in South America. Some guys tried bodyguard work but found being at the beck and call of some Arab's wife boring, no matter what the pay packet.

I had my house at Loch Lomond where I felt safe and at one with the world. It was a solitary existence, but it suited me.

I had taken a part time job working military shows around the world. I worked for a very well-known glass company. Indeed you probably have some of their products in your own house. Little known is that they also manufacture very specialist lenses for satellite systems and sniper sights. The money was okay and I got to see some of the old faces, who worked the same circuit.

That aside, I had grown tired of smiling sweetly at foreign generals and I was ready for a bit of real action. I put to the back of my mind the fact that the money for this job probably came from a gangster. I was bored shitless and needed to feel part of a team again.

The tannoy announced the last call. Around thirty passengers were left in the row. Most were twenty-something, well dressed and slightly stoned. I joined the back of the queue and shuffled forward until I handed my boarding pass to an uninterested ground crew. I found my seat and, just as I'd thought, the plane was rammed with over-excited clubbers.

Straight after take-off I put on one of the £2.00 headsets to drown out the noise and listened to Terry Wogan. Within ten minutes I was sound asleep.

I knew we'd started our descent into Manchester. Even after years of flying in every possible type of plane and helicopter my ears popped and woke me every time.

A hostess walked along the aisle making a final sweep of the passengers, collecting cans, bottles and crisp packets, at the same time, checking seat belts were fastened and seats were in the upright position. She had beautiful long dark hair tied back in a ponytail and the most striking bright green eyes. She looked Irish. She sported that wonderful clear, pale skin that the Emerald Isle seems to produce.

"Any rubbish there, sir?"

I drifted briefly.

"Sir?"

"No," I said," her accent making my next question stupid but my mouth opened and it came out. "Are you from Ireland?"

"From Dublin, why do you ask?"

I smiled.

"You have lovely hair and eyes."

She looked at me, not knowing if I was the proverbial dirty old man, seemed to decide against it, and gave me a smile in return.

"Why thank you sir, please fasten your seatbelt."

In the 1980s and early '90s Northern Ireland was at the centre of a massive political row over the so-called 'shoot to kill policy' by the military.

Rick was heading a four-man team out there. We had set up a surveillance of a PIRA weapon stash. I'd been dug in at a farmhouse in the middle of bandit country for several days. Confident that the weapons were there and several players were visiting, we were convinced that we could get a good result. Rick ran the op, he, two other Regiment guys, and me all pissed off and wet through.

We were compromised by a bloody dog. We hadn't seen it. One of the players had brought it with him during the night and all hell broke loose on our approach. Tactics went out the window and the firefight lasted forty minutes.

To cut a long story short I was shot in the leg and it all got messy. Rick killed five terrorists that day and saved all our asses. When the dust settled we found that two of the Provos' team had been women.

Two young pretty Irish girls, with nice dark hair and green, unseeing eyes.

Shaking the images from my mind's eye, I gave the hostess my
headset and returned her smile.

"I won't need these," I said.

We landed with a bump at Ringway and it took nearly an hour for
the baggage handlers to do their job.

Once outside the terminal, I took a cab to Salford Quays, feeling
good about meeting my best mate again. The two dead Irish girls
were safely returned to that secret place in my psyche but I noticed
that my foot was tapping to nothing in particular, the extra
adrenaline reminding me that this was a dangerous job. I felt alive
for the first time in months.

Rick Fuller's Story:

Finding the right calibre of staff for a job like Joel's was never easy. There was no time. The other side, the Dutch, had the gear, the boat and the cash. They'd be expecting some form of investigation, even retribution. The job was to recover a great deal of money, stolen from a truly evil gangster with a huge ego. Trouble was, the thief was the biggest gangster in Europe, and other than our darling Susan, not a living soul appeared to have ever seen him.

Top quality people were never available at the drop of a hat, unless, of course, you were paying large sums of money. Fortunately I was. Tanya was on her way from The Moss.

Des had just arrived from Manchester International Airport. His Glasgow flight had passed without incident and he was sitting in my lounge sipping black coffee laced with the best Irish single malt.

He was a fine chap. His wiry Scots frame stood barely five foot ten topped with dark brown wavy hair that was turning salt and pepper. His face was so weathered it looked like he'd left it out in the rain each night. His piercing blue eyes followed my every step. Not quite as quick as they used to, but still too quick for most.

Des's forte was surveillance. His idea of a good time was sitting in a freezing hole in the ground for days on end, shitting into a plastic bag and watching big daft Irishmen come and go. He could also empty a 9mm SLP, one handed, into a target the size of a biscuit tin from thirty yards. You did not fuck with Desmond.

Since his more than honourable discharge from the Regiment, Des had been freelancing for various arms suppliers. He sold sighting systems and surveillance kit to Arabs, who would never know how to use it. It was not Des's idea of fun.

I had scarcely told him the bare bones of the job on the phone when he'd snapped at it. Des had always been a fear junkie. It was the only drug he ever needed. I liked that and I liked him. He was a class performer, my solitary friend.

My only complaints were his clothes. He had never known how to dress. Lord knows I had tried to educate him over the years but to no avail. Other than good quality Irish brogues he appeared to shop solely at Marks and Sparks.

I had been a busy chap, booked all the flights and arranged some currency. I'd made as many enquiries about Susan as I could without upsetting anyone and had also paid a visit to my stash out in the country. My stash was my insurance and my legacy.

I'd arranged for Des and Susan to travel together on British Airways. Tanya and I would go KLM. If we did get a welcoming committee we would be harder to hit as two couples arriving at different times. I had been briefing Des. I'd told him as much as I could about Joel and Susan. We knew the Dutch boys would be able to identify her as she had been the courier or broker on the two previous successful deals. Only Des and I would know the full SP. He was the only person on the planet I totally trusted.

As I finished the briefing Des's wrinkles doubled to a smile. His Greenock accent had softened over the years.

"This is gonna be a wee bit sticky, mate," he drained the remainder of his Gaelic, "and I reckon I've got the short straw baby-sitting Joel Davies's missus."

"Fair go, Des, but you know Tanya's temper. She would top her before we got across the Channel and we are going to need both ladies for this job."

Des burst into a laugh. He'd met Tanya before and knew exactly what I meant. The Jamaicans were not noted for their patience with petulant, pampered whites.

He lowered his tone. "What if she's been in on the deal with the Dutch since the marriage proposal? If so, we'll be compromised from the start, we could be walking into a minefield."

I nodded in agreement.

Des had come to the same conclusion as I. What if Susan had decided to go into business for herself? What if her marriage to Joel and the two previous deals had all been bait for the big payday? If so, she was the ultimate grafter. If she was a con artist, she had made over a million pounds in less than two years and lived in luxury whilst earning it.

"She gets no contact with anyone outside the team unless it's to Davies himself. Either you or I must be present even then."

Des nodded. "What about Davies himself? Does he trust her?"

I felt my mouth turn at the edges.

"Who the fuck knows, Des, he wouldn't be the first to be conned by a pretty face, would he?"

The doorbell announced Tanya's arrival.

She strode in with a broad grin for Des and me, rested a manicured hand on Des's shoulder and pecked me on the cheek. She wore a black, figure-hugging, two-piece tailored suit by Karen Millen. It caused a deep wrinkling of Des's brow. She dropped a single suitcase onto the carpet and poured herself a brandy without invitation.

Tanya knew the outline of the job. That was all she needed, that and her fifty grand fees. She swallowed and wiped her lip carefully with her index finger. This time the nail was black to match her suit.

"So, boys, we're going on a holiday to Amsterdam, eh?"

I told her the travel arrangements. She nodded.

"This Susan Davies, can we turn our backs on her or what?"

Des piped up, and as casual as you like said, "The first sign of a problem and I'll slot her."

We both knew he meant it. Only I knew it couldn't happen. We needed her. Well, for the time being anyway.

My entry phone beeped and I lifted the receiver. I saw the black and white image of Susan Davies. Even two inches tall and out of perspective she looked stunning. A lift ride later and she arrived at the door flanked by what she would describe as her 'security', which consisted of a fat dickhead carrying a mountain of luggage.

He was red-faced and out of breath. If this guy had to help you in a barney he would be as much use as a chocolate fireguard.

Des eyed him with mild amusement and turned to our esteemed guest.

"So, Susan, I take it you are Susan? Is this your personal porter?" It took a second or two for the tub of lard to realise he was having the piss taken out of him. As the light came on he dropped the cases and squared himself at Des.

"I'm Mrs Davies personal security. So shut it."

Des raised his hands in mock surrender.

"Deepest apologies, pal; personal security? My word, you must be important."

Susan had no time for the show at all. I could see the change in her. With no Joel Davies about there was something different. A tiny change maybe, but it was there. And it wasn't what I expected.

She reached out and planted the palm of her hand slap in the centre of the big fella's chest. There wasn't a hint of nerves there at all.

"Stop all this macho shit, will you! You can go now, Eric."

Eric looked puzzled, he was obviously expecting a jolly to The Dam, but Susan nodded to the door and he turned to leave.

I decided to push the envelope a bit.

"Before you go, son," I motioned to the ridiculous amount of luggage on my living room floor. "You'd better take all these cases with you, Eric."

Susan was on me like a rash. Her personality changed again. In fact it seemed she had more of them than your average mental patient.

"That," she pointed, "is my luggage!" Her hands moved to her hips and I saw Des raise a smile out of the corner of my eye.

"Mine!" she continued.

"It is nothing to do with you or anyone else, understand, Colletti?" She was on a roll and pointed straight at me. Her Dutch accent more pronounced than ever. She was so close, I could feel her breath.

"We need to get this straight. Before I go anywhere with you and your little team of cronies, you need to remember that you work for my husband, Joel Davies. Remember him?" She cocked her head,

"You do remember him, don't you? The guy that pays you all? The scary guy with the big house? The guy that would have the three of you killed without a second thought?"

She glanced at each of us in turn.

Tanya was pouring a second brandy. She raised the balloon to the light and inspected the liquid colour before taking a measured sip. Des simply smiled broadly back in Susan's direction.

He crossed his legs and motioned to each of us with an outstretched palm.

"As you can see, Susan, we're all fuckin' terrified."

The confidence in her voice wavered slightly. Her pointed finger wagged up and down but it had lost some of its force. She made a vain attempt to regain her composure.

"In Joel's absence, you work for me."

She tailed off. There was an awkward silence.

I smiled.

Tanya moved with all the grace of a ballerina. Her left foot connected with Susan at about calf height. Simultaneously Tanya pushed Susan backward. Both Susan's legs flew from under her and she landed on her arse on my Persian rug. It looked fairly painful, but I got the impression it was only Susan's pride that was dented. In fact she fell quite well.

Big Eric was lumbering toward Tanya like an overweight heifer. Des and I exchanged a look that allowed the show to go on. He was within six feet of her, when Tanya drew an exquisite Derringer pistol from her jacket. She extended her arm. The engraved silver barrel met Eric's forehead and stopped him dead.

This was a good start to the campaign, I was enjoying myself, and from the grin on Des's face, so was he.

Eric the Flabby stood rooted and sweating. Tanya raised one eyebrow that asked the obvious question. I broke the silence.

"Is that a .22, Tanya?"

"Uhh, uhh."

"It will still make a hell of a noise."

Tanya was having none of it.

"Turn up your hi-fi. No one will hear."

Eric was shaking. Susan seemed remarkably calm.

I turned up the sounds and barely heard Eric cry out. Didn't he like the White Stripes?

I had recently installed the system. It was the dog's bollocks. So small you hardly noticed it. It didn't interfere with the look of my living room. Yet it was so powerful, over a hundred watts RMS per channel, it would cover the gunshot with ease.

Then I remembered. I had just had my rug professionally cleaned. It was pale grey, with black and gold Persian panel, beautifully hand woven, and pure wool.

"Just a minute, doll."

I walked to my utility room and gathered some plastic sheeting used by my decorators. I placed a single sheet about eight feet square behind Eric.

"Ask him to step back a little, Tanya. I've just paid an arm and a leg to get this rug cleaned."

She nodded at the blubbering hulk. "Step back, fat boy."

He complied. A tiny red circle had appeared on his forehead from the barrel of the Derringer.

I do like it when people take pride in their equipment. Tanya must have parted with a princely sum to obtain such a weapon. She pulled back the hammer on the deadly beauty. It made a *clickity click* sound and Eric's bowel control failed him. Susan had seen enough.

She screamed at Tanya, "Stop this nonsense! For Christ sake, stop it now!"

The point had been made to the person who mattered. Tanya looked to me for the signal, and holstered as quickly as she drew. I grabbed Eric by the hair and pushed him toward the door.

"Fuck off before you stink out my house."

I closed the door behind him and turned to Susan who, to my surprise, had regained her composure.

I selected one suitcase.

"Now, Missus Davies, I'll try to remember that I work for your husband whilst you pack this single bag, no more. You have ten minutes."

I pointed to a grinning Scot resting his bones on my sofa.

"You'll be travelling with Des here. He has your ticket and your best interests at heart." I looked her straight in the eye. "I've known your husband for a long time. I know exactly what kind of man he is and what kind of woman you are. We are here to do a job. I don't give a shit if you want to be here or not. What I can tell you, is that the three of us would rather be without you. The best thing you can do is keep your mouth shut until the time comes for you to ID the man that stole from your husband. Fail in that department, honey, and nothing will protect you. The only person in charge here is me, understand? Now pack that bag."

She didn't answer. She simply stared straight at me, her blue eyes flashing contempt. She raised herself and started to arrange her luggage.

I was particularly taken with her Christian Dior shoes.

I didn't bother to check exactly what Susan had packed, even though I admit to a certain curiosity. Her taste in clothes was obvious for all to see and I'd bet it dented old Joel's chequebook. What she paid for her underwear would have kept a family of four in clothes for a year.

Everyone was travelling under their own name except me. I can never relax if strangers know my identity. It's a personal thing.

We had split into our relative couples. Tanya and I were leaving thirty minutes prior to Des and Susan and from different terminals. I left the Range Rover in covered parking and the two of us relaxed in the KLM first class lounge. We drew some attention, but I put that down to the fact that Tanya was not only beautiful but black. The sight of a mixed race couple still raised an eyebrow in the UK.

We both double-checked a very athletic looking single white male reading a Dutch newspaper, but he left on a flight to Frankfurt. Our nerves were starting to hone the rest of our senses. The ability to turn tension into intelligence is a great advantage; a physical and mental state that makes an invisible enemy visible, the very special gift that keeps people like us alive.

The first call for our flight sounded from the public address system. I drained my Evian over ice and walked from the lounge to the bathroom. The flight time, Manchester to Schiphol was only an hour and twenty minutes, but I disliked using the toilet on aircraft.

The first class rest rooms were clean and presentable. They had black marble tiles and shell-shaped washbasins which I found a little ''80s'. I appeared to be the lone user of the facilities and I entered a cubicle at the end of the row of three.

I sat.

Within seconds I heard footsteps on the tiled floor. They paused and then the next cubicle door opened. I couldn't help but listen to the noises.

Something was wrong. The noises were wrong. The hairs on the back of my neck started their journey upward. I had no weapons. We had just cleared security. As quietly as possible I reached for my trousers. Anyone would have trouble defending themselves with their trousers around their ankles and their dick hanging out.

There was a sudden scrabbling noise. The person in the next cubicle was agile and quick. Before I could complete my task, my assailant was over the divider. I was knocked backwards onto the pan, trousers still at my ankles.

Tanya grabbed my hair hard enough to remove some by the root and forced my head back against the wall. She was as strong as an ox. She planted her mouth on mine and pushed her tongue to the back of my throat. She was standing astride me and reached down to grab my crotch. She handled me roughly. Her breath was all I could hear as she sucked and bit frantically at my neck. I raised a hand to touch her but she pushed it away with more strength than the average male. Stepping back, she was breathing hard.

She smiled. "You were a little slow there, baby, you need to sharpen up, or I'll have to find myself a new plaything."

It was Tanya's idea of a joke.

What was even funnier was the look on the face of the guy that saw the pair of us emerge from the single cubicle with me covered in Tanya's lipstick.

The Dutch are notoriously casual towards recreational drugs, sex and art. Some of their ideas make perfect sense. Others defy belief. Amsterdam Airport, though, was like any other major international, with lots of people and lots of security. It would have been madness to bring weapons or anything else through a place like Schiphol. I had personally arranged for our hardware to be left in a luggage locker at the airport. The contact was all my own and nothing to do with Davies. This was exactly the way I liked it. The drop and the weaponry cost me ten grand. I knew it would be an expensive job. I quietly did the sums.

Until the weapon stash was collected we were totally vulnerable. Our only saving grace would be that any attempt at a hit would be very dangerous in the airport complex.

Tanya had grown increasingly uncomfortable in the arrivals hall. Jamaicans have these peculiar mojo moments that I find weird. It's not that I didn't believe some of the black magic stuff. I did a tour in Africa and saw some really strange shit there. It's just that I preferred to deal with the 'here and now' and not what might happen. I wandered around in duty-free.

As we waited for Des and Susan's flight to land, I stocked up on aftershave. I bought the new D & G, Hugo Boss and CK. I wasn't sure about the CK but it was a bargain. I shopped whilst Tanya pensively checked for any tails, and rubbed rabbits feet or whatever. We watched the others clear customs. No one else appeared to be skulking around so we walked separately to a café by the luggage lockers. It was a typical airport design, all open-plan with a poor menu, dreadful coffee, and extortionate prices.

Why is it, that you always find a spotty, unkempt and intellectually challenged youth serving in these places? After my passable attempt at Dutch, the little bastard serving ignored me. I'd suffered this treatment in Holland before. I was on a stag trip to Amsterdam with some army mates and we'd walked into a small bar where the Dutch locals drank. When we eventually got a beer we were asked to sit in a small separate room away from the rest of the drinkers. As I said, the Dutch are a strange mix. Tanya's definite rudeness paid off and we got two cups of truly awful coffee.

Des and Susan sat three tables from us. I got up and walked to the left luggage room; the key arrived at my flat in Manchester just three hours after I knew I was visiting 'The Dam'. Now that is service for you.

A swift walk down two flights of stairs and I was in the locker room. It was busy with mainly student types. People were dumping their larger suitcases and travelling light into the city. Most would be day trippers. Some of them were excited and talked openly about the drugs they were about to buy in the many legal coffee shops once they got to the centre. I did a double take as one meat-head dropped down the steps and seemed to do nothing in particular. Several moments later, he was joined by his girlfriend who had just dropped her case in a locker and they left, hand in hand. I gave myself a mental slap. I was starting to get as bad as Tanya.

Paranoia, self-importance's first cousin.

There were hundreds of identical steel doors. I found the one with my key number and removed two large black suitcases. I strolled to the gentleman's toilet. I didn't expect another visit from Tanya. Directly on cue, Des took the next stall to me. His Irish brogue pushed under the partition. He tapped out my initials in Morse. I slid one of the cases to him under the stall and made my exit.

Our nakedness was over.

The plan called for Des and Susan to take the train to Central station and from there, a cab to the hotel. Typical of Amsterdam the hotel was called 'The Koch' which was a five minute stroll from Dam Square and the heart of Amsterdam city life.

Tanya and I walked to Avis.

"How's the mojo, Tanya?" I said trying to lighten her mood.

"Don't mess with the magic," was all she said and strode on in front, the conversation was over.

I rented a BMW 325i. It was a brand new car; black with caramel coloured leather seats.

Once the paperwork was completed we loaded up and made for the city. The motorway network from Schiphol takes you under a runway approach and as we stuttered through traffic I watched the bizarre sight of a Boeing 747 taxiing over our heads.

The traffic cleared. Tanya stamped on the accelerator and the German saloon responded nicely. I sat in the back and checked the contents of our armoury.

The case contained two Heckler Koch MP5K's with sliding stocks; they had Ultra dot aim point sights and Maglites fitted.

Beautiful.

They took an extended magazine of twenty rounds, two of which were taped to each weapon. The MP5K is light enough to use one handed and operates on single shot, burst of three and fully automatic. At the flick of a switch, this weapon is the ultimate urban killer. It is deadly accurate to a hundred yards on single shot, an ideal weapon in a running battle on short burst and a great room-clearer on automatic.

Sitting either side of the MP5's were two Glock 9 mm SLP's. Not my ideal choice of weapon, I preferred the SIG or H and K. The plastic Glock felt too light and flimsy but it was short notice for my man and all the weapons took identical ammunition, which was a bonus.

I loaded the two Glocks, handed one to Tanya, and pushed the other into my waistband in the small of my back. I felt instantly more secure.

I was checking the remainder of the case, night vision goggles, audio transmitters, de-bugging gear and other bits of ancillary kit, when Tanya piped up.

"Green Audi A6, babe. Two cars back. It's been with us since the airport."

I checked and it was there. Two goons were in the front, and I could make out one in the rear seat. All wore suits and sunglasses. They certainly looked the part.

I leaned between the front seats and spoke into Tanya's right ear. "Take the next slip road off and let's see what they got."

Tanya punched the pedal and the BMW did as it was told. She glided past two vehicles and the car hit two hundred kph before I blinked. We were the outside lane and a big Alfa saloon was blocking us. Tanya dropped the Beamer down to fourth, and undertook it. She was red-lining the rev-counter. I looked back and the big Audi was still in sight. He was a tail, no doubt.

"He's still there, babes."

The BMW was screaming. The slip road was coming up. One hundred metres and we were still in the outside lane of a five-lane highway. Tanya threw the car right and chopped anything in her path. I heard a horn blare and then saw a puff of tyre smoke. She almost made it, but clipped a small red saloon in the nearside lane with the boot of our car.

The BMW wiggled slightly but the German engineering had it right and the car straightened under Tanya's deft touch. We were on the slip road okay but travelling much too fast. I saw stationary traffic looming. Tanya stood on the brake. The ABS automatically kicked in. It sounded like automatic gunfire. The whole car was shaking and I was flung forward against the seats. We were not going to stop in time, and I didn't fancy a trip through the windscreen or bouncing around inside a rolling car with two loaded sub machineguns. I saw a gap.

"Go left, left, left!" I screamed and pointed. "There, now!"

The manoeuvre was tricky and we hit a kerb hard. The car lurched upward and the engine howled as we left the road completely, the rear wheels spinning free. As the wheels touched down and traction returned, Tanya fought for control. The car snaked wildly left and right, but she straightened in time. We now had to negotiate two fuck-off concrete supports. I decided the car would fit. Tanya's rabbit's foot was working overtime and some.

"Go between!" I shouted.

A split second later, courtesy of Tanya's bottle and talent, we emerged into sedate traffic minus both wing mirrors and a section of rear end trim, not bad considering.

The Audi was gone, we were in the clear.

I rang Des's mobile. He answered immediately. He and Susan had arrived at the hotel without drama. I warned him about the Audi and described the goons as best I could. Tanya parked the BMW. I took an incendiary canister from our case of goodies and slipped it under the front seat. Before it went off, we were in a taxi.

So, the Dutch boys knew we were in Holland. If that was as a result of their good intelligence, we had a leak. No one knew our travel arrangements other than the team. Or had they just been waiting and watching for us? Had we been sloppy at the airport? Obviously all roads eventually led to a security leak and Susan Davies. How she'd done it, with Des watching her like a hawk, was another matter. Still, the first little problem had been overcome and I should have been in a good mood. Why was I not? Well, I left my new aftershaves in the fucking car, didn't I?

Our adjoining suites at The Hotel Koch were comfortable and quite large by Dutch standards. I was not impressed with the décor, though. I think Joel Davies had a hand in the interior design. Whoever had the idea to put two types of wallpaper, separated by a flowery border, on a solitary wall? Looking at it gave me a headache. Add to that, terrible furniture that was obviously designed by Sven Goran-Erikson and you get the picture.

We all sat together with a room service tray of tea and average sandwiches. After a shower and a change of clothes I felt a little better about my recent loss of duty-free goods. I was wearing a lightweight French Connection suit with an open neck cotton shirt and very comfortable new loafers by D&G.

Tanya was near naked; she had discovered a gym in the hotel and had been working out. I admired her new SPX trainers and the cut of her triceps.

Susan was singularly petulant and, according to Des, hadn't spoken a word since leaving my flat. More importantly she hadn't been out of his sight until they were in the hotel. Des was adamant she couldn't have been in touch with the Dutch. So she had to have tipped the wink before we left.

She too had changed and now sported a pair of khakis by Donna Karen. Her still unfettered breasts were covered by a tailored shirt by Abercrombie and Fitch.

Des looked like an advert for the Grattan catalogue.

I'd called a briefing.

"Okay, we haven't much time. Somehow the Dutch already know we are here and it won't take long for them to find us again. This is a small city. Des has done a quick assessment of the target premises and the Dutch team haven't moved the Landmark. It's still in the same position we expected it to be. We must assume that the product has been removed from the vessel. In all probability it was never loaded or already sold. All we can do is keep observations on the target premises and hope one of our players turn up. Let's concentrate on recovering the boat and/or one of the players. As soon as we know more, I'll make a decision about the timing of our entry to the premises. If they decide to move the Landmark before we are ready, we'll follow and do a hard stop."

A hard stop was the last thing you would wish for. It was a method of containing a moving vehicle and neutralising the occupants. A specialist team from the Regiment would plan and train for a hard stop for several days prior to executing it as it was such a difficult and dangerous task to complete. Normally three cars with four team members in each would practice stopping the target vehicle over and over, normally on the runway at Hereford. Every possible scenario would be tested. The timing, the place and the occupants would all be known in advance. If the Landmark was moved before we were ready, we were in the shit. We were only four, and had no way of training for, or planning the stop, and no intelligence as to how many faces would be inside the vehicle towing the boat.

Susan looked up, her hair back to a lovely auburn, minus the gel. "What do you want me to do?" she asked.

Des was in first, his voice sharp and to the point. "You, my lovely, don't need to do a fuckin' thing for now. The sole reason you're here is to ID the boss man, what's his name? Stern? Consequently you are a necessity, sweetie."

I could see Des really didn't care for Susan. He was a good Catholic boy and hated women who slept around, especially for wealth.

She leaned back in her chair and covered her face with her hands and exhaled. She seemed deep in thought for a moment and then straightened her pose, palms showing.

"Look, I can't do this. I'm not going to do this! I told Joel before he dreamed up this pathetic trip, I couldn't identify David Stern. You have no idea how powerful this guy is. I would never be safe again even if he thought I'd considered betraying him. Just by being here with you probably means I'm already dead. I'm an administrator, a pen pusher, you know? I help to grease the wheels on the machine. I'm not a killer or a gangster. I can't fire a gun or use a knife and I don't fucking want to."

This was Susan number three we were seeing. This was the vulnerable female. The innocent girl caught up in a situation that was out of control.

The cracks were barely visible. She was good, I'd give her that, but I was unimpressed and I felt the need to point out some facts.

"Aren't you the wife of Joel Davies? The most notorious cocaine baron outside London, a man who has risen from nowhere to become one of the most feared mobsters in Europe? Just three months after you split with your anonymous Dutch dope grower, you marry Joel in England and, as we all know, two years down the line, you now broker multi-million pound cocaine deals. Not only that, but you single-handedly put him together with public enemy number one, the most infamous and evil gangster outside Russia, David Edgar Stern. The last two deals must have increased the nose candy levels of Manchester threefold. I'd say you're some piece of work, love, so don't play the innocent eh?"

She almost spat at me, "I set up the deals for Joel because he asked me to, because I love him. He knew about me and where I came from. He didn't give a shit about my past, who I knew or whatever. It was business, just business. He asked me to do it, so I did, simple."

Des poked in.

"Funny you just happened to attract two cocaine dealers eh? Still I suppose it's like birds who serial shag footballers."

She shot Des a glance but ignored the comment.

"As soon as Joel found out I'd met David Stern, he wanted me to arrange a meeting with him. Stern never meets face to face with his buyers. At first Joel took his refusal to meet as an insult, a lack of respect. But money talks with Joel and once I brokered the first deal, he forgot all about any petty one-upmanship. He just counted the cash."

Tanya stretched her hamstrings and joined the fray.

"When did you last see this Stern guy, then?"

Susan shook her head. "Months, not since before the last deal was done. I was flown to Columbia. He was there for a few hours. He's harder to find than Osama Bin Laden. This latest deal has been done without any involvement from David. All negotiations have been done through the couriers. I've spoken to him by phone once more this year, that's it."

Susan looked genuinely uncomfortable.

"I'll tell you, as soon as I heard the news that the Landmark had been stolen, my blood ran cold. I was really scared, and so should you be. If you think I am going to identify Stern, point the finger, you and my husband have made a big mistake."

She picked up her bag, rooted nervously for cigarettes, and continued. I couldn't be sure if the nerves were real but the information was interesting.

"Compared to David Stern, Joel is small time. He could buy and sell him twenty times over. Joel has no idea what he's messing with. Stern probably just got tired of Joel's constant bartering and decided to teach him a lesson. He does it with everyone once in a while. Joel should just accept it. I tried to tell him but…"

Tanya stood upright. "I think this Stern guy decided he wanted you to help him fleece your new hubby and you were only too pleased to help. How much was your cut, sweetie? Come on, less of this fuckery, you are in this man Stern's pocket."

Tanya looked at me, her Jamaican accent cutting through. "You crazy to trust this one Stephen she's a *bladclat*."

Susan went to light up. She shrugged her shoulders and I caught a glimpse of the real woman, cold, hard, eyes like glass. He lips grew thin and the edge returned to her voice.

"I don't care what you think, any of you. I know I want to stay alive though. And there's no way I'm going to identify David Stern, so why don't you go sightseeing or something, see Amsterdam before you die."

I walked over and snatched the cigarettes from her hand. She had just quit.

"This is a no smoking room, and you will do as I fucking tell you. We are here to do a job, earn our cash, and go home in one piece. To me, Stern is just another contract."

She was about to speak but I pressed my index finger lightly onto that gorgeous mouth. I felt her lips turn upward in a smile and then fall as she saw my expression of loathing. The mere touch of her mouth against my finger made my stomach tighten. I removed it a little too quickly.

"Now, tell me this, how did Stern know we were in Amsterdam?" She displayed flat calm and shrugged again. "It wouldn't surprise me if Joel's house is bugged. David is a very careful individual. Like I said, I think you should take in the sights and then run as far away from this as you can."

I recovered my composure and my personal space. I felt anger rise in my throat. My words fell from my mouth in measured but furious tones.

"I'll tell you this. Stern made a mistake when he upset Joel Davies. It could well be his last. Not because of Joel, but because of me. Just ensure you don't make the same one or you'll join him on a slab."

She looked at the floor to hide a smirk, and then addressed the whole room. Her tone was so sarcastic I was ready to physically restrain Tanya.

"I'll tell you this, ladies and gentleman. Your chances of ever finding Stern are zero. Getting close enough to kill him will be impossible. He has property and people all over the world. Joel's little show of force will be a minor annoyance to him, and you," she pointed a long finger inches from my nose, "he would eat you for breakfast."

I was never one for unnecessary violence, but I could feel the time fast approaching.

"What you know, or think you know, isn't important. You set up this crooked transaction. You were the one who smoothed the waters. It was you who took the money to Stern's goons on every deal. How did you contact him? How did you persuade him to deal with a psycho like Joel in the first place? I just wonder which fucking drama school you went to."

Susan sat in petulant silence. The two-faced bitch had a point, even if it wasn't put in a way that would endear her to the group. David Edgar Stern was a serious player in a serious game. I had only ever heard his name mentioned in the highest circles of criminality. Other than Susan Davies, I had never actually met anyone who had seen him. Even the Dutch police were without a photograph. He was a legend without a face.

Our task was to persuade Stern to show himself, draw him out into the open, and the only way to do that was to embarrass the man, steal what he considered to be his. I also had a feeling, that while we had Susan Davies, we had David Edgar Stern's full attention. She was my bait. I felt sure that no matter what happened he would seek her out. When he did, we would find him. Then we would kill him.

Des was busy planning the next stage of the operation and I spent a long time on my mobile phone to some old contacts.

Tanya took Susan off to find us transport and some less conspicuous lodgings. The hotel was fine for the night, but too many people see you in a hotel. They were going off to the south side of the city posing as two gay women in search of a quiet rented house.

Tanya had no problem with her role. The dusky maiden had a wicked look in her eye as she took Susan by the hand and led her to a taxi. I had the feeling she would give our guest a hard time for an hour or two.

Susan looked slightly pale and drawn and hadn't changed since the afternoon. The realisation of her situation appeared to weigh heavy. For the first time she'd seemed defeated. Whether the emotion was real or faked, I honestly had no way of knowing.

The girls gone, Des set about preparing his kit for his observations. We had the exact location of the Landmark on two hand-held GPS units. Des had already been out, surveyed the location displayed on the tracking system, and as expected the big boat was exactly where it was supposed to be.

Believe it or not the fact that the boat was there concerned me, I wasn't quite sure why.

Des had chosen his spot for the main observation and had taken a few quick photographs. I'd downloaded them and was studying the screen on my laptop. The digital pictures were excellent.

Des pulled on his kit.

"I'm off then," he said.

I nodded. "Keep your head down, mate."

Des hesitated. It was something I'd never seen him do. It sent a signal to my brain that I didn't like. First I'd had Tanya and her mojo working at the airport. Now I had Des, pussyfooting about on my carpet.

"What is it, Des?"

He shook his head and his accent took me back to our first meeting. Before we had both married our women. Before we had both killed a man.

His words stuck in his throat so much that he spat them machine-gun fast.

"Susan Davies is all wrong, Rick. You know it and I know it."

"I know that, Des."

He still shuffled.

"Yeah, but I've seen that look on your face. Why has this job got so much importance to you, Rick? This is a big fucking risk man. You know I'm with you all the way, but fuck, this one is, is… "

He trailed off. I stood and faced him.

"Never mind about Susan, she's nothing I can't handle. Get me the pictures I need, pal. Let's make some money."

Des nodded and left without another word. That was Des's way of telling me we were in the shit. It wasn't the first time, and he was usually right.

Des Cogan's Story:

The Amsterdam night had turned bitterly cold. I turned my collar against it and strode on. I walked via typical Amsterdam bridges. Their wrought iron rails silhouetted by the moon, cast dark shadows on the murky water. I evaded tall brusque cyclists hurrying home for their evening meals. Well-heeled men in long overcoats and women, power dressed, pedalling rather than driving home. Clumps of tourists blocked my path as they studied maps or gawked at the architecture. It was going to be a long night.

I put all worries about Rick and Susan to the back of my mind and, as ever, got on with it.

I gained access to the thirteen-storey block of flats overlooking the scene by simply pressing all the intercom buttons until a lazy resident let me in. Then I climbed the fire escape to the roof. I was carrying a fair amount of gear, and by the time I reached my spot I was breathing hard. I made a mental note to get some more exercise when this job was over.

I set up my kit. A digital camera with a night-vision telescopic lens gave me a perfect view. I could see the Landmark was on a trailer, inside a large container storage depot. There was a great deal of activity. Heavy vehicles were delivering and collecting their loads in a constant stream. Cranes and heavy lifting gear moved containers from one part of the yard to another. There were dozens of employees. If this was one of Stern's legitimate businesses, it was an ideal cover, hard to identify anyone and loads of space to hide. It would be ideal for any smuggling operation. It was situated some fifteen kilometres out of the city and was surrounded by a twelve-foot wall, a fortress in its own right. There was a security office on the gate, and one small Portakabin structure was visible from my position. Inside the yard, just nestling next to that very cabin, was the Landmark. I had the whole spot covered. I started snapping away.

My home, come rain or shine, was that roof. I was in permanent contact with Rick at the hotel and continually took digital pictures of all the staff entering or leaving via the gatehouse. Anyone showing an interest in the boat would get special attention. I could instantly download the shots onto a palm-size PC and send them directly to Rick by mobile phone. The chance of any of Stern's crew monitoring these cyber transactions was unlikely. All Rick had to do was sit in the warm and compare my shots to the pictures Joel gave him of the Dutch players. If we could get a match, Bob would be your father's brother. Well, that was the theory. It was a place to start. To be fair, I kind of preferred being on the roof, rather than in the hotel.

The yard would probably run twenty-four hours a day and, as they said at school, I was it. With that in mind, I had packed lots of emergency rations and fluids, thermal blanket, waterproofs and, the containers for my bodily functions. When I left the observation point, so would every trace of me.

I'd used public transport to get to the observation point, visited several locations, and doubled back on three occasions, before arriving at my final destination. If there was a tail, I was confident I'd lost him. With all the doubling back and checking, the fifteen-kilometre journey had taken me two hours.

It started to rain steadily. I tucked myself into my poncho and tried to concentrate. I'd felt nervous on my way to the point. It seemed as if every man and his dog were looking at me. It seemed that I, the grey man for so many years, was standing out like a big daft Jock in Holland. It was, of course my own insecurity. After a lay-off like mine the senses get dulled and you lose that edge. I could not afford to lose mine for long. After all it was my second visit to the plot and I should be getting used to the drama.

I could hear trams lumbering below me taking people back to Dam Square. Their laughter floated upward through the rain and it cheered me up.

It was getting dark and the rain became more persistent. One of the things I learned in all my time in the Regiment was that the enemy, no matter who, didn't like the rain. They got lazy and sought cover. It was the best time to operate if you had the resilience.

I didn't mind the rain. I'd spent the last several years in it, fishing in Loch Lomond just for fun.

So there I was all nice and settled. The rain was falling around me in steady droplets. I had an 8 million pixel digital camera, a palmtop, a mobile and a Glock 9mm. pistol. The whole lot was kept dry by my wet weather gear. I took the first picture and settled down for the night.

Rick Fuller's Story:

With Des in position, I was alone for the first time in a while and immensely thankful for it. I had become used to my own company and relished the privacy that came with it. People found that selfish but I preferred my own companionship. Despite the tacky décor, the room was comfortable enough. The bellboy had just delivered grilled chicken with lemon butter, shallots and baby potatoes so I settled, ate and relaxed. The food was passable. I found a classical music station on the hotel radio. It played *Finlandia* by Sibelius. It was dour and depressing so I switched until I found another. I wound up the volume, Bizet, *Farandole*, from *L'Arlesienne*. Lighter. Better. I lay back on the sofa, closed my eyes and the darkness began. It swirled around me like an ill wind, each twist and turn dragging me down deeper and deeper to the darkest place a human can endure. A place that scares even the bravest soul.

It was always the same dream. I am standing next my car in the driveway of my house. The front door is open. Something pale is lying just inside. My heart is racing as my adrenalin levels peak out. I try to run to the door, but the stone driveway turns first to a vile liquid and then to a swirling, steaming void beneath my feet. Putrid hands grab and tear at my ankles, pulling at my shoes, wrenching them from me. My bare feet burn and I hear screams of agony beneath them. I am terrified to look down but I am drawn to the tumult below me. My heart is close to bursting, pushing itself upward and into my throat. My chest is being crushed by a massive unseen weight as two rotting female corpses climb my legs and pull me downward. I am filled with despair and look again to the open door. The pale form is still there. Then, I see her face.

Everyone dreams. It's just some dream better than others. I suppose I should have been thankful when Susan shook me awake, her voice chasing my personal dragon. Before I had assimilated her identity, my reactions had overtaken my thought process and I had pointed my Glock directly at her head. I heard my own breath and felt the blood pound in my ears. Adrenaline made my legs twitch. It gets everyone.

Susan seemed scared by my reaction and my facial expression. The dream hatred hadn't left my countenance. The subject of my recurring nightmare always left me hating just that little bit more. It dehumanised me piece by piece.

"Christ! It's me!" she screamed.

I looked furtively around the hotel room, not knowing what I was looking for, then lowered the weapon and took a drink of water. I could see that we were alone and Susan had entered via the adjoining suite doors.

"Tanya?" I barked. "Where's Tanya?"

Susan pouted and placed a finger to her lips. "Shhhh, she's sleeping." She closed the door quietly behind her. "You sure you are okay?"

I nodded and felt mild embarrassment. I pulled myself back from the edge and concentrated on where the girls had been earlier.

"Okay. Did you find a place for us to stay?"

"Yes." She oozed with a newfound confidence that rattled me. "If I had been one of David Stern's boys, the dream you were having would have been your last."

She was right of course.

We all make mistakes. I should have locked that door. I should have been awake. Perfection is for the movies. Errors of judgement in this business can be fatal. The first thing that struck me was I had no recollection of Tanya informing me she was going to take a break and sleep. She had let the spoilt bitch out of her sight. I hoped that it would be the last of our cock-ups. We couldn't afford too many.

I set up my kit and waited for Des to send the first shots. The laptop had booted and the connection was made. Files would soon be downloading.

I ignored Susan's presence as she stood in my peripheral vision. Dreams were put aside and I wanted to get on with the job at hand, but she disturbed me. She had showered or bathed and wore nothing but a white hotel towel. Her hair was dripping on her pale shoulders. She was serious and stunning.

She looked at her bare feet. "I'm sorry."

I waved away the apology. I mean, what was there to apologise for? Typical of a woman, they had to analyse everything. She was persistent. I just considered it an act, another of her many personas. In fact I considered everything Susan did to be an act.

"I mean it. I'm sorry I disturbed you."

I gave in. I was impatient for Des's pictures. "Okay, accepted."

She looked happier, walked to the sofa, and sat a little too close to me for comfort.

"Who's Cathy?"

I felt like I'd been poked with a cattle prod. I took a deep breath but still couldn't help myself. She had a triumphant look about her. There was no trace of true compassion on her face, only the half-hidden happiness fuelled by the knowledge that she had the upper hand. I struggled to keep my voice level, keep my hand covered. But my tone held more venom than I would have liked.

"That's none of your business, Susan." I gestured toward the door. "Now why don't you go back to your room and get some rest."

She moved away a little, sat side on to me, and crossed her legs. She was insistent and showed no sign of giving up.

"Is that your wife? Cathy? Are you married? I mean, you wear a wedding ring. And your name, Colletti, that's not your name either, is it?"

Too many questions; I kept it as light as I could.

"Shakespeare said, 'What's in a name?' Romeo and Juliet, wasn't it?"

She placed a hand on my knee. The usual knot did its job in my guts. "You don't trust me, do you?"

"No."

She played aimlessly with a lock of damp hair.

"I want to help Joel, honestly I do." She raised her eyes to mine. "I love him, but I'm scared of David."

I had to remove her hand. "Good." I changed my position on the sofa, making further casual contact difficult. "Joel can trust you. I'll remain firmly on the fence until this is over."

She was not easily dissuaded. Her tone lightened further. She was almost giddy.

"If you pull this off, what will you do with the money, Colletti? I mean, you aren't exactly broke, are you. I've seen the clothes, the car and the flat."

I smiled as sweetly as my disposition allowed. I decided to fight back, to hit where it always hurt a woman.

"No, I'm not broke, Susan, and neither are you. The difference is, I know what I am. Do you? I suppose you don't actually feel like a prostitute? Is that because the money isn't left on Joel's bedside cabinet? I mean you're not a streetwalker, are you, more of a high class call girl. I'll bet you've fucked some high ranking guys eh?"

She flared at my comment and her Dutch accent reappeared all too professionally.

"I'm Joel's wife, not his whore! I have a PhD. I am a fully qualified pharmacist." She jutted out her chin and looked as ugly as someone like Susan Davies could. What about you, Colletti? High school dropout? Parents in jail? Sent to a care home? The world didn't understand me, so I just went around killing people for a living? I don't need to mix with the likes of you. You're nothing but a mercenary. No honour, no country, a low life murderer."

I had long since become immune to insult. I had been my hardest critic for far too long. Any guilt I had left inside my body was reserved for another. What did concern me was how close to the truth Susan was.

"Why don't you get dressed, stop playing games and I'll tell you when I need your services."

She was angry. The little girl hadn't got her own way. She pointed at me, an action that got to me even when made by someone as striking as her. She was in mid-sentence of some verbal diarrhoea when my patience ran out and I grabbed at her. I intended frogmarching her to the adjoining door. It was instinctive and I hadn't planned it, but in my haste her towel fell downward and over her breasts. I heard a sharp intake of breath from her and the bleating stopped.

She stared straight at me, her eyes burned. Two naked blue flames flashed and darted. She made no attempt to cover herself. In fact I was sure she arched slightly to improve the view. Her expression showed nothing but confidence and satisfaction.

I moved slowly, deliberately. She stiffened slightly and I felt her guard slip for a second. I took the towel's edge between thumb and forefinger and restored her modesty.

As I did she followed my hand with her eyes and then returned them to mine. Any failure in the confidence department had been repaired and restored. She grinned.

"Did you like what you saw, Mr Colletti?"

"I'd have to be blind not to see. But like you said, I'm a married man. There's something about you, something unpleasant, something not right. You're like most beautiful things, Susan, you come with a high price. I'm happy to let Joel pick up that particular bill. I'll console myself with the knowledge that the money I save will buy me a Ferrari."

To my amazement she wasn't fazed. In fact her confidence grew further. She purred,

"I've seen the way you look at me, Stephen."

My skin crawled and I couldn't contain myself.

"Do you get off on men who kill for a living? Is that it? Is that why you're hitting on me? Or is it so I'll drop my guard and you can warn Stern I'm coming?"

Once again our eyes locked. It was her turn to show herself. She pulled her towel slowly downward until her naked breasts were on show again. Susan grabbed at my hand with surprising speed and held it against her. Her nipple hardened to my touch. I went to draw away but she leaned into my palm and squeezed my hand into her flesh.

She took a sharp breath and moaned slightly. Her face was inches from mine. The perfection of the blue in her eyes held me transfixed and I hated myself. Her mouth was open slightly, wet and inviting. She showed no fear, only pleasure. I could feel the heat of her on my face. She was the picture of sexuality. Her whole body oozed it. The towel had fallen at my feet. She was naked and exquisite. Her voice was calm between breaths.

"I'd like to keep you alive, Mr Colletti."

Her tongue slid from her mouth like a lizard catching a fly. She licked my bottom lip.

"You are the only man I have ever seen that isn't scared of Joel or David Stern. You're not scared of anything, are you, Stephen? That's what I like."

I stepped backwards, picked up her towel and threw it at her. She caught it without looking.

"I don't mess with married women, especially one whose husband is about to pay me a great deal of money."

She stood defiant and held her towel at her side. She displayed her nakedness to me in the austere hotel room light. For many years, I had only seen beauty like it in a dream, a dream that became a nightmare every time. The dream she had interrupted moments earlier. She turned with the grace of a bird in flight. "Have it your own way."

The adjoining door closed behind her and I was once again alone. I put my head in my hands and felt tears prick my eyes. She had discovered a weakness in me that I had kept secret for ten years. I had told her I was still married. Why?

Then, in the darkness of my tears, Cathy looked up into my face and smiled. She had a smudge of earth on her cheek from digging the garden. My tears flowed freely and washed her from view.

My hands were still shaking slightly as I rebooted the laptop and started to download the files that Des was sending me. I looked out of the hotel room window. It was a dark, dismal and cold night for June. Raindrops slid along the pane following each other downward in their own private crazy game of chase. I stood to look out and saw people hunched under umbrellas as they made their way to the local cafés and bars. I thought of Des. It was not a night for sitting on a fucking roof.

I gave myself a mental kick up the backside. For a moment, I felt for him up there. Then I remembered his favourite theatre was the Arctic. I'd never met a guy who actually enjoyed being cold.

Minutes later the bleep of the PC told me that the first image was ready to download. The kit that Des had brought along was amazing. He was two hundred metres away from the target, on a roof, in the rain, and the shots were so clear and bright I could read the time off the subject's watch if I'd wanted.

The images came thick and fast. Overall views of the yard were first, together with shots of the roads leading to and from the plot. I was as good as there.

Then came the Landmark, it was still in the same position as in the afternoon shots, except someone had covered part of it with tarpaulin. Were they getting ready to move? As if to confirm my suspicions, the next three shots were of several men and a powerful Toyota Land Cruiser 4x4. It was big enough to tow the Landmark. More pictures, as usual Des and I were on the same wavelength. A sense of urgency formed in his work. Four more shots of the boat appeared on screen in quick succession. Men in wet weather gear pulled more tarpaulin over the vessel. Des then sent close-ups of all of them. I couldn't match them to Joel's pictures. Not a single known player. Leaning against the Toyota was a big bull of a man with a white-blond crew cut wearing small, round, gold-rimmed glasses. He was speaking into a mobile and held a newspaper over his head to shield himself from the rain. I again checked the four mug shots Joel gave me. No match.

I knocked on the adjoining door and Tanya appeared looking fresh, clean and ready.

"What's happening, man?"

I was already packing gear in a holdall. The thought of committing the team to a hard stop weighed heavy on me, but I had no choice.

"We're off, Tanya. The shit has really hit the fan. They look like they're going to move the Landmark."

I pushed a magazine into an MP 5, cocked the action, released it, and checked the safety.

"It's time to get Joel's boat back if nothing else." I gestured into the darkness behind her. "Get Susan together. It looks like it's a hard stop."

Tanya turned down the side of her mouth.

"I dunno man, t'all seem too quick to me."

I knew what she meant but we had no choice. A hard stop was exactly what we didn't want. It always happened on every job. Something always went tits up. I'd had it happen to me in Ireland, in Columbia and in Bosnia. The best you could do was to just get on with it.

"Maybe we're just lucky, eh?" I said.

Tanya looked unusually nervous. Not something I was used to.

"Ain't no luck on this job, babe. I can feel it in my bones. Nothing feel right tonight."

I ignored the mojo and a small tingle shot down my spine.

"What car did you get me?"

Tanya seemed to cheer a little and smiled. "A Volvo S80."

I frowned at the word Volvo. How can any self-respecting collector drive a fucking Volvo? She disappeared briefly. Her mojo had taken a back seat, realism had taken over and I could hear her giggling in the background. She knew what I was thinking. When she returned she was pulling on motorcycle leathers over cotton trousers. Before I could ask, she chirped, "Oh and a Ducati 900 for me."

I watched as Tanya left in a plume of tyre smoke. Despite the wet weather, she was positively flying on the Ducati. Her orders were to back Des up prior to my arrival and keep a tail on the cruiser if it left before we regrouped. We'd had no practice. We had the bare outline of a plan, nothing more.

That aside, my humour was restored slightly as I had underestimated the Swedes. The Volvo S80 was as sweet as a nut. The 2.4 litre 5 cylinder 20-valve engine put out 180bhp. It handled well enough and felt as safe as a virgin in a convent.

Susan sat in the front seat and stared over with those blue eyes. I sensed a hint of fear, but it was short-lived. Her sheer presence bothered me but I hadn't the time or the inclination to worry about her at that moment. I'd asked her to read the map I'd given her, and surprisingly she used her local knowledge to our advantage. I don't know if you've ever driven in Amsterdam, but it's a fucking nightmare. Trams, cycles, one way systems and stoned pedestrians, what a mix!

Five hundred metres from Stern's yard we slowed and collected Des, who slid into the back seat, a wet and sorry-looking soul. He stowed his surveillance kit and checked his weapons. No MP5 for Des. He loaded a Winchester pump action shotgun with 'RIP' rounds.

"It won't be long before they move now, mate," he said, double checking his Glock. "Tanya is about a click from us to the north of the yard. There's no sign of an escort, nothing. The blond guy in the glasses is the main player. He's organised the team and has been barking out orders for the last hour. The good news is it looks like just three guys in the Toyota."

I nodded. Stern's men knew a team was in the country, but he wouldn't expect us to be able to trace the boat so quickly. It would be too much to ask for the goods still to be on board. No chance. That said, I'd known doors left open before.

Our only plan was to follow at a discreet distance using our two vehicles, Tanya's Ducati and our Volvo. All we could hope for was a quiet stretch of road where we could do the business as best we could. Once we had the Landmark and the towing vehicle, Tanya would deliver it to Rotterdam docks, where Joel's team would take over. Once Joel had his boat on the way, Des, Tanya, Susan and I would return to the Dam and wait to see if Stern came out of the woods once his pride had been dented. Then it was time to find big bags of coke, even more bags of money, and the main man, David Edgar Stern. Payday beckoned.

There was a sudden burst of static from our comms and the car was filled by Tanya's voice. The Jamaican drawl was unmistakable. The Landmark had just passed her position with three men on board. Within minutes Tanya had dropped back from her position as observer on the cruiser and we had the point. To have a successful tail, it was essential that the point was changed over at regular intervals so the bad guys didn't get nervous. Anyway, the Landmark was so big they couldn't see too much behind them and could hardly lose us in a chase. It was the one good point I could think of as I mapped out the stop in my head.

We were on a motorway and the cruiser was managing a respectable eighty kph. Our visual contact consisted of a pair of taillights in the far distance. Slowly, slowly, catchee monkey was the order of the day. Susan hadn't uttered a word and seemed as focused as any in the car. Des seemed to nod slightly in the back seat, his shotgun resting across his chest.

Thirty silent minutes drifted by and we saw the Toyota and its valuable cargo signal to exit the motorway. We took a chance and got a little closer. I saw the lone headlight of the Ducati appear in my rear view mirror. Swift and purposeful movements from Tanya showed she was ready to commence the proceedings.

The new road seemed ideal. We hadn't met another vehicle for over five minutes. The road lighting was minimal. A deep drainage ditch at either side of the road made for careful driving.

Susan remained quiet but her eyes flicked around the car. She looked a little nervous. I handed her a balaclava mask.

"When we stop this thing, I want you to wear this at all times. Stay in the car and keep your head down, don't move and you'll be fine." She eyed the mask, then me. Her manner cold, she crossed and uncrossed her legs. Was it genuine nervousness? I got the feeling she was secretly enjoying the whole thing.

"Why not just follow for a bit longer, they might stop soon anyway?"

I thought it a strange thing to say.

I pushed the comms pretzel and Tanya answered instantly. She was using a 'hands free' inside her helmet and I could hear the purr of the Ducati.

"Hi, baby."

Her casual tone gave me strength and I felt myself smile. My confidence rose.

"Okay, Tanya, time to do this thing. If you have a clear run for one kilometre, go for it."

Within seconds Tanya flashed past us on the powerful motorcycle. We saw, rather than heard her wind up the Ducati as she passed our prey. The front wheel lifted and the bike's staggering power was transferred to the rear. It was a show just for the Dutch. They would still be commenting on her poor control when they found the bike and Tanya strewn across the road in front of them.

People are predictable. Men are the worst offenders. I mean, think about it. You work for a very dangerous man. He has entrusted you with a quarter of a million pounds worth of boat, a stolen boat for that matter. You are delivering it somewhere, in the knowledge that if you fuck up, you're dead.

Nonetheless the three buffoons in the cruiser stopped at the sight of a beautiful black girl sitting next to a prostrate red Ducati.

Their wheels had barely stopped turning when we pulled alongside. I made a quick check to see if Susan was masked, as despite my misgivings it was still important none of us could be identified.

I was out of the Volvo. For a split second I was vulnerable until I rolled over the bonnet and got cover from the car engine block.

Des was out and I heard the sound of the Winchester. The 'RIP' was away. So called because the round punches a hole in the first thing it hits and then delivers a block of CS dust into the hole. This time it was the rear window of the Toyota Land Cruiser. The Dutch guys were already fucked. They were blind from the CS and could hardly breathe.

They staggered from the vehicle coughing and choking. The more they rubbed their eyes, the worse it got. With CS, you feel like gouging out your own eyeballs to rid yourself of the irritation.

Tanya had the whole of the front of the scene covered with her MP 5. Des had ditched the shotgun and trained his Glock at the emerging rear passengers.

The driver jumped out holding an Uzi. Tanya double tapped him, and I saw two dark stains appear in the Dutchman's chest. He went down in silence without getting a round away.

Slick and quick, like a well-oiled machine, Des was barking at one guy to lie down but the sap seemed either too scared or didn't understand the Greenock accent. I had the second man covered. The safety was off on my H & K. I could see through the haze of CS that he was scared to death.

I noticed a flash of light. It was off to my left, behind Tanya. Headlights, the last thing we needed. Before I knew it there was gunfire, lots of it. It was heavy calibre automatic weapons, probably 7.62.

From the darkness, six rounds tore into the bonnet of the Volvo, missing me by feet. I turned and started to lay down rounds in the direction of the attack. My heart lurched. The attackers were too close to Tanya. She was silhouetted in the headlights of an unseen vehicle. She had no cover at all. We just hadn't planned on the cavalry and I swore under my breath. Susan! We'd been set up! Our friend Stern wanted his girl back.

I heard the crack of Des's Glock to my right and cries from the area of the Toyota. The Scotsman was playing percentages. The two guys in the cruiser were dead where they lay, under the circumstances, two less men for us to worry about.

More big stuff flew in my direction and I was knackered for any cover other than the Volvo's front wheel. The 7.62 rounds would probably slice through the rest of the car. I remembered Susan was inside and crawled backward to her door. I wasn't going to let her get killed in the process. She was our only ace in the hole. As I opened it she was cowering in the foot-well screaming in Dutch. I gathered she was swearing. I heard more covering fire from Des and the big stuff subsided a little. I reached up and pulled Susan out without looking up. She hit the tarmac hard and I saw she was bleeding. I couldn't tell from where.

I heard Tanya's MP5 and saw she was prone behind the fallen Ducati which was her only chance. I poured rounds over her head at a saloon which looked like the Audi from yesterday. At least two men had left it and were firing controlled bursts in Tanya's direction. She stopped firing to change magazines. I fired again over her in the direction of the muzzle flashes. It was a vain hope as I couldn't properly see the positions of the shooters, but it was the best I could do.

Her mojo, her protection, had stopped working. I watched helplessly as a line of automatic fire marched relentlessly along the ground toward her. Each round sent small pockets of dust up into the air, like drops of cold water falling on a hotplate. Then, I found myself in some B movie cheap slow motion shot. The procession of bullets bounced forward. Now, I could see the shooter in faultless focus. The perfect moon again. The man was smiling as the action on the AK47 in his grasp flew forward and backward. Spent cartridges were ejected from the weapon as bullet after bullet flew from the red hot muzzle. His blond hair, which fell across his left eye, was blown temporarily off his face with each recoil. Then, my heart tried to leave my chest. It tore at my ribcage, climbed my windpipe and made for my throat. To my horror the first of Blondie's rounds reached their target. The black full-face helmet Tanya wore exploded like a dropped peach. Kevlar was never a match for the ArmaLite. I felt physically sick. Her body bucked as the following rounds entered her in a line down her spine.

She didn't feel them. Her brain had stopped receiving pain messages. But I felt them. Each and every one ripped into my flesh. I suppose I had been kidding myself the last two years. For a moment my body was frozen.

Without my knowledge, I had grown close to someone and once again they had been taken from me.

Des was working like a man possessed. He fired burst after burst in the direction of our attackers. He rolled between each set of fire to confuse the enemy. The technique also made him incredibly hard to hit in the smoke and darkness.

I pulled myself together. The relentless training, first with the Regiment, then my own personal, darker, regime, kicked in. The loss of a friend, even a lover, in battle, was part of the deal. I looked for cover for us all and knew that we had to make the gully at the side of the road. Without the ditch for protection we would die like grouse on the Glorious.

Just like Tanya.

I grabbed at Susan who was still cowering, but the tirade of expletives had ended and she was silent. The air stank of death and battle. I was nearly deaf from the gunfire. Anything other than a shout was blocked by a high-pitched ringing sound. My ears thought I'd just been to see Motörhead.

There were ten metres of open ground to the ditch. Ten meters, in which Blondie and his mates could slice us in two. Susan was injured and appeared traumatised. I knew she would slow me, but I dragged her to her feet and screamed at her to run and get cover. She did. It was a breathtaking turn of speed and I watched as she dived headlong into the ditch.

The boys with the AK's were having a field day and rounds exploded in front of my feet, shards of tarmac tore holes in my trousers, as I ran for cover myself. I made an almighty leap to the ditch and I was hit by three feet of freezing shit-coloured water. Seconds later I heard, "Des! Des! Des!" and the Scottish lunatic came flying in on top of me. I have to admit I was pleased to see him. I looked left and right into pitch black.

The gunfire subsided slightly and I risked a look up over the ridge of the stinking ditch. I saw nothing but shadows. Des immediately popped up thigh-deep in water and emptied his clip in the general direction of the Audi.

"How many you think?" he said, panting.

I had it all in my head, I always did. For some reason I could see the battle in my mind's eye. A recollection only likened to photographic memory, I could place every enemy I'd seen in their last position. The most frightening thing was, I would never forget any or their faces. From Armagh to Amsterdam I would recall every last one. "Originally four in the Audi, plus the three from the cruiser," I said, my voice echoing inside my skull. The whistling blocked out most of everything important.

Des was checking his weapon. "Reckon only two men left alive, heading to the Audi. How are you for ammo?"

"Fuck all."

Des gave me the look that told me he was in the same boat. We had to get the fuck out of there, we both knew it. Where the hell was Susan? The foetid water in the ditch made any movement difficult and slow. We could hear footsteps and shouting maybe twenty metres away. Both of us ducked low into the freezing ditch. Then, even though my ears were shot, I heard Susan's voice. It was unmistakable even in my poor state.

I popped up to look. The two men left standing had her by the arms and for the first time, I saw that they were not in overalls as I had first thought, but uniform. Specialist shit, not the standard stuff, like some tactical police unit or other. I'd seen the gear before and I was racking my brains when Des got real close and whispered, "They've got Israeli Special Forces kit on."

Both guys looked sorted. Blondie and his best pal carried heavy calibre machine guns. The friend walked backwards as he held Susan and trained his weapon in the direction of the ditch but he couldn't see us in the dark. The guy looked wired but stayed on his task. He was a pro, no doubt about it. There had just been a small war. Hundreds of rounds had been fired.

Susan looked calm as they helped her toward the Audi. She was limping slightly. The blood I'd seen on her was from a superficial leg wound. She seemed okay. I heard radio transmissions, and then saw what I should have realised from the start. Susan took the handset and started speaking into it, her tone measured and calm. It wasn't Dutch either, well not exactly, it was Afrikaans, and she was pissed off. I couldn't understand what she said, but I got the impression she wasn't happy we weren't lying dead in the road.

The three walked past Tanya's body on the way to the Audi and the blond uniform stuck the boot into her midriff.

I knew he'd pay for that one.

We had no way to get to Susan. No ammunition and no cover. It would be suicide and that came extra. We weren't getting paid by Bin Laden. Des was looking at his hand-held GPS unit. We both carried one, together with the mobile phones.

"I reckon," he began, "we are twenty clicks from the nearest town. We need to split up and…"

My mind was on Susan and the soldiers. How far away were more of Stern's guys? What if he could muster air support and track us down? Even more strange, they were leaving their colleagues dead on the ground? Who did that? Not even the worst Mafioso left their dead. There was only one answer. They had a clean-up team on its way and I'd bet next month's pay Susan had just called it in.

Des shook me by the arm. "You listening?"

"Yes."

"Well, we gotta move."

We heard the Audi's tyres screech as it drove into the night and I looked over the top of our cover. The air had cleared and there was an eerie silence except for the odd metallic clink from the ruined vehicles. Des climbed from the freezing water of the ditch and crawled toward the devastation. I followed his wet trail. My head was in turmoil. Why hadn't they started a search for us?

I told myself, I didn't care.

The perfect moon popped out again just for our benefit and Tanya was suddenly surrounded by shimmering black. Her heart had pumped on long after the initial rounds struck her. To the left of where the Audi had been, lay two bodies in uniform.

Des reached Tanya first and took the MP5 from her dead hands. He checked the mag, gave me a 'thumb', and approached the bodies lying in the darkness.

He rolled the first with his foot and then quickly knelt at the second. "This one's still ticking," he shouted.

I walked by Tanya. Her face was hidden by her helmet and I was strangely grateful. I paused for a moment and looked at her lifeless form, before I joined Des and inspected the living, a man in his prime, lying gasping for breath. He wore the same uniform as the others in the Audi. I would have put him in his mid-thirties and he sported a military style flat-top. On his left side, he had an entry wound just below his collarbone and a second to his ribcage. Red bubbles formed at his nose with each shallow breath. I guessed he could only be using one lung and was finding breathing an interesting concept.

Des pulled out a first-aid pouch and checked his pre-loaded syringes. He selected adrenaline and administered it to the unfortunate bloke. The reaction was instantaneous. The boy almost jumped to his feet but Des was ready and cradled him tightly. Everybody always remembers when John Travolta gave the shot to Uma Thurman in the movie *Pulp Fiction*. Well, this was a close second.

Des spoke in quiet measured tones as I looked nervously about for the cavalry. "Steady, son, settle down now, you'll be fine."

The boy's eyes were wild. He was shitting himself and the excess adrenaline had tripled his heart-rate. He started to shout. Des put his hand on the boy's mouth and made a hushing sound. After a few seconds the guy obeyed. So would anyone. Believe me.

"Speak English?" whispered Des and released the grip.

"Please....," blurted the guy in perfect Queen's. "Leave me here."

I couldn't make out the accent exactly, but thought it sounded American, maybe Canadian.

"How long before your friends get here?" said Des, as if asking directions to the park.

The poor bastard summoned some bravery from somewhere deep inside his gut, did a fair impression of a smile, and told Des to go fuck himself.

Des was ruthless. He searched for the guy's rib entry wound with his thumb, found it, and plunged the stumpy extremity in up to the first knuckle.

There was a wet plop and the boy made a strange gurgling sound. Des's thumb had plugged the entry wound and there were weird and wonderful things happening to the boy's body. He wasn't quite sure if he should scream or breathe.

He chose to do the former.

"How long and how many?" repeated Des.

There was another gagging effort and a cough that threw blood and snot over Des. The boy was really struggling for air.

"Minutes…" was all he could manage before chucking more of his lungs over Des's jacket.

The boy fell unconscious. Des looked at me, between brushing bits of lung off his soaking coveralls. "Well? I say we fuck off."

Guess what?

We did.

I started to unhook the Landmark from the Toyota as it was the only serviceable vehicle. Joel's prize boat was a real mess. Dozens of 7.62 rounds had devastated the luxury vessel. Des did a sweep and collected as many weapons and as much ammunition he could, together with everything he and I had brought to the hard stop. Also, at my request, he checked Tanya for any ID. There was none. As a professional she shouldn't have carried any, but Des checked anyway. I couldn't bring myself to do it.

The Toyota still reeked of CS. Contrary to popular belief it isn't a gas but an irritant and clings to everything it touches. The seats in the cruiser were rife with it and my nose and throat started to itch immediately.

I fired up the car and Des trotted toward me. As he reached the wounded man he stopped and knelt. Des whispered something to him I couldn't hear and I saw the briefest movement and flash of steel.

Seconds later, Des jumped in the car.

"He's gone," he said.

Now you may consider Des's actions harsh, but it was just part of the war. We were in deepest shit, and until we knew what the fuck was going on, all we had was each other. We couldn't risk the boy giving any information to his buddies.

My mind made a brief trip back to Manchester.

Joel was going to be really pissed when heard this one. He really was out of his depth with Susan and Stern's crew. He'd completely underestimated her and how powerful and professional this group were. She was part of the plan, no doubt. Joel had to know and quickly.

I mulled over what we knew. The guy Des had just put out of his breathing difficulties looked ex-army to me, maybe even ex-Special Forces. Joel had now lost his wife, boat, coke, and a big pile of money.

As for Susan and Mr Stern, they had just upset a psychotic multi-millionaire who would undoubtedly pay vast sums to anyone who would avenge this little lot.

Probably more scary was one of the most ruthless Yardie gangs in the UK would be buying EasyJet tickets to Amsterdam the instant they found out about Tanya. I knew her brothers would never forgive her killers.

Stern's biggest problem though, was neither Joel, nor the Richards brothers.

He had really upset me.

As I drove the cruiser, Des was rooting through the cabin for anything of use or interest. The rear nearside window had gone and the draught blew bits of paper about the interior.

We had enough petrol and, due to Des's expert scavenging, we had a serviceable weapon each with a few rounds. Not enough, but beggars couldn't be choosers.

Finally Des sat beside me and pulled out his dreadful pipe. It was a habit he had never been able to break. I gave him the sternest look but he didn't give a shit and lit it anyway. A plume filled the cabin before being sucked out of the broken window. Neither of us had mentioned the cock-up on the road, or Tanya, and we travelled in silence for a while, deep in our own thoughts.

"They knew we were gonna hit the boat, didn't they?" said Des eventually.

"Hmm, yes, I reckon so."

"Susan was in on this from the beginning, then?"

"Certainly once she found out Joel wanted her to ID Stern, maybe much earlier, who knows? Maybe she opted for the safest route and jumped ship. Either way, Joel will want her back alive."

I spun the cruiser left and onto the motorway and I felt my voice falter for a second.

My friend saw it.

"I want to finish this job, Des, for lots of reasons. It was shit about Tanya, she was a good mate. We need to have a beer for her when this is all over."

Des nodded in silent agreement.

I rubbed the back of my neck and considered I was getting too old for the mountain of shit we were going to climb. Then my brain came to life.

"I can't see Joel getting anyone else, I guarantee it. He might be an arse, but he knows we're the best he's got. With Tanya dead, the Richards brothers will be sending death squads to Holland the second they get the telegram and I'm more pissed off than I'd care to mention."

I looked at Des as he took a pull on his pipe. I asked the obvious. I just needed confirmation I wasn't in a James Bond picture.

"Did you see Susan grab that radio handset back there?"
Des checked the magazine in what was Tanya's Glock, and pushed it into his waistband.
"Aye, I saw."
"Did you hear what she said?"
He exhaled plumes of smoke out of the window, wiped his teeth with his tongue, and savoured the taste of his favourite shag.
"Nope, but I gathered that someone had fucked up, and got to the party late."
"Yeah, I reckon Stern's plan was to take us all out, leave Joel without protection, and then attack his business. I tell you, Des, he doesn't just want to rob Davies of his money," I pulled my mobile from my pocket. "He wants him wiped off the face of the earth."
I punched Joel's private line into my handset. There was a long silence, then, a metallic message. I hardly heard Des's voice.
"Do you think that Susan could have been in on this from day one?"
I let the message repeat in my ear.
"Dunno mate, it's possible." I said absently.
The robotic voice was clear. Joel Davies private telephone line was disconnected.
We needed to be out of the country, soon as. The moment I hit the red button Des knew. He bagged his bloodstained jacket and chucked it out the window. We had to dump the cruiser ASAP as it did a fair impression of a mobile cheese grater. We were wet, filthy, had no money or passports and no transport.
We managed about thirty kilometres before we decided our luck was at a premium and turned off the motorway. We found a nice looking suburban area and parked the cruiser in a large car park that serviced four blocks of private flats. The perfect moon made one last effort to frame our sorry-looking souls and we could see our breath in the chill. Des had found a length of plastic parcel binding and a screwdriver in the cruiser. All we needed was an old-ish model car to boost.
Sure enough we found an '80's Ford Escort just ripe for the picking in a corner of the car-park, shaded by conifers. Whilst I kept a casual eye out, Des folded the parcel wrap in two and pushed it between the door frame and centre pillar of the car. Seconds later he had wiggled it over the old-fashioned door lock button and with a deft tug, we were in.

The screwdriver took care of the ignition barrel. Within ten minutes we were back on the road.

Wet stinking overalls and brushed nylon seats. I was more pissed off than ever.

Stern's crew would come after us, no doubt. Joel was either dead or on the run. This was the mother of all takeovers. We had a window of opportunity to get some miles between us and them. Also, we didn't have any petulant passengers to contend with, so we'd be much harder to find.

Des drove in silence I turned up the heater, got my head down and said a little prayer to the nice dream God.

When I woke, the first signs of dawn shone into the old car's filthy windscreen.

We had pulled into a supermarket car park and Des had worked more magic and got us both a brew.

"Where are we, mate?" I stretched and took the polystyrene cup. "And how'd you pay for these?"

"We're less than a mile from Rotterdam and I found some change in the glove box."

I took a sip of tea. It was probably shit but to my bird cage bottom of a mouth, it tasted great. My clothes had dried on me and I was left caked in mud that smelled as good as it looked.

"You're a star, Des."

"Yeah right." He rummaged in his pockets and produced three Euros.

"This isn't gonna get us over the water though."

I took another drink of the warm brown liquid that passed for a brew.

"True, but I think I know how to manage it."

"How?"

"Well," I turned to him. "You're going to have to punch me for a start."

He did, and it fucking hurt.

Another thirty-minute drive brought us to the port of Rotterdam. With the Escort left burning all trace of us some two kilometres behind, we wandered the concourse close to the ferry terminal, keeping one eye out for any sign of anyone who looked like one of Stern's cronies.

The ferry port of Rotterdam teemed with travellers. Dozens of unwashed hippies with braided hair, smelling of petunia oil, mixed with cheap-suited businessmen.

What looked like an organised party of American cruise ship pensioners was being led toward a coach. They were probably there for the Dutch Flower Festival and I watched the tour guide with interest.

He wore a navy blue uniform with gold trim. The jacket was slightly too small for him, but he was smart with a grey crew cut and a big white smile. I shivered at the thought that he would have to keep thirty overweight geriatrics happy for days on end, listening to their endless complaints. He looked like a good guy, an all American boy. He'd probably served his country too. I could see it in his movements. His stature gave him away.

The clear morning had turned cold, and the stiff breeze was causing havoc for the elderly passengers. They held on to all manner of hats with thin, veined hands whilst the tour guide helped the coach driver to load masses of luggage into the hold.

Finally a couple of the old dears pointed in our general direction. One covered her mouth with shock at our appearance. Des and I staggered along, both covered in mud and the usual bumps and grazes associated with a fire-fight. I sported an obvious fat lip courtesy of the Scot. He was shouting obscenities at the old buggers and doing a fair impression of a drunk.

Within seconds, the coach driver was prodding at his mobile for the coppers. My tour guide watched us impassively, totally unfazed by the din. For a split second he caught my gaze. He had pale grey eyes that matched his crew cut. His tourist smile broadened and became real. I staggered left and Des and I fell to the floor with a fair wallop. I hoped it looked as real as it felt.

The American strode over, doing his best to hide a limp, and knelt by our exhausted bodies.

"Say, you guys better get lost before the cops arrive." He held out a ham-sized hand to me. To my surprise I took it and he pulled me to my feet with ease. The guy was strong as an ox.

"Thanks."

"No worries. You guys English?"

"Ah'm no English," growled Des in thick Greenock.

He shrugged patiently. "Brits then."

The guy looked me up and down. He knew something wasn't right. "Wherever you're from, you'd better go now, the Dutch harbour police aren't noted for their hospitality."

Des sat back onto the concrete. "Fuck 'em," he slurred.

Once again the big guy shrugged and smiled. "Suit yourself, buddy, just moderate your language around my old folks, eh? Elderly people deserve a little respect."

I nodded and Des mumbled an apology. "Aye, sorry there, big man." The guide offered his hand again. This time my arms stayed locked in place. The guy looked mildly embarrassed.

"Jerry Mahon," he said, tucking his hand back into his pocket.

"Navy Seal, before I lost my kneecap."

I heard a voice below me.

"Des Cogan, drunk and happy, before I lost my wallet."

The three of us burst out laughing. It was the most natural laugh I'd had in years. The guy turned and limped away. I would never meet him again, but he was one of the good guys.

Before he had reached his coach, I heard the first police siren. Seconds later a meat-wagon came into view, driven by a very sour-faced cop. The van was closely followed by a squad car which contained four uniformed officers.

We were unceremoniously dumped onto the cold concrete by the contents of the car, cuffed, with a little too much vigour, and driven to a holding centre that looked like a training centre for suicide bombers.

Neither Des nor I had been prisoners before. We had decided on a story, part truth, and part fiction. This was the standard operating procedure of the Regiment. It was accepted that any man would eventually give in to torture. A holding story was essential. Once the enemy bypassed the tale, lives were at risk.

We stuck to our task. We had flown to Holland via Amsterdam. Our passport swipes would confirm it. We had travelled to Rotterdam and we had been duped by a man in a large saloon car. He had purported to be a taxi driver and had turned out to be a robber. He had stolen our luggage, our money, our passports, indeed everything of worth. He had forced us to stand in a freezing ditch as he drove away. We were poor destitute white European tourists.

We were treated like the latest batch of Eastern Bloc illegal labour. Seventeen hours in a freezing cell did little for my humour.

You need photographic ID to get on a ferry. That or the relevant documentation from the coppers to say you've been robbed. After twenty-six hours of dicking around, we smiled sweetly as we got it. Once aboard, we ate from a decent buffet, courtesy of a Dutch police voucher and dressed our minor wounds from the ship's pharmacy.

Later Des and I climbed the metal stairwell to the upper deck of the ferry. As it lolled along, piercing the dull grey sea with its blunt nose, my thoughts turned to Tanya. My mind played horrible tricks as she flashed into my conscious, wearing fabulous clothes and a wonderful smile.

I had known her for four years and we had been intimate for two. I knew it wasn't love, but she knew too. She accepted me for what I could give. She never asked me for more. It was enough for us both and she understood.

The Regiment had its own way of dealing with loss. In general, you accepted it and had a piss up. There was usually an argument over the ownership of the soldier's boots.

Tanya would be no different. My mind would not allow it. I would miss her, that was true. I knew that I had to meet David Stern and I wouldn't rest until that day came. My doleful thoughts and fat lip were lifted by a familiar figure striding toward me carrying two brews. Des looked pissed off. The coppers in Holland had given him some clean jeans that were all of three sizes too big. He looked a proper twat. That said, it wasn't the denims that were bothering him. "You're going to take Stern on, aren't ye?" He shook his head in irritation as he handed me black tea. "You always were a mad bastard."

I looked into the distance and saw the first shapes of the English coastline. "I can't let the fucker get away with this though, can I?" I said to no one in particular.

The wind made my eyes water. Des stepped in front of me to get my attention. "What you gonna do about that bitch Susan? She wanted all of us dead on that road, mate. No question. If we'd not been on our game, she would have succeeded."

I took a drink from the polystyrene cup.

"She had bottle, though. More than I gave her credit for. She could easily have been killed back there. She handled herself pretty well." My guts turned over.

"You have to admit it, Des, I should have seen her coming."

"Aye, maybe."

I leaned over the rail of the boat and took a few good breaths of sea air. "I think Joel's already dead."

Des nodded slowly.

"Maybe, but he's no great loss though, eh? He disnae concern me. Live by the sword an' all that. What concerns me is what happens next like."

"True." I could see why Des was reluctant to get involved any further. I changed the subject.

"So what are you going to do now, Des? You'll get your cash as planned, of course."

He waved his hand dismissively. "Me and you need to have wee drink for Tanya. Then I'm going back to Scotland to catch some fish. You know where I am if ye need me."

I'd lost the best part of sixty grand in expenses, the weapons, surveillance kit and wages. I'd been shot at, been forced to stand in a freezing dirty ditch, Susan had pissed me right off and Joel, my best source of income, was probably in several pieces holding up a section of the M60.

I always had Des.

The crossing to Hull took us just shy of twenty-four hours. I really wanted a shower, but even if we'd had a cabin, we couldn't have risked some hairy-arsed Dutch drug dealer coming flying in during routine ablutions. So we sat and stank.

Rules, you had to have rules. If you stuck to them, you lived longer. Once back on home soil I organised two seats on an internal flight from Hull to Manchester simply by blagging twenty pence for the phone and being able to memorise Mr Colletti's credit card details. Our flight would take a little under forty minutes. We were flying BA. I liked BA. They did it right.

When you sign up for the Parachute Regiment, not only do you agree to jump out of an aircraft, but any aircraft HM Army suggests. In some countries, planes fall out of the sky before you can jump. Believe me; never fly on a Russian aircraft. I was once stuck at Charles de Gaulle and the only available flight was Aeroflot. I managed to obtain a seat, but when the air hostess started a collection for spare parts for the plane, I was off. Jumping out is one thing, making sure the thing stays in the air is another. I trust us Brits, personally.

Still, I digress. Des and I sat drinking in the less than comfortable lounge of Hull Airport waiting patiently. Two real Hooray Henrys boasting 'rugger shirts' insisted on quaffing 'champers' as if grapes were endangered. They were lolling at the small bar and were unfairly abusing a young girl who was serving them.

She wore the BA uniform, which I had to say, was flattering. She had long straight black hair to her waist and typical doll-like Philippine features. Her attempts at politeness were lost on the overpaid louts as they continued with Chinese restaurant humour.

"Say fried rice!" one of them ordered.

"Fried rice, sir," answered the girl. This seemed to tickle the boys no end.

"Flied lice! Flied lice!" they bellowed. One made chicken impressions and added, "Chicken flied lice!"

Rules you have to have rules. I was in no position to make any kind of scene. The grey man had bigger fish to fry as they say, so I, like the waitress, listened to the inane shit. Everything was bearable until 'Geoffrey the fried rice man' decided to invite me into their soiree.

"Have a drink, old boy, you look like you need one. We'll pay if you're skinters." He sprayed me with spittle. I declined, politely. I could hardly comment about the state of my apparel as I looked like the monster from the blue lagoon. I hoped he'd got my message.

He insisted.

I declined again.

He insisted.

I couldn't help myself.

I stood and faked a clumsy trip over Des's outstretched feet. The table in front of me, together with my drink fell forward. I tumbled with it, adding all my weight to the pivoting furniture. The table edge landed squarely on Geoffrey's kneecap, pushing the patella down his leg to around mid-shin. He made the most bloodcurdling sound I'd heard in a long time. I, of course, the tramp-like soul, full of regret (and mud) apologised profusely. His numb friend even told me it wasn't my fault, 'just an accident, could have happened to anyone.'

Des smiled and shook his weary head. As the paramedics treated poor Geoffrey, the beautiful Asian girl stood in some shock. Then she looked over, put a delicate finger to her lips, kissed it and blew in my direction.

Our flight was being called. I apologised to Geoffrey again but he was in too much pain to care. I looked back but the British Airways girl had gone; one of the good guys, you meet them wherever you go.

I boarded, feeling much, much better.

<u>Manchester, The Northern Quarter, 2006.</u>

"I need a fuckin' drink." Des was severely pissed off. His weathered brow was creased in temper. It was unusual, Des didn't lose his temper, he was never just 'angry'.

The pub we'd opted for was an Irish theme job called Finnegan's and was in need of a re-fit. Des had picked it as he said it would do good grub. The countless drunken feet that had danced on the furniture had taken their toll. The place was pretty lively. A DJ with a '70's haircut and a beer belly blasted out good time music from a small stage in one corner. The place was popular with the student fraternity and I spotted too many woolly jumpers for my liking. Hardened drinkers lined the bar. Brickies and scaffolders with red faces threw pints of Guinness down their necks. Small groups of mainly overweight women cackled their way through vodka and Red Bull, which appeared to be the trendy drink.

Des and I found a quiet snug and settled in. The Scot ordered the 'All Day Irish Breakfast' and two pints of Caffreys. I had an espresso. I was intending on a recce to Joel's gaff later and I wanted a clear head.

We blabbed on about old times like a pair of wounded veterans and Des worked hard at getting pissed. Finally, Des had consumed enough and, as usual, the floodgates opened. It was a story I'd heard before, too many times before.

"It was never the same after you went, mate," he slurred, "you know I'm straight, straight as they come."

"Forget it, Des."

"Bollocks. You will never forget or forgive, not after Cathy."

I didn't want the conversation. It was a part of my life I needed to forget. The dreams were enough. The reality was just too much to bear.

I remember as I pulled into the drive I could see that our front door was open. The window on the Cavalier was still misted despite the heater and I couldn't quite focus. The sodden trees were being whipped around by the breeze. I felt the cold on my shoulders from my earlier drenching between DIY store and the vehicle.

I remember stepping out of the car. The open door was not that unusual. Cathy would often be pottering around in the garden. We lived in a very safe area.

I moved around to the boot and opened it with the key. I gazed at all the orange and white plastic bags inside and my stomach churned. I held my head in position staring at the collection of home improvements. My neck was locked, because I had seen.

All my life, ever since my first memories, I'd had the ability to freeze a scene in my mind. One glimpse was enough. I could tell you numbers, colours, name plates, anything you wanted. For some it was on a page, for me it was in the real world.

And I had seen her.

She lay face down; her right arm flopped over the front step. Hair covered her face, but she was naked.

I couldn't find the courage to raise my head toward the door and take a second glance. I squeezed my eyes tight shut and said a prayer to a God who had never listened to me and never would.

It was no use. Each facet of the doorway thundered through my head. Flashes of extreme detail tore into my skull and strangled my heart. Her left shoulder-blade had been pushed out of her back by an exiting bullet. Her flesh was torn away in grotesque pieces as each white hot cartridge had taken her life.

From somewhere outside my own body I heard a scream. I know now it was my soul deserting me.

It has never returned.

In the following weeks and months after Cathy's murder, Des was a rock. I was completely on my arse. If it hadn't been for him, I would have ended up in the loony bin for good. But I think that was the Army's plan.

I sat looking at the drunken Jock who was my only friend in the world.

"You're right, Des, I'll never forgive."

I gave him a playful slap.

"Come on, fuck Joel's pad, let's get pissed."

I awoke with a hangover for the first time in years. The hotel room smelled like a brewery and the sunlight hurt my eyes as I opened the curtains. It had been a night of bad dreams. Cathy had visited me for good measure. At first, just after she was murdered, she would fill every dream, but more often, every nightmare. The last few months I'd had more sleep. It was just every waking hour that was a real bastard.

I realised I should have done my job and checked out Joel's house and that it had been a bad idea to get leathered with Des. If Joel was dead, it put a whole new complexion on the game, and the Richards brothers needed warning that something big and ugly could be brewing. I also regretted that I'd stayed in the Novotel. It was like kipping in a Burger King.

By ten a.m. I'd managed to get myself home and sorted.

I punished myself with a ten kilometer uphill run on the gym treadmill and finished with four sets of bench press exercises. I had worked so hard that my muscles twitched under the skin and my hands shook, not with alcohol but with adrenaline. I lay in the hot Jacuzzi until my heart rate returned to normal and my head was clear. Breakfast was masses of fruit, cereal and eggs.

I had just about decided on my wardrobe for the morning when my flat door exploded open.

Mr Stern's boys had come to call, and they didn't look happy. I reached for my Beretta but it was pointless, two serious looking faces stood feet from me. One I knew immediately. He had white-blond hair that fell across his left eye in a side parting. His sparkling blue eyes followed my every move. The man who had killed Tanya with expert precision made no secret of the fact that he was armed. He was pointing an Uzi directly at me at hip height. I knew that if he pulled the trigger it would cut me in half before I even drew my gun. "Richard?" he questioned in a clipped Dutch accent. "That's the name, isn't it? Richard Edward Fuller to give you your full title, ex of her Majesty's Special Air Service? Poor little orphan type, joined the Parachute Regiment as a boy soldier?"

I stayed silent. It was obviously a rehearsed patter. My skin crawled due to his close proximity and I felt genuine hatred for him. He started to wander around my lounge, picking up items at random. Whilst his silent partner trained his big bore handgun at me.

Blondie wore flesh-coloured latex gloves.

He rediscovered his sarcastic tone.

"You resigned from the Regiment before you were kicked out, I believe.

Nasty business about your wife."

I nearly lost it there and then. The piece of shit had no right to talk about my wife. He could see my rage building inside me. Everything I had learned in my years of service was being tested to the limit. If I exploded he would have even more of an advantage. These were his mind games. The physical stuff was just around the corner. He laughed dismissively. He held all the cards, after all.

The Dutchman stepped sideways but kept his eyes firmly on me. "Stop trying to look so tough, Richard. What are you going to do now? Bleed on me?"

He thought he was really funny.

"You went a little crazy after the Irish shot your wife, didn't you, Richard? She was naked when you found her wasn't she? It was you who found her, wasn't it, Rick?"

He took two steps toward me and gestured for me to take a seat. I did as I was told. My mind was racing as I tried to get a handle on the situation. How had they found my flat? Of course, it was Susan. I knew that stupid bitch would get me into trouble. My address was one thing, but how did they know my identity and background? Joel had no idea. I was sure of it, so it couldn't be him. I had to presume he had been their first port of call and that he was dead. Then I remembered Susan's little outburst about me being in care as a kid and it all started to fit into place.

Blondie continued inspecting my possessions, keeping his Uzi pointed in my direction at all times.

"You like the good life, don't you, Rick? Good clothes, good wine, fast cars? Shame about your nigger girlfriend, eh? Fancy that, you, a pure bred Englishman fucking a black."

His last word was flecked with the same Afrikaans accent I had heard from Susan. The guy looked relaxed and tanned as he spoke his tirade of shit. He was immaculate and his voice was completely level. But there was anger there under the surface, expertly controlled, but there. I got the impression that he could explode into violence at any second. He looked the epitome of the pissed off gangster. The fucker just needed a white cat to stroke and I would have felt like an extra in a Bond movie.

"So what do you want?" I asked. I kept my voice level, even subservient.

He shrugged as if it was a question that was unimportant to him. "I have to say that you and your friends made a pretty good job of our boat. It's going to cost a small fortune to make it seaworthy again, if we ever manage to get it away from Customs. You killed some very good friends of mine too. My boss is very angry. He never thought you would ever turn up again. This visit, though, is a cleaning up exercise, Rick. The boss wants you to know it's nothing personal, just business."

Now my mind was working overtime. How had I turned up again? Had I met Stern before? How did he know my past?

Blondie took the lid from my brandy decanter and sniffed at the contents. "Were you close to Joel Davies, Richard? Mr. Manchester?" He looked straight at me and his thin lips turned upward into a smile.

"The big fat fucking joke squealed like a pig when I finished him. Not that it will concern you much. You do realise you've had your day too, Richard. What are you now? Forty-five? Forty-six? You're a bit past it. You should have retired. This was one job too many."

He motioned toward his silent partner. "This is Max. I will look after matters here. When I'm finished with you, Max will pay your friend Des Cogan a visit, another over the hill has-been. I'm sure you'll provide us with all the information we need to find the little Scottish prick."

He poured himself a drink. "I think it best you do that sooner rather than later, Richard. There is no point in unnecessary suffering. You know the drill, been through the training eh? If you are a good boy, it will all be over quickly. All the remaining ties between us and this operation will be severed within days. We will simply walk away and leave the remainder of the Manchester scum to it."

He stood close and I considered an attempt at stripping the Uzi from him. Max was on to me and just shifted slightly to make life impossible. Max stepped in close and they grabbed an arm each and quickly tied my hands with plastic cuffs. I didn't see the point in struggling.

I gave it my best shot. Under the circumstances I had to try and buy time.

"Let me and Des sort this out for you. I'll smooth the waters with Tanya's brothers. No one, not even Stern, needs a war with the Yardies." Max stopped briefly, gave me a sickening smile and spoke for the first time.

"Rick, you have no idea what is going on. Don't even try to understand." I'd never been captured. Obviously I'd known lots of guys that had. I'd heard all the tales about Iraq, even read the book one of the boys did about it. I was in Belfast when the Provos captured two Det guys after driving into a funeral procession by accident. They killed them both, eventually.

In the Regiment we were told that no man would stay quiet under torture for too long. Therefore just as Des and I had used the day before in Rotterdam, we always had a cover story ready prior to an operation that we could use as a delaying tactic. The interrogators didn't believe the tale for very long, but it could buy you some time and hopefully keep the rest of your guys in the field safe for a while longer.

As Blondie and Max chattered away in Dutch in my kitchen I was trying to think. Where had I met Stern before? He knew everything about me. I pushed him to the back of my mind and concentrated on the problem at hand. I figured that the easiest way out of this was to give a false address for Des and hope that some opportunity arose for me to escape or disable the two goons.

They had relieved me of the Beretta and now had me tied to one of my dining room chairs by both ankles and wrists. They'd done a good job too and the lack of circulation to my extremities was starting to cause me pain. I could just about feel my toes but my fingers tingled as the bloodflow ground to a halt. This I knew would be temporary unless they left me for any length of time.

Blondie walked in carrying a kettle of boiling water, and my blood ran cold. He was a big man as you might expect. The fine blond hair that fell across his forehead was well cared for, no ten pound haircuts for this guy. He had added gold-rimmed glasses which made him look younger. He smiled to reveal perfect white teeth.

"Rick, I don't need to tell you what scalding water does to the skin. I'm sure you have had medical training. The body can withstand an enormous amount of pain. Although the problem is, as more and more areas are scalded, there is the risk of the person dying from shock and lack of fluid. I want you to tell me where your friend is in Scotland. Max will then travel there, and, when he returns, having dealt with Desmond, I will ensure that you do not suffer unduly."

I was about to go into the blubbering fool act and give him the phoney address when he poured the contents of the kettle over my right leg.

I think I was screaming. The pain was horrendous. My ears popped as my blood pressure hit the roof and my heart went into crisis mode and pumped like a freight train. I felt the searing heat of the water but shivered uncontrollably as my body went into shock. Within seconds my trousers were welding themselves to my skin.

The Dutchman leaned forward and put his face so close to me that I could feel his breath.

"Now, Rick. I promise you that you will tell us the truth. The next kettle will be for your left leg. Then I'll fry your bollocks. If I need to keep you alive after that, I have an IV and adrenaline in the car. This is a one chance opportunity, Rick."

For the first time in my life I knew I was beaten. I couldn't take another kettle. Des had promised himself a fishing trip and he could be away. He had a place just off Loch Lomond. It was off the beaten track, very remote.

In the end of course, my only hope was Des. I figured that if he could slot this Max guy before he suffered a similar fate to me, then we had a chance. He would definitely come straight here. If the roles were reversed I would understand. In fact I would want Des to send them to me. I felt the need to cry but I couldn't.

I gave Blondie the address.

I didn't know how long Max had been gone but the first signs of morning were in the sky outside. My torturer was called Stefan. He'd introduced himself as he had stuck some morphine into me a few hours back. It had helped the pain but it had returned with a vengeance and I shivered uncontrollably. I could hear him dialling numbers into his mobile but he spoke only Dutch. I could hardly feel my hands or feet at all. The only thing that was keeping me conscious was the pain in my leg. Stephan's mobile gave me an idea. My own unit was in my back pocket and I could just feel it with my right hand. From memory I felt for the buttons as best I could. The centre button 5 always has two ridges and from there I could work out what was going on. Slowly and deliberately I pressed the control button to unlock the keypad. I sent a numbered text to Des and hoped it made sense. If I didn't survive and he did, he would know what to do.

Stephan walked into the kitchen again and I heard the kettle being filled. I felt sick, my legs twitched and I thought of Cathy, of how we had planned a baby, of the way she laughed at my stupid antics; the smell of her hair. I tried to picture her face but each time I only saw her lying in her own blood in the hallway, a simple hallway with ordinary furniture. I had never really cared for anyone or anything since that very day. And now I knew it was my turn to join her. I suddenly didn't give a shit about Stephan, Max, Stern, Susan, anyone. If he was going to slot me I just wanted him to get on with it. The goon walked in carrying the kettle. He looked pale and pissed off.

"I am disappointed in you, Rick. Your friend Des is not in residence at the address you gave me."

My body was shaking so much, my voice sounded like it belonged to someone else. I wanted to tell him to go fuck himself. I wanted him to pull out the Uzi and shoot me. Instead I saw the kettle and I knew what was coming. "He's fishing," I blubbered, "he'll be out on the water. You need to give it time."

"Time is something you don't have my friend."

I think I begged before he poured.

After Stephan had scalded me for the second time, the pain was so bad that it obliterated everything else. He hadn't even bothered to ask me any more questions; I think he just wanted to hear me scream. I realised that I was in a vehicle and we were moving. I had been hooded and my hands were tied. Even if I had been free I didn't think I could find the strength to stand never mind run. Each time the vehicle hit a bump or turned a corner my legs felt like the flesh was being torn from them. I presumed it was some kind of van from the noise inside but to be honest I was close to not caring. There was a faint smell of engine oil and some other chemical I couldn't identify. My only hope was that somehow Des was on his way or that Stephan got stopped by the law. I never thought I would be glad to see a copper.

The road started to get more uneven and the pain shot through my body in vile spikes. Suddenly the vehicle lurched to a halt and I heard the driver stop the engine. The back doors were opened and someone grabbed my feet. I screamed in agony and almost passed out again.

My hood was removed and I saw Stephan staring at me. He was a little wild looking but managed his sick little smile. Now I know you might say that he was only doing the same job I had done for the last few years. It's true I had disposed of many people. The one thing I couldn't understand was the enjoyment in his eyes. He revelled in my agony and I felt the surge of adrenaline that total anger brings. If he untied me, despite all the pain in the world, I would rip off those glasses and gouge out those eyes as my last act.

He obviously noticed my feelings.

"Don't even think about it, Richard."

He produced a large bore handgun, probably a .45

"We're going for a short walk."

Walk! The guy had to be out of his fucking mind. He grabbed me by the shoulder and sat me up on the edge of the van floor. There was a sticky fluid covering both my shoes which I presumed was a mixture of weeping burns and urine. I felt ashamed that at some point I had wet myself.

Stephan seemed to get an even bigger kick as he realised my own discomfort. He simply pointed the .45 toward my damp groin and sniggered.

"Maybe I should have made a washroom stop en route, my friend."
I couldn't help myself.

"Why don't you just fucking do what you're paid to do, sonny, and stop this shit."

His face boiled up with anger and he hit me a good one with the handgun. It caught me across the cheek and I felt blood trickle down my face. To be honest it was worth it.

"Walk!"

He grabbed me again and pulled me out of the van. My legs gave way immediately which angered him even more. "Get up, you asshole!"

I tried to ignore my pain and looked around to get my bearings. We were in the country. A similar spot to where I took Alfie to be disposed of. It looked like moorland and I couldn't see a single building. To make matters worse it was pissing down. A minor thing, you might think under the circumstances, but believe me that was how I felt. I checked out the van. It was an old Transit. As the rain splattered my face I looked for a second vehicle but I couldn't see anything. It raised my spirits slightly as I presumed Max was still looking for Des or better still Des had found Max.

"Get up!" screamed Blondie.

It was starting to look like an episode from a bad drama. I mean if the guy had been such a pro, he would have known I couldn't walk. All the shouting and screaming was only going to attract attention. Even up on the moors there might have been ramblers. He was a dickhead.

I just lay on the ground in major discomfort but I was not going to help him top me. He grabbed my hair and turned my face toward him.

"Get up or I'll take off your trousers."

I knew what that would entail. It would take off my skin with them. It would be as good as flaying me alive. I was not going to let him do that. He would have to kill me there on the road.

Stephan made a grab for my belt and with all the strength I could muster I lifted myself with my stomach muscles and butted him firmly in the face. He fell forward dazed and I rolled until my body was on his. My only weapon was my mouth and I sank my teeth into his cheek. I felt like fucking Hannibal the cannibal but it was all I had. He screamed and hit me again with the .45. I felt the pain but didn't let go. He couldn't get enough leverage to knock me out as our faces were locked together. I tasted copper and bit harder. I needed to get to his nose. If I could get locked on just under his nostrils, around his top lip, I could do enough damage to render him unconscious. Then he raked his foot down my right leg and all my plans were dashed. It was all over. White hot pain tore through my body and I released my grip.

It was pointless.

Stephan forced the .45 into my mouth.

"You fucking piece of shit," he spat.

He put his hand to his face and inspected his own blood. I could feel the sight of the weapon digging into the roof of my mouth. I didn't want to see his face but I couldn't look away.

I closed my eyes and thought again of Cathy. This time her smile was perfect. There were no bullets, no blood and no screams.

Stephan pulled the trigger and my world went black.

Des Cogan's Story:

It doesn't matter if you catch anything. Fishing is about calm and concentration. To relax in the beauty of the situation and to pit your wits against one of God's wily creatures is one of life's pleasures.
I bought the house on the Loch with fishing in mind, when I left the Regiment in 1998. I was married back then, but when I was away working my wife Anne found that the isolation was difficult to cope with. As time passed, she secretly got pissed off with me under her feet when I was at home too. She missed her friends in Hereford. It was a difficult and painful time, the thought of divorce was hard. No one in my family would ever consider such a move. Anne had other ideas. To add to my marital difficulties, I was trying desperately to get to grips with not being a professional soldier. I'd never known any other job.
One of seven brothers, I was brought up in a three-bedroom tenement a bus ride from Glasgow city centre. My staunchly Catholic family scraped for every penny, but still had change for the plate at Mass every Sunday. I'd watched all my older brothers scratch around for work, whilst after school I ran errands for anyone with two pennies to rub together.
One night my eldest brother Tom had a friend over for supper. All us boys were ordered to dress in our chapel best and my mother had cooked a joint, unheard of other than on a Sunday. All the boys were excited at the event, but had no idea who our special guest was.
Tom's friend turned out to be James MacAfee. He'd joined the Scots Guards as an infantryman and sat at our meagre table, resplendent in his uniform, green beret tucked under his left epaulette. My father beamed from ear to ear as he questioned James about his various exploits.
From that moment, I knew what I wanted to do.
His red hair was cropped short and even though he had barely passed his eighteenth birthday he cut a formidable figure in my eyes. He was so smart and clean and brave. Moreover, he had something I wanted.
The respect of my father.
My whole family made a very special effort to welcome him to our home. It was genuine affection.
When James was killed at the battle for Tumbledown in the Falkland Islands, he was twenty-three.

I'd often wondered if the claustrophobic yet loving home I came from, led me to specialise in such a lonely area of warfare. I'd certainly had enough of sharing a bedroom with three mischievous brothers.

When our family attended the funeral service for James MacAfee in 1982, I was already serving myself and had just completed selection. As we gathered around the doorway of the chapel on that breezy summer morning, my father tapped me on the shoulder.

He looked at me, his rugged face bursting with pride, the very same way he had looked at James at our table five years earlier. He gripped my arm. "You take care of yersel', son," he said.

Before I could answer he had stepped off to give his personal condolences to the McAfee family.

He was a man of few words, my father.

Now I had all the space I would ever need.

I think Anne had liked it best when we were back in Hereford, she had her friends and I was away a lot. The marriage finally ended in divorce and the split was acrimonious. I got the wee cottage in Scotland and the clothes I stood up in. She got our holiday cottage and the chance to live back in civilization. Anne married again six weeks after our divorce was final.

My father died a year later, my mother is still convinced it was the shame of the divorce that killed him.

I genuinely still live with the guilt.

The only other person close enough to know all this, and that the cottage on the Loch was my home, was Rick.

Rick or Stephen or whatever bollocks the boy was calling himself. He had remained my only mate through all this time and I loved him to bits, but to be honest, I had become happiest when alone.

Just me, the rain and the fish.

It was a full five miles to the nearest shop and I ran there with an empty Bergen, collected supplies, had a brief chat with old Mrs. McCauley and ran back with it full, three times a week. It kept me fit without the need for a gym and I got to speak to another human being.

It was enough.

In all the years I had lived there I had never seen another motor vehicle on the road other than lost tourists and the monthly gas and diesel trucks that supplied my cottage with heat and light.

So it was a surprise to me when I saw the Range Rover that morning, crawling along the road, not a mile from my place.

One guy was inside. He was very blond and serious looking. He didn't see me, but I saw him. He certainly wasn't a tourist. Tourists didn't have hand-held GPS systems, they had a TomTom.

Maybe it was a sixth sense or just years of distrust but the moment I heard the engine coming toward me I slipped off the road and dropped myself out of sight. The guy was a player. I'd bet my life on it. I felt a shiver of apprehension. I needed to speak to Rick.

I did what I did best. Kept my head down and waited. There was no mobile signal out by the Loch so I was completely alone with the situation. There was no immediate reason to approach the guy. I decided to wait for him to piss off, and sure enough, after about an hour I heard the burble of the Range Rover again and the blond dude passed by without a hitch. I started back home without my shopping. I had a sticky feeling that this was all about Joel Davies, David Stern and a whole lot of cocaine.

My worst fears were confirmed when I reached the cottage and found the door busted in. I didn't have much of value thanks to Anne and there didn't appear to be anything missing, but the hairs on my neck were standing to attention. The boy had been through my desk for certain but I kept all the sensitive stuff in a gun cabinet in the loft. I checked the access door and it was untouched. He'd missed it. The only way the guy knew I was there was to have obtained that information from Rick, and the only way Rick would have told them, and not warned me, was too hard to think about.

I grabbed the house phone and tried Rick's home number. I got a long continuous tone. I then tried his mobile. It rang and then went onto answer-phone. I started to feel sick. You will have heard or read all the Regiment stories of how, when we lost a guy on an operation, we argued over his boots and had a piss up in his honour and all that. The truth was I never got used to loss.

I sat down to have a smoke on my wee pipe and a think. As it turned out I didn't have long to muse. I heard the crack of big tyres on gravel. The Range Rover was back.

All my weapons were kept in the loft. It was a throwback from when Anne was there. She hated to see guns in the house. I took the stairs two at a time, lifted the hatch and unlocked the box. I heard the car door slam outside. He wasn't a very careful boy. He obviously didn't rate my chances.

The first thing I could lay my hands on was a Remington pump action shotgun. I used it to shoot small game around the cottage. It wasn't the subtlest weapon in the world but it would have to do. I'd got myself in a good spot on the top of the landing. The solid brick interior walls of the old cottage were good cover, and I could see the front door which was flapping about in the wind from the boy's previous visit.

I slipped the safety button just behind the trigger guard to the fire position as the guy stepped into view.

He saw me in an instant and made a grab under his coat. That was enough excuse for me. I let go the Remington and remove most of the boy's left kneecap. I had to give him credit, he still went for the weapon until I put a second cartridge into his foot.

After a careful walk down my stairs, I bent down next to the powerless guy and removed his weapon from the shoulder holster, a SIG 9mm pistol.

"Now then, matey, what the hell are you doing in ma house with a big fuckin' gun?"

The boy was shaking and his lips trembled as he tried to speak.

"Go..to..to hell."

His accent was Dutch and my mind shot back to the road in Amsterdam where I had to push my thumb into the player to obtain information. It was like being back in Belfast with wounded Provos. I pushed the barrel of the pump action shotgun under his chin and kept my voice level even though I wanted to slot the bastard there and then.

"In case you're no aware, sonny, this shotgun here has a six shot magazine and nothing would give me more pleasure right now than to use all the remaining four to kill you."

I leant onto his bad ankle with my knee and the old trick worked a treat again. The pain kicked in and he spoke through gritted teeth.

"You know who I work for and why I'm here, so you'd better," he took a shallow breath, "let me go now."

I held his SIG in front of his face. "Yes, you're here to kill me, son."

The boy nodded, his face resigned to his lot.

"So just because you work for a drug dealing scumbag, I'm supposed to crap myself, dust you down and let you shoot me, that it?"

I tried hard to control my rage and swallowed hard. "Before we go any further, boy, you start talking about my friend down in

Manchester. He isn't answering his phone and I'm a wee bit concerned like."

He didn't look scared. He wore the look of a man already dead, and I knew the answer before he spoke. They were two words that changed my world.

"It's done," he said.

As I packed my gear I thought it ironic that the fish I would eat in the coming months would have fed on the young Dutchman. The Loch had claimed another victim and the world turned.

I'd cleaned the area where he'd lain of obvious bloodstains and fixed the lock on the front door. I intended to commandeer the Range Rover and his GPS too. David Stern, a man I had never met or ever wanted to meet, had ordered the murder of my only friend. I had no choice in my course of action. Revenge is an ugly emotion. It often leads people to behave in ways they never thought possible.

For me there was a void in my life that could never be filled. Did I want revenge? Call it what you like, I was going to find Stern, and kill him. But first I had to bury Rick.

I needed money to do what I had to do. I'd been well paid the last few years and I'd been careful before that. I knew I could raise about thirty grand but it would take a week or two to organise. I'd got some walking around money and some weapons. Together with what I'd lifted from the boy, I felt secure enough. I could lose myself in Manchester a damn sight easier than in Belfast. Besides, the Dutch kid had no photograph of me either in his clothes in the car or in his phone. By my reckoning the main players in this scenario didn't have a likeness of me and that was my biggest asset. Only Susan could ID me and if she got close enough for that I'd slot her too.

My first duty though was to Rick and that in itself would be a problem. Once I started snooping around in his affairs I would be visible. I knew that Rick trusted Tanya and her close family. I would need some help and the best place I could think to start was Tanya's brother, Georgie Richards.

It was getting dark as I reached the outskirts of Manchester and my mood was blacker than the sky itself. I found myself in Rusholme surrounded by Indian restaurants, and realised I hadn't eaten in over twelve hours. I needed some grub and some kip before I could start to look for Georgie.

I saw that there was a hotel coming up on my left, The Woodland. It looked like a typical business class hotel and there were plenty of curry houses around for some food. That, and a few drinks to aid my sleep. I might not have been able to fight over Rick's boots but I was damn well going to have a drink for him.

I pulled into the Woodland's confusing car park and opted to leave the Range Rover around the back out of sight. I had packed all the weapons and ammunition I possessed into a sturdy suitcase and I was glad it had wheels as it must have weighed sixty pounds.

I dragged it and other light luggage into the small carpeted reception which was fairly busy with visitors. I had to wait in line, but within half an hour I'd sorted out a room. I, unlike Rick, used my own name, but I did use an old safe house address from the Regiment days rather than the cottage in Scotland.

The receptionist was pleasant enough and a decent room cost me sixty-five pounds bed and full English. She explained that the hotel was busier than usual as Manchester United were playing a European tie at Old Trafford.

She even flashed me a smile. Had I been feeling myself, I'd have been flattered.

Once in the room I removed my weapons stash from the case and laid it on the bed. It was an accumulation of all sorts of kit I'd collected over the years.

Two pistols, a 9mm Browning I kept as a souvenir after my last tour in Northern Ireland, and the SIG I commandeered from my Dutch assassin. The Remington shotgun with the extended magazine and shortened barrel; a Heckler & Koch Mp5k 9mm machine pistol and enough plastic explosive and detonators to make a hole you could drive a truck into. I'd packed half a dozen flash bombs, a pair of night vision glasses, a good digital camera and the commandeered GPS.

Add the boxes of 9mm ammunition and 12-gauge cartridges and you can understand why I had to split the lot up and stash it.

I decided that the best thing was to separate the haul into three working sections, then if one was found it wouldn't be a total disaster.

I hid the Remington and the Browning under the seats in the Range Rover. I deposited the Mp5k and the flash-bombs in the hotel left luggage and left all the remaining kit in a suitcase in the room. All except for the SIG and a couple of magazines of 9mm of course, I didn't feel that safe.

By the time I'd sorted all that, had a shower and changed my clothes, I was starving.

Rusholme, Manchester, is a vibrant but garish area, full of Asian shops and restaurants. It's nicknamed 'The Curry Mile' and it lives up to it. There were hundreds of curry houses to choose from, and not being a local, I opted for a busy one.

The standard of grub and the service was great and I wolfed down poppadoms, mango, bhajjis, chicken vindaloo pilau rice and a pint of Cobra.

I was starting to feel better, my head had cleared and I tried to assess just what the previous couple of days had been about.

The only person capable of finding Rick so quickly was Susan. She was obviously part of David Stern's crew. The visit from my Dutch friend was obviously a clean-up exercise. It'd happened before in Rick's business, but it didn't make sense to me as it was very expensive. The only thing I could think of was that the boys had come with the orders to hit Davies. Maybe topping us was some kind of punishment or warning for even having had the balls to go up against him. I had to assume Davies was already dead. The worrying thing was that it meant I was the only one left alive that knew about the Amsterdam connection.

This was all spinning around in my head when I noticed a guy at the next table reading a copy of the *Manchester Evening News*.

Splattered across the front page was a picture of Tanya. The shot sent a wave of realisation into my head. It had only been three days since she'd been killed. I couldn't make out any more information from where I was, and I didn't want to risk drawing attention to myself by staring at the guy. The grey man remit suited me fine. So, I paid the bill and went to find a newsagent.

I didn't have far to go. Four doors down, was a Late Shop. A Pakistani guy in national dress sat behind the counter playing with black prayer beads. I picked a copy of the *MEN* from the shelf and dropped it in front of him as I counted change.

"A terrible thing these black people running around, killing people and selling drugs," he commented as he took my money.

A bit rich, I thought, considering over eighty per cent of the country's heroin arrived via Afghanistan and Pakistan, but I didn't comment.

Ten minutes later I was sitting back in the bar of the Woodland devouring the lead story and another lager.

The writer had obviously taken the information from a wire service. Second-hand words, translated from Dutch. They knew who Tanya was and that she had connections to Jamaican drug gangs. There was no mention of other casualties. Stern's team had obviously cleaned up very well. According to the British press, this was a lone woman shot dead in Holland with no clue as to her killer. The only veiled suggestion from the writer was that Tanya had been previously associated with contract killings in the Manchester area.

I put the paper down Took a long drink and fumbled for my wee pipe. Rick hated my pipe. *Well, ya wee shite*, I thought, *this one's for you, mate.*

I was just about to light it when I grabbed at the newspaper again. I shuffled through to the announcements section, and there, I found what I was looking for. A much smaller picture of Tanya headed a single column. Words of condolence and lists of family members followed. Then a date, her funeral was arranged for Thursday, two days' time. It seemed I wouldn't have to look too far for Georgie after all. I just wondered what my reception would be like.

I had just forty-eight hours before Tanya's service and I needed to get myself organised, so I tried to put any thought of Rick's own funeral, or where his body might be, out of my mind. I found that so difficult. Not just because we had been friends for many years, but because we had looked out for each other in the most terrible circumstances, and triumphed.

I drained the last of my pint and ordered the next with a wee whisky on the side. I was just getting the taste. Once the drinks arrived I proposed a silent toast to my mate.

I'd bet most of you reading this have had a number of people in your life that you trusted. I mean absolute one hundred and ten per cent pure loyalty. A husband, maybe a boyfriend, sister, father, or lifelong school friend?

How many times in your life have you been let down by family, friends or partner?

We forgive our family, even close friends and lovers can be forgiven. But when it came to the relationship between Rick and me, forgiveness took on a whole new meaning. In the field I could rely on Rick without question. Outside the field he was a fuckin' nightmare.

Let me put it this way. It was Christmas 1980, we were young squaddies and had home leave; we'd both just passed the first stages of selection. We had seven fantastic days before we would be off to the Far East for jungle training.

We were driving from Hereford to Greenock to spend the holidays with my folks. Rick's family, well, his mother and father anyway, were dead. He had been brought up in care and he had bad memories of all holiday times. For weeks before he'd been giving me the big sob story about being alone at Christmas and Hogmanay. So, I got my folks to agree to take in another mouth. Not an easy task, I can tell you, especially as my dad never forgave the English for Culloden and Rick kicked with the wrong foot, if you know what I mean like. Anyway, off we set in my pride and joy, my Mk 4 Ford Cortina. It was metallic bronze with a beige vinyl roof and I thought I was the dog's bollocks in it. Rick had persuaded me to let him drive.

We must have stopped fifteen times on the way up to Scotland; fifteen different pubs and a pint in each one. Suffice to say we were so pissed that the staff in the Roe Buck, about ten miles south of Carlisle, finally refused us a drink.

Not before Rick had found a pretty girl to talk to. When we walked back outside, we found six local lads sitting on my car. One was the boyfriend of the girl. Rick, who before he met Cathy was a notorious womaniser, had been chatting up the wrong lassie. A fracas ensued. Rick and I got seven bells kicked out of us as we were too pissed to walk, let alone fight. They also kicked fuck out of my Cortina.

To make matters worse, the coppers turned up and nicked us for scrapping and being drunk. The MPs picked us up from Carlisle Police Station and kept us in the brig at Preston until New Year's Day.

My mum and dad didn't speak to me for near on six months and I got fined two weeks' wages. To add insult to injury, it cost me two hundred quid to get my car fixed. It was never the same and I sold it on my next leave.

Yeah, that was Rick for you.

Bastard he was.

You wouldn't believe how many times we laughed our bollocks off over that tale whilst we were banged up by the Queen's Lancashire Regiment. On New Year's Eve one of the MPs sneaked us a bottle of scotch into the cell. We sang *Fields of Athenry* and told old jokes till our sides split.

I picked up my whisky.

"Cheers, pal."

I have to say I awoke a little fuzzy. My first task was to find somewhere to live that was safe so I could store my kit more securely. I had no idea how long this job would take. I also needed a motor for daily use. I decided that despite Max's Range Rover being hot as the proverbial, it was too big an asset to lose, so I would only use it in an emergency. Still, I had to stash it somewhere, it couldn't stay where it was and neither could I.

I'd had my breakfast and lots of coffee so I turned to the trusty *MEN* again to look for a car. I gave myself a budget of a grand and looked for a big, quick saloon with lots of tax and test. The last thing I needed was to be compromised by the local police just for having a dodgy tax disc.

I circled a couple of old 2.0 lt. Audis and a newer Mondeo and got on the mobile. The Mondeo was a clocked ex-taxi and the kid selling it got right up my nose. If someone is going to talk shite to me, they'd better make it good. I'd lived in it.

The first of the Audis was a cracker. An old boy called Henry was selling it and he'd looked after the car like it was a favourite child. I wagered that the car had never exceeded the speed limit in its whole life. It was up for twelve hundred pounds in the paper and I'd turned up with the intention of paying the grand that I'd allowed myself. The truth was the old boy took me into his house, made me a brew and took me for the whole twelve hundred. The car was worth it and he was a good old chap.

After talking to a number of machines and even more Indian call centres, I sorted third party insurance cover on the car. Once I was all legal I drove back to the hotel. It was always worth taking the time over small details like car insurance. The amount of jobs that I'd seen compromised by coppers chasing Regiment observation cars for petty shit didn't bear talking about. Once in the car park I removed the stickers from the back window of my new purchase. You would be surprised how many people ID a car by silly stickers and I'd never had a dog, even for Christmas.

I strolled into the hotel reception, hands in pockets and head full of questions. I booked myself another three nights' accommodation with the singularly attractive receptionist who seemed to work twenty-four hours a day. I figured that would be enough time to find a flat of some kind.

Once again I settled into the cosy bar and had a pint.

Before I had drained half of it, my thoughts once again turned to Rick. It wasn't the fact that he was dead, it was that his body would be lying in a ditch somewhere. The old habit of bringing home your mates was hard to break. I had scoured my old copy of the *MEN* for any news of a body turning up in suspicious circumstances and bought a new early edition but there was no news of my old buddy. I lit my pipe and tried to think of a plan of action that would still keep my cover. I couldn't go to Rick's flat as Stern's guys could be watching it. I knew Rick had a lock-up somewhere in town, but I'd only ever been there the once and it was dark then. I hadn't a clue where it was.

I was getting all frustrated when my mobile vibrated in my pocket. As God is my witness my heart leapt when I saw Rick's number appear in the text message box. Every hair on my body stood up. My hopes were quickly dashed when I saw the time stamp on the message was two days old. Living in the back of beyond meant my message service was sometimes days behind. It had been sent the morning after we got back from Holland. The content of the message, though, puzzled me.

It read: 8565490*54333

I racked my brains trying to think what it meant.

I was never any good at solving puzzles but took out my own mobile and stared at the keypad. If I was in such a hurry or it was dark, what could these characters mean?

I took out my pipe and wrote the figures out on the top of my paper. Was it a phone number? The star could have been meant to be a 7 or an 8 or a zero so I changed it to an 8 as a guess. It still didn't make sense.

A balding man in a business suit was at the next table reading *The Times*. He looked up at me and obviously saw my puzzled expression.

"Difficult clue, old chap?"

"Kindae," I replied. I couldn't see the harm so I showed him the figures at the top of the page. He wrinkled his brow for a while and then spoke.

"Is it something to do with a map?"

"What makes you say that?"

The man leaned forward. "Well, if it wasn't for the zero it would be a map reference."

I looked at my mobile keypad again and, yes, if Rick had meant to type a space rather than zero, it would be a map reference.

I thanked the guy and rushed to the lift.

Once in my room I poured over a large scale map of the area.

856549 854333

If I had it right, the reference was in a country park area just outside Bolton called Belmont. It was maybe fifteen miles away. It had to be worth a look.

I gave my new car a spin but got lost a couple of times until I used the GPS. It took me forty-five minutes to find Belmont Country Park. Had the circumstances been different I would have noticed more of its beauty. It was one of those wild early summer days where the wind chilled the air yet the sun shone and made everything clean to the eye. I pulled the car onto a picnic area car park that had police signs plastered around warning of car crime in the locality. I looked at the GPS and figured the exact spot the numbers referred to would be about half a mile from where I was standing. I pulled on a sweater and set off to walk.

I walked around a fine looking reservoir and started the climb. Other than a couple of fishermen the place was deserted.

I began to notice all the beer I'd been drinking as the walk got steeper. I could feel my breathing labour and I started to push myself a little. Finally I found what I was looking for. It was an old well with wooden boards over the top of it. It had probably been the local farmers' only supply when it was dug. I looked about to see if there were any walkers in the area and when I was happy, removed the first board, prising it up with my knife.

I shone a Maglite inside but the darkness defeated the beam and I could see nothing. Then I noticed a nylon rope fixed to the side of the wall. I pulled on it. It was heavy as hell, nearly as heavy as my suitcase full of gear. This had to be Rick's stash. Five minutes of sweating and looking for snoopers and I had the item in my hands. It was Rick's old Bergen from his Regiment days and I felt a pang of sorrow as I noticed the small changes he had made to the shoulder straps. I remember calling him a pussy when I'd seen the extra padding he'd added to save his blistered shoulders during selection. I re-fixed the boards on the well top and stared at the Bergen. I suppressed the urge to open it there and then and opted to strap it on and tab back to the car.

Despite the over-indulgence of the last couple of days, all the running I had done in Scotland stood me well for the task. Anyone who has tried to carry forty kilos plus weight for any distance would tell you it's bloody hard going, and it took me twice as long to get back to the car as the outward journey.

Finally, I dropped the Bergen in the boot of the Audi and opened the top. For all intents and purposes I looked like a rambler changing my clothes or shoes.

Sitting on the top of whatever was beneath was a letter. It had my name rank and serial number hand-written on the front.

It was Rick's handwriting and I could feel that the envelope was well filled. I'm not sure how to explain the feelings that I was experiencing as I sat in the car opening the letter. Anger and bitterness flowed through me one moment, closely followed by deepest sorrow and affection. The whole clutter of extreme emotions made my hands shake as I removed the sheaf of paper from within. The letter had been written the day before we left for Amsterdam. I felt like I'd raised the dead.

Dear Des,

The chances are if you are reading this, I am already dead.
I decided that if the shit really hit the fan one day then I needed to sort out my affairs.

Having so many names and passports made it difficult to walk into a solicitor's and make a will, so this is mine.

You are my only real family and everything I have is now yours. At the end of this letter are all the details you will need to access numbered bank accounts together with the deeds to my houses and the registration documents of all my vehicles. You are now a very rich man. I know you'll spend it wisely. You always were the sensible one.

The two memory sticks contained in this envelope contain intelligence reports I've assembled since leaving the Regiment. They are encrypted. The password to unlock the files is the name of the pub we got thrown out of in Carlisle that fated New Year.
If, for any reason, you need this information, use it carefully.

I know what I've become these last few years. The only time I've felt alive was when crazy jobs were offered to me. It would seem that I took one too many. I should have known better.

We used to be quite alike, you and I, Des. You with Anne, your fish, and that bloody pipe. Me, fixing up the old cottage in Hereford and looking to start a family with Cathy.

In those days all I could think of was her, and having a son. Then she was taken from me.

If it hadn't been for you, I would have blown my brains out that weekend. It was at that point our lives changed and I went on a mad obsessive spiral while you stayed strong.

I suppose this is an apology for turning into an arsehole.

A rich arsehole nonetheless.

Treat yourself to a new fishing rod with my cash.

Rick.

PS: No fancy funerals. My boots are in the bottom of the Bergen.

Tears pricked my eyes, and I looked around the car park feeling embarrassed. I felt like a boy who had been given the cane at school and had cried when the others had stayed firm.

Then I remembered my father at James McAfee's funeral. He knew he could have been burying his own blood that day, but he'd been strong. Death was just part of life. If you had faith, then it was a natural progression, God's will. I pulled myself together and tried to think of Rick and Cathy united again.

I read the letter twice more and then flicked through the pages, somehow hoping that there was some kind of mistake. I popped the two memory sticks in my top pocket, memorised what I had to and burned the letter there and then. I watched the paper curl up and blacken on the floor at the side of the car. Eventually the wind took the weightless fragments and there was nothing. It felt like some kind of ceremony.

I set off driving in no particular direction, trying to get my head in gear. Until I had read the letter there was one small part of me that wasn't completely sure Rick was dead. Now it was definite. I was even more determined to get to the bottom of the Amsterdam job, and to find Rick's killer.

I would need a computer, and from the figures I'd seen on Rick's paperwork, it would seem that I could now afford one.

After several detours due to my lack of concentration, I found myself back in Manchester city centre. I parked the Audi close to the Arndale, the site of one of the IRA's biggest mainland bombs. It seemed that, financially at least, the Irish had done the people of the city a favour as new structures gleamed in the sunshine. Much of Manchester's newfound wealth stemmed from that incident and numerous expensive penthouses and apartments lined my route.

My stomach complained and I again realised that I hadn't eaten. I took a bite in the nearest café before shopping for a laptop computer. I managed to find something that would suit me fine for under five hundred pounds including a small printer, all the time thinking about what might be in the Bergen and what secrets were on the sticks in my pocket.

By five p.m. I was back in my hotel room with Rick's possessions spread on the bed and the laptop charging in the corner.

Indeed his boots were at the bottom. When I saw them I said a Hail Mary for the first time in years. It was followed by a good dose of Catholic guilt.

The Bergen had obviously been an emergency pack for him, which for some reason he'd very recently turned into his last bequest.

As a result I now had another couple of weapons, a .222 rifle and ammunition, plus a little six round pistol, and some medical supplies including morphine.

There was ten thousand pounds cash, a bag of solid gold coins and two sets of car keys, both unmarked.

Having the keys was one thing, collecting the cars was another, as I'd yet to find anything related to Rick's lock-up.

The laptop brought me from my thoughts by announcing in a metallic voice that the battery was fully charged. I sat the machine on the dressing table and inserted the first memory stick into a USB port. I tapped in the password, 'Roebuck', and the encrypted files became visible. There were dozens relating to the Regiment, MI5 and 6. Most names I had no recollection of, except one, Charles Williamson. I clicked on his folder and several other files appeared. They seemed to be code names. They were tagged as you might expect military operations to be named. Desert Storm etc. I knew of Williamson, he had an infamous military background. He'd commanded troops in Ireland, Bosnia and Iraq. He was known as a real hard case.

For some reason, known only to him, Rick was convinced that Williamson had a hand in the shooting that led to Cathy's death. It was an obsession that ultimately led to Rick's resignation from the army. Rick's mental state was shot in those days, and the date that the files were last modified suggested that they hailed from those dark and terrible times. I remember calling in on him in the summer of 1997. I found him in a shit tip bedsit just outside Brighton. He hadn't washed or shaved in weeks. The room was acrid and its grime-filled carpet and walls were covered in photographs and pages of scribbled information relating to Colonel Williamson and the secret services.

He was manic.

His powerful frame was thin and hunched. A small two-ring stove remained useless in one corner. A filthy fridge contained seven full bottles of vodka. His eyes that once burned with fight and intelligence were yellow and dead. He was a tortured soul in every essence.

I'd tried long and hard to turn him around. Colonel Williamson was one of the good guys. A hard case yes, old-fashioned yes, a womanising big-drinking bully yes. But he was Queen and Country before all and would never have done a deal with the IRA.

Rick had convinced his shattered brain and body that there was a conspiracy against him. Nothing I could say would change his mind, and there was nothing he could say to change mine.

Grief did terrible things to him.

I visited him when I could.

Then, four months and seventeen days after the shooting, he disappeared.

I didn't see or hear from him again for thirty-two months.

He shook my hand as Stephen Colletti at a charity garden party in aid of Manchester Mothers against Gun Crime. I was doing close protection for some second rate government official. I tell you, I nearly fell over.

He was fit and tanned, even fitter than I'd remembered. He wore an expensive suit, and I noticed he'd had lots of dental work. The Hollywood smile didn't fool me though, it didn't reach his eyes. He left a sliver of paper in my palm with his mobile number and a message.

Thought I was dead, eh? it said.

I scanned the rest of Williamson's folder. One file looked out of place, but I decided old soldiers could wait, and changed sticks.

I opened a can of Guinness I'd bought at the local off-licence, lit my pipe, inserted the second stick and began to read.

As I scanned yet more of Rick's delusional theories, the name of that strange Williamson file, wouldn't leave me. 'Hercules' Pillar'.

Lauren North's Story:

<u>Revolution Bar Manchester</u>.

Jane and I sat in the 'Rev,' sipping the first drink of many. The third Friday of every month had religiously become the 'girls' night out' for our unit. Six qualified nurses between twenty-eight and thirty-nine were scattered around the trendy vodka bar. I looked about and realised we were all lacking a little designer class for such heroin chic surroundings.

Dianne and Audrey went for the bare midriff with false tan look; Philipa went with the 'I'm totally desperate' ensemble of miniskirt and high boots and Carol wore the same little black dress she wore every bloody month. Jane always squeezed into something two sizes too small for her voluptuous form, which made her huge bosom look freakish, and I wore a trouser suit I bought for my sister's thirtieth. She is now thirty-seven.

The Revolution sat on Oxford Road, just a short walk from the railway station. The tall steps and the cobbles were a bugger in stilettos, but it was a fun place to start our Monthly Mancunian Mission.

A mission of alcoholic forgetfulness with deeds best forgotten by Monday. We all got a return ticket for the train from Leeds. Most of us would make that journey. Some, usually the same ones I might add, found solace in the arms of other equally desperate thirty-somethings, dressed in equally desperate fashion faux pas.

The 'Rev' as the locals called it, was a newly refurbished affair. The building itself was quite old and the Victorian ceiling roses and plaster covings were still visible. A Japanese DJ played funky house and the sickeningly thin waitresses pushed drinks promotions.

When not devouring pepper vodka and cheesy nachos, our job was to run the Leeds General Infirmary HDU. The High Dependency Unit was hated by some. If patients ever regained consciousness, it was a bonus. Most didn't, severe brain or spinal injuries saw to that. Over half of our patients died within a week of arriving on HDU. I suppose you could call it depressing. Maybe, but I enjoyed talking to the patients and caring for them. I really believed they could hear me and that in some way I was helping them. Jane had been my closest friend throughout my nursing career. We had worked the unit together for five and a half years. The night turned into a mix of good old gossip and a mountain of vodka. It was difficult not to talk shop at the best of times but the week had seen some interesting events and Jane and I were putting the world to rights, whilst the guy from the land of the rising sun played *Café Del Mar* and Dianne and Audrey got chatted up by two guys with even stronger self-tanning moisturiser.

All the fuss was over one new patient and I knew all the staff had been whispering about him. Two days earlier, a male had been admitted to HDU in a flurry of police activity. His face was heavily bandaged, so much so, that only one eye was visible. He had undergone reconstructive surgery to his mouth and face and was being fed intravenously. Both his legs were badly scalded. He had suffered some kind of brain damage and was comatose. Hospital consultants were assessing his condition.

The thing that intrigued Jane and me was the constant police supervision he got. Okay, most of the time it was a young copper who just sat and drank tea by his bed and tried to chat me up, but with the prognosis of the patient being poor, I presumed that the cops weren't expecting him to escape. They were expecting someone to finish the job.

Jane and I ran through all the possibilities as to the poor man's past, whilst finishing the last glasses in a tray of shots.

"I bet he's a gangster," chirped Jane as she waved over to a bright orange stick-like waitress to get two complimentary slammers.

"Bit old," I said, "he must be in his late thirties. Most English gangsters don't last that long."

I could see Jane was surprised by my level of knowledge, when it came to organised crime in the north of England. "I read a lot of crime novels," I shouted over the din. "Funny it's not in all the papers though."

Our waitress and free slammers arrived on cue. She placed the free shots on the table. Jane downed the first and gave me a cheeky wink. "He may be over thirty, but what a bod, eh!" She gave me a comedy nudge in the ribs and I smiled happily.

"You have a one track mind, love."

She pulled her top down over her ample hips and straightened her hair with a bright red fingernail.

"Well we can't be all like you, Lauren. I suppose you want us all to act like ladies around you, do you?"

She grabbed at the empty shot glass, which for some reason had been bright blue, and inspected it. She giggled mischievously.

"They've started calling you Miss Iron Knickers in the canteen." Pulling at my arm, Jane reached in for privacy, smiling wickedly. "I mean you haven't had a bloke in years! I'll tell you, love, if I looked like you I would be getting a damn sight more action than you are at the moment."

"I'm happy," I replied through a fixed, 'I'm going to kill you' smile. "And...I don't need a man to be happy!" I shouted just a little too loudly.

I was sure a mere child of less than twenty viewed me with pity from his leather pouffe. Jane arched her back and surveyed every single guy in the room with the expertise of a hawk.

"Well I bloody well do, and I'm hoping tonight is the night!" Jane let out her trademark guffaw and I recalled why I loved her so much. Jane was fun, always smiling, always the same. Whenever I had needed her, she'd been there. And, my God, had I needed her the last four years. I smiled back at her and gestured to a geeky looking guy at the bar.

"He looks interested."

Jane's head nearly swivelled off completely. She turned to me and leaned across the table so our faces were close.

"Not much to look at, but did you see the package in the jeans!" We both broke out into fits of laughter. The shots took hold and the tone of the conversation got lower and lower. I knew Jane better than anyone and I also knew that we would go home alone this Friday, just as we had every Friday.

Jane talked a good game but, like mine, it was a lonely one.

Des Cogan's Story:

I awoke feeling knackered. I had been up till daft o'clock sifting through the more recent files I'd found on Joel Davies. I had to hand it to Rick; he'd done a good job on the guy. Family history, alarm codes to his house, registration numbers of vehicles, mistresses, likes and dislikes, I felt like I'd known the guy for years. Then of course there were the pictures. I now had a face to put to the name. He looked like a bear to me.

The list of Rick's hits was lengthy, starting with Joel's own family right down to any poor bastard that stole a gram or two from him. He had certainly ruled with fear and used Rick as his constant weapon of choice.

There was a small section on Susan but no more than her name, date of birth and mother's name. Her maiden name had been van der Zoort. This had been highlighted in red by Rick. I presumed recently.

Susan van der Zoort. The name certainly did fit a Dutch girl and if I wasn't mistaken the 'van der' bit meant she was descended from money.

One thing did puzzle me. There was nothing at all on Stern, our Dutch big hitter. I realised that it was the last job Rick had done for Joel but if he was Joel's chief supplier Rick would have had some reference to him somewhere earlier in the text. There was none. Without doubt Stern was 'the' international man of mystery.

With the information that I had, the weapons, transport and now cash, I felt I was nearly ready to start work. All I needed was some bodies to do the job with. I would have much preferred to use guys from the Regiment, but Rick had few friends there after his spectacular fall from grace. And not many ever believed Rick's theories of Army Secret Service involvement in Cathy's murder.

The only place I could think to start was Georgie Richards and I wasn't looking forward to the meeting. Despite my misgivings about walking into a Yardie wake I had to prepare for the tasks ahead.

I needed a flat and once again my trusty Manchester evening paper gave me the information I needed. After two hours on the phone I finally had a shortlist of flats to see that were available immediately. I certainly couldn't stay in the hotel much longer. Before I could go flat hunting though, I had to check out the cemetery where Tanya's funeral would take place.

I'd downloaded both of Rick's memory sticks onto my laptop and encrypted them as best I could using Windows software. I destroyed the copies, stowed the computer in left luggage and set off to Moston Cemetery.

The rain hit me as soon as I left the lobby and by the time I'd made it to the car I was soaked. I had packed some good waterproof gear for my visit and I would need it.

Moston was a downtrodden area of Manchester but the cemetery itself was well maintained and situated between two mature wooded areas. It was a big place and there must have been over two thousand graves. I parked a good distance away and walked to the gates. It was pouring, and the place was deserted except for two men who were digging a fresh grave in the south east corner of the cemetery.

It had to be for Tanya. I checked where the funeral procession would enter and found a spot where I could observe without being seen. It would involve getting there before first light and, if this weather was to continue, getting very cold and wet. It had always been part of my life, sitting in holes in the ground. I actually enjoyed it.

I knew that there would be a police presence at the funeral, some uniformed and some not, so it was imperative that I did the job right and didn't get compromised.

I was happy that I had found a good obs point, yet depressed by the sight of so many graves. They were a constant reminder that I had been surrounded by death most of my adult life, yet I had never got used to loss.

I walked back to the Audi formulating my next move. I had six flats to look at but I decided my next task would be to dump the Range Rover somewhere in town. It was just too hot and just about the only thing left that could compromise me. Once that little job was out of the way I could go and house hunt.

The Rover was where I left it at the rear of the Woodland Hotel. I felt it was best to leave the Remington and Browning I had stored in it earlier, under the seats, and use the car as an emergency vehicle if things went pear-shaped.

She fired up first time and I set off looking for a long stay car park. I was pretty sure I'd seen a place on Portland Street on my earlier shopping trip, so I drove through the university district towards the city.

As I got to Oxford Road I knew I had company.

A dark blue Lexus saloon with two guys aboard had been with me for too long. I felt the tell-tale tingle of excitement, but also the fear of being completely alone.

I took a sharp left just before the railway station, and did a right under the arches. Sure enough the two boys were still behind.

I'd done my advanced driving course in a Range Rover. The police instructors called it the mobile jelly mould because of its handling characteristics, but if you drove it right it performed well enough.

I couldn't be sure if the guys were police or not. I was about to find out.

I floored the accelerator and burst out of a line of traffic heading toward the Palace Theatre. The car behind mirrored my move and stuck to me like glue. There was no attempt at defensive driving from my pursuers so I dragged the Remington from under the seat. I knew it was loaded and the safety was on. I needed to lose these guys quickly and with the minimum fuss. The idea of slotting them both in the middle of a Manchester street was a non-starter.

The lights ahead were red and there were two lines of queuing traffic. I batted down the outside of them and flew through the junction against the lights. I missed a taxi approaching from the left but clipped the front of a green saloon that was travelling a little quicker. I heard the sound of brakes and a blaring horn, but I was off and away. The Range Rover was an automatic and the engine screamed as the gearbox went into kick-down.

The damage to the car seemed superficial and it handled itself through the next junction as I took a hard left over the tram tracks and toward Piccadilly. I looked in the mirror and saw the Lexus was still there, but it sported some damage to the front. I kept my foot firmly on the floor. As I reached seventy mph he closed in on me. I hit the brakes hard.

The Lexus slammed into the back of the Range Rover and my seatbelt cut into my chest, winding me. I hit the accelerator again and with some difficulty pulled the Rover off the car behind. The Lexus was a write-off and I could see that one of the guys inside was badly injured. The driver was fighting with an air bag. I knew I had them, but was also aware of the growing crowd of shoppers staring in my direction. I could have walked over to the pair and taken my revenge there and then. I also decided that it was too risky to try and lift one of the guys. It would have been ideal. Information was king in the game I was playing. But I had a nosey crowd and with camera phones being so popular I buggered off quick sharp.

The virtually undamaged Rover bubbled away in the middle of the road. Within thirty seconds I was off and walking. I'd lost the car and worse still the weapons inside. The police would find the car, and them, very soon. It had turned into a very bad day before I could even make a start. Within hours the police would find my fingerprints and some fibre samples from my clothes. They may even find some DNA.

I didn't have a criminal record so they had nothing to match the prints to; it just meant that I had to stay out of trouble for the rest of my life. Not easy in my game.

I caught a cab back toward the Woodland Hotel. I jumped out a couple of hundred yards from the place and bought a baseball cap and a scarf. Then I did a recce before risking entering the lobby. I had changed my appearance sufficiently with the hat and scarf so as to put off any snoopers with just a description of me. I packed everything I had and paid a final visit to reception to pay my bill. It had to be there and then. I needed another safe place.

My mind turned to the Lexus as I collected everything I'd stored in the left luggage. The boys weren't coppers. That was for sure. The place would have been teeming with the squad as soon as the chase started if it had been coppers. If I had been followed by a police surveillance team there would have been at least two other vehicles in the tail and I wouldn't have noticed them till the team did a hard stop on me. That's the way they worked.

No, they were definitely not the law. I did have a sneaking suspicion that one of the two boys had a radio earpiece but I couldn't be sure. Would Stern's boys be tooled up with shortwave comms? How did they find the Range Rover so quickly?

I put it all to the back of my mind and concentrated on stowing my kit. I had to find somewhere quickly and prepare for the funeral. It was three p.m. I had twelve hours to be on plot.

Lauren North's Story

The mystery patient appeared to be more popular than ever. Two surly detectives had been to see the consultant neurosurgeon in charge of his case around four p.m. The specialist had told the officers that there had been no change in the man's condition and that the prognosis of them ever being able to talk to him was fifty-fifty at best. The dour-looking men looked even more upset when they left.

I was on a twelve-hour shift, due to finish at three a.m. and Jane was busying herself with the collective nightly medication for the unit. As I walked past her desk she hissed at me to stop.

"What's going on with the Invisible Man?"

Jane had christened the patient with the film character's nickname due to the facial bandages which all but covered the man's face.

"Nothing," I replied, knowing that there would be a follow up from my friend. She leaned forward with a conspiratorial tone.

"I told you he was a gangster. Detectives, eh? Under guard and now detectives."

"Don't go making a mountain out of a molehill, Jane," I said sharply.

Jane knew I disliked policemen, especially detectives.

"I think you have a soft spot for our invisible friend, Lauren."

"Don't be ridiculous."

"Well what did the coppers want then?"

"I don't know, they saw the specialist and he told them his prognosis and that was it, they left."

Jane looked crestfallen at the lack of gossip and went about her duties filling syringes.

From my station desk, I sat and stared at the man lying there, in the half light of the ward. I watched as his guard stood, stretched and shuffled toward the staffroom. When I was certain the young copper had gone for his break, I stood and walked to the end of his bed.

Our mystery man was surrounded by the best of modern technology. His heart rate, blood pressure and breathing were constantly monitored. He was nourished by intravenous drips. He had been heavily sedated when he arrived, but within twelve hours he was breathing unaided without any ventilation or sedation. His pupils reacted to light but he was totally unresponsive to any other action. My mind worked overtime.

He held no possessions. No clothes and no jewellery. Most patients, even if they had no visitors at all, had some possessions. A watch or a diary, anything at all. This guy had zilch. The police had taken his shirt away for forensic examination. I'd overheard one of the detectives talking about finding two blood types on it. His trousers, underwear and socks had been removed by the burns unit and incinerated.

Then I noticed he was wearing a wedding band. A plain gold band, the simplest of rings. I walked to him, sat next to his bed on a plastic chair and spoke in quiet even tones as I did with all my brain-damaged patients.

"Hello, and how are we feeling today?"

I didn't expect a response and got none.

I imagined who he might be. My mind wandered and fancied he would have a beautiful wife, and, for some reason, money. Almost absently I said to myself, "Where is your wife, mister? What is her name?"

Nothing.

"I'll bet she misses you. I bet she's worried."

I took hold of his hand and cradled it in mine. It was smooth and his nails had been manicured. I mused that they were in better condition than my own. The ring was clean and on further examination I realised that it was only present as it couldn't be removed. His hand was swollen from some trauma and the ring was tight. There were lesions on his wrist. He'd been bound.

"I wonder why she hasn't visited you?" I spoke my thoughts under my breath, watching for the return of his guard.

His one visible eyelid flickered slightly, common with all patients, and I looked at him closely for the first time.

He was a big man, broad shouldered and powerful. He carried no excess weight at all. He looked like he had a gym membership somewhere and used it well. Despite his obvious desire to look after himself and the very expensive manicure, he had never bothered with the fashion of waxing his body. He had a hairy chest and I almost smiled at myself for thinking Pierce Brosnan or a younger Sean Connery was wrapped in those bandages.

I decided that someone must be missing the man. "Someone important, I think."

The burns to his legs were severe looking. I was no expert on burn injuries but I thought he may need grafts to repair the damage. One thing I had decided. This was not an appalling accident. He'd been tortured terribly. I lifted the dressing near to his right ankle and saw that his feet had been tied as well as his hands. My mind whirled. What kind of person ends up this way? Was he a gangster after all? As I sat contemplating my mystery man, his consultant appeared at my shoulder.

"Any change, Sister?"

Mr Kahn was an imposing figure. He was a Sikh, well over six feet topped with a pure white turban that matched his starched coat. He was a most respected neurologist, but a terrible bore.

"Are we expecting a change, sir?"

Kahn crinkled his nose, pushed his glasses back toward his eyes and then stroked his impressive beard. "This is a most interesting case, Sister. I have only ever seen one more like it in my entire career. A most interesting scenario indeed."

I was even more intrigued. Kahn's reputation for boring the pants off anyone who would listen had spread around the whole hospital. So much so that he rarely had the opportunity to tell his war stories. I bit the bullet as my curiosity got the better of me.

"Really?"

"Yes, when I studied in the USA I came across an identical injury. The man was dead, of course. It was a suicide case."

"Oh." I said, blankly.

"The poor man in question had parked his car in a McDonald's car lot to watch his estranged children enter there. His wife had prevented him from visiting them after a very messy divorce, you see. He had lapsed into a severe depression and he was on strong medication. He watched his children enter the burger bar, saw that they looked happy and smiling without him, and decided to end it all. I suppose he felt they didn't need him. Very sad, you know."

"So what happened?" I mentally rapped my own knuckles for seeming too keen. Kahn looked a little surprised at my enthusiasm, but continued.

"The man took a handgun and, intending to end it all there and then, put it into his mouth. So!"

Kahn pushed his index and middle fingers into his own mouth to demonstrate and then attempted to speak.

"I'm sure you have seen this many times on the movies, Sister?"

I nodded furiously, completely enthralled with the story. I could barely hide my glee at the thought that Jane was missing this.

Kahn removed his fingers and sat on the end of the bed, carefully avoiding the man's burned feet.

"Now then," he smiled. "At this point, the poor man lost his courage. He didn't want to die after all. He lost control and started to weep. The trouble was there were parents and children entering the restaurant who could see all this. They reported the man's behaviour to the police. Within minutes the LAPD were there and surrounded the man's car. As the first officer leapt from his patrol vehicle the man panicked, pushed the weapon back into his mouth and pulled the trigger. BOOM!"

Kahn laughed as he saw me flinch at his description of gunfire but quickly became animated as he continued his tale.

"The police officers were just as hyped up as the man in the car. Hearing the gunshot, and fearing for their own safety, they fired on the man's vehicle. Six officers in all emptied their weapons into that poor man's car."

"Bit pointless," I quipped.

Kahn shook his head from side to side and made a strange pouting shape with his mouth as if sucking an imaginary sweet.

"Not at all, Sister; you see when the post mortem was carried out, the cause of death was found to be a direct hit to the man's heart. Yes, the man had placed his own weapon into his mouth, but when he pulled the trigger the bullet struck his wisdom tooth and exited through his cheek."

Now I was enthralled.

"Really and he would have lived?"

"Definitely. Indeed, as I was to learn, the behaviour of a bullet is not as straightforward as you might think. The man would have lived and he was not alone. In the USA there are over ten examples of this type of injury."

I closed my mouth as I was beginning to feel like a fish.

"And our man here?"

Kahn shrugged.

"He has been deliberately scalded with liquid and then someone decided to finish him off. Whoever his tormentors were, they obviously don't read *The Lancet* or they would know what we do now."

He belly laughed as if this was the funniest thing on the planet and I made a note to myself never to date a doctor again.

"Will he regain consciousness?" I pressed.

"It is possible. You see when the bullet struck this man's tooth, the velocity and power of the impact would have been massive. Similar to brain injuries suffered by casualties of high speed motorcycle accidents. He may do, but what state he will be in, if and when he does, is in the hands of God."

I was about to ask another question when the young constable that was charged with the man's protection returned. Kahn nodded courteously at the officer and left. As he did he tapped the bridge of his nose with his finger.

I somehow didn't need reminding to stay mum.

"Good evening, Constable." I said primly.

The young guy wasn't interested. He was bored.

"Just been for a brew," he muttered.

I walked back to my desk and sat tiredly. Jane was over in a flash.

"What's happening then?" she hissed.

"Nothing, Jane." I pulled off both shoes and rubbed my feet. I wasn't really listening. I had so much going on inside my head.

"Awww, come on, Lauren."

I looked at my friend and lowered my voice.

"Okay, he's been shot in the mouth."

Jane nearly burst but managed to keep her voice to a whisper.

"I told you! I bloody well told you, he's a gangster."

"Maybe, maybe not."

"Maybe, my arse, he's Al Capone."

We both laughed like a pair of schoolgirls.

The policeman didn't notice.

Des Cogan's Story:

Moston Cemetery Manchester.

It had taken me a couple of hours to get all my kit into the Audi and find another hotel. I had moved away from the centre of town and found a small family-run place in Didsbury. The whole thing had passed without drama and I was glad of it.

By three a.m. I was on plot in the cemetery and in a good covered position to watch the whole of the funeral without being spotted. It was a cold night but dry and I had managed a brew and a few pulls on the old pipe. I'd brought a video camera and all my usual toys. All that was left to do was to wait until the mourners started to arrive. By observing the funeral, I would get as much information as I could. I had my stills camera too and would make full use of it. There were bound to be some interesting faces around. Then, after the service, I planned to follow the family back to the wake, introduce myself to Georgie and hope for the best.

Other than the odd owl and distant passing traffic, the place was quiet as a graveyard should be. I'd never been spooked by graves or dead bodies. My family were fiercely religious and although I gave my mother nightmares by failing to practice my Catholicism, my faith held me in good stead when it came to death and its associated superstitions. In all my experiences, in action over three continents, the only people that did me any harm were very much alive.

So when, just before five a.m. I heard the sound of a vehicle behind me, my ears pricked up and I slid deeper into cover and pulled the SIG from my holster. I had definitely not banked on company. Two men got out of what appeared to be another Lexus and my pulse rate increased. They climbed the fence behind me and started to walk steadily toward my position.

I flicked the safety from the SIG. They were about a hundred meters away and through my night vision binoculars I could see they were carrying a holdall. They walked in silence, closer and closer to me. I could feel the first pricks of sweat on my back. One was taller than the other. Both looked fit and organised. From the angle they were taking I figured that they would pass within feet of me. I lay, silent and ready.

The footsteps grew louder and louder. Then they stopped. One spoke, the accent was American.

"Over there."

The taller of the two pointed in the direction of the newly dug grave. He stayed put, whilst the smaller man continued his task.

He walked so close to me that I could have touched him.

I knew he was heading for the hole in the ground but I couldn't risk any movement with his taller mate so close. I was flat to the floor. I could hear his movements but not see them. After a couple of minutes he started toward me again.

This time he was on course for a direct hit.

I had one guy in front of me and one to the rear. I was in shit. I couldn't believe that out of all the places in the cemetery they could have chosen to enter they had to pick where my obs point was.

I pointed the SLP toward the walker. He was silhouetted by some distant streetlights. He would be first and I would spin to take the second guy if need be. He was ten paces from me. Nine, eight, seven…

The Yank behind spoke, "I'm here, Stephan."

I could see the goon clearly now. He couldn't see me. He was a bullish-looking guy with blond hair swept over his face. He wore glasses and I could have sworn I'd seen him before. He also had a bandage or dressing over his right cheek.

The taller man's voice had moved to my left and it took Stephan away from my position. I held my breath and finally they started away. Within a couple of minutes both men were back in their car and the drama was over.

I removed a plastic bag from my kit. I needed a crap.

The morning was spectacular. The beautifully tendered lawns were resplendent in the early sunshine. The sky was the brightest blue, sliced into provinces by the white spirals of aircraft trails. I could feel the cold morning air burning my nostrils, but I revelled in it and took deep lungfuls of crisp Manchester daybreak mixed with newly cut grass. The owl that had kept me company through the night had gone.

I needed to check exactly what Stephan had been up to at the graveside but by the time I was sure the two heavies had left for the night it was light, and I was going nowhere. I lifted myself into position and took a look. Through my binoculars I saw a wreath had been placed at the graveside.

By six a.m. the ground staff arrived for work, followed by early visitors to their dead. Gaunt grief-stricken men and women interspersed with resigned regulars. They came and went. Some stayed just long enough to leave flowers, some stayed to talk to the gravestone. Maybe it was a birthday or anniversary. Maybe it was a weekly occurrence. Whatever their purpose, they were as close as they could get to the people that had once been blood or lover.

For an hour I watched the start of Tanya's 'mourners' arriving. The boys that were first to arrive weren't grief-stricken. They were on BMX bikes. They wore colours too. This was a public show. The Richards' reconnaissance team. One rode straight to the graveside and checked the newly dropped wreath; he picked it up with a single gloved hand, read the message and dismissed it. He rode on. I felt better, good enough to have a sip of coffee and a nip on the pipe. At least the wreath was inert, maybe there was recording equipment inside. One thing for sure, Stephan and his chum weren't visiting the cemetery at three in the morning for the good of their souls.

The BMX crew were all between thirteen and sixteen years old. These boys were some of the most dangerous people to walk the streets of Moss Side. The colours and the single golf glove signalled to their peers that they were armed. Street shootings were at epidemic proportions and these boys were a big part of the problem. By the time the cortège had pulled into the cemetery, the BMX boys had dispersed out of sight and had been replaced with serious muscle. I counted fifteen guys. All wore black greatcoats and wore sunglasses. If I hadn't known better I would have said they were CIA.

The procession itself was led by a large black woman in her late fifties who I presumed to be Tanya's mother. She was in obvious distress. Two solemn young men held her by the elbows and coaxed her the last few meters to the graveside. Just behind them was a beautiful young girl in her teens. She was the spit of Tanya. I decided this was the immediate family and one of the two boys must be Georgie. I took several pictures of both guys. I would have to convince them that Tanya wasn't dead just because of a daft Jock. The highly polished black coffin was carried by six bearers all identically dressed; they, in turn were followed by mourners carrying large floral tributes, their fabulous colours framed against a backdrop of black. I scanned the crowd for faces. Two very obvious detectives held up the rear. There was no noticeable presence from Davies's crew, which pleased me.

The crowd circled the grave. A preacher spoke and five gospel singers sang hymns. The coffin was slowly lowered into the grave. The outburst of emotion could be clearly heard from my position.

Then the bomb went off.

At first I couldn't see or hear anything. My eyes slowly started to focus and as God is my witness I wish I'd stayed blind. I'd seen soldiers with bad injuries. I'd been in battle, but this was different. The first thing I saw was the remains of a small boy. He'd have been five, maybe six years old, no older. He landed fifteen feet from me. He had been blown a full sixty meters from the graveside. His legs were gone and his body twitched as the life drained from him. I was frozen. Through the smoke I started to hear the screams of the injured and bereaved.

I thought my head would explode. Why hadn't I checked that wreath myself? Why did I stay in cover?

There was more ghastly screaming and a distant siren. It was that wail that brought me back. The siren. Maybe it reminded me of Ireland, my family's homeland. The place my grandfather was born and raised. He moved to Scotland to avoid the violence. I, in turn went back to help stop it for good. It was the country where I saw my first action and first killed another human being. The place where I first saw the slaughter a bomb can cause.

Don't ask me how, but I gathered my kit together and stowed it against a tree, leaving me dressed in jeans and a sweater. Then I ran to the carnage. God forgive me, I had morphine in my pack but dared not use it for fear of being compromised.

The wreath must have contained plastic explosives together with a timer, or it had been set off by remote control. If it had been activated by a tremble switch it would have gone off when the BMX boys touched it. In all the chaos I had forgotten to check the road for any activity. If the bombers had been behind me in a vehicle, waiting for the moment, they would have seen me pack up. I pushed that horror to the back of my mind and concentrated on the one in front of me.

The bomb had created a second gaping grave. The hole itself was empty, it was what surrounded it that tore at my heart. I counted six obvious dead. The injuries were so horrific that identification would be difficult. There were body parts strewn everywhere. Part of someone's arm and shoulder dangled from a marble cross. Two gospel singers, who had been feet from the centre of the blast, were standing rock still, apparently untouched, at the graveside. Was someone looking out for them? I'd like to think so, but years of the kind of shit I'd witnessed told me different. It was luck, pure and simple, not fate, not God, just luck.

I started to work on the casualties and tried to block out the screams from my head. I could hear a young boy pleading off to my left. A large piece of debris was lodged in his stomach. He would most probably die within minutes.

I turned from him and worked on a kid who had lost a hand. I knew his agony would quickly turn to shock and he might die along with the poor guy behind me, but his chances were much better and I was only one man.

I could hear the sirens getting closer but I couldn't stand the screams of the gut-injured boy any longer. I ran back for my gear and my morphine.

Fuck it, I thought, *ID me, you bastards, come for me. I'm ready.*

It took me less than a minute to get my bag. I got to the kid. Big tears fell down his face, his eyes wide with fear and agony. I loaded the syringe and pushed it into the child's arm.

Before he felt the effect he arrested. I held him until he stopped breathing.

When the first police officers arrived they were sick. Physically and wrenchingly sick. They were useless and the mourners who were fit enough bellowed at them to get their shit together.

In all the distress I was the professional. For years I had seen and done things that most people wouldn't dream of. It was my theatre and I had to get on with it. I decided that my cover would be that I was a doctor, that had been walking by and hopefully I would be able to steal away in all the trauma.

It took forty minutes for all the serious casualties to be removed. My hands shook and I was covered in blood. A paramedic asked me if I was okay. I told him I was, that it wasn't my blood. He gave me a thermal wrap and sat me in the back of his ambulance. Then he sat opposite me and burst into tears.

Tanya's mother, brothers Georgie and Michael, nephews Shelly, Bonny and William were all part of the dead. Bonny, at eighteen months old, was the youngest to die. In all, eleven people had lost their lives in an instant. Many more would be severely disabled for life. All would be affected, forever. Me included.

A casualty with severe head injuries was wheeled into the ambulance with me. The medic was ashen-faced but coping.

"Will you treat him en route, doctor, while I carry on here?"

I nodded, tried my best to pull my shit together and started to work on the guy. The doors were closed and we were on our way.

The guy was in big trouble. I had been given medic training in my Regiment days and I was as good as anyone in the back of an ambulance but this guy was seriously hurt.

I shouted to the driver.

"How long before we get him to a hospital?"

The driver shouted back over the wailing horns.

"Gonna be forty minutes, nearest bed for this type of injury is in Leeds. We're going to Leeds General."

We arrived at the hospital in a flurry of activity. I counted nine ambulances with Greater Manchester liveries parked outside. Some of the casualty staff tried to treat me but I waved them away. After briefing the casualty doctor I sat on a chair at a nurses' station and closed my eyes. I had been awake all night. I was knackered. I needed food, drink and sleep. I also needed some fresh clothes and a shower.

I asked one of the nurses if I could use the hospital facilities to clean myself. After about an hour she showed me to a small bathroom and I was able to shower. I had spare clothes in my pack. I placed the old ones in a bag and took them to the incinerator. Then, with a little difficulty, I found the staff canteen and went to eat. It seemed that all the police effort was being concentrated on Manchester and therefore my cover story had not been tested. No one asked for ID and I offered none. Everyone was shell-shocked. It would take a while for the cops to get to Leeds. As soon as I'd had some food and a hot drink, I intended to do one. I needed to think and get my head down.

I got myself some cottage pie and chips and was washing it down with a hot cup of tea when I got myself some company again.

This time it was most welcome.

Her name badge announced Sister Lauren North. She walked to my table and sat without invitation. She was beautiful.

"You don't mind, do you?" she chirped.

"Not at all, hen."

She smiled at me briefly and tucked into her meal. There was a silence until she lowered her fork and asked,

"Are you new here?"

I swallowed more tea and used my cover.

"I don't work here, I've just brought a patient over from the incident in Manchester. The bomb, you know?"

She seemed fascinated.

"Oh my God, yes, terrible, isn't it? They say it was gangsters."

"Do they?"

"Well yes, they say that the people who were killed were Yardies," she pushed a piece of tomato in her mouth and chewed vigorously, "and they're gangsters aren't they?"

Her innocence amused me at a time I needed it most. I resisted a smile.

"I suppose so."

She ate some more, but stopped abruptly. She leaned slightly closer, a move I found most pleasing, and lowered her voice.

"We have a gangster on my ward right now," she hissed.

I played the game.

"Really, is it Al Capone?"

Lauren looked slightly cross when she realised I was teasing her but remained undaunted.

"Well that's what my friend Jane calls him." She tapped her fork on her plate. "But I know for certain he is. Not Al Capone I mean, but a gangster."

"And how do you know that then, Lauren."

Her eyes gleamed, she was enjoying her moment and I could smell her. She was a truly stunning creature. I just didn't think she knew it.

"Well, there was this guy in America who tried to kill himself with a gun. He put it in his mouth, pulled the trigger, but he didn't die of it."

I looked puzzled.

She shook her head.

"What I mean is, this guy on my ward, well someone put a gun in his mouth and pulled the trigger, but he didn't die either."

I still looked puzzled but didn't care. She was a sight to behold.

"Gangsters poured boiling water on his legs to get him to talk, and then they put a gun in his mouth, thought they'd killed him and left him in the road. Someone found him and brought him here, no one knows who he is and…"

I stood up and I could feel my heart race. My mind slapped me down instantly. The coincidence was just too bloody obvious; too cosy.

"Where is he?" I snapped.

"What?"

"Where is this man? Can you take me to him?

"Well, I, I mean, I suppose I could." Lauren seemed perturbed by my reaction but I couldn't help myself. I'd left my grey man impression back in the blood-soaked dirt in Moston.

I stopped, raised my hands and took a deep breath, forcing a smile.

"I'm sorry, Lauren, what I'm trying to say is, in a very bad tempered way, would I be able to see his wounds?"

I fought my way back to regular breathing. "You see, I am writing a paper on unusual gunshot injuries."

She seemed to relax a little.

"Erm, okay, I don't see why not. They'll have taken off his dressings now. I believe he's pretty bad though. I haven't been up yet."

I offered my hand together with a genuine grin and coaxed her to her feet. I let myself feel good for a few seconds.

"I'll be okay, trust me, I'm a doctor."

She stood, brushed down her uniform with clean hands, her nails clipped short and un-varnished. She gave me a look that told me I was slightly crazy.

"I suppose I can take you then, but just for a few moments."

We walked briskly along disinfected corridors. Lauren's sensible shoes clicked as I spoke.

"I'm Des, by the way."

"Really," she said.

Lauren North's Story:

The cheek of the guy! I mean, I'd sat across from him in all innocence and told him the best bit of gossip Leeds' side of the Pennines and he just took the Michael out of me. The next minute, he changed personalities faster than Robbie Williams on jellies.

I knew he was looking at me, as he kept one step behind me as we walked. On the plus side he was a handsome man, a bit mad maybe, even scary, but handsome. On the minus side, he was a doctor and I had made myself that solemn promise.

No more doctors.

As we strode down the corridor towards the lift, he was talking incessantly, asking questions about the patient's prognosis. If he was writing a paper, he certainly took it seriously.

He was a bit small for me, but well put together. Not in a muscular way but his veins were pure wire.

A rough diamond too. Not exactly your doctor type. I could hardly contain my smile. If I'd fallen over a heroic figure that regularly volunteered for duty in some war-torn African state and was writing a book on his findings, Jane would be absolutely livid.

We got in the lift.

"Where in Scotland are you from?"

He seemed impatient and distant for a second.

"The Gorbals."

"I see, is it nice there?"

"No."

"Oh."

"I'm sorry," his face creased into a smile, "as you can imagine, I've had a traumatic day."

I suddenly realised how damn insensitive I'd been. I mean the guy had just been to a bomb blast. He could even be traumatised himself and I was accusing him of schizophrenia.

"No, I'm sorry." I placed the flat of my hand on my chest and took a deep breath, suddenly embarrassed.

"I'm just amazed that you want to see more injuries today."

The lift stopped and he smiled again.

"Thank you for your concern, Lauren, I'll be fine, now, which way?"

I walked Des to the cool, quiet ward. It was a seven-bed unit. One was empty, awaiting the arrival from surgery of a bomb blast victim.

He stopped at the entrance to the ward. Something was troubling him. I thought it might have been the uniformed police officer sitting by the patient's bed. I stepped forward and spoke to the young constable.

"Constable, this is Dr..." I fished for a surname.

"Cogan," Des obliged, stepping close behind me.

"Yes, Cogan," I blurted. "He needs to examine the patient."

I nodded at our man who'd had his facial bandages removed. A smaller dressing covered the wound on his cheek.

The policeman seemed to get the message, folded his newspaper and strolled toward the staffroom.

Then something troubled me.

I couldn't place my distress at first, and then it came to me. It was Dr Cogan's hands. When he had taken my hand in the canteen, they were like oak. Not like doctor's hands at all. I knew, I'd been married to one.

"You okay?" I asked.

He just stared at the bed containing the mystery gangster. He didn't approach, just looked.

I took his hand again, I don't know why. I felt the strength in it and he squeezed mine in his. I suddenly realised that I'd been in this very same position many times before. Des was behaving like a relative.

"Do you know him?"

He gave no reaction.

"Doctor?"

He seemed to snap out of his dream-world but his voice was flat.

"Is it okay to inspect his wounds now, Sister?"

I looked around for any sign of the consultant or the duty matron. I began to feel very uncomfortable.

"I suppose so."

It was the first time I had seen the patient without his dressings myself as they were removed whilst Jane and I were off duty. His facial features were severely distorted. His left cheek looked like it housed a Jaffa orange.

Des moved slowly to him but rather than start his examination, sat on a chair at the side of the man's bed. He placed his hands to his face and rubbed his cheeks. He seemed speechless.

"You do know him, don't you?" I whispered.

He just nodded.

"I think you'd better go." I said.

Des looked at me. His ice blue eyes bore into me. They didn't plead, they demanded my attention. His voice was low and even.

"We need to talk, you and me. There's nothing to be scared of. He isn't a gangster and neither am I. Do you believe me, Lauren?"

I smiled nervously, not knowing what else to do. I thought about calling security, but there was something about Des Cogan that made me trust him.

He stood.

"What time do you get off work?"

"Eleven o'clock, why?"

His face changed again and he smiled. "Let me tell you a tall story over a wee drink."

I heard myself say yes.

Des Cogan's Story:

I was in total shock. I couldn't believe Rick was alive. The jammy bastard had done it again. Once more he had cheated the Reaper. I had to say I was over the fucking moon. Everything seemed peachy. It was the closest thing to a religious experience I had ever known. My mother would have had me down the chapel every night for a month. I almost skipped down the corridors, a big smile on my face. Then, without warning, a picture of the young boy, blown into my path by the cemetery bomb, tore into my mind. I stood still, my head swimming. I thought I might faint and sat heavily on a bench seat, my eyes squeezed tight together in an attempt to obliterate the horror.

I waited and waited until he released me. My balance was restored, my Karma.

I had a friend once. He was a Polish Airman, from Krakow. He was a very dour guy, never prone to outbursts of emotion good or bad. One day we had all been celebrating something or other and Jack was sitting quietly in a corner with his orange juice. I sat down beside him and asked him why he wasn't joining in the fun. It was then he explained Karma to me. He used the analogy of a pendulum, with joy at one extreme and pain at the other. He tried to keep his Karma steady with the most moderate of swings in any direction. Swing too far toward joy and gravity would ensure that an equally painful event was around the corner.

Jack was centred, literally.

My pendulum had just had a field day and Jack's theory had proved all too correct. I regained my feet and started to get my head together. The job had taken a turn for the better but it was still a live operation. I knew what Rick would want me to do and I intended to do it.

I had no idea if I could trust Lauren, but I had no choice. She seemed a pretty sorted person but whether she would bottle it later in the day and tell her boss or the police, only time would tell.

I took a black cab from outside the hospital to the nearest Travelodge, having arranged to meet Lauren at eleven-thirty at a bar in the city centre. I sorted a hire car with the receptionist. It was delivered whilst I slept. Despite being totally exhausted, I didn't sleep well.

After two hours of tossing and turning I took the hire car and drove back to my last hotel in Didsbury, Manchester. I nervously picked up all my kit and drove back to Leeds, which would have to be my base for a while. Rick was my first priority. Fuck Davies and Stern. I needed my mate back in action.

I risked a smile as I realised the bastard would want his boots, and all that money back. He could have it with pleasure.

After an uneventful drive back to Leeds I did my best to secrete the weapons and kit in the hotel room. The hire car would do me for a couple of days. My Audi back in Manchester was just too risky.

I felt the need to clear my head and went for a run. The area was hardly conducive to rural life but exercise was exercise. I'd been running for forty minutes at a steady pace. The Travelodge was close to an industrial estate. I'd passed numerous car sales pitches and warehouse premises, glaring neon signs reflected on the wet tarmac and occasional ropes of bare white light bulbs illuminated cheap Fords and Vauxhalls. Fluorescent banners boasted 'low mileage' or 'one owner'. I increased my pace. I could feel my body start to relax and my breathing fell more into step with each stride. It always took me the first five miles to settle into my rhythm. Once I found the zone I could run marathon distances. I found myself running towards Chapeltown. This was the notorious red light area where The Yorkshire Ripper had plied his bloody trade. Leeds looked a rough old town to me, and coming from a weegie that wasn't too complimentary. Thankfully it was also a place where I could disappear for a while, until I knew how Rick would fare. I turned for home at sixty minutes. I arrived back breathless and made a mental note to do more fitness work as soon as possible.

I showered, shaved and found some passable clothes to wear. I had to admit, that despite everything, I was secretly looking forward to meeting Lauren.

The helpful girl on the reception desk organised a cab for me and I set off to my arranged meeting. It was either quite a way around the ring road or the driver was taking the piss. Either way I was totally lost. I decided that it wasn't worth the hassle to argue with the cabbie.

Eventually I arrived fifteen quid lighter and an hour early. I couldn't be totally sure that Lauren wouldn't have organised a welcoming committee for me so I did a full recce of the gaff before I got comfortable and settled with a pint. The place was pretty quiet for the time of night. It was called 'The Font' and was a typical city bar, all bare wood and mood lighting. It was three quid for a pint of Stella and I mused that it wasn't that much of a surprise the gaff was half empty.

I found myself what looked like a comfy sofa that kept my back to a wall and gave me a good view on the entrance, and sipped my reassuringly expensive brew.

At eleven twenty-seven p.m. she arrived.

She wore a black woollen coat over her nurse's uniform. She obviously hadn't had time to change and looked a little harassed. She hadn't seen me and I left it that way for a few moments until I was sure she didn't have any company. When I was certain she was alone I stood and caught her eye.

She smiled at me, opened her coat to reveal more of her work clothes and shrugged her shoulders in apology. "Sorry, Des, I just didn't have any time to change. The guy you came to the hospital with went into arrest just before ten."

She took on a resigned look. "We lost him."

The bomb had claimed its twelfth victim. "He was badly hurt, Lauren."

She sat. "Yeah, I suppose, but he was only young, wasn't he?"

I found a waiter and Lauren asked for a red wine. Finally we sat together and I took a good look at her. I figured she was in her mid-thirties. She could have been anything from thirty to thirty-eight. It was hard to tell. She was at least five feet ten and I was pleased to see she still wore her flat sensible shoes from work. She had dark hair that just touched her shoulders. It looked thick and shone healthily in the candlelight. Her eyes were a stunning light green and, despite her long shift, they sparkled as she spoke.

She had a touch of Yorkshire in her voice, but it wasn't her birthplace. There was something else in the mix, a bit of a southern quality, a bit of English rose. Her tone was defiant. She took a sip of her wine and looked me in the eye.

"I haven't got a clue why I'm here, Des. I should have gone to the police really."

"That's an option," I said.

She lifted her glass and took a bigger drink. She had a full petal-shaped mouth but I couldn't detect any lipstick. Indeed I couldn't see any make-up at all.

She wiped her mouth with the back of her hand. It was almost a masculine gesture.

"I have to say, I'm intrigued; stupid, but intrigued. I mean, a woman on her own, risking life and limb, not to say anything of her career, just to help two guys I have no connection with, both of whom could be Scarface himself. It's not clever."

"I told you, I'm not a gangster and neither is Rick."

She took a large gulp of her wine and waved the empty glass at the waitress.

"So you say. Well, I suppose that's all right then. I always trust people that have a bullet hole in their head and that are being guarded by the coppers. Not to mention someone posing as a doctor, because you're not a doctor, are you, Des?"

"No"

"Well then." She moved her hands around in small circles to emphasise her point.

"That's obviously why I'm helping James bloody Bond and his Scottish sidekick."

Her wit was mixed with genuine fear. I could see it. I smiled at her and she fell silent.

"Just give me a few moments. I will tell you the truth, I promise. I have no one else that can help me. If you want to walk away after you hear what I have to say then so be it. You can do that. I won't try to stop you or hurt you. Do you believe that, Lauren?"

She nodded and took her second glass of wine.

I took a deep breath and began.

"Rick isn't a gangster, he's an ex-soldier. Rick and I served together in Northern Ireland and too many other battlefields to mention. I've known him for twenty-six years. He's my best mate. He comes from Hertfordshire. His father was a soldier, as was his grandfather. Both were killed in action. He was brought up in children's homes as a result but he was a clever lad. He could have gone to Sandhurst but refused. I met him when we were in the Parachute Regiment together. We were never the type to get involved with anything criminal. We were posted to Ireland to work in a small team the army called a multi-agency unit. Our task was to observe several IRA cells who were involved in funding the terrorists' weapons operation. Their largest single form of income was the trade in illicit drugs. Heroin from Afghanistan, cocaine from Columbia and cannabis from Europe. Our job was to watch and listen, but when we were sure we had the main men, it was our job to kill them."

Lauren spat wine onto her coat and rubbed it furiously.

"Shit, sorry, erm, okay, go on."

"That has been our life, Lauren. Rick and I were the kind of men who kept the balance in terrorist wars. Publicly, governments always had to play fair. The terrorist boys could do what the hell they liked. Drugs, prostitution, extortion, torture. Shit, even when we caught them we had to pay for their legal team out of our taxes. It was a way of balancing the books. Eventually, of course, the press got hold of what they called the 'shoot to kill' policy in Northern Ireland and tactics changed. I went to fight another war. Unfortunately Rick didn't."

Lauren raised a brow. "He didn't?"

I shook my head and felt a twinge of sadness. "Rick lost his wife. She was murdered by the organisation. The IRA. It sent him crazy for a while. I thought he would top himself. It was awful.

"Rick blamed the secret service for the death of his wife. He never believed the IRA found his home without inside help. He turned into a man who I no longer knew. Guys who leave the Regiment do things when they retire that most normal people would never envisage. They become bodyguards, sell weapons even fight for other armies as mercenaries."

I took a big gulp of my lager, wiped my mouth and went into the hard bit. "Rick went to work for a really nasty character. He was his debt collector. They even called Rick that: 'The Collector'.

"He'd spend thousands on cars and clothes but he was miserable. He had a penthouse and all the money you would ever need. He kept working, taking dirty money. He took bigger and bigger risks. Finally he needed a team to go and collect a boat from Amsterdam that had been stolen from his client. He contacted me and asked if I would help, be part of his team.

"To be honest, I was bored and needed something to do, so I agreed. Four of us went to Holland to get the boat and it all went pear-shaped. We were set up. One of our team was killed. A girl called Tanya Richards.

"The people killed by the bomb, this morning, were all her family. It was her funeral. It's been five days since Amsterdam. In that time, Rick has been tortured, scalded with water, shot in the mouth, to all intents murdered and dumped in a deserted lane. A man tried to kill me at my home in Scotland and Tanya's family has been wiped out by a bomb the IRA would have been proud of."

Lauren was dumbstruck.

"So the people with the boat in Amsterdam, killed all those poor people?"

"Possibly"

"And the man who tried to kill you?"

"Yes."

"Did you, erm, did you…?"

"Kill him? Yes, Lauren, I had to."

She looked blankly at me and bit her lip. The story wasn't going well.

"And what about the fourth person that went to Amsterdam? Is he okay?"

"She," I spat, "Susan Davies, wife of the infamous Joel Davies. Well, our Susan was an altogether different matter, Lauren."

As I let the tale unfold, Lauren seemed to relax a little. I talked until the early hours. We were the last people to leave and, as I promised, I told her everything I knew. Death, drugs and all.

We were both a little tipsy by the time we stood waving down a taxi. Lauren hugged herself against the cold. Her pale face began to show pink extremities. She turned to me.

"I've been thinking," she slurred, "if I'm going to help you, we have to have a cover up."

I laughed. "You mean a cover story."

She stamped her feet. "Yes, one of those. I mean my friend Jane will cotton on in an instant if you just keep turning up all over the place. So, we have to have a cover up, erm story."

"And what will that be?"

The taxi pulled up and she jumped in. I closed the door for her and she wound down the window to speak.

"You'll have to be my boyfriend," she giggled.

The taxi drove away, leaving me warm as toast on the pavement.

Lauren North's Story:

My head felt like it had been stuffed with cotton-wool as I walked into the ward the next day. Despite being definitely tipsy I had found it near impossible to sleep with all the information ticking over in my head.

No matter how I looked at it, the two men, one a patient, and one a fake doctor, were criminals. They had been working for a drug dealer and had killed people. You could dress it up any way you wanted but as far as I was concerned that was the truth.

So my decision should have been straightforward. No mystery, no second thoughts, but I was having them. Was it because Des was one of the most fascinating men I'd ever met? Was it because every time he brushed my hand with his last night I shivered inside with excitement?

He scared me to death. I mean, he was so cold about killing. It was black or white. Him or me. No thought for the law or family.

And yet he was so gentle and kind. He genuinely cared for his friend, the man lying in front of me in the cool ward, battered and scarred.

But it was the cold light of day. The candles were out and those twinkling blue eyes were somewhere else. I knew I needed to grow up, get a life and find a man who wasn't a criminal. I needed to go to the police. That was it, decision made.

First though I had to change Rick's dressings.

He had a new constable sitting by the bed and I asked if he could leave us during the procedure. I figured my tale of international drug running and gangsters would be wasted on the probationer and could wait until I ended my shift. He gladly went off toward the staffroom and I drew the screens around my patient.

I lifted the sheet from the bed to reveal Rick's legs. One was damaged from the kneecap whilst the other was from mid-thigh. He must have suffered terrible pain. Des believed that whoever did this was trying to find out where his house was in Scotland. If this had happened to me? My God, I couldn't even start to imagine his agony.

I was removing the second dressing when I saw Rick's fingers move. It wasn't just a reaction to the pain of having the dressings removed. He'd cupped his hand upward and was beckoning me. His eyes were closed, I looked to his monitor, but it was normal, no sign of any change, but his hand continued to coax me toward the bed. I stood, motionless for a while my own heart was racing. I found some courage and sat at his side. My hands were shaking.

He opened one eye. His left was still swollen shut.

"Where is he?"

His voice was quiet and hoarse, distorted by his injured mouth.

"Who?"

"The man who was here with you yesterday. Where is he now?"

"You were awake yesterday?" I frantically looked around to ensure that there were no gaps in the screens. He moved his body slightly as if he'd waited an age to do so.

"Yes, now where is he?"

Now the cat was most definitely amongst the pigeons. All my good work and sensible decision making went right out of the window as I heard myself whisper, "He's here in Leeds. I know everything. Des told me last night. Now, be quiet. The guard is back."

I couldn't see the policeman, but I heard him sit on the chair just outside the curtains. I was faced with the choice of pulling the screen aside and telling all to the constable, or keeping my mouth shut. To this day, I don't know why I decided to keep quiet, but, I did just that.

I knew the procedure of re-dressing Rick's burns would be extremely painful. For a comatose patient, it was not a problem, but conscious, he would need serious pain relief. I couldn't obtain any drugs from the pharmacy without announcing to the world that Rick was awake. Therefore he would have to bear it in silence.

As if reading my mind, he looked at me and nodded slowly.

My hands trembled as I began. I could barely imagine what he was feeling. Each tiny movement must have been agony as I removed his old dressings, piece by piece. Each step, each section of gauze removed part of his damaged skin with it.

It was the longest thirty minutes of my life. Rick remained silent throughout. I found tears too persistent to prevent.

When I had finally finished I drew the curtains to be greeted by the guarding policeman.

"You look pale, love, late night last night?"

I did my best to stop my hands from trembling. "Something like that, Constable."

I scurried to the loo to be sick.

I sat in the ladies' cubicle for what seemed like an age. Everything that had happened to me over the last twenty-four hours twisted my neck muscles and made my head pound. My hands tingled and my stomach felt empty, yet bloated all at the same time.

Des excited me. I had to admit that to myself. He treated me like a woman, but an equal. Something I'd forgotten in the years since my divorce. The violence was so real though. I recalled the night out in Manchester when Jane and I had discussed the identity of our mutual patient. How we had laughed at the prospect of having some kind of celebrity on our own ward. Now it was all too factual. These were cold and calculating men in a world, the likes of which Jane and I had only ever read about or seen in the movies.

This was Robert Di Nero and Al Pacino territory. The pair may have been soldiers first and foremost, but I couldn't kid myself that they weren't breaking the law. The man lying in the bed in my ward had been subjected to the most horrific torture. I couldn't understand how could another human being could be capable of such vile behaviour. What fuelled them and drove them to torture? Was it drugs, money, power? Yes, power, the only thing really important to men.

Money itself was not enough. Power was absolute. With power you could change the world.

I cupped my chin in my hands and stared at the toilet door. Des had told an amazing tale. It was like an episode of *Spooks* or something. The murder of Rick's wife had been the catalyst for all this grief. Had that one event not occurred, Rick would probably be raising a family in some southern coastal resort and Des would be resigned to catching fish. There would be no gangsters; no drugs and no murder left in either them.

Could I really buy into that? And where to now? That was my next question. What was the next instalment in the saga?

I was returned swiftly to reality with a firm knock on the cubicle.

"You all right, Lauren?"

It was Jane's voice.

"Yes, I'm fine, I just felt a little sick, that's all."

I opened the cubicle door. Jane stood in the fluorescent glare, arms folded, looking concerned. I knew her emotion was genuine, but there was another motive to her seeking me out.

Scandal. She lived for it.

I couldn't tell her, that the reason I felt sick was Rick, our international man of mystery was wide awake. So, I would just have to tell her something about Des and hope it placated her fixation for gossip. I managed a weak smile.

"I had a few too many wines last night."

Jane looked suspicious. "Oh that's where you were then. I was ringing your mobile half the night. I was worried. You never switch it off normally."

"I'm sorry, Jane, I was in such a rush, I never switched it back on after work, and I went straight out." I felt my face colour. Jane was on to me like a rash.

"You've met a man, haven't you?"

There was a trace of sadness in her voice, as if she had been dreading the moment when I would meet someone. She did her best to hide it but failed. She brushed herself down mentally and smiled. "Tell me all about him."

I walked to the sink to scrub my hands.

"He's called Des and he's a doctor," I blurted, finding myself, ever so slightly deeper in the plot. Jane threw her hands into the air in a manner any lay preacher would have been proud of. "Oh Lord, another doctor!

"It's not like that," I said, defensively enough to arouse Jane's suspicions even further.

"Really?"

"Yes really, he, he's been at the hospital treating another patient, the one from the Manchester bomb blast, you know?"

"Mmmm."

I felt like an extra from Bridget Jones.

"See, when I told him about our celebrity patient and his injuries, well, he was so excited, you know, he's writing a paper on gunshot injuries and, well I brought him to the ward and, and, well, we hit it off and, erm, I'm kind of dating him. Kind of, if you know what I mean."

I felt totally deflated and my cheeks burned.

I'd kept it brief but this only stirred Jane's curiosity even further.

"Kind of? You mean he wants a shag but no commitment kind of?"

"No, he's not like that!"

Jane was flabbergasted. "Ha! The first man on the planet who doesn't want sex. How long have you been seeing him? One night?

One night and 'quote' you're dating? You, ice queen of Leeds General, are dating? And a bloody doctor to boot? What happened to 'never again, Jane' eh?

Her eyes narrowed to a squint and she pushed her ample chest out in triumph. "I don't believe you. There's something else going on, something you're hiding from me."

"It's true," I countered lamely.

"No." Jane wiped her palms together in dismissal. "It just doesn't wash, girl. I know you far too well for this nonsense."

I felt my temper rise.

"What do you mean, Jane, nonsense? I like him. He's the first man I've met in years that treats me like a human being rather than a pair of legs with decent tits."

Jane cocked her head to one side and eyed me dubiously. She tapped an index finger on the centre of her palm repeatedly as she spoke. "Well, Marge from ICU saw you with your 'man' yesterday in the canteen and she says he looks a right hard case. She said he looked like a copper or worse."

I managed to keep any emotion from my face, but felt my cheeks tingle as blood made its way to the surface of my skin. I pictured Des's worn handsome features and could see where Marge was coming from. I played dumb.

"He does a lot of fishing and outdoor stuff. He doesn't look much like a doctor, I have to say."

"Outdoor stuff?" Jane practically spat the words, "You can't fool me, dear, you are up to something."

I couldn't take any more interrogation. I turned on my heels, gave Jane a playful tap on the bum and said, "Not yet I'm not but give it time."

I couldn't see, but as I walked away I would have bet a month's wages that Jane's mouth would be open like a trap.

As my shift dragged on, Jane shot me the occasional look but didn't mention Des again. Rick hadn't moved or given any indication he was awake.

When ten o'clock came his police guard was collected by a red-faced sergeant. I strained to overhear their conversation. Rick's security had been downgraded to regular drive-by patrols as manpower was scarce due to the bomb in Manchester. From the sergeant's tone, the forces surrounding the area had been stretched to the limit assisting Greater Manchester Police. The national newspapers had reported severe racial tensions as a result of the misconception that the police were not taking the incident seriously. From what I had seen, they were taking it very seriously indeed. Despite this, forces with large Afro-Caribbean communities were on alert as large groups of youths were forming on the streets. There had been ugly scenes in Moss Side, Toxteth and Brixton.

I walked to Rick's bedside and sat.

"My shift ends in an hour," I said as quietly as I could. "But when the consultant comes at eight in the morning he will know you are conscious."

Rick opened his good eye and looked at me. Now I knew he was awake, even lying in a hospital bed he scared me.

"Tell Des to get me out of here tonight."

"That's impossible," I hissed. "You need specialist care; the move alone could send you into shock. He can't."

"Just do it."

"No."

"If you don't tell him to move me I'll be dead anyway."

"No one knows you're here."

Rick moved his head slightly. He did his best to moisten his dry mouth. "Come on, girl. Do you really think I put the gun in my own mouth? What? You think the guys who did this will stop looking? Des found me, you know who I am and our friend over there is a nosy cow. It won't be long before you give in and tell her. The only time three people can keep a secret is when two are dead. The people who did this will come here and kill me and walk away as if nothing happened."

"Don't say that."

To my surprise he closed his eyes and moved his broken body again. I could only imagine his agony.

"Sorry, love, I'm just a bit stressed out today, there was no gravy with the Yorkshires."

I smiled at his dry wit. I tried to put myself in his position and realised just how vulnerable he was. Then I shuddered. How in heaven's name would Des get him out of the ward, never mind a city hospital? They would be seen and stopped without question.

"I can't do it, Rick, I can't even have anything to do with it. I'd get caught."

He took my hand gently.

"Not if you kill me first."

Des was waiting in the car park of the hospital as I walked down the hospital steps. He had a big smile for me and held the door of his car open as I got in.

"Hello, Lauren, you okay?"

I shook my head and felt tears on my face. Two days ago my life had been normal. I was a reliable honest employee and a bloody good nurse. I was alone, but fairly comfortable with it. Now I was mixed up in this terrible mess and could see no way out of it. Even if I walked now, people would find out that I had met Des, talked with him, brought him to the ward, and been for a drink with him. Questions would be asked that I couldn't answer easily. I was scared and in big trouble.

I sat and stared straight ahead. I could feel hot tears but I couldn't do anything to stop them. I watched the first spots of rain drop onto the windscreen. Slowly each droplet formed a film across the glass, distorting all beyond it. My tears finished the job. I closed my eyes and sobbed.

I turned my head, knowing that my soul was laid bare. "Rick's awake," I blubbered. Inside my head my voice sounded tired and I suddenly felt drained. I tried to wipe my face with my hand. "He's crazy, wants you to get him out, out of the hospital."

I turned to Des and took his hand, my voice a full on tremor. "I can't help you, I'm sorry."

"I know," he replied, his voice laden with understanding.

"I mean the police would catch me."

I felt strangely stupid, pointing out the obvious, but I felt I had to reason with him.

"The move could kill him, Des. I don't know the full extent of his injuries and neither do you. We would be the ones that got the blame if he died as a result."

I felt my pulse quicken and heard myself raise my voice. I sounded manic.

"I'm talking manslaughter, Des. I'm not cut out for this. I'm a nurse for fuck's sake, not a soldier."

Des put his arm around me and held me tight. I felt the warmth of his body and his wiry strength. I could smell his clean shirt and a warmer manly trail from his skin. Somehow I needed his strength. I wanted to be strong like him, even though he was at the centre of all my problems. I knew I should pull myself away from his embrace, open the door of the car, and step out into the rain and run to the nearest copper.

But I didn't, I didn't pull away, I didn't run into the rain. His soft Scots voice filled my ear.

"Don't worry, hen. I'll sort it out. You don't need to do a thing. I'll take you home and cook you some food. Then I'll sort it."

Then he smiled. The broadest whitest smile.

"He's awake then?"

I wiped my face. "Yes."

"And how does he seem?"

I couldn't think of what to say. I hadn't examined him. I found a tissue in my bag and blew my nose. Then I blurted like some sixteen-year-old,

"He's mean."

Des roared with laughter. I mean, he was the clown outside the fun house at Blackpool. Tears streamed down his face. It took him a full minute to calm himself.

Then he stopped and held me again.

I looked up at him.

Des wasn't just calm. You know the, 'I'm a big hard soldier and my mate needs me', sort of calm. He was serene. There wasn't a trace of fear, or worry, or anger. The only time I'd seen that kind of happy in a man, was my time in maternity.

Then, he simply turned from me, had one last chuckle and started the car. "He's as mean as a scrapyard dog is our Rick," he said to no one in particular.

Des Cogan's Story:

Lauren's flat was nice enough. It sort of went with her, reflected her personality. It was organised on the surface, but like the duck, paddling like fuck underneath.

I have to say that the presence of a little female company was a most welcome distraction. My over-active brain was dragging me to shadowy places I didn't want to go. The bomb; my failure to check the package left by Stephan; the aching guilt; the screams and the death. It seemed determined to make me suffer. Lauren was a sparkle in a dark sinister world.

I stood in the warm cosy kitchen and boiled potatoes for supper. I'd decided to play safe with the food and was making 'mince and tatties' for Lauren. It's a traditional Scottish dish that my mum would make for me whenever I was home on leave. As I pricked the spuds with a fork I weighed up my plan for the night's forthcoming events.

The potatoes were just perfect so I hunted for a ladle. Several pans fell on the floor as I opened the kitchen cupboard.

"Sorry!" Lauren piped from the living room. "I need to tidy those!"

It was another example of Lauren's 'paddling like fuck' moments.

I put off the urge to rearrange her kitchen and finished serving. I carried the two large plates of steaming honest grub into the lounge and sat on the floor next to Lauren. She had changed into her dressing gown and her hair was still wet from a shower. She had chosen Michael McDonald for music and prodded a cigarette burn in the worn rug with her nail.

"I used to smoke," she said absently, then took the plate and smiled. "Thank you, this looks lovely."

We ate in silence for a while. I could smell her clean hair. I heard her lay down her fork, and then she said, "How are you going to get him out?"

I swallowed some food.

"You don't need to know anything, Lauren, and it's probably best that way too. All I need from you right now is some idea of the treatment he's going to need."

Lauren looked at her food, seemed to decide she'd eaten enough and put her plate on the floor. She appeared to tense slightly.

"The move will traumatise him for sure. I don't know exactly what will happen. He could have a severe reaction or, with some pain relief, he might be okay. Did I tell you that he lay completely still whilst I changed his dressings? He must have been in agony."

"Yes, you did."

That didn't surprise me; Rick always had a high pain tolerance. His ability to bear sheer agony wouldn't help him if he caught an infection and septicaemia though. I gave up on supper too, pushing my plate along the carpet.

"What about care after the move, how specialist is it?"

Lauren rested her hand on my shoulder. It felt good. "He's going to be a high dependency case for some weeks. I'm not a burns specialist. He could be high dependency for maybe a month. He'll need a number of dental procedures to repair his facial damage. As for his legs, to be honest, Des, I'm not sure. Infection will be the biggest problem."

I thought for a minute. I needed all the information I could get from Lauren, without involving her directly. "What I really need to know, Lauren, is how long before he'll be fit to work?"

I thought I'd electrocuted her she stood up so swiftly. My mince and potato leftovers added even more damage to the rug.

"Are you fucking crazy!" she shouted. "You just found out that your best friend, who you thought was dead by the way, is actually alive. With a little TLC he'll be good as new in a couple of months."

She waved her hand about like a dervish. Her voice went up a tone. "Now all you can think about is getting your old sparring partner back, so you can fuck each other up again, add a few more scars to brag about, kill a few more bad guys. Or are you the bad guys? I don't really know who you are, do I? What's next for you two? Let me guess, you're going to keep this bloody massacre going. You won't rest, until this Stern guy, or whoever, is dead. Will you? The only fucking reason you're here, being nice to me, is that you need me. You don't care for me; you might want to shag me for a bit. But, let's face it, Des, you're using me like you use a gun. When the job's done, you'll get rid. Jane was fucking right. Why don't I ever listen?"

I knew I was crap at this kind of conversation. All I could do was sit and pay attention. Let her go off on one. I knew that if I said anything at all it would make it worse. It would be pointless. If I'd said that she was the most beautiful woman I'd ever been close to, or that I thought she was cute, or funny, or honest. I would have messed it up, or it would have been the wrong time.

So, I did what I always have done when the going got slightly tough with a woman. I stood up and walked out.

As I reached the lift I heard Lauren's footsteps. I turned and she stood in the corridor. Her arms were folded across her chest.

"He said something." She hopped from foot to foot as if she were cold even though the corridor was warm.

I swallowed and spoke quietly. "Who, Rick?"

"Yes, Rick."

She looked at her feet.

"He said something strange."

I waited.

"He said I would have to kill him to get him out."

"That's all?"

She nodded and fought back tears.

I turned and pressed the call button. The down light illuminated. I could feel Lauren at my back. Then she spoke. "Des?"

"Yes?"

Lauren's temper had disappeared she'd calmed down in an instant. Her voice was level and sensible.

"Please, Des, don't come back here. I'll take my chance with the hospital; I'll plead insanity or something. I mean, I, erm, I did, I mean do like you, and everything but, well, It's all just too much for me, this macho shit. I don't get out much. Drug barons and torture aren't that romantic, in real life, I have washing to do and stuff."

I had to smile. She was right, of course.

Then she looked straight at me. Her beautiful features couldn't hide her disappointment, and I thought she might cry. .

"I mean it, Des," she said. "Please don't come back."

I stepped into the lift and turned to face her but she had already gone. As the doors closed I pondered how many times in my life I had made the same mistake. I would meet someone good, honest, beautiful, and fuck it up royally.

I was destined for loneliness.

It was a solitary tedious drive, but I made it back to the Travelodge and tried to put Lauren to the back of my mind. If things went wrong on a Regiment operation, there were specific routes to follow, people to contact. I was in real trouble and totally alone. I'd had medical training of course, but any type of long term care for Rick would be a place I'd never been.

Not only did I need somewhere to take him, somewhere safe and quiet and clean, but I would have to depend on someone else to advise me on long term care. I couldn't just sit about for a couple of months either; I needed to work on catching the bastards that killed all those kiddies.

First up would be some transport. When I'd been out running I had seen a garage on the way into the city that sold camper vans. They were the nearest thing to a useful vehicle I could think of. I'd stolen a few rides in my time, although most had been with some legitimate military reason. It seemed, if you got involved with Richard Fuller, all legitimacy went straight out of the window. If I could steal a camper, it would make a good ambulance, I was sure of it.

I decided to leave my hire car at the hotel and walk the four miles or so to the camper pitch. It took me the best part of an hour. I had a little trauma when a local police car took an interest in me but after a stern glance the guy carried on and left me alone. I always found running or walking helped me categorise things, get my head in order. As I trapped along it was raining steadily and I was pretty miserable and wet. I thought of Lauren all warm and lovely in that cosy little flat. As I walked I told myself; I had known her one night; I hadn't even kissed her so how could I expect her to behave any differently? Why did I feel butterflies when I thought of her? I knew the answer to that one too but I slotted it away. I wasn't meant to have a relationship, it was as simple as that. The butterflies would soon turn to bile, I knew from experience. By the time I got to 'Dawson's Campers' I had left women behind and got my mind back firmly on the job at hand. The pitch was around a thousand meters square, with a permanent brick structure just about dead centre. It held two very up-market models which were lit by spotlights. A cardboard cut-out family smiled at me from the awning of one gleaming holiday home. Other than the two dimensional family, the whole place seemed deserted. The only visible security was an ageing camera mounted on one corner of the main building. That didn't seem a problem as it pointed toward the newer vans, away from the one I'd selected. Still, getting nicked was never a good idea so I did a full circuit of the place, just to make sure all was well, before going about the job. I selected a ten-year-old Ford Camper with double doors to the rear. It took me thirty seconds or so to get in and another minute to break the steering lock and hot-wire the engine.

The diesel motor rattled away like a good one and I noticed that the kind people that had traded it in had left me a full tank.

I was fairly confident that the van wouldn't be reported stolen until the morning so I settled back and drove back to the Travelodge, drying off on the way.

Once back in my room I set up the kit I would need. I loaded two syringes with morphine and placed them in a plastic box in my inside pocket. I rooted through the rest of the medical kit until I came across an old bottle of my ex-wife's sleeping tablets, there were just four left. I crushed them, added a little warm water to the bottle and dissolved the mixture. Then I selected the SIG SLP and a spare magazine which tucked into my belt in the small of my back. I dived into Rick's old Bergen and took a thousand pounds in cash from the bundle for sweetener money. The rest of the kit took me ten minutes to load into the camper. I paid my bill like a good boy and set off to the hospital, my mind flying in anticipation.

Rick had given me the clue I needed to get him out. All hospital morgues and pathology labs tend to be secreted out of sight of the general public around the back of buildings. If Rick 'died' then that would be my escape route.

The rain was insistent. It battered the camper as I lumbered through light early morning traffic toward the hospital gates. The cabin was warm and cosy enough but I felt a chill as I pondered my task. I had to get Rick away from the ward before Stern's men found him and finished the job.

It was two-twenty a.m.

Despite the hour, the hospital car parks were busy and there was plenty of activity. This was a plus to me as I didn't stand out like a spare prick at a wedding.

I drove to the rear of the building until I saw the tell-tale signs of death. I looked for a chimney that would form part of a furnace. All large hospitals had an incinerator that disposed of various body parts and contaminated materials. All the bits and pieces the doctors cut out of us. They burned everything from gall bladders to amputated limbs, ingrown toenails to unborn children. It all had to go somewhere, it was just that people didn't want to see it.

The incinerator was always close to the pathology department. In turn the mortuary was always close to pathology. I saw the chimney, and just to the left of it, two large plastic swing doors. It had to be the place.

I parked the camper as near as I dared to the mortuary entrance and pushed the heavy doors. They made a swishing sound as they closed behind me. Muttering to myself, I strolled casually into the mortuary area. I always found that if you looked like you knew what you were doing, most times no one bothered you.

The place seemed deserted, and bright strip lights illuminated my way as I walked by two viewing rooms. They were small chapels of rest used by the police to lay out bodies so relatives could identify family or friends in a more humane place than a path lab table. Both were empty, there was no bad news for the families of Leeds that night.

The place was silent. I was, once again, around the dead. The memories of the funeral gave me a little nudge, but I didn't allow myself to be swayed from my task.

Another set of swing doors took me to a refrigerated area where dozens of large drawers held corpses. Each drawer displayed a name plate just like a filing cabinet in any office. The place gave me the creeps. I had seen plenty of death and gore in my time, I'd never been frightened of dying, but I still hated hospitals.

Then I found what I was looking for. There was a small staff room. It had probably been a storage cupboard that the staff had commandeered.

It held a few lockers. A portable television stood on a makeshift stand. There was brew-making kit and a couple of old chairs that looked suspiciously like commodes. Within seconds I had my disguise, a full porter's outfit kindly left hanging inside an open locker. It was slightly big but beggars couldn't be choosers, eh? Then I sat and made a brew.

You may think that it was a bit risky but I felt confident that any visitor would be a lone one and I was far enough down in the bowels of the hospital not to disturb anyone if I had to disable a nosy porter. The brew was important as it was the home of my sleeping tablet mixture. I made two black teas, milk and sugar on the side, slipped in the mixture and set off toward the HDU with a whistle and a tray of deep sleep.

I took the elevator to the third floor but walked to the intensive care unit which was next to HDU. I poked my head around the door and saw three nurses. One took a quick glance at me and smiled. I returned the gesture and gave her a quick friendly wave, turned on my heels and walked to Rick's ward.

I virtually marched into HDU with the tray of drinks at shoulder height. I walked past Rick's bed and he seemed fine.

I counted two nurses. The first was in her late forties, maybe older, and was very overweight. The second was younger and attractive. Call me cynical, but not being the handsome guy at the party, if the job involved sweet talk, I always went for the fat one.

"Hiya!" I chirped, but half whispered. "I'd made tea for the girls in ICU and there are two left. So I thought of you lot here with the cabbages."

I gave the fatty my best Scottish twinkle and added, "Milk and sugar?"

In perfect unison both women said, "No sugar for me," and then giggled slightly. My God, it was all going too bloody easy. I poured milk into both teas and handed them to the nurses.

I concentrated on my older prey again. "Drink up, it won't be that warm now."

Both sipped their tea. The young one wrinkled her forehead and said casually, "I've not seen you before."

"Nah, I've only been here two weeks. I've never made it away from the path lab yet."

"Oh," said the pair, again in perfect time.

"In fact, I'm off there now, girls. I'll collect the cups later, okay?"

"Great," was the chorus and the pair started to worry me. They must have been some kind of relation, maybe mother and daughter. They probably lived and worked together, spent so much time together that they became inseparable like those identical twins you see on the telly, the ones that speak in unison all the time.

Whatever the reason, it was a strange encounter.

Just as got to the exit I turned again and in my best Lorraine Kelly gossip tone I whispered.

"Which one is the gangster, by the way?"

The older woman rose from her desk and I thought I detected a slight stumble.

"Number four here."

I could tell she was quite excited that she had someone else to share her gossip with. She walked over to Rick's station. I turned and joined her.

"Big fellow, isn't he," I quipped, hastily taking in as much as I could about Rick's medical state. He was being fed intravenously and he had a catheter, but the rest was monitoring gear.

"He is, but he's no trouble." The nurse guffawed and elbowed me in the ribs to make her point.

I laughed with her and noticed she was definitely unsteady. I checked over my shoulder just in time to see the younger nurse drop her tea cup and fall unconscious in her seat.

The big nurse took on a puzzled expression before dropping to her knees. I helped her to her desk and she went out completely, farting loudly in the process.

I walked back to Rick.

"Alright, mate. Can you hear me?"

Rick opened one eye.

"Good to see you, Des, get me the fuck out of here."

I took out my little plastic box.

"I'm going to have to hit you with some morph before I move you, mate. At least you won't feel anything till we get mobile."

Rick moved his body slightly.

"Just do it, let's get going."

I wasted no time. I found a vein and pumped enough of the drug into him to knock out an elephant. I stripped back his bedclothes and removed his catheter. Then, I took out his drip and lifted his forearm to stem any bleeding. It was all going well until I removed the monitoring gear. In my haste I'd forgotten that the heart monitor had an alarm system and I hadn't disabled it.

The second I removed the first sensor from Rick's chest it went off. The alarm was deafening.

I would have a resus team on top of me in no time. I heaved Rick's dead weight into the wheelchair at the side of his bed. He groaned slightly as I propped his feet onto the supports. Then I legged it quick time to the lift. Buzzers were going off all over the bloody place and I could hear the hurried footsteps of emergency staff getting nearer and nearer.

I changed my mind about the lift and went for the stairs. I only needed to get one floor away from the melee, and then a porter pushing a sleeping man in a wheelchair might not seem too bad. Well, it was the best I could do.

I pushed Rick along the corridor until I saw the green and white sign for the stairwell. I knew the next act was going to be hard. I was going to have to haul fifteen stone of dead weight down two flights of stairs in double quick time. I opted for backwards and pushed the swing door open with my backside, looked over my shoulder and negotiated the first steps. I took all of Rick's weight onto my chest. By the time I'd bounced down the first flight one at a time I was panting like a greyhound and sweating like a racehorse.

As I made the bottom of the second flight my legs burned with the effort and my heart pumped hard. I wiped my brow before casually pushing Rick out onto the ground floor.

As we negotiated the X-ray department, I confiscated a blanket from a nearby trolley and covered Rick's legs with it. Then I whistled my way to the lift which would take us to the mortuary and our escape route.

By the time the hospital security guys had dealt with the two unconscious HDU staff and even noticed Rick's empty bed, I was at the back door of the Ford camper van.

With all of my strength, I lifted Rick from the chair and laid him on a single bunk inside the camper. I covered him.

"You okay, mate?"

He groaned. The morphine had done its job.

I jumped down from the back of the van, keys in my hand and plan in my head, straight into the arms of Lauren North.

Rick Fuller's Story:

Despite the painkillers, I could feel the bumps in the road. It was a really strange experience. I had suffered burns to just over eighteen per cent of my body. Hospitals categorise burn injuries by degrees. Mine were first degree, the same category as severe sunburn. Some fucking dick-head with an Oxbridge PhD had decided that. I bet he'd never had boiling water poured over twenty per cent of his body mass. I was lucky though. I'd been wearing boots. Had I been barefoot, my burn injuries would have been far worse.

As for my gunshot wound, to be fair, the surgeon had done a great job. He'd sorted the dental side of it out on the table. What was left of my wisdom tooth was removed at the same time he repaired my cheek. He'd also left a painkilling pad at the site of the operation. Something I'd been glad of the last day or so.

So why, as we drove along, could I feel the road and not my injuries?

Who knows?

The roof of the camper was starting to glisten with condensation. Des and the nurse were sitting up front and I could just hear the radio.

How the hell did Des find me so quickly?

Why the hell was the sister there? I had lots of questions.

My last definite memory was Stephan pulling the trigger. I had some vague pictures of people around me, later on, maybe in an ambulance? Whether they were the good souls who found me on the road or hospital staff, I couldn't say.

Being on the road in a camper van was similar to an ambulance and I actually felt okay. I know that sounds pretty weird coming from a fucked up bloke who was being driven to Scotland in a stolen second hand Transit. But I did.

The morphine sorted my pain and I was with the only person in the world I trusted.

No worries.

I slept without hurting.

I awoke to near silence. The van was parked and empty. All I could hear was my own breathing and distant motorway traffic. I presumed we were in a motorway service station and Des had gone for a brew or whatever.

I was well delighted at my exit from the hospital. Des had played a blinder. How the hell he'd conned the nurse into the plan I could only guess. I had to hand it to him, he was good.

I heard another car approach the parked van. Headlights illuminated the interior of the camper. They lingered. They stayed too long. I heard a car door open, then the voices.

I started to feel uneasy. I couldn't walk, and I couldn't cry out. Then I heard Des and the key in the lock. The interior light came on, and finally, he and Lauren peered at me from the sofa opposite.

"How ya feeling, pal?" whispered Des.

"Are ye hungry, mate?"

I did my best to speak out of the side of my mouth that worked.

"No, ta, but I could go some water."

"No problem," said Des. "I've even got you a straw."

He rooted in a carrier bag, found a bottle of Evian and a box of straws and held it for me. The water tasted good. I'd been fed intravenously the past few days and my throat was dry as a bone.

"Cheers," I said.

Des knelt by me. He poked a thumb in nursie's general direction.

"We've been and hired another motor. I used one of your snide driving licences just to be on the safe side. Funny thing, though, your credit card didn't work. We had to use hers."

I didn't take in the information. I should have. It would have saved time in the end, but I was too drugged to notice.

I think I managed an "okay", and fell into a deep sleep again.

By the time I awoke, it was daylight, we were travelling on a country road and I could just see the green of the hedges fly by and some bright blue sky. I twisted my head to look for Des but couldn't see him. The nurse drove. She noticed my movement in the rear view mirror, and shouted over the engine noise. "How are you feeling?"

It was a very jolly hospital voice. The swelling to my face was going down but I still found speech hard. The morph had all gone and I was perhaps a little blunt.

"Where the fuck is Des?"

Lauren alarmingly swerved the camper and suddenly we ground to a halt. She leapt from the driver's seat and sat heavily opposite me. The sofa across made a second single bed, if anyone could ever bear to sleep on something all yellow tartan and fake pine.

Lauren wasn't pleased with me. I could tell.

She sat in silence for a moment as if considering what to say. She was a classically beautiful woman. She was Bathsheba. Raven-haired with no hint of make-up.

She appeared not to notice her own splendour but it was there, like something she'd carried inside her, something that was allowed to be noticed by others but never completely supposed. She looked past me at first, as if focusing on a distant object. Her voice was quiet but precise. She left a gap between each word.

"Where, the, fuck, is, Des?"

That one line seemed to give her confidence. She grew in stature as she repeated the same line.

"Where, the, fuck, is, Des?"

Any hint of nerves faded with each staccato delivery. This was a woman who had fought many a verbal battle. Somewhere behind those eyes was a past with too much pain, eyes that had fought a war and were not afraid to fight another.

She dropped her head in her cupped hands, her face inches from mine. She focused on me, sharp as a rapier, voice level.

"I'll tell you where Des is. He's taken the hire car to his old house by the Loch. Know it? Stern's guys already have that address so we can't go there."

Her green eyes widened and she had the slightest hint of derision in her tone. Her words hit me like a brick.

"I believe that one was down to you, Rick?"

If she'd been a man I'd have knocked her out.

"Des has organised a safe place to stay. We're about ten miles from it now. He'll meet us there after he's collected some gear from home. He can't go there again. Well, not until this is all over."

My blood boiled at her insolence. I raised myself from my bed for the first time. I felt my usually strong arms quiver under the strain. My head swam. I took a deep breath and managed a full sentence.

"And you know what all this is about then, eh? Sister?"

"Lauren," she tapped her chest with an unpolished nail. "That's my name, and yes, Rick, I think I know where we are all at." She stopped short, and for a second I thought I saw a flaw in the performance, a trace of fear maybe?

I couldn't hold myself in position any longer and I fell back on my pillows panting and in pain.

"Sure you do."

She looked concerned but stood, and walked back to the driver's seat. Once she'd started the engine and strapped herself in she turned, and delivered her prognosis in her slightly Surrey tone.

"Without my care, the possibility of you getting back to full health again is pretty shitty. If you think you've got me sussed and know why I'm here helping you, you're very wrong."

She turned the wheel of the camper and we started to move.

"Cos I haven't a fucking clue myself."

Lauren North's Story:

It didn't bother me that Rick was a mean bastard. I suppose anyone would be, if they'd been in his shoes of late. But he wasn't going to take it out on me. I was used to men who were mean bastards.
My ex-husband was a successful doctor, a specialist. He was respected throughout his profession. To the outside world he was a good, honest man. No one, my mother, Jane, no single human, knew he beat me. Even his longest and closest friends never knew of his violent outbursts.
And I don't just mean a one-off slap in the middle of a drunken row. I mean a systematic yet frantic punishment should things not go his way. This was always followed by weeks of him being the perfect fucking human being.
Now, if you saw Des and Rick it wouldn't take you long to realise that they were two extremely scary guys. Yet I knew, just knew that I was totally safe in their company despite everything that was going on. No matter what was to come. I was in safe hands with them.
I had made a decision, and even though slightly insane, I considered it to be the right one. I told myself, I'd be there to see Rick through the first few days of his treatment. Once he was stabilised and out of any danger, well, then I'd turn around and go on holiday as I'd planned. It was a purely clinical decision.
Back in Leeds, after Des had left my flat, I'd stared at the closed lift doors for ages. I stood there with wet hair, dressed in a five-year-old dressing gown. It had a very fetching iron burn around arse level. I realised that I'd had a gorgeous guy back at my flat for the first time in living memory and I was dressed like a bag woman. I looked at my feet and was horrified to confirm I was wearing Snoopy slippers. Since becoming single I'd dated one man for three awful hours. I'd drunkenly snogged a doorman outside The Ritz in Manchester, and had my backside felt by a couple of overzealous patients.
That had been the sum total of any excitement in my life for the last three and half years. For a woman of my age it was a bloody long time. I was in my prime. I'd read it in Cosmo.
As Des exited my block, and with him, any chance of further excitement, I turned, went back inside, and started to wash dishes. After the water had finally drained, I prodded some peas down the plughole with my finger and I realised the truth. I didn't want to have a relationship with Des. I didn't want a boyfriend or a lover or

a husband. I just wanted to be in his world for a while. I'd listened to his amazing story on that one fascinating evening, and, I was ashamed to say, it excited me. It was physical. I could've been part of his world if I'd wanted, but I chose safety, as I always did. That's why I chose my husband Phillip. He was safe, from good stock. Safe as bloody houses, I was.

It had all ended as quickly as it had started and Des was gone. I'd frightened him away.

I rang Jane.

"Alright?" she chirped.

"Not really."

"What's happened now?"

"Nothing."

"There must be something, you've got that 'nobody loves me, everybody hates me' tone."

"No." I tried to sound a little happier. "I just rang for a chat, nothing wrong with that, is there? Ringing a mate for a chat?"

"Okay." Jane let each letter drag. She didn't believe me.

"I am okay, honestly I am. It's just well you know how it is with me and opportunities. I get a prospect of some real excitement in my life and I push it away."

"This is the new guy we're talking about then, eh?" I heard Jane reach for her cigarettes and take the first long drag. "This Jock?"

"Scot," I countered.

"Whatever. So he's dumped you then?"

"He didn't dump me, I sort of dumped him. In fact there was no dumping at all."

"Hmmm."

"It's true!"

"Yeah?"

"Yeah."

I felt as close to tears as I could, but as usual none came, "Jane, I need to banish some ghosts, once and for all."

There was silence other than the static of the phone in my ear.

"I need to get on a plane right now, where nobody knows about me, where nobody gives me pitiful looks and where Phillip and his fucking cronies don't sneer across the dining room at the crazy frigid bird in the corner."

I heard Jane take a deep breath. She was about to go into her 'Support Lauren' speech, the same one she'd delivered to me on countless occasions in the past. Jane was my personal self-confidence counsellor. Before she could start, I heard myself say.

"I'm going to take some leave, right now."

I was owed four weeks annual holiday and I decided to take two of them from that night. Jane tried to argue about the staff rota, but I had made my decision.

In my mental wanderings I'd forgotten that Jane and I had planned a holiday in Greece together. I'd promised her two weeks in Crete, but I needed to stand firm. I needed to go.

I tried to explain the inexplicable to her but of course I couldn't. I just had to get away from Leeds for a while, that was it. I was going to go to the ward right that minute and tell the on-call unit manager what I was doing.

When I'd finished, I heard Jane stubbing out her cigarette, as she exhaled slowly.

"Suit yourself."

The phone went dead.

I cursed my useless self all the way to the hospital.

I thought I'd done the hard part when I'd convinced the unit manager to let me change my leave at a moment's notice. I virtually hopped down the last few steps to the car park, mentally booking my holiday on the net. I'd always promised myself a trip to Egypt and the Pyramids.

I was almost to my car when I heard the unmistakable sound of the resuscitation team alarm flooding out of the open casualty doors. It always filled me with dread, that dreadful siren. I pulled my keys from my bag and opened the car door. I was glad that I didn't have to deal with any death for a few well-earned nights. A little devil on my shoulder, the one you should never listen to, told me what the alarm meant. I just knew it had something to do with Des. Des and Rick. I knew he was there, in my ward, stealing my patient. My heart raced and I started to run. I ran around the side of the main building toward the path lab. I had no idea what I was looking for until I saw the camper. Come on, who goes to visit a sick relative in a camper van?

Within seconds I saw him.

Des was pushing Rick with all his might towards the van. I was so close I could see Des was pouring with sweat and smiling.

His face was a real picture when he jumped right into me ten seconds later.

"Lauren! Jesus H Christ, love, you frightened the life outta me."
I didn't speak but looked at Rick moaning steadily inside the van.
"He's a very poorly man, Des."
Des closed the back of the van. There was obviously no time for sentiment.
"You know I've got to move him."
I must have been out of my mind. "Where are you going?"
"Scotland."
I opened the passenger door and climbed in. The cab smelled vaguely of pipe tobacco.
"I've never been to Scotland. Is it cold?"

I checked my map and made the final turn toward Hillside Cottage. Rick slept as the camper bounced along the track to the house.
If I had ever wanted to escape, to find peace and solace, Scotland would have been my place. The mid-morning sun flashed in fresh puddles ahead of me and I blew a low whistle as the whole of Hillside came into view. The cottage had everything you might ever dream of. Its stone-built whitewashed walls were fixed firmly to the Scottish landscape by thousands of ivy fingers which covered a full two thirds of the house. The living structure supported a recently thatched roof. I suppose the place may have needed a lick of paint, but unbroken views of the whisky trail, as far as the eye could see, more than made up for it. A large private walled rear garden pricked my girlish imagination. The cottage had it all.
The place belonged to Des's ex-wife. She had inherited the place as part of their divorce settlement. I couldn't help but feel a little jealous as I compared my grotty Leeds flat with the relative rustic charm of Hillside.
Des had been forced to contact his estranged partner to get access to the place, and from the telephone conversations I sensed it had been a tough job for him. He was one of those men who wore his emotional heart on his sleeve.
He had used the story that holidaying American fishermen had approached him for accommodation. She had only been too glad of the four hundred quid a week offered. The conversations had been businesslike. I got the impression Des was somehow saddened by her detachment.
I pulled the camper to the rear of the cottage and killed the engine. I heard Rick cough but he stayed asleep.

I sat listening to Rick breathe. The sun was suddenly dragged upward and sinister black curtains of cloud took most of the daylight.

I'd never witnessed such a frantic change in weather. It was if the sky had suddenly become embarrassed at the beauty beneath and attempted to preserve its modesty.

Then it rained.

Ten minutes later, the sound of the downpour hammering on the roof of the camper was covered by engine noise and Des pulled into the drive.

"This is it then?" I chirped as I jumped from the van, shielding myself from the torrent with a newspaper.

"Aye, nice isn't it?" Des hid his sarcasm badly and didn't seem to bother about the downpour and just got wet.

"The place cost me a fortune. Now I'm paying to bloody rent it." Des unlocked the front door. I followed and dropped what possessions I had in the middle of the lounge floor. The cottage had the chill that always comes from a house having lain empty, but I spun around in the centre of the living room and took in the decor.

"Very nice, Des. Mrs Cogan has extremely good taste."

I stopped still and saw that Des looked slightly hurt.

"Sorry." I sounded weak and felt stupid.

"Nae bother," he said. "Let's see to getting the big man inside."

I felt suitably chastised. With some effort we carried Rick carefully to a downstairs bedroom. He was still drowsy. I got what medical supplies we had together on a dresser worth more than my entire collection of house contents, and Des got straight on with lighting the fire.

Rick looked pale. He'd had all the morphine he could take. I could see he was in some pain. I sat beside his bed. "How do you feel now?"

"I'm okay." He stretched his neck painfully.

"Can I get you something?"

He lifted himself slightly. "A brew would be great, tea, no sugar."

"Tea it is."

I turned to leave the room, but Rick took my arm. He looked straight at me. His voice was soft and kind. I didn't believe he could produce such a sound. "Thank you, Lauren."

"Erm, no problem," I said. "I'll bring you some paracetamol with the tea. I'm afraid that's all the pain relief you can have for a while."

"Okay," he said, as matter-of-fact as you like.

I motioned toward his scalded legs. "We'll have to start physiotherapy on those first thing tomorrow."

I saw him grimace, so I added, "Be thankful it wasn't your bollocks."

He smiled. It was the first time I'd seen it, and despite the swollen lips he lit up the room. I shook the shiver from my back and closed the door behind me. I walked into a small, tiled kitchen. It, like the roof of the cottage, had been recently refurbished. You could still smell new wood. A stunning Aga cooker was surrounded by beautiful oak and stainless steel. Des's ex certainly had style.

Des himself had pre-empted Rick's request and was boiling a fancy chrome kettle.

"He okay?"

I shrugged. "He's in a bit of pain but he seems good enough considering."

Des rummaged around in cupboards for mugs and I unpacked groceries obtained from unknown sources.

"He's a good bloke really, Lauren."

"I know," I said. "Why don't you take him his tea and I'll finish the fire."

Des nodded and I tapped along the polished wood floor to the perfect country lounge. I sat and stared as the first flames found their way through the jet coals. I added some wood and poked at it, not really knowing what I was doing. For the first time we were all together under the same roof and safe. I was exhausted. I felt my insistent muscles complain as I rested back on the sofa. The warmth of the fire grew and I was engulfed by it. I could barely hear Des's voice echo along the hall, as he talked to his best friend. I was falling into the deepest sleep, strangely content.

I awoke to find Des had put me to bed in a beautiful attic room. He'd been the perfect gent and I was fully clothed minus shoes.

I stepped onto more stripped wooden floors and shuffled to a small en suite bathroom. Once again, no expense had been spared and yet it was just quality for its own sake. No flash.

I could hear voices and smell bacon. Both attracted me in equal amounts, so I hurried my shower and pulled on jeans and a sweater. I negotiated a spiral staircase that would beat most Sherpas and marvelled at Des's ability to get me up it the night before.

"Morning!" I shouted as I hit the bottom.

Des met me with a smile and a cup of tea. "Breakfast is on."

I cupped the drink in my hands

"Have you seen Rick?"

He threw a thumb over his shoulder.

"He's where you left him, except he's got my laptop and he's working."

"Working?"

"Don't ask. The guy's fucking barmy."

"He needs to rest. The physiotherapy sessions for new burn victims are a killer."

Des shrugged. "Up to him, never was anything I could do with him." He walked back to the kitchen whilst I stuck my nose into Rick's room.

"Hi," I said.

Rick was propped up with pillows and he scrolled through documents on a computer on his lap.

"Hi," he returned. Any hint of the soft voice from the previous night had disappeared with the dawn. I nodded toward the silver Apple on his lap. "You need some rest."

He nodded, "We're doing my legs this morning, yeah?"

"Yes."

"Well, I reckon I'll be fit for nothing after that, so I thought, I'd do this now."

"True."

"So get your breakfast, and I'll see you later."

I was about to speak but he was back to the documents on the screen and I knew it was pointless. I wandered back to the kitchen. Des was dropping bacon onto kitchen roll and buttering fresh bread.

"I've seen most of those files of his," he said. "There is nothing there that is going to lead us to Stern."

I shook my head.

"I'm really not interested in what happens next, Des. As I told you on the way up here, as soon as Rick is out of any real clinical danger, I'm off back to Leeds, and this is all over for me."

"Fair enough."

Des looked a little hurt again and I wondered if he had read something more into my presence. I couldn't blame him for that but I needed to put the cards on the table.

"It's not that I don't like you, Des."

"I know."

"I mean it. I do like you, but I just don't want to get involved with a guy at the moment."

"Especially one that could be dead next week, eh?"

Before I could answer he smiled at me and handed me a bacon sandwich. "Here. Get this down your neck. After you've seen to Rick, I'll show you the sights."

Rick Fuller's Story:

I scrolled through page after page of text, hoping to come across some clue that may lead me to Edgar David Stern the myth. I was more convinced than ever he was just that, a myth. Joel Davies had been dealing with him, through Susan, for some time. She had brokered several smaller deals prior to the Amsterdam disaster, obviously tasters for the big sting.

I had heard Stern's name mentioned by various other villains, but nothing other than Robin Hood stories. No one had met him or dealt with him other than Joel Davies. And he had never met or spoken with him. The only direct link to him and his organisation was Susan. She had turned out to be the surprise package of a lifetime, beautiful, dangerous and elite.

Des had found me by a terrible accident. What he had seen at the cemetery defied belief. I couldn't get my head around the ferocity of the aftermath of the Amsterdam job. Not only had Stern's guys followed all the players of the Dutch disaster, and attempted to kill them, but the planting of an explosive device at a civilian funeral was way beyond anything any European drug baron had ever orchestrated.

From what Des had described, Stern had wiped out the leadership of one of the most powerful drug families in the north of England in one move. We had to assume that Davies was either dead by Stern's order or in hiding. What did that mean on the streets of Manchester? I'll tell you what. About half a million customers looking to get high. Not something to be sniffed at if you are a drug dealer, if you forgive the pun. The void would need to be filled and my guess was our friend Susan and her pals were working on just that.

As I mused, Lauren stepped into the bedroom. She had that nurse-like tone back; the same one from the camper. She insisted on being badly dressed, wearing poorly cut, cheap denims. Despite it all she was still attractive in a clean sort of way. I kept my thoughts to myself as I knew that she was about to hurt me. It was a pain that would enable me to walk and run again. Something that just days earlier, I could only have dreamt of.

The therapy was needed as burn tissue tightens and restricts movement. Most people have suffered a minor burn or sunburn, so understand how tight and sore the skin feels afterward. In the case of my burns, it was the area around my knees that would give me trouble.

Lauren rolled down my covers and gently removed the dressings from my legs. It was the first time I'd got a good look at them and it wasn't a pretty sight. My left leg looked worse than my right. Most of the top of the thigh was one large blister. The remainder from my kneecap to my ankle was blood red. Smaller white blisters had formed on the inside of the calf. I got the distinct impression that I wouldn't be wearing my Calvin Klein shorts this summer.

"First," said Lauren, wiping her hands with a sterile cloth, "I'm going to apply an anti-biotic ointment to the whole area of each leg. We'll do this each morning from now on. I won't be replacing the dressings. I want to get some air to the burns."

"Okay," I said.

"It will be quite painful but we can't risk any infection as we have no medical back-up. If you get infected you will get septicaemia within hours and you'll be dead within days, understand? "

I nodded. She raised my left leg slowly and rested my ankle on a clean white towel. Then she gently applied the cream. It actually felt soothing rather than painful. It seemed to take away some of the burning for a moment. I lay back and let her get on with it.

Each leg took several minutes to cover. When she'd finished Lauren washed her hands again.

"Now for the hard part. We need to get some movement back into your legs. We'll start with ankle rotations and work up to the knees." She cocked her head to one side and her hair fell to her elbow. "This will be unpleasant, Rick."

She was right too. She cupped my heel in one hand and my toes in the other and started to turn my ankle. Even though the ankle itself hadn't been affected, the scalded skin above felt like it was being torn off. I let out a gasp as the rotations got wider. Lauren seemed either not to notice, or was resigned to causing me necessary grief. The whole process took over thirty minutes. By the time it was over I was soaked in sweat and shattered.

Right on cue Des popped his head around the door.

"Ye coming for a run yet, ye big Jessie?"

I couldn't even manage a reply, but flicked him a very shaky pair of fingers.

"Charming, eh, Lauren? Ye enquire after yer mate and that's all the thanks you get."

"I think Rick is a little sore right now, Des." Lauren gestured towards the door. "But I'll go for a jog with you."

"Jog!" Des seemed amused by Lauren. "I don't think so, love."

Lauren seemed to take the bait. "I'll have you know I jog three times a week."

Des smiled his knowing smile. "The girl wants to get some in, eh, Rick?"

I was coming down from my adrenaline rush. The pain was easing a little.

"Just take it easy on him, Lauren. He's over forty now."

Des guffawed, "Eh! At least I've not taken to my bed with no more than sunburn and a toothache."

"Fuck off the pair of you."

I listened to them sorting out their running gear. Des with his boots and Bergen, Lauren with her Reeboks and trackies, the pair were slagging each other off even before they had even started. It was all good natured banter. I felt a pang of jealousy, at not being able to share the jokes. As I listened to Lauren take the piss out of Des's knees, I couldn't help but wonder why someone like her had got so involved with us.

I mean, the thing was far from over, and from what Des had told me, he hadn't hidden anything from her. So she was either crazy about him or just plain crazy.

Well, if Des was looking for a new woman in his life, he could do worse.

She was adamant that as soon as I was out of any real danger, she was off. I didn't believe that, and neither did she. Des could have organised the meds and done the physio. If I'd suffered any real setback, or contracted a serious infection, Des would have had to dump me on the NHS and hope for the best. Simple as.

So why was she really playing nursie?

I put Lauren to one side and turned back the clock to Amsterdam, Susan and David Stern.

Lauren North's Story:

Jesus, the guy was a bloody gazelle. There I was thinking that we'd set a slow pace. Tabbing, Des called it. Murder, I named it. We'd been going for about an hour at something between marching and jogging pace. Des had loaded a big green rucksack he called a Bergen with so much stuff I thought we were going on a weekend trip, never mind a run. The Bergen was strapped to his back and he showed no sign of fatigue.

I was blowing like an old kettle. I'd reckoned we'd done about eight kilometres, mostly uphill and we hadn't turned for home.

"When are we going to head back?" I gasped.

"About another four clicks and we'll have a break."

Oh my God! That was a minimum twenty-four kilometres by my reckoning. I'd never run further than ten in one go.

"Turn back if you like," he said, with a hint of 'smug bloke' in his voice.

"No. I'm okay, I just like to know where I am, that's all," I lied.

"'Kay," Des chirped.

Twenty minutes later I was near exhaustion and thankfully Des slowed to a walk.

"We'll take a rest here, and have a brew."

I could hardly breathe and he'd brought half the bloody kitchen with him. He sat on the grass and unpacked a small primer stove, bottled water and plastic mugs. He settled to his task whilst I took lungful after lungful of air with my head between my knees. Once he'd got the water on he had the audacity to light a small pipe. He blew a plume of bluish smoke into the air and rested back on his elbows. He beamed in my direction.

"Not as fit as ye thought, eh?"

"Obviously."

I heard mild irritation in my voice.

"Never mind," he added. "Soon have you in shape if you train with me and Rick."

I sat beside him, my breathing returning to normal. I was suddenly aware of the view. So much beauty surrounded us. The morning air was still, crisp, clean and fresh. Wisps of white cloud were translucent, unable to hide the intense blue of the sky. Rolling green hills that had looked so daunting when we arrived now looked lush and welcoming.

"There's no chance of that. It is beautiful here, Des, but I can't stay. I have a life and a career in Leeds."

"None of us can hang about here forever, Lauren. I was just suggesting you might want to stay until Rick was fit."

"That could be months."

"Weeks," Des corrected.

I watched him reload his pipe. I took a deep breath and heard myself say, "I'm going back home in ten days when my leave runs out. You won't need me then."

Des checked the water and rooted for teabags. His voice, flat and matter of fact. There was no hint of displeasure or disappointment. "Suit yourself, hen, it isn't a problem. What you did for both of us was beyond anything that we could have expected. If you go in ten days, we'll wish you well. If you want to stay on a while and help out, that's okay too."

I didn't know what to say, because I didn't know what I felt. I was enthralled by the two men that had been thrust into my life. I was bored with my petty existence in Leeds. But I wasn't sure I wanted to throw everything away. I had friends, a home and a job I loved.

"Just pour the tea," I said.

Des found his smug face again and handed me a brew.

"We'll take the short way back."

I couldn't help myself.

"We bloody well won't!"

Four weeks on, I was keeping up with Des on our daily runs. He had added circuit training to his regime and I was fitter and faster. Rick was walking around the house like a caged, bad-tempered lion eager to join in.

He'd suffered a small setback in the first week after he had attempted to climb the stairs and torn the skin on his left leg. Since then his recuperation had been remarkable and he was able to walk unaided. I had removed the stitches from his cheek and he had been left with a star-shaped scar the size of a two-pence piece. He split his time between exercising his upper body, poring over his computer and being grumpy.

Why hadn't I returned to Leeds? Because I'd never felt so alive. I found that I could enjoy the company of men without feeling the pressure of a relationship. I discovered that I liked to fish and I established that I could shoot too.

It was like living with my two handsome older brothers, who just happened to be your favourite anti-heroes.

By week six Rick was running and punishing his body in a way a tri-athlete might when preparing for the Olympics. His determination to be fit was only matched by his obsession with finding the man I had grown to know as Edgar David Stern, his femme fatale Susan and his henchman Stephan.

Rick had been cooking dinner when he called Des and me into the kitchen. I had been in Scotland for almost three blissful months. What I didn't realise was, that moment, that meeting of three people thrown together, seated around a kitchen table in Scotland, would change my life forever.

Rick Fuller's Story:

I felt pretty good. My legs were still scabbed and itched like hell but apart from that I was in good shape. Des and Lauren had been out fishing most of the day. I had spent my time sorting out what kit we had. We were okay for weapons and ammunition but cash was becoming an issue and I was fed up wearing clothes that had the name Fred or George inside them. I had decided that a trip to Manchester was the order of the day, get my wardrobe sorted, pick up my day car and pay Joel Davies, or what was left of him, a visit. We had been holed up for close on three months and I figured that even someone as vindictive as Edgar David Stern would have moved on and found bigger fish to fry. Still, it was safety first so I'd split what kit we had between Des and me and put a Sig and a box of 9mm to one side for Lauren. Then I called a meeting in the kitchen.

"You're giving me a gun!" Lauren looked shell-shocked.

"It's just for your own protection, hen," Des soothed. "Just in case we get split up."

I picked up the pistol. There was no point in fucking about. The girl had put some work into her fitness and even displayed some skill with a weapon. I needed to see a bit more commitment.

."Are you in or out, Lauren?"

There was a brief silence. She pushed her hair away from her face, puffed out her cheeks and exhaled.

"In," she said sharply and took the SIG.

I didn't dwell. "Right," I said. "We have to presume that the boys in blue will have some interest in us all. Me, as I was found with a bullet hole in my head, Des as he stole me from the hospital, and you, Lauren, as you disappeared the same day. We also have to presume they have photographic ID from CCTV at the hospital."

"Aye, deffo," said Des.

"You think we're wanted?" asked Lauren.

"I don't think we'll have warrants, we haven't actually committed any offence, but a nasty detective could try and get a perverting the course of justice charge on us. I think they might like to talk to us all, and I'd rather not spend a night in Bootle Street cells. So with that in mind, you might want to think about changing your appearance and we should all travel separately tomorrow. The CID may have put a track on our bank accounts, so it's best we don't use them right now. If you need cash it will have to come from the pot or one of my bogus cards."

"Aye, if the thing disnae bounce," added Des.

"Bounce?"

"Remember, on the way up here we tried to use your snide card and it bounced."

I had completely forgotten. In my drugged state the fact had left me. I stood up, found the laptop and plugged it into the telephone socket. A minute later I punched in the security code for Stephen Colletti's credit card account. To my horror it sat at zero. I tried three further accounts all with the same result. Finally I tried my numbered Swiss account. I was penniless.

Lauren put her hand on my shoulder. "How could this have happened, Rick?"

I shook my head. I was in shock.

"I don't know, but I'm going to fucking find out."

I slammed the laptop shut. "We've got just over five grand in cash, plus the gold coins which will raise another five. We'll take three separate trains to Manchester. You two go to Oxford Road Station. Des, book yourself into the Novotel. Lauren, you find the Ibis. I'll use the Britannia. They are all close to the station. Find a Phones 4U and each of you buy a pay-as-you-go mobile on Vodafone. Any make, but make sure it has a USB connection. The RP will be O'Shea's bar on Portland Street ten p.m. tomorrow. Don't book anything in advance either by phone or the net from now on. And cash only. Any questions?"

Lauren opened her mouth but didn't speak. There was no way I was going to pussyfoot around with her. She'd volunteered her help. She was one of the team. I looked her in the eye.

"Lauren, this is for real. We aren't planning a social outing. The reason you're holding a 9mm pistol, is because this is going to get very messy. If you want to change your mind and get the train to Leeds, do it now."

She just stuck out her chin and pushed the Sig into the waistband of her jeans.

"I said I was in, didn't I?"

Des stood up. "Let's clean this place and get the fuck out of here."

I didn't have much gear to pack. Des had sorted me out some underwear, a couple of shirts, a pair of jeans and some trackies. God knows where he got them, but suffice to say I felt like a born again catalogue shopper.

We had a collection of weaponry and medical supplies which I'd wrapped in pillowcases and stowed in an old suitcase I found in the cottage. My old Bergen was back and I loaded it with what clothes I had, the laptop and my old boots.

Des and Lauren dropped me at Glasgow Central railway station a little after six-fifteen a.m. I bought a Virgin one way ticket to Manchester Piccadilly, got myself a brew and a paper and waited. I was travelling to a different station than the others as I wanted to go straight to my lock-up on Oldham Street, pick up a motor and the spare keys to my flat, and stow the weapons.

It was a typical Scottish, October morning and I felt the cold as I hadn't a coat. Thankfully the train was on time and I had a seat with a table all to myself. The thought of making small talk with some dickhead from Salford just didn't appeal. I drew the occasional look from other passengers; I gathered my angry scarred cheek made for a talking point.

I pulled the laptop from the Bergen and studied Joel Davies's file for what felt like the millionth time. The only thing that stood out to me was Susan's surname. She had used it on her wedding certificate, which Joel had proudly mounted in the house. Van der Zoort just rang a bell but I just couldn't figure out which one. It certainly wasn't of poor Dutch origin to fit the underprivileged little junkie's moll story. Then again nothing in this whole caper fitted. It was a typically Dutch royal name, yet I'd bet Susan was not Dutch, I believed she was most probably South African. I knew the name. I'd seen it somewhere.

As soon as we settled we needed to get into Susan's old house. Joel was probably dead but it was that house where I intended to start our search. From there Stephan and Stern would get the treatment. I wanted my hard-earned money back.

I closed the lid of the computer, and then my eyes. Two hours later I awoke to see the familiar skyline of Manchester. I was home.

It took me just under ten minutes to walk to my Oldham Street lock-up. I entered a nine digit security code into the locking mechanism on the front door and stepped inside. It seemed an age since I had collected Joel's Porsche from Bootle Street nick, and of course, dealt with Jimmy. The Escort van that I used that night was there, together with three other cars and various bits of kit that needed to be tucked away from the prying eyes of my delicate Quays neighbours. Everything from pneumatic door openers to 'Stinger' tyre deflators were concealed in this place. Of course the jewel in the crown was that I'd never had the opportunity to give Joel the 911 back and there it sat like a healthy bank account. I felt at ease for the first time in ages. I was fit again. I had a second chance at life, and once I had dealt with the Dutch connection, this place would be redundant. I would retire.

Honest.

At the back of the lock-up was a small office with an old fashioned safe. I turned the combination and pulled open the heavy door. I removed the spare keys to my flat and the keys to a black Vectra V6 that I hadn't driven in over a year. I also took my genuine driving licence and passport. I was Richard Fuller again, and intended to remain that way for as long as possible. There was a thousand pounds in cash nestled on the top shelf. I stuffed it into my pocket and shuddered at the thought that someone, probably Stern, had stolen over a million pounds from my bank accounts.

He'd pay for that.

I opened the Vauxhall and it fired up first time. Salford Quays was ten minutes' drive away and I was looking forward to a shower and to wearing some decent clothes. I figured that I could only risk one visit to the flat. I decided to grab the bare minimum. A few Paul Smith casuals would do the trick. I tuned the radio in the Vectra to Key 103 and trod on the accelerator. Within minutes I was heading along the Mancunian Way towards my home.

I parked the Vectra about half a mile from my block and walked the rest of the way. I went straight to the underground garage. As I opened the heavy barred gate to the cold parking area, I felt my chest tighten. My two private spaces were empty. My classic white Aston Martin DB5 and my Range Rover were missing. I jogged to the lift and entered the security code to get me to my penthouse. I pushed open my flat door. The flat had been stripped of my furniture and every possession I had. I was in shock. I was so angry, no, more than plain anger, blind rage maybe? Fury? Hatred?

No criminal organisation on earth was capable of this kind of asset stripping. It took the police years to seize assets in the public domain, let alone strip cash from carefully hidden numbered accounts. This was the work of someone more powerful than the police. I paced about the interior of what had been my beautifully furnished bedroom. At that moment I noticed a sheet of paper casually left on the floor.

It was an estate agent's blurb. My flat was for sale. I folded the sheet of paper and stuffed it into my pocket. I stopped briefly and looked out of the panoramic window of what once had been my lounge, the city spread out in front of me like a concrete carpet.

"I'm going to find you, Stern. If it is my last waking moment, I am going to find you, and kill you."

I drove the Vectra hard towards Cheadle and Joel Davies's house. I needed to sort my head out and decide on a plan of action.

Within the hour I had found myself a spot where I could observe the front gates of his considerable home.

It took me forty more minutes to see all I needed.

Lauren North's Story:

I'd settled myself in my room at the Ibis, done as Rick had requested, and bought a pay-as-you-go phone. A nice pink Motorola. It was charging on the bedside cabinet whilst I showered and changed.

I felt really uncomfortable being in possession of a gun. Although I'd done lots of shooting with Des the last couple of months, it was always a fun thing, punching holes in tin cans and stuff. This was very different. I was being carried along by an energy that I couldn't, or didn't want to fight. I checked my watch and saw I had half an hour before the scheduled meeting at O'Shea's.

I couldn't decide whether to take the SIG with me. I eventually decided against it, and concealed the box of ammunition and the pistol in my suitcase. I tucked my new phone in my jeans pocket, pulled on my anorak and walked to the lift.

I could hear O'Shea's before I could see it. Banging Irish tunes bounced off the office blocks opposite, before disappearing off towards the canal and Manchester's infamous gay village.

I stepped into the tiled hallway of the bar. Two large shaven-headed bouncers looked me up and down, issued a polite 'good evening' and pushed open the interior doors.

I was hit with a wall of cigarette smoke, clinking glasses and a boisterous crowd. There were half a dozen booths to my right, filled with a mixture of student types and Celtic football fans. Obviously a televised game had recently ended, and judging by the mood of the Catholic side of Glasgow, Celtic had been victorious.

The bar then crooked left and I faced a stage, occupied by five guys and a lone female sporting guitars, fiddles and whistles. The backdrop announced the band as 'The Bogtrotters.' They were just starting a rousing rendition of *Black Velvet Band*.

A large group of green and white hooped shirts were gathered in front of the band, and clapped and cheered every move.

Finally, I saw Des sitting at a table to the left of the stage. He waved at me and smiled. Rick sat to his right, he didn't acknowledge me; he simply checked his watch implying I was late. I wasn't.

"Drink?" asked Des above the din.

"Bacardi and Coke please," I shouted as the band got to the chorus.

I sat opposite Rick. "You okay? You look pissed off."

He pointed toward his half empty glass of what appeared to be water. "When we've had this we'll move on, it's too noisy here." Des returned with my drink and a pint of Guinness for himself. He'd read the situation. "I like it in here, there's no point in moving now, mate. Let's just organise the morrow and have a few beers eh?"

"Were not on a fuckin' jolly here, Des, these bastards we're going after are serious players, we're not here to have a fuckin ceilidh. Getting pissed and having a good night out is low on my priority list, my old son." Rick bared his teeth. He looked as scary as hell. "I've a feeling about these fuckers. These guys are big, massive. They can do things the fuckin' CIA have difficulty doing. But I'll tell you this, the bastards are going to pay."

Des shot me a reassuring look. He leaned over the table toward Rick. "Dinnae get shirty now, pal. We've all given up a lot to see this through."

"You," Des pointed a finger, "said not to check our accounts. But if I were a betting man, I'd say you have, and you are cleaned out, just as I figured when we tried your card three fuckin months ago. I also reckon," Des pointed between us, "that we are in the same boat. Wouldn't you? I'd wager that Lauren and me here haven't a pot to piss in either. I know something's no right. I knew as soon as that bomb went off in Moston. We're not here to get legless, we're here to sort out what happens next. So wind yer neck in, big man."

I thought Rick was going to explode but Des faced him without a hint of fear. I'd seen fights before. We all had. My heart was in my mouth. I knew if these two went off, it would take a lot more than the two bruisers on the door to stop them.

"For God's sake, you two," I heard myself say. "You're like two big kids. Des, go to the bar and get Rick a proper drink."

I thought Rick was about to punch me, but I couldn't stop myself. I slid in next to him, so close I could smell his cologne. I gripped his wrist and leaned in his ear. It was the closest I'd ever been to the man and his sheer presence scared me. It was too late to back down. I went for him with both female barrels.

"It's all been about you for a long time, hasn't it, Rick?"

He turned. His eyes burned into me. He didn't speak. I sensed we were alone at the table. Des must have gone for that drink. I couldn't look to check. I was simply mesmerized by his gaze. I took a breath and persisted.

"You haven't a thought for anyone, have you? All these years you've been alone, the solitude, it's eaten your heart. There's more to life than cash, and cars, and women."

I gestured toward Des. "What about him? He's put his arse on the line for you more times than you can remember. He can't go home. I can't go home, and all you can think about is your fucking Paul Smith wardrobe."

I knew I had already gone too far, but it just came out.

"We didn't kill your wife, Rick."

I had found his Achilles. I saw his expression change. The rage fell from his face and his eyes lost their fire. It was replaced by the most incredible pain. He no longer saw me. No longer heard the music or complained about the smoke.

He was alone with his sorrow.

Des came to my rescue and sat. He slid a large single malt whisky across the table. Rick turned his head and stared at the drink. A moment passed. He took the glass and downed the golden liquid. He stood.

"I've parked a Black Vectra on the NCP on Hulme Street, opposite the Salvation Army hostel. That's the RP, four a.m. I'll brief you both then. Don't get pissed."

And he was gone.

Des Cogan's Story:

My train journey had been torturous. It was my own fault. I'd missed my connection at Carlisle and ended up on the Blackpool to Manchester Airport train. Jesus, they never changed. They still had filthy carriages, with not enough seats to go around, noisy engines and a jarring ride. The table in front of me was covered in graffiti and inhabited by a woman and two kids who all smelled of vomit. I'd travelled on trains all over the world. Ours were slightly better than Sri Lanka's.

I just knew Rick and Lauren would have made their timetable and would be sitting pretty in their respective hotels by the time I'd made Oxford Road. It didn't help that the train stopped every fuckin' ten minutes. Chorley, Adlington, Blackrod and God knows what other one horse towns.

Finally, just before midday, my rust-bucket attempt at a train pulled into Manchester and I stepped onto an equally grubby station platform. Oxford Road was a grand sounding place but in comparison to its neighbour, Piccadilly, it was very much the poor relation. Its overgrown railway tracks to the north and a filthy pale green fence to the south set the scene, and three aging platforms awash with disgruntled passengers told the story. Oxford Road was in pretty poor shape.

I'd been dying for a brew since Preston, but ignored the station coffee shop as it looked similar to the station itself. Instead I walked a few yards down the station approach and found Java.

It was a little independent coffee house, not connected to any chain, like Nero or Starbucks. Best of all, it still allowed lepers like me to smoke inside.

I ordered a cappuccino and a cheese toasty, grabbed a gratis copy of the *Daily Mirror* and lit my wee pipe. Two young guys behind the counter insisted on calling me 'mate' every other syllable, but the coffee was good and the sandwich did the trick.

I read the paper, drained my pot and walked the couple of hundred yards to the Novotel. I stowed my kit, had a shower and by the time I'd fannied around looking for Phones 4U and bought the obligatory item, I was ready for a pint.

Rick hadn't said anything about keeping a low profile, but it wasn't in my nature to stand out. I decided to go straight to a pub I knew.

'The Monkey' was as quirky as its name suggested, just a short walk from where Rick was staying.

I had a couple of pints of average Guinness, smoked a little too much and allowed my mind to wander. My conscience spent its time chastising me for my sins in the graveyard in Moston. The little boy with the stomach injury sneaked into my head and wouldn't leave me alone, and then for some reason I was transported back to the Sudan and a village massacre we came across whilst patrolling with the local recruits.

More young lives snuffed out, horribly mutilated by murderous tribesmen.

I drained my pint and ordered a large whisky. I rubbed my face with my hands and wondered why I tortured myself, best not to think too much eh?

I left The Monkey and made it to the Irish pub, O'Shea's, and was hoping for better vibes and company.

I should have known Rick would kick off.

Rick Fuller's Story:

"Rick! Rick!"

I could hear Des shouting after me, despite that fucking music. The tourists and the Celtic fans might go for that shit, but to me, Paddy rebel songs weren't entertainment. Once you've seen your wife with the side of her face missing, Irish music in general loses its quaint charm.

Why arrange the meet in an Irish boozer then?

Because, normally, I could take it. I'd lived with it for years. I was better than it. It was convenient.

"Rick! Fer fuck's sake, hold up."

I couldn't stop walking. I passed the doorman and knocked his shoulder with mine. He gave me the evils. If he'd said a word at that point, I'd have blown the whole job and slotted him.

"Rick!"

I was on the street walking fast and the cold hit my face. The area around my new scar tingled as the air played with brand new skin. I strode on across the junction toward Piccadilly bus station and my hotel. Two obviously gay men held hands in front of me.

I turned to the right into Canal Street and the music changed to Kylie and Shirley. Despite the cold, the street was busy with revellers. Straight couples mixed with transsexuals. Shaven-headed lesbians laughed with suited Japanese tourists, it was a smorgasbord of humanity, all bent on having a good time.

I heard Des, he hadn't given up, "You stubborn bastard, stop."

A guy, my size with a number one crew cut, dressed in nothing but leather chaps and a waistcoat, took one look at Des chasing me and called out,

"If I were you, darlin', I'd slow down a bit. He's just gorgeous!"

I stopped. REM blasted from the bar on my left. Two pretty young girls staggered from the doorway and snogged passionately yards from me. I was in another world.

My anger subsided; the Irish music no longer haunted me.

I turned to see Des walking through the crowd. He'd left his coat in the pub. He sported Levis, a white, cotton Lacoste T-shirt and a whiter smile. He thumbed over his shoulder in the direction of O'Shea's.

"Get back in the bar, yer bollocks."

He stopped inches from my face. I lowered my voice as much as I could in the din of Canal Street.

"Look, it's got nothing to do with you and Lauren. I'm going to my hotel, Des. That's all. There's no hidden agenda."

Des gripped my forearm. There was no revulsion at his touch. I welcomed it.

"Come on, just one more beer."

I stalled. I knew what I'd become. I knew Lauren was right. What was the true worth of my recent loss? How could it compare? It was cash, dirty money too. Des would give his life for me. He had, once again, saved my arse. I put my arm around him.

My brother in arms.

"Come on then, let's fuck off."

We walked down the remainder of Canal Street to cheers and wolf whistles from the balcony bar. We knew how it looked but I kept my arm around Des all the way to O'Shea's.

Lauren North's Story:

It was good to see the boys relaxed.

We had denied ourselves all alcohol during our three-month stay in Scotland. The punishing fitness regime we had all completed had been at the expense of any form of R and R. I knew my body had changed shape. The jeans I wore were slack around my waist but tight on my thighs. I had biceps and triceps for the first time in my life.

I looked at myself in the grubby mirror of the pub toilets. I was still Lauren, but a fitter, stronger Lauren. It was my first real comprehension of what I was about to become.

A crowd of teenage girls bounced into the room behind me, full of attitude. One pushed me roughly to get a look in the mirror. Without warning, adrenaline hammered its way around my body and I felt the rush. Better than sex, they say.

I turned toward them, instantly on my guard. All four fell silent and looked at me. Then I saw it. I saw the fear in their eyes. They were actually frightened of me.

"Excuse me, ladies," I said as they parted like a sea. I pushed open the toilet door and walked back to our table, smiling.

Despite all Rick's posturing we had a ball in O'Shea's. We drank and we danced. We laughed, yes actually laughed.

We became close that night; something unsaid; something immeasurable; something exceptional.

If you were to ask Des or Rick about the defining moment in our relationship, I reckon it would be the night in O'Shea's.

Sometimes, it is the smallest thing that makes you realise you have made the right choice. It can be something as simple as a look, or a shared joke. I felt at home. I suddenly realised just how lonely I'd become before meeting these two men. There is a song. I can't remember who sang it or anything else about it other than one line. It went, 'I'm tired of being alone and calling it freedom.'

There's nothing free about planning your life around a shift rota and the television pages; nothing liberating about cruising singles bars with people as sad and alone as you in the hope of some fleeting excitement; and nothing healing about taking a beating for expressing an opinion in your own home. No, walking into the canteen and sitting opposite Des had been liberating, healing and exciting. All the very things I had sought, the very things I had promised myself as a young woman were now in my hands and the beauty of it all was the men in my life wanted nothing more from me than trust.

Before we all knew it, the lights in the bar were raised and the band was packing away their instruments. I checked my watch and saw it was one a.m.

Rick raised his glass.

"To the three of us."

"To the three of us," we mimicked.

Des had a glint in his eye. He was the happiest I'd seen him.

"Here's tae us," he proposed. "Them that's like us. Damned few, and they're all deed."

We all drained our glasses. I felt like part of the Three Musketeers. Little did I know what being part of the team would mean, and what difficulties were to come.

The RP remained the same. Four a.m. at Hulme Street car park. No allowance from Rick or Des for the late hour. I lay in my bed and stared at the anonymous ceiling. I couldn't sleep; part fear, part excitement.

We were to pay a visit to Joel Davies's house.

Was he still alive? Was his house in the same state as Rick's flat? Or had Stern gone through the whole of the Manchester drug scene like a plague of locusts, devouring all in his path, taking anything of value and wiping out all living things in his way, carving his own path to fantastic riches and power?

This action could put our heads above the parapet for the first time since Rick and Des's return from Holland. Once we started this operation our cover was blown and we would be visible. If you were an enemy of Mr. Stern it appeared to be a very unhealthy state of affairs.

It was the only lead we had. Let's face it. Everyone else connected the Amsterdam job was probably dead.

At three a.m. I gave up any idea of sleep and took a long hot shower. I scraped back my hair and dressed quickly. Finally I removed the Sig from its hiding place, took thirteen rounds from the box of ammunition and carefully filled the magazine as Des had taught me. When the last bullet was loaded, I pushed the magazine into the butt of the gun and slid back the mechanism. This action chambered the first round and made the gun ready to fire. I applied the safety and pushed the weapon into the waistband of my jeans.

Once again I found myself in front of the mirror. Half of me felt like Al Pacino, the other half, like a delirious fool.

With one last deep breath, I pulled on my coat and headed for the lift.

Rick Fuller's Story:

I got just two hours kip before the receptionist called my room at three-thirty a.m.

For the first time in years, I felt really alive and ready to do business again. Somehow, the scene in the pub had cleared my mind.

I'd become a man who owned everything, but had nothing. I used to look at rich guys, driving around in their flash cars, and say, *fuckin' hell Rick, one day, that'll be you there, mate.*

Manchester made that little dream come true.

I'd started out with the intention of making a quick buck, and maybe doing one to Asia. Running away from my problems seemed a good idea at the time. But I stayed in Manchester, and made more money than I could have ever imagined.

Now, I had a big hole where a five-hundred-pound gold tooth once lived, and legs that looked like the surface of Mars. Suffice to say, I hadn't a pot to piss in, but if I was honest, I wasn't fucking arsed about any of it. None of it really mattered anymore, all I knew was at last I was around people of substance. People who genuinely cared about the same things as me.

I don't know if it was the bullet from Stephan's gun, that selfless care that Lauren brought to me, or Des just being, well, Des, but I felt good.

Really good.

I'd packed everything I could into a small holdall. Entry devices, camouflage, recording equipment and spare ammunition, anything that we might need for a covert entry to the house.

If we could get in and out without drama it would be a Godsend, although from what I'd seen earlier, it would be a miracle.

I kept that little gem to myself.

If we had to fight our way in and out then so be it. It was the worst case scenario, but I was in the mood to do some damage.

To gain entry to a house like Joel Davies's, you needed a considerable amount of skill, bottle, and inside knowledge. I knew enough about Davies's security to get us inside. I had codes for the gates, entry doors, garage, even his safe. My biggest hope was Joel's old computer was still there.

If it was, we'd nick it. Knowledge is king, my mate.

We had enough weaponry to start a small urban war and when I got the chance, I intended to use mine.

For ten years I'd been convinced that the Secret Services had sold me to the enemy and instigated Cathy's murder. They had worked hand in hand with a terrorist organisation to meet their own ends. I knew that everyone thought I was mad, that I was fucked up in my own world of grief, but I knew that governments didn't play by the same rules as us mere mortals. They had different agendas; they had targets and budgets that could not be broken. Failure was unacceptable.

The one thing that I never told Des, or any living soul, was what I saw that night in Ireland at the DLB.

Despite my silence, forty-eight hrs later Cathy was torn to pieces by the IRA. There was no question which organisation carried out the killing. But who ordered it, and held the information to enable it to happen was a different matter. Was it a warning or was I supposed to get the good news too?

Either way, the murderous bastards had returned to their hole over the water, leaving me alive on the outside but very much dead within. That morning Des had whisked me away and, not to put too fine a point on it, I'd been running ever since.

Now, a decade later I had a familiar feeling in my gut. It wasn't pleasant.

I recalled that Susan knew about my past in Amsterdam. Then Stephan read my life story to me, before trying me out as Gordon Ramsey's next big dish.

He could only have received that information from one place.

Once again I'd studied the data that we had at our disposal. A major criminal organisation had access to military records of the highest order. No question.

These guys had the power to asset strip bank accounts from all over the world. The power of the organisation came from the highest sources of business or government.

On leaving the hotel, I walked briskly back toward Oxford Road and onto Hulme Street. I passed by regenerated warehouses which lodged some of Manchester's student village. I eventually saw the Vectra, bathed in sodium light, surrounded by rusting chain-link fencing. The car park gates were left ajar permanently. National car parks had grown tired of replacing locks. The street was deserted.

I opened the car, stowed my bag and checked my watch. It showed three-fifty a.m. I sat in the driver's seat with the engine off. The last thing I needed was a nosey copper.

At three fifty-five Des came into view. He sauntered along past the grubby Salvation Army hostel. A single bulb appeared on the second floor and bathed him in light. I heard a raised voice from the building. Some tortured soul barking at the moon.

Des reached the car. I popped the boot using the remote switch and felt a blast of cold as Des sat alongside me.

"Alright," he said.

"Yep."

"Lauren is just behind me. I saw her crossing at the Palace Hotel."

I motioned forward.

"She's here now."

Lauren didn't stride with Des's confidence, but she looked positive enough.

"You think she's up to this, Des?"

Des nodded.

"She's a natural, Rick. Trust me."

I did, so there was no more to be said.

The rear door of the car was pulled open. Lauren threw her bag on the back seat and flopped down after it. I could smell Tisserand and for a second I thought of Tanya.

"Sober?" I asked.

"As your proverbial judge, mate," she said. She looked at her watch, smiled at Des and added, "What are we waiting for?"

Des turned to me.

"We off then, boss?"

I started the engine and pulled the car onto the road.

We rode in silence, each member of the team deep in their own private thoughts. I stuck rigidly to the speed limits. The last thing we needed was a pull. We would have all gone to jail for a long stretch with the firepower we were carrying. It took thirty minutes or so to get to our next stop, the LUP or 'lying up point,' as it was known in the Regiment. It was a safe place to sit and kit up. I had selected it from memory.

Davies's house was nothing less than a fortress. It was surrounded by eighteen hundred feet of eight-foot wall, covered by thirty CCTV cameras. Motion sensors covered large parts of the grounds. I knew where, I'd designed his security. That, in itself, meant the security system posed little problem even if someone had decided to change his security codes, I had the override. I was pretty confident.

I'd visited Joel's old house straight after my devastating visit to my own Salford Keys pad. It had been most enlightening. The house was very much inhabited.

Several vehicles came and went in the short period I was there. The people driving those cars were our enemy. The suits, the cars, the haircuts. Yes deffo, Stern had taken Joel's home from him, just like he had taken mine. In Joel's case, though, the team had taken root. Despite my anger, I knew we had to attempt a covert entry and at least endeavour to stay under the radar for a while longer.

The LUP was situated some five hundred meters from the main house. It was a small car park at the rear of two shops that served the village. Both shops opened at a reasonable hour and both were of the lock-up variety with no one living above. The car park itself was shrouded by mature trees. With a little luck we would be safe there until daylight. We could sit, brief and kit up.

Once we were parked, Des got out a small flask and we all had a brew whilst I went through each team member's respective tasks.

I had a full floorplan of the house and grounds. Davies had given them to me when I had reviewed his security. I had scanned them into my home computer and they were saved with all the other stuff I'd left in my Bergen. To the rear of the house was a raised section of rough ground that acted as a natural vantage point. Des was to set himself up there and watch the rear. Despite the high wall, the annex that housed the staff and the CCTV monitoring station could be seen from there. Should there be any signs of life in the CCTV room Des could tip us off before we started the entry. The two poor bastards that had been Joel's staff probably held up the same section of motorway that he himself did.

The hope was the annex and the monitoring room would be in darkness. Once inside we would steal anything of use and get the fuck out before anyone was wiser. If Joel's computer was still lurking around it would be a bonus. Information, at this stage, was king.

We had shortwave comms for two but not for Lauren, so she would have to stay with me. When the all clear came from Des, we'd enter the grounds through the front gate. Once we'd made the front door we would have to hold. Des had to get from his observation post, scale the rear wall and make to an entrance on the east side. That would take him seven minutes.

On my call we would enter the building simultaneously, locate a computer that had been useless to the new occupiers for the last three months, and steal its hard drive.

Easy, eh?

As soon as I'd finished my spiel, Des was out of the car and pulling on his camouflage gear. I watched him check and re-check each piece of kit he carried, which included the .222 rifle should he need to drop anyone from a distance. Finally, he gave me a quick 'thumbs up' and pressed his comms pretzel twice. I returned the gesture to inform him the shortwave was working in my ear and he disappeared into the night.

Lauren sat motionless in the Vectra. I popped my head into the open window.

"Get your kit together, we'll move as soon as Des is on plot."

She didn't speak, but simply stuck to her instructions, and started to pull on her overalls. She was indeed beautiful. There, at four in the morning, bitter cold, no make-up, with little sleep, she shone.

"You nervous?" I asked.

"A little," she said, and gave a brief smile.

"Everyone is. I mean, even experienced guys in the Regiment get nervous. It's a good thing. Use it, Lauren. Use it to your advantage; to stay focused."

She slid from the back seat, stood, and faced me. She held the silver SIG in one hand and two spare magazines in the other. The black Special Forces overalls she wore hid her figure, but nothing could dull her radiance.

"I'm sure you and Des will look after me. Besides, I never felt like this when I was changing bedpans."

She pushed the magazines into pouches in her suit, pulled on her balaclava and adjusted her hood.

"I'm ready," she said.

I pushed the rear door of the car closed and locked it using the remote. Even though I knew all my kit was in the right place and working perfectly, I checked all the pockets on my overalls to ensure nothing was going to fall out or make any noise.

I rolled down my balaclava and pulled up my flameproof hood to match Lauren. I gestured her over and we checked each other, just like divers do before entering the water. Not even the SAS can see behind their backs, and a loose flap can ruin everything on a covert entry.

I heard two short bursts of white noise in my right ear, which told me Des had got himself in position. I motioned to Lauren and, using the shadows of the high walls surrounding all the properties in the area, we walked into the darkness of the street.

There was the slightest hint of daylight in the sky and the solid black of mature branches swayed above us in the breeze.

Over five silent minutes passed until we reached Davies's electric gates which cast a striped shadow against us.

I motioned Lauren to stay in the darkness whist we waited for Des to report in. Within seconds I heard the shortwave click and Des's voice.

"All quiet, Rick."

I punched in the six digit entry code I had personally written for my old boss, and the gates silently opened. We were in. No turning back. My heart rate increased as we carefully made our way across the pathway. We had to avoid any censors which might set off the security system. I had studied the layout, and knew the location of every one. By the time we had reached the front door I was sweating under my hood. It felt good. For the first time in months, I was back in business, back doing what I did best. This time, though, my motives were totally different.

The house had two large bay windows to each side of a centrally placed main entrance. A pair of very solid looking oak doors, beautifully varnished and sporting large oval brass handles, barred our way. A rectangular keypad glowed green to the right of the doors.

The place was in total darkness, which I found slightly unnerving. Lauren was in a crouch to the left of the doorway, her arms outstretched, pointing her pistol at the firmly locked doors.

I waited and listened. People forget their ears when they get scared. That's why you hear of people who have run out into the path of a speeding car when being chased by some bruiser or other silly drama.

It's the first sense we lose when stressed. You can hear your heart and your lungs working fucking overtime, but not the express train that is about to kill you.

So, in this scenario, you wait, let your heart rate fall, let your breathing return to normal and, most of all, listen.

A minute went by. As I tuned my ears into my surroundings, concentrating all my efforts into my audible range, I felt a chill. Somewhere to my right, probably close enough to touch, was a dog. Not just a dog, but a fuckin' big dog, and it was just getting ready to rip my head off.

Animals, of any sort, are your worst fucking nightmare. At best they make enough noise to wake the dead. This bastard had done the opposite. It had tracked us silently and was ready to go for the kill. An adult German Shepherd dog's bite has the same pounds per square inch power as a gristly bear. You do not want to be bitten by one. He will take out skin, muscle, tendons and even break bones if he has a mind to.

If this guy attacked, before Lauren or I had stopped screaming, our target would be awake and laying down rounds on us.

Now I know what you're thinking. Killing a dog is not good. It isn't, I've always liked dogs. It's just this one had to go.

Lauren was physically sick on the ground as the animal twitched and bled to death on Joel's gravel drive.

In a previous life, I was taught how to kill a dog silently.

"Get it together!" I hissed.

She glared at me with some degree of disgust through the holes in her balaclava. Then with as much dignity as she could muster, wiped her mouth with the back of her hand and resumed her position. I was beginning to believe Des's remarks about her bottle.

I approached the keypad to get us into the main house. I entered the digits.

There was the smallest click and then a mechanical whirring as the locking mechanisms drew back.

The door clicked open and a crack of light escaped into the porch.

We wanted to get in and out without a trace. We had the element of surprise and we were armed to the teeth. We were on top.

I'll tell you this, and listen carefully.

Walking through that door was like walking into hell.

Des Cogan's Story:

The second I heard gunfire from the front of the house I loaded a c4 charge, pushed it onto the back door frame, took cover and pressed the fire button. The rear exterior door of the house was blown twenty-five feet into the back kitchen. On its way it destroyed most of everything in its path. At the back wall various pots, pans, spices and the rest were clattering to the floor. Through the dust and shite, I charged forward, cleared the kitchen and covered the first interior door.

This was not a job you should do alone, but I had no choice.

I pushed out my right leg and opened the interior door to reveal a sitting room in darkness.

I rolled to a large armchair and scanned the area, I arced the Glock across the full width of the room, confident it was empty.

Then I heard AK47's and I knew we were in the shit big time.

Lauren North's Story:

My heart felt like it was about to leave my chest. I was sweating in places a girl never sweats, and I still felt acid burn my throat from vomiting. When the charge Des had used went off, despite the ear protection Rick had given me, my world went silent for a few moments.

We had stepped through the front door into a hail of bullets.

Something, maybe the dog, had disturbed them.

Rick was through in a split second.

I followed him using pure instinct.

It was a war.

The hallway was open plan. The black and cream floor tiles glistened in the half-light and made me feel like a pawn in a chess game. A central marble staircase rose up majestically to a balcony which, in turn, ran in a semi-circle around the back of the house. Every upstairs room was accessed from those stairs. I counted eleven doors.

I could see two men running down the steps. Two of the eleven doors above them were opening and I could hear shouting.

One man on the stairs was blond.

He had a fine muscular body and wore only black boxer shorts. He had a bad scar on his cheek. He also had a machine gun.

Rick Fuller's Story:

I saw him straight away, Stephan, the fucker who tortured me, the guy who poured kettle, after kettle of boiling water over me, and then laughed as I screamed my bollocks off.
Happy fuckin' days.
A heavyset guy was just behind him. He had a pistol of some kind. He looked out of it, as if he had been sound asleep. Even so he was working on killing us all and emptied a full clip in our direction.
The Dutch was much cooler and hadn't fired a shot.
Not laughing boy.
He ran straight toward me, armed with a Kalashnikov.

Des Cogan's Story:

From the rear sitting room the gunfire was horrendous.
The unmistakable sound of 7.62 short high velocity rounds still made my blood run cold, even after all those years.
There was so much being fired that plaster dropped on my head as I made my way toward the battle. Fine ceiling roses dusted me so much, that by the time I opened the door to the hallway I looked like a Scottish ghost.
Rick and Lauren were pinned down by the front entrance. They both had some cover from two large stone plant stands, but they were in the shit. I entered from under a massive stairway which seemed to lead to a balcony I couldn't see. How many targets were laying down fire was difficult to say.
I banked on five.
I legged it under the stairs and slid in as far as I could.
I was completely hidden under step two.
I could see Lauren but not Rick.
The gunfire was constant but my heart was raised as I heard the return from my comrades. It wasn't over. Not just yet.

Lauren North's Story:

I caught sight of Des. He looked like someone who worked in a bakery.
He'd hid himself under the fabulous stairs out of sight.

The noise was unbearable. I felt a trickle of sweat in the small of my back, as the marble tiles around me were shattered by gunfire. I was now totally deaf.

Two other men had emerged from the upstairs rooms but stayed on the landing above. They had automatic weapons and were firing bursts at Rick and me in turn.

They were determined and I was terrified.

All I had to protect me was a big plant pot, and it was getting smaller by the second.

Rick was firing at the two guys on the stairs. He hit the dark one immediately. The guy spun around, firing a pistol at nothing in particular. A fountain of blood burst from his thick neck and doused the black and cream tiles red before he fell.

The blond muscled guy jumped over the banister to my left and was running to a door. As he did he looked me in the eye. He appeared to be enjoying the whole thing. He made my blood chill.

Des, hidden by the stairs, saw him run and fired in a prone position toward him. I saw each bullet dig into the tiled surface around the blond man's feet. Somehow, he was protected. Somehow, he reached the door. Somehow he was gone.

Rick left his cover to give chase. It was foolish. He moved too soon. Des had not yet got into position to cover him.

Two armed men remained on the balcony. One leapt down the steps toward Rick, arms outstretched, police style. A semi-automatic pistol pointed to kill.

Rick only had eyes for the blond man.

The man on the stairs had a clear shot.

Not as clear as mine.

I fired.

The gun kicked in my hand. The first time I had ever fired in anger, I instantly knew I had killed a human being.

The round hit him in the centre of his chest, just how Des had taught me. Somehow I saw it. He looked surprised. Then fell. Despite my impaired hearing I heard a hard slapping sound, as his bare flesh hit the cold steps.

His body slid downward one step at a time until he was ten feet from me. Over the gunfire, I heard his breath escaping and saw his lifeblood seep from under him.

Rick ran in front of me without a second glance. His body crouched against the fire from the single remaining man on the balcony.

Like the blond man, he was gone from my sight.

Des was there before I knew it. He pushed me backward and fired two bursts toward the balcony.

The final man fell and suddenly there was silence.

A door to my left opened and Des twisted violently to cover the threat.

He dropped his weapon as he heard Rick's pissed off voice say, "He's fuckin got away."

Rick staggered back into the hall, his chest heaving for breath.

Looking at me, he saw death at my feet.

Something inside me gave way. Rick strode forward but stopped short of holding me, and I fell to my knees and wept. Great hacking sobs filled my head and covered the high pitched ringing in my ears.

Within seconds I was lifted back onto my feet by two strong arms.

Des pulled off his hood and looked me firmly in the eye. His spectacular blue gaze dragged me back to reality.

"You okay?" He gave me a 'thumbs up'.

I think I gave it back.

"You injured in any way?"

I shook my head. At least I didn't think I was injured.

He shot a glance at the man I had just murdered.

"Good job," he chirped. "Just like I showed you, hen, eh?"

I cried even harder.

Des grabbed my chin with a gloved hand. It hurt, he was deadly serious and his eyes were like ice.

"Lauren! You did well! You hear me? You did exactly what we asked of you. You covered us just as we planned! You saved Rick's life, for fuck's sake!"

He was covered in white plaster dust, his hair was stuck to his head with sweat, but he gave me the biggest smile, tapped me neatly on the cheek and said, blasé as you like, "Part of the team now, babe."

Somehow, and don't ask how, but I felt his strength flow into me. I felt steel that I had never felt before. I dried my tears with my sleeve and holstered my pistol.

"We've got to get out of here," I said.

Des shook his head, then, gestured toward the open doorway.

"No, sweetheart, I'm going help Rick and you're going to lose all that vomit outside so you don't leave a pile of DNA for the cops."

He tapped the side of his nose knowingly.

"Then we are going to get on our toes."

At that he strode off.

I stepped over my victim and went to find a bucket and mop.

Those were the last tears I ever shed for a dead man.

Rick Fuller's Story:

I was seriously fucked off that I'd lost the Dutchman, but I had to get over it and get on with the job. It was already pear-shaped of course. Laughing boy would soon have all our cards marked. Even though he was wearing nothing but his skids, he would soon have Mr. Stern out of his bed and in a very nasty mood indeed. I'd left Lauren and Des having a heart to heart on the rights and wrongs of shooting someone. I figured that she would get used to it, knocking about with the likes of us. I'd never been good with crying women. How my wife ever put up with me, I'll never know. She brought me out of myself somehow. She taught me how to express my feelings, how to deal with emotions. But she was never able to help me deal with tears. When she cried, I just stood there helplessly, frozen to the spot. If her tears needed comfort, she was the one forced to seek me out and hold me close. That was in that previous life I told you about.

Time was of the essence. We needed to look for anything interesting, and preferably, Joel's old computer. Joel and the two old geezers that were his staff were obviously no longer of this earth.
The yearning to meet the Flying Dutchman was as great as anything I'd felt since Cathy. I needed to meet him again and settle that old score. First though we had to get to Joel's office and hope his computer was still there; anything to give us a Scooby where to find Stern and Susan.
I went straight to Joel's office and it appeared untouched. I found his safe, opened it with the combination I had acquired in my previous role as his collector and dropped the contents into a plastic bin liner. There was a lump of cash and documents, together with a semi-automatic pistol. There would be time later to find out exactly what. I was quickly joined by Des, who started to remove the hard drives from Joel's computer which mercifully remained.
Des took the cover from the tower and Lauren burst into the room holding a mop.
"I think you need to see this," she said.
We followed her in silence to a room on the west face of the house. When I had visited Davies previously, it had been a games room, with a snooker table and tacky trophy cabinets.
It had been transformed into a communications centre.

I don't mean a couple of phones and a computer. I mean 'Houston, we have a problem'.

Des let out a low whistle.

"This is fuckin' CIA, pal."

Lauren North's Story:

For the next ten minutes, I felt like the proverbial ham butty at the bar mitzvah. I'd cleaned my vomit from the steps of the house and collected all our spent cartridges as the boys had requested.

Rick and Des ripped all they could out of the control room. Each had a small toolkit with basic screwdrivers, pliers and stuff, and they were feverishly unscrewing covers from six computer towers.

I strolled from the room feeling strangely calm and walked into the now silent chequered hallway. I could see the outline of my victim at the bottom of the stairs. For reasons known only to my delirious mind, I was surprised to see he had not moved in any way. I stepped over him for a second time without paying him further attention.

Walking into the office where the guys had been earlier, I found it ridiculously green; carpet, chairs, curtains, horrible.

I walked around, not looking for anything in particular. Finally I strolled into a small hall.

My eyes were drawn to a framed document hanging in pride of place. A brass light fitting illuminated the gilt frame. This was a very important piece of paper to Mr. Davies.

I was even more intrigued.

As I moved closer I could see the document was framed with a delicate pattern. It was a marriage certificate. I lifted it down and read the names. I noted the date.

He and Susan had signed this paper, so had two witnesses.

Davies just didn't strike me as the kind of man to be sentimental.

After all, he paid Rick to top half of his own family.

If this was so priceless to Davies then the document was important to us too.

I didn't realise at the time, just how important.

I tore the backing from the frame, folded the certificate and pushed it into the pocket of my overalls.

The first sirens brought me back to reality.

Suddenly we were on our way. Rick and Des worked swiftly and effectively. I had been briefed on every possible exit plan. Each contingency arrived in my head in the correct order. I knew exactly what was coming.

Rick had repeated it over and over. It was no use getting in, if you couldn't get out.

I stripped off my weapons, kit, boots and overalls and threw them into a holdall which Des collected. He handed me a pair of casual flat shoes and a hairbrush.

He led me quickly to the back garden and bunked me over the back wall. Dressed in jeans and a T-shirt, I brushed my hair as I walked, threw the hairbrush into a convenient skip. Even though I knew they were there, I checked my pockets for my mobile and money. Thirty seconds later, a full minute and a half before the first police car arrived, I was heading to the Metro and looking forward to a hot shower back at my hotel.

The tram was full of commuters dressed for the office or bank. A few, more casually attired folk appeared to be going shopping. Two obvious uniformed nurses hung onto the overhead rail to prevent them from staggering around as the tram lurched toward the city centre.

I felt a twinge of guilt as I remembered my own previous life. Life before Des and Rick; I hadn't been able to contact Jane. It would have endangered her, just as much as me.

Nursing had been my life after my divorce and what had it offered? Graveyard shifts and crap pay, sore feet, lecherous doctors and the occasional night out with the girls.

Life was totally different now. I was in shock, yet I was full of excitement. There was no turning back.

One of the nurses caught my eye and smiled. I looked down at the floor.

No eye contact. It was another of Rick's rules.

I spent the rest of my time staring out of the window and watching the Manchester landscape pass me by.

The suburbs had given way to Chinese wholesalers, car valets and boarded-up pubs. Then, as the real city got closer, fine penthouse apartments, coffee shops and vegetarian restaurants lined the route.

I got off at Piccadilly Gardens and strode across the square, past the fountains and into Starbucks.

I bought a latte and a blueberry muffin from a very handsome French guy behind the counter and sat scanning the *Telegraph*, secretly waiting for the text to say Rick and Des had made it away safely.

At 8.04hrs my phone vibrated in my pocket. I opened the text message. It read, *Chop-Chop*.

Back at the hotel I caught two hours' sleep in my clothes and awoke feeling like I'd run a marathon dressed in one of those Disney costumes. My T-shirt was plastered to me and my hair was wet with sweat. I felt suddenly vulnerable. Switching on the television, I sat motionless on the end of the bed, feeling the chill of the air con drying my back whilst some morning game show numbed my senses.

My brain gave me an abrupt jolt as the news item appeared on the screen. I rooted out some headed notepaper courtesy of Ibis, found a ballpoint and began to scribble. Within twenty minutes I had left all my worldly goods to my sister and two men I'd known less than a season. I wasn't sure if my scrawl would be legally binding, or indeed if I had anything of value to leave Rick or Des after Stern had his way, but it made me feel so much better.

I stood and stretched my back, feeling the tendons crack and the vertebrae open and close. Then I did the same for my legs and before I knew it, set about punishing my aching body with two hundred sit-ups, two hundred squats and two hundred tricep dips before a cold shower. I stood naked in front of the wall mirror in my plastic room and felt rather smug about what I saw. My muscles twitched from exertion and as I pulled on my clean clothes I felt a rush of self-confidence tear through my veins. The confidence my husband had systematically taken from me had been restored by Rick and Des in a matter of months. I almost bounced to the elevator.

Rick's text was a little code we'd decided upon, just to be on the safe side. Even though the mobiles were unregistered pay-as-you-talk jobs, we didn't take any chances.

'Chop-Chop' meant he was back at his hotel, everything was okay, and we were to meet at a pub called The Chop House at four p.m.

Des Cogan's Story:

I'd had a little drama exiting the house and had suffered a broken nose in the process.

Everything went to plan at first. I'd bunked Lauren over the wall, collected all her gear and within seconds climbed the same wall myself. A five hundred meter tab brought me to a safe area I had organised before the entry, where I packed my rifle, Lauren's handgun and all the entry clothing into my Bergen. I then pulled on my old Parachute Regiment uniform, complete with red beret and marched off down the street, like a fuckin' war hero.

Whenever you were home on leave as a squaddie, the coppers never bothered you when in uniform. It was perfect, Rick was a fuckin' genius and I was home and dry, striding along the road with cop car after cop car screaming past me.

All would have been peachy had I not run into three Muslim brothers who took exception to a British soldier in uniform on the streets of Manchester.

I took the smack in the nose, and the embarrassment of the abuse, without retaliation. It was not a time to draw attention to myself. I'd never served in Iraq, too warm for my liking. I felt sorry for the fuckers that had to. I'm no racist. Live and let live, I say. Jesus, I'm a Scot, I'm from the most persecuted country in the Western world. The English have fucked us about for centuries.

The guys that punched me, spat on my uniform and abused me, were English born and bred.

No change for a Scot there, then.

Rick Fuller's Story:

I was at the Vectra before the first wooden-tops arrived. Our exit went far more to plan than our entrance.

Despite the drama, we had all been wearing hoods and balaclavas and so couldn't be identified by Stephan, I felt confident we had fallen on a wealth of information. The hard drives we had recovered had the data that would lead us to Stern. I felt it in my bones.

It took me an hour to clean my weapons and reorganise my kit. When I was happy with my work I stored it all out of sight, leaving a loaded SLP under my pillow. Knowing Stephan was in town made me nervous enough. Having just wiped out a small part of Stern's

English empire made me doubly so. I lay on my bed and sent two text messages.

Then, I watched the news to see what coverage there had been on our Cheadle incident and got nothing. I picked up my pay-as-you-go and flicked onto the web browser and selected Reuters News. Again, zip. My hair started to do its standing up trick. An all-out gun battle in a sleepy upmarket suburb of Manchester should have been big news. The press ought to have been crawling all over it.

I turned up the volume on the small television and changed to BBC News 24. It had taken its time but the story had finally broken. The very attractive Indian woman reading the bulletin was stone-faced. Behind her beautifully styled hair was a still picture of Joel's front door. It had a lone police constable guarding it. Across the image, red impact font screamed, 'Mass Murder.'

The anchor had a clipped London accent, softened deliberately for her job. Her impassive face only deemed any hint of emotion necessary when totalling the body count.

"Residents of an upmarket Cheshire suburb were this morning in shock, as they awoke to the sound of gunfire. Armed police officers were dispatched to a usually sleepy Cheadle residence to find a scene detectives described as 'sickening'."

There was only one thing for it.

I rang Spiros Makris.

Not only was he the master of disguise when it came to documentation, but he had the IT knowledge that we needed.

His phone rang once.

"Hello?"

"Spiros?"

"Fuck me, Richard, you are supposed to be really dead this time, and I'm asleep."

"It's eight-thirty in the morning, you lazy Greek bastard."

"It's also Saturday, you *malaka*" (wanker).

"Spiros, I need total documentation for three people and I have seven hard drives I need looking at."

Makris was silent for a moment.

"Listen, my friend, even though my heart is now full that you are still alive, from what I hear, your old boss Davies is pushing up daisies, you know? Sleeping with the fishes? Dead as fuckin' doornails?

"I gathered. So you watch the TV."

Makris lowered his voice slightly. There might have been a hint of real embarrassment in his tone.

"I don't want to be disrespectful, Richard, but I also hear your credit isn't too good this month."

I'd had enough of the posturing.

"Can you deliver, Spiros? Can you get us three sets of good docs, the new stuff, the biometric type?

"Sure, you know I can."

"And the hard drives?"

"Maybe, depends on encryption and, well..."

"And what?"

"And one hundred thousand pounds, my friend."

"Leave it with me."

I hit the end button. I could raise that kind of money but would it be worth it? This was no time to worry, I closed my eyes and slept for the first time in three days.

Within minutes I was back in Hereford lying in bed with Cathy. The dream, so realistic, so vivid, I could smell her hair on the pillow next to me. My face turned to hers as she slept peacefully and I felt myself smile, a real smile, full of genuine happiness. She stretched, still deep asleep, to reveal her tanned shoulders and breasts. We had just returned from the South of France and spent seven glorious days in the sun. I reached out to touch her, to caress her hair, taking great care not to wake her. I stroked her temple with my thumb. A sudden cold wetness covered my nail and dripped down my thumb to my wrist. Cathy's beautiful tanned face was gone and an unrecognisable mush of blood and bone was in its place. I was flung through time and space by unseen devils, back to the garden of our house, to the open door, the pounding in my chest was unbearable and I knew that nothing could prevent me from reliving her death in full Technicolor. What was left of my conscious begged to wake, but it didn't come and once again the tears flowed.

I woke in a pool of sweat. I'd bitten my lip and there was blood on my pillow as if I needed any more realism. My hands shook as I sat up and brought my head back to the present. I didn't know if other people felt genuine hatred the way I did, the way I still do, but if they feel that emotion with the passion I feel it, I am sorry for them. It is a destructive emotion. But regardless of its vicious power I sought vengeance every single waking hour of the last ten years. I knew it was slowly destroying me, destroying Richard Fuller. Even Stephen Colletti was touched by it.

Despite my shaking limbs and nagging doubts about the kind of money Makris was asking for, I did a full hour of core yoga, before showering and dressing. I didn't shave as I knew I would need to change my appearance sooner than later and a beard would be a start.

I clothed myself quickly in a pair of Levi casual cotton trousers that were the star of my recently devastated wardrobe. I topped them with a plain white open neck shirt by George, which I had discovered to my horror, was a supermarket label.

Then, pulling on a black bomber of doubtful antecedents, I surveyed my form in the cracked full length mirror fastened to the rear of my hotel room door.

I looked like a villain, and a cheap one at that. I secreted my SLP in my waistband at the small of my back and it struck me that my appearance was about spot on.

Being a rogue was one thing, but a cheap rogue was a totally different matter. We needed cash, lots of it, and quick.

Mr. Thomas's Chop House was reportedly the best gastro-pub in England. Egon Ronay said so, and who was I to argue.

It had just about everything you could want from a city centre boozer, which was reflected in the clientele. A mix of corporate suits pored over the substantial menu and well-dressed city visitors quaffed pints of real ale. Muted conversations were almost made inaudible by Rufus Wainwright's latest single, protesting American foreign policy. A uniformed waitress with a frilly white apron looked me up and down. She smiled weakly before offering me a poorly positioned table. I was convinced it was the George shirt. I took a disdainful look at the offered seating and reverted to type. I had scanned the room and decided a window seat would suit my guests just fine.

"I'll take the table for four in the window," I said in a matter-of-fact tone. The girl was about to protest but I was already drawing my chair and making myself at home.

Frilly Apron thrust a menu into my hand and gave me a cruel look. She was of Eastern European origin, quite nice-looking in a scrubbed kind of way.

"Drink, sir?"

From the accent I guessed Slovakian.

I scanned the starters and without looking up said, "Stella Artois, a bottle, no glass." And she was gone.

The drink arrived chilled and it tasted just fine, I had just taken the neck from the bottle, when Des flopped down in front of me wearing a sweater that looked like his mother had knitted it and a broad smile. Frilly was on to him like a rash and he ordered a pint of Spitfire bitter.

He waited in silence until the drink arrived.

"Take it you saw the fuckin' news," he said, wiping foam from his top lip.

I nodded.

"Once Lauren gets here we need to work out how to get our hands on some serious coin. I've been on the phone to Makris and he wants a hundred thousand to unlock the hard drives and get us three sets of docs."

Des let out a low whistle. "Fuck me. Nice work if you can get it. Even with the gold coins and every bit of cash we have we could only raise half of that. But we need to move and fast, mate. Whoever is in control of this shit will be out there right now, wanting to snuff the three of us out like a candle, and get their computer drives back quick sharp by the fuckin' way."

I took some more Stella and a slightly paranoid glance out of the window, and wondered if my vain seating requirements had been the best idea I'd had in a while. Before I answered I saw Lauren saunter past and into the bar. She had a relaxed smile on her face. I had marvelled at her capacity to learn the killing craft in such a short space of time, indeed to become another person. She looked amazingly fit and her triceps bulged as she dropped both palms on the table and leant in to speak. She had definitely just worked out.

"Everyone okay? Seen the news, I take it?"

Both Des and I nodded sombrely in agreement. Lauren, on the other hand, seemed unworried by the TV revelations. Indeed she was buzzing with excitement. She was dressed in tight jeans and a white vest which proclaimed 'fit as fcuk' in silver lettering.

She sat, and Frilly was at our table before we could say another word. Lauren was dismissive and simply waved her away.

"I can't eat at the moment."

"A drink, madam?"

"Cranberry juice, ice, no lemon please."

Neither I nor Des had seen this side of our new partner before. Des held a wry smile as he watched her.

"So what's the crack then?" she said.

I placed my hands on the table and lowered my voice. "I know a guy who will get us new ID's and decrypt all the hard drives we have, but he wants big money. He knows how dangerous it is for him. He wants a hundred thousand for his trouble."

Lauren's cranberry arrived and she sipped it. She wore no noticeable make-up.

"We can't stay here much longer, that's obvious. We need to get those drives looked at and we lower our profile whilst that happens. I say we find the money."

Des and I looked at her and nodded again in total agreement.

She shuffled along the seat closer to me and I could smell Chanel No5.

"Look, why don't we get a price for the new ID's, get the fuck out of here and then try and sort the hard drives ourselves?"

Des leaned back in his seat with the broadest grin. "Ye gotta hand it to the lassie, by the way. The most important thing now is for us to get our heads down."

I spun my empty Stella in front of me. "I can get the cash, no problems. I still have Joel's Porsche 911 in my lock-up, that's worth seventy thousand at least, but before we go and spend, spend, spend, I have another idea.

Lauren looked me straight in the eye and I thought I detected a hint of excitement. "Go on," she nodded toward Des. "We're all ears, mate."

I pulled the estate agent's flyer from my pocket, the one I had found on the floor of my flat and handed it to my two colleagues. Lauren let out a low whistle. "Nice gaff, six hundred thousand for a flat, eh? Whose is it?"

"Was it," I countered. "It was my flat before Stephan took me for a ride in the country, and now it's for sale."

Lauren leaned in, barely able to contain her enthusiasm. "So when do we go and have a look at the agency then? There has to be a lead to Stern there."

Des shook his head. "Maybe, hen, but not necessarily. These guys can set up so many bogus companies and bank accounts it could take months of unravelling and we could still be no nearer."

Lauren turned to me. "But we are going to have a look, right?"

I waved my bottle and my stomach rumbled as Frilly walked by with two plates of glorious-smelling food.

"Yes, we'll have a look at the place, probably best if you and Des go and check it out this afternoon. It's got to be worth a try before we do anything else." I felt myself smile, an unusual sensation. "But first we need to eat, I'm ravenous."

Lauren had the broadest grin too, the cat had her cream.

"You know, guys, suddenly I'm hungry too."

Lauren North's Story:

I'd never ridden in a Porsche before. Come to that I'd never shopped in Karen Millen or worn Giorgio Armani shoes either.

Des looked very handsome in the outfit Rick had chosen for him although he didn't look too happy about wearing a pink shirt, even if it was a Dolce and Gabbana original. I was amazed at Rick's fashion sense and knowledge. After our meal we had walked along Deansgate and shopped in places I had only ever dreamed of. In less than an hour we had spent close on three thousand pounds, and by the time Rick sat me in the bright red sports car my head was swimming. I was beginning to realise the power of money and the kind of life he had been used to. I also realised that he was still terribly unhappy and that the old saying was probably right.

Rick was not being a spendthrift for its own sake, of course; if you were going to view a six hundred thousand pound penthouse then you had to look like you could afford it.

Des wore a lightweight navy two-piece suit from Hugo Boss and the infamous pink open-necked shirt. I was power-dressed to the max in my Karen Millen charcoal number and I had to admit that the clothes, the car and my new found fitness regime made me feel incredibly sexy for the first time in years.

The car was hard to get into and even harder to get out of, my skirt being pencil-tight with no room to hide my SIG which was stowed in an equally impressive Gucci clutch bag.

Des fired the car into life and we pulled out into the Manchester winter with Rick's orders whizzing around my head.

We would be at Crowder and Madden Estates within thirty minutes and Mr. and Mrs Cogan were in the mood to buy.

After a few minutes in slow traffic the road opened up and the car hit the expressway with acceleration that took my breath away.

"You look nice," said Des, in his short clipped Glasgow accent.

"And you are very handsome, Mr. Cogan," I replied, watching the hard Scot blush.

"Ach," he said awkwardly, brushing his hand down the lapels of his jacket, "this kinda thing is no good tae me, Lauren. I'm a simple kinda guy, you know. I'll probably rip the bloody thing before we get to the poncing estate agents anyway."

I patted his knee playfully. "Never mind that, you are a fine looking man, you should look after yourself a little more. Maybe when all this is done you can get yourself a nice woman to share that cottage up north."

"Maybe I don't want to find one," he glanced over at me. "Maybe she's already here."

I couldn't help but smile. "Maybe."

We travelled the remaining miles in silence, both thinking our own thoughts. I have to be honest; romance was not on my agenda, finding Stern was. That may seem harsh to you but I wanted to see the whole thing through, then, well, then I could think of other things. Des was a nice handsome guy but I relished my freedom and my newfound confidence. I didn't want to spoil what we had. In my experience, sex spoils any good friendship.

The estate agency was situated in a twenty-plus-storey building in the green quarter of Manchester.

New money.

Thrusting execs eating sushi and drinking smoothies by the bottle walked purposefully along pavements that a few short years ago they wouldn't have been seen dead on.

Des parked the 911 on a ridiculously expensive meter and we strode into the lobby of the building hand in hand, every inch the successful couple in search of new lodgings.

According to the wall planner, Crowder and Madden were on the third floor so we took the lift with me holding the flyer for Rick's flat in one hand and my Gucci bag complete with 9mm pistol in the other.

As the doors opened we stepped into a small, sparsely furnished waiting room with a receptionist's desk. Several aerial photographs of monstrous properties in exotic locations adorned the walls. The perma-tanned receptionist who had obviously never eaten a potato in her life smiled sweetly enough to get our attention.

"Good afternoon, guys, and how are we? What can Crowder and Madden do for you today?"

I was nearly sick. Des seemed impressed by the girl's obviously surgically enhanced assets and stepped into the breach.

"Well, err," he leaned over to see the girl's name badge that teetered on her mountainous cleavage, "Madeline, we'd like to enquire about a property you have for sale here in the city."

He put on his cheekiest smile, took the flyer from me and handed it over to the girl. She batted her eyes in Des's direction and the pair of them flirted silently before she spoke.

"Ah, the penthouse on the Quays, yes a lovely property, but I'm afraid this one is now under offer."

"Oh no!" I didn't need to feign any upset as I was gutted we might fall at the first hurdle. Des walked over to me and put his arm around my shoulders.

"Don't worry, darling, let's see what we can do. Madeline will help, won't you, dear?"

"I'll try, we do have several other properties…"

"No," Des cut the woman off in mid sentence. "We like this property, Madeline. Besides the owners may wish to take another bid if it is more financially rewarding than the one on the table. Why don't you contact them for me and see if they are open to another offer?"

Madeline shook her head and lowered her voice as if telling a great secret.

"I'm sorry, folks, but this property is owned by a Crowder and Madden subsidiary offshore company. Mr. Crowder deals with all their sales directly and he is out of the office at the moment."

Des pressed on as I eyed the stunning villas pictured on the walls and pretended to be comfortable.

"Can you ring Mr. Crowder and ask him when he might return? My wife has fallen in love with this property and we are very keen to buy."

"I'm sorry, sir, but Mr. Crowder is in Spain viewing properties and won't be disturbed. Besides we at Crowder and Madden have very strict rules when it comes to our transactions and it would be unprofessional to accept another offer on a property at this stage."

I was thinking that the bullshit smelt worse with each syllable. This was the first estate agency I'd ever known that wasn't into making more commission. I was looking at a picture of a large villa in the middle of refurbishment nestled at the foot of the Rock of Gibraltar. Des was insistent. "Surely you have the details of whoever owns the property? Maybe I could…"

Melanie was not for turning either. "Sir, Mr. Crowder deals directly with that particular side of our business. Technically the property is owned by us. Our offshore investment arm purchase many repossessed properties and sell them on via our agencies. But as I said, that property is sold. Now, if I could interest you in another similar penthouse…”

Des turned on his heels and spoke into my ear.

“Nothing doing here at the moment, hen.”

I nodded toward the picture of the half completed villa with what was going to be two large swimming pools. “Nice if you have the money eh? Swimming at the foot of one of the Pillars of Hercules.”

I decided I would try my luck on Melanie myself and turned to the woman. Before I could speak, Des grabbed at my very expensive sleeve.

“What did you just say?”

“I said nice if you had the money but...”

“No not that, after that, about the pillars?”

“Oh the Pillars of Hercules, you know the myth, one pillar was the Rock of Gibraltar and the other was the Moroccan coastal mountains. Hercules is supposed to have used his super-strength to push the pillars apart, creating the Straits of Gibraltar which have been fought over ever since.

Des rubbed his chin thoughtfully.

“Let’s go,” he said.

“One minute.” I turned to our smiling if unhelpful receptionist. “Do you sell property for other individuals here or is it just this mysterious foreign snatch-back merchant?”

“I beg your pardon.” Melanie pushed out her huge bosom and gave me an incredulous stare. “We are a bona fide agency with very strict policies and procedures. There is nothing underhand in our dealings.”

“I take that as a ‘no’ then. This agency is just an outlet for the bigger guy who buys up all the repossessed houses for a cheap price and you sell them on at a pretty profit.”

“Since when was making a profit been illegal?” The voice came from a very smart-looking man in a three-piece suit. I placed him in his mid-sixties. He had pure white hair swept back in a style slightly too modern for his years. His eyes were bright blue and they darted between Des and me devouring information at a rate of knots. He walked from behind Melanie’s desk purposely toward me and extended a perfectly manicured hand. I didn’t see which door he’d emerged from. “Edward Madden,” he announced.

I managed a smile but the guy gave me the instant creeps. I made the expected introductions. “Lauren, and this is my husband Desmond.”

Madden looked Des up and down and offered his hand once again. "You are a very lucky man, Mr?"

"Cogan."

"Ah, Mr. Cogan and what part of Scotland are you from?"

"From Glasgow, Mr. Madden." Des gave me a look that told me we were leaving and smiled at the very suspicious-looking Madden.

"I'm sorry we have no time to chat, Mr. Madden. I understand the property my wife and I were interested in has been sold. Lauren was just a little disappointed and got upset, that's all. So, we'll bid you good day and continue our hunt elsewhere."

Madden smiled to reveal a Hollywood set of teeth. "That's a shame, sir, we always try and accommodate our clients if we can, maybe if you leave your details with Melanie here we can put you on our mailing list."

I grabbed Des by the hand and we made to leave. "That won't be necessary, Mr. Madden, I prefer to know who I am buying from and it seems that is not the way in your business."

And we were out, leaving Madden standing rooted to the spot, paranoia thrashing through us both. I checked for tails as Des drove us back to town. There were none but my heart rate told me we had taken a step closer to David Stern. Edward Madden did not strike me as an estate agent. The company was as straight as a nine-bob note.

As we parked, Des was already on the phone to Rick, something had clicked in his head and it involved Gibraltar and a file on Rick's laptop. Des was very excited, and as it turned out, he had every right to be.

Rick Fuller's Story:

Hercules Pillar Gibraltar, that little file from ten years ago. I'd read and re-read it, even printed some sections. I sat and watched Des rigging Joel's hard drive into a tower and then up to my laptop.

There was a crackling sound as the drive prepared itself, the screen loaded and demanded a password.

Lauren sat with me as we gazed at the empty box.

"I know the first eight digits, but not the last eight," I said, matter-of-factly.

"What are they?" Lauren asked.

"11091962."

She wrote the numbers down and mumbled something.

"What?" I said.

"It's a date of birth. Eleventh of September 1962."

"What?"

"The number sequence is a date of bloody birth."

"Might be."

"There's no 'might' about it."

At that, Lauren urgently rooted in her bag and produced a folded up piece of paper. She spread it over her knee and then tapped at the keyboard.

"I knew this was important," she said as the screen came to life. "It's the marriage certificate of Joel and Susan. It was on his wall for more than sentimental reasons." It bore two dates of birth 11/09/1962 and 08/08/1974 and it opened Joel's drive. I took the document from Lauren and stared at it. Then I looked at my printed notes and found another major clue to the identity of David Stern.

After several hours of searching Joel's data, I somehow managed to control my trembling hands and made some tea. Lauren, who seemed upset from the visit to the so-called estate agents, played nervously with her hair and had watched the proceedings in solemn silence.

I handed out the cups of very poor Typhoo and motioned Des to sit down. This was my show. Des and Lauren were waiting to hear all about the Stern Empire.

They were about to be disappointed.

I stood with my back to the computer screen, like some sales guy about to deliver a seminar, except this was deadly serious.

Des and Lauren sat on the two single beds my room offered and looked tired. They needed to see the end of this and so did I. Without closure, we wouldn't be able to live any kind of normal life; I mean, just being able to function without looking over your shoulder had become of major importance to all three of us. I knew my recent life hadn't been ideal but neither had Des' or Lauren's. We had gone up against a powerful organisation the authorities didn't know existed. As a result we hadn't any money and couldn't return to our homes. The word reprisal had taken on a whole new meaning to us all. As a result, the only thing that mattered to us all was closure, our spirit and friendship.

I heard myself start to speak.

"Until you guys told me about the picture on the wall in Crowder and Madden and explained the history and the myth of Gibraltar, I was never really quite certain who my real enemy had been all these years. Now I know who was responsible for Cathy's murder, for Tanya's death and for all those poor kids in Moston Cemetery. God only knows how many more they have killed."

I sat heavily on the lone hotel room chair and rubbed my face with my palms. I forgot all about being professional and briefing my team, now it felt like a confessional and Lauren and Des were my priests.

I started slowly. Lauren drew her knees to herself and cupped her chin with her hands, as if sensing that something huge was about to happen.

"Ten years ago," I began, "We stole several kilos of pure cocaine from the IRA. This was done under the direct orders of my Regiment Commander and therefore 10 Downing Street. I delivered those drugs to a secret location. A dead letter box."

Des looked up from his cup, caught my gaze, and I knew he remembered the job. I knew he remembered lying in that stinking field for hours on end whilst we stole our booty. And now he would know the whole truth.

Lauren looked shell-shocked.

I cleared my throat.

"Two Regiment colleagues, Butch and Jimmy Two-Times, knew I went back to the drop-off point; they knew I went back because something wasn't right. What they didn't know was I identified the collector."

Des looked at me in disbelief. He had no idea.

I felt suddenly drained. I locked my fingers together, rested my palms on my head and closed my eyes. I took a deep breath, exhaled through my nose and told the tale I had kept secret for ten years.

"Colonel Charles Williamson collected that package. At the time he was the most powerful soldier in Northern Ireland. I didn't divulge that information to anyone. There was a man with him that night, a tall thin blond American called Goldsmith. Did they see me? Was I compromised? I will never know for sure but I have to presume I was."

I now believe Williamson or Goldsmith ordered the slaughter of my wife as a simple reminder that to deviate from orders meant severe punishment."

I did my best not to think of Cathy but how could I tell the tale without bringing back her memory?

"I had only been home from that operation a day or so. Her God, not mine, only granted me one day before Cathy was murdered. No doubt, the gunmen were meant to take me out too. They missed me and now, ten years on, the people who ordered that hit, have found me again and are trying to finish the job. They want me dead, no question."

I looked toward Lauren and saw she had tears in her eyes.

"We are all in extreme danger."

There was a silence as we considered our situation.

I felt the muscles in my neck tighten. A burst of acid threatened to reach my throat and I swallowed hard. Images, memories, flashed across my eyes like newsreel. Cathy's naked corpse, Tanya's bucking body and Stephan's sick smile.

The same old pain and hate engulfed me, the pain that I have tried to explain to you before, the pain no one can understand.

In the name of my agony, I have done terrible things. I have shown people what real pain felt like, what true hurt does to you, but they still didn't understand, they just screamed.

Des broke the spell and my ghosts were driven from the room.

"Go on, big man, get on with it but."

I studied Des's face. The last months had ensured it had grown even more ravaged by life, but in his eyes was a man I hadn't seen in years; a man who felt suddenly alive again.

We both needed this job for different reasons. I felt my edge return with each second I looked at him. For ten years I'd been alone; a leper at first, then later, a ghost of my former self. I knew what I was, what I had become, but Des didn't judge me.

I saw the glimmer of a smile before I spoke.

"The file, codenamed Hercules Pillar, consisted of several lengthy confidential files the largest of which was a consultation document between the USA and Britain. There were details of some trial actions in Belfast in the late nineties together with results. Also some personal correspondence between Williamson, and the man who he became increasingly involved with, Gerry Goldsmith Jnr: The tall blond American I mentioned earlier."

I found pictures of the two men in a folder and dragged them onto the screen of the laptop.

"Goldsmith was an ex-Navy Seal turned CIA officer who had a special investigations brief directly from the Pentagon. His orders were to drastically reduce the amount of drugs on the streets of the United States. He had control of a huge budget by British standards, millions of dollars. But Goldsmith had a plan to win the war and not spend the Government's money. He was the all American hero. He was John Wayne and Will Smith all in one package. All sides of the US Congress were behind this face.

Goldsmith realised that the biggest drug dealers were also terrorists and dictators, so he developed a plan so ancient in its formula and so simple in its execution that he couldn't fail.

"His idea?

"Divide and conquer.

"He codenamed the action 'Hercules Pillars'.

"He needed a theatre to trial his theory and he selected Belfast as his ideal testing ground. Lots of poverty, lots of guns, lots of drugs and most importantly to Goldsmith, not in his own backyard.

"The first operation listed in the file was to destabilise two factions of a notorious Republican family. This was actually sanctioned by both the US and UK governments; in fact, the first operation was so successful that several others were executed after it, including the one Des and I were involved in.

"In one operation documented in the file, just as in our action, drugs were stolen from a very well-known IRA sympathiser, Thomas McEwen, and dropped in a DLB. What wasn't known was in both cases, a second Regiment team were handed that same stolen package.

"They delivered it to a rival dealer, chosen by Goldsmith, at a fraction of the street value. In McEwen's case it was his cousin, Patrick O'Hara. Then the Chinese whisper boys got the word on the street that it was one and the same gear. Finally to top things off McEwen's eldest boy was found shot in the head at the back of the local bookies courtesy of the SAS.

"The blue touch-paper was lit, all Goldsmith and Williamson did was sit back and watch the two families kill each other.

"Less than a month later, when both were weak enough, the RUC moved in and finished the business end by busting the remaining runners and riders."

Lauren drained her tea and looked for a place to put her cup. "Sounds like a good plan to me."

I was feeling better.

"It was, and it worked well until Number 10 got cold feet around the old 'topping Paddies on purpose is not cricket' thing. Williamson and his chum tried a few more jobs that winter but when questions were raised in Parliament about the shootings in Belfast of eight teenage men inside a week, the hatches were well and truly battened. The Yanks were far less squeamish about blood on the streets, especially when it was not their sidewalk it was spilled on. Not only that, Goldsmith and Williamson were getting more and more gung-ho in their approach, and were starting to become something of a pair of very loose cannons to our intelligence service. There were also murmurings about what was happening to all the cash that had been 'recovered' as a result of the listed ops. Our 'touchy feely' New Labour government needed scandal about as much as a dose of the clap. Two months after our op, and Cathy's murder, the Goldsmith plan was shelved completely and he and his family returned to the States."

I needed a drink but there was nothing to hand. I licked my lips and went on.

"Williamson was not a man to be put off easily. His relationship with Goldsmith was beyond the stage of mere comrades. Both had seen great results and enormous profits. Fortunes could be made. The operation more than paid for itself. Any monies and property recovered would far outstrip the cost of the manpower and equipment. I suspected, as did Whitehall, that it did far more than that.

"Goldsmith and Williamson knew it did far more than that.

"It created an empire."

I finally found a bottle of water and took a deep drink.

"Our pair were royalty in the making. Both men 'retired' within months of Cathy's death and virtually disappeared off the map. Rumours that they were running deep cover ops for one of the major agencies were rife for a while. Goldsmith was reportedly seen at a Basque Separatist Movement meeting in '97 where two major players were shot to death. There were no official sightings of Williamson after August 6th 1996 when he buried his mother. He had no other living relatives. Goldsmith, however, had a son and a daughter. Both were born to a Dutch wife, Helena van der Zoort."

Lauren nearly jumped out of her skin but I motioned for her to sit.

"I know! The name on the marriage certificate and Goldsmith's Dutch wife! I fuckin' know now, don't I? And it's no coincidence."

Lauren gave me a stern look, stuck out her bottom lip and nodded furiously.

I drained the cold Buxton Spring water. It loosened my throat and I felt it drain all the way to my stomach. Then I let go my bombshell.

"I believe Williamson and Goldsmith created the myth. David Edgar Stern, the un-photographed spectre we seek is just that. A spectre, a figment of two very powerful men's imaginations."

Des raised both eyebrows but stayed silent. Lauren looked unimpressed by my theory.

"Hell of an assumption there, Rick."

I ignored her scepticism and pressed on.

"I became untouchable to all my ex-army colleagues within a month of me leaving the service. They helped with my intel at first but I was too drunk to do much of anything after week three.

"It was the personal stuff on the Hercules file that I'd ignored. I was so convinced the answers lay in the business end of the deal. Death drugs, money etc, that family pictures, that sort of thing, didn't register."

I turned to the laptop. "That is until now. The old '96 file had some shots of two kids. The pictures were mailed from Goldsmith to Williamson at Christmas that year." I pointed to the screen and the miniature images of two ten-year-old kids made no impact on my diminutive audience.

"Then we got access to Joel's computer and with it Susan's email and documents. Susan's mother, Helena Van Der Zoort, was a socialite and femme fatale. Her son, Stephan bore an uncanny resemblance to his father with white blond hair whilst the daughter took her almost gothic appearance from her mother. Helena died 'tragically' and alone in an LA apartment; the children had long since disappeared with their father."

I hit the right arrow on the laptop and a snapshot of a teenage girl and boy filled the screen. "This shot was taken in 1999, a full three years after my last intel. This picture was important to the Goldsmith family as Susan had kept it for over ten years."

The image framed two coltish kids standing poker-straight in full army fatigues. It looked like some kind of Cadet Corp gathering. Neither child was smiling. The boy had white blond hair that fell over his face. He needed no introduction to me.

Lauren jumped to her feet. "That's bloody Stephan! The guy from Joel Davies's house!"

Des was not so quick but walked deliberately to the screen and examined the picture closely. He tapped the monitor with his fingernail. His voice was quiet but venomous. "And that little bairn there is Susan fuckin' Davies."

I stood and my head swam.

"We need to find Gerry Goldsmith Jnr and Charles Williamson."

Des Cogan's Story:

The revelations hit me like a hammer. Deep inside, despite the relationship between Rick and myself, I had never really wanted to believe that Williamson, a respected army officer, a man's man, had been involved in anything so deeply disturbing. It was one thing to do some dodgy jobs once you retired, Jesus, glass houses and all that, but to apply your power and influence whilst a serving senior officer; to actually use Her Majesty's Forces to murder and steal for your own advantage, well that was another matter entirely.

I had always been convinced Rick's theory had been the ranting of a disturbed and bereaved soul.

As far as I was concerned, my best mate in the world had just fallen on the hardest of times. He had lost his wife in the most unspeakable of circumstances and, in turn, had lost his way. I had always told myself that it was so. It had kept me sane the last ten years.

At that moment, that picture, the two bairns, those unsmiling, youthful 'All American' children, bathed in sunshine and middle-class Massachusetts values, opened wounds and turned all our lives upside down once again.

The man who stood in front of me was not my blood, nor did he believe in my God, but he was something else to me. Rick's shoulders were extraordinarily slumped. I grabbed his T-shirt and pulled him upward.

Our eyes met.

My voice was calm but my heart raced in my chest.

"We'll find them, mate, and nail the fuckers to the wall."

Lauren North's Story:

Rick had printed out copies of the Gibraltar file for each of us. He'd also Googled all he could find on the Rock and any properties in the area that had been sold, or were currently for sale by Crowder and Madden.

I returned to my room with his instructions ringing in my ears, dropped the substantial file on my bed, switched on my pink Motorola and began to read.

After two hours I needed to clear my head, so I pulled on my jogging kit and a very unflattering woolly hat and hit the street.

I swung left onto Sackville and immediate right toward St Anne's Square. It was eight-forty p.m. Diners, theatregoers and street people all bustled around the tram-stops bathed in fluorescent light from advertisement boards. I pounded past them, any hope of a show and dinner as far from my mind as it could get.

Next, the Midland Hotel's lights bathed the pavement in front of me. The Stones had stayed there the night before after another final date in a final tour at the MEN Arena. A tacky white stretch was double-parked and the doorman was remonstrating with the driver. My breathing was beginning to find pace with my feet and I felt the first flush of endorphins spur me forward. I ran past the famous Coronation Street Soap set and I was flying.

My mind turned to Gibraltar.

Gibraltar or 'The Rock' was named Mount Calpe by the Greeks, with Abila Mount sitting on the opposite side of the strait in Morocco. Hercules pushed the two apart and made the strait the entrance to his home, that being the Atlantic Ocean. Him being a Sun God of course.

It's been brawled over ever since; the Moors, English, Spanish, Dutch, French and Arabs have all spilled blood over the six-square-kilometre rock.

It was of key importance in the First and Second World Wars and its economy still relied heavily on the fact it is a working naval base and free port.

I did a left and headed toward Salford, I felt a slight chill as the city fell away. A burned-out old cinema cast an eerie shadow on my pavement but there were still plenty of cars and people around. Besides I still had my Glock tucked into my trackies.

We were going to Gibraltar to find Goldsmith and Williamson. Never mind it's ancient history, Gibraltar is a massive secret intelligence base. The Rock contains over fifty kilometers of man-made tunnels that had been cut into that cliff face since 1782 and there were more satellite dishes on the top than Roman Abramovich's yacht. What goes on inside those tunnels is one of the reasons the Spanish are never getting it back. Rick's theory was that the 'David Stern' drug base was in those tunnels and on that rock. After reading the file, I pretty much agreed with him. The problem was, we were three, and the people we were up against were heavily armed and many.

I saw a McDonald's appearing on my left and took it a signal to turn back, ten kilometers should take me less than forty minutes. I had the feeling I was going to have to run a lot further in the coming days. I turned on my heels and my thoughts turned back to my breathing, my head clear.

Tomorrow was another working day and Rick had to pay a visit to a Greek forger. Before I did anything else, I needed to change my appearance, get some passport photos and think of a new name and identity.

We were to take a massive risk and leave all the hard drives we'd stolen from the Davieses' house untouched. No matter what was on there, we just couldn't afford the Greek's price to decrypt them. So, Rick was to swap Joel's Porsche for three biometric passports and a weapon stash near Malaga. We could always use the hard drives for bargaining chips later if need be. Everything else was a shot in the dark. Would we find what we were looking for in Gibraltar? Who knew?

I showered and dried my hair with a towel, pulled on a sweater and jeans, found my purse and walked to Tesco. I felt really strange pottering around the little Metro store, a box of Nice 'n Easy hair dye and a packet of Jaffa Cakes in my trolley and a loaded semi-automatic in my trousers. For some ungodly reason, I bought a lucky dip scratch card at the checkout. Once outside, I walked briskly along Oxford Road rubbing furiously and winning a tenner in the process.

I stopped off at a twenty-four-hour chemists, got chatted up shamelessly by the Asian guy behind the counter, and bought a pair of point-five reading glasses.

Despite all the massive changes to my life over the last months, it was good to know some things never changed. I got back to the hotel only to discover I had bought red hair dye by mistake.

I cut myself a new fringe with blunt nail scissors and stood in the shower to apply the colour, which incidentally quite suited me. Once dry and dressed, I popped on the glasses to complete the look.

I nearly fainted when the knock on the door came.

I drew the Glock and clicked the safety to the fire position, pointing the weapon downward as I approached the spy-hole in the door. My heart raced and the gun felt suddenly slippery in my grasp. I supported my right wrist by gripping it with my left hand just as I had been trained to do. I made my approach as quietly as I could and I released a slow breath in the last few paces.

I pressed my eye to the hole and saw Rick, hands in pockets, studying his shoes patiently.

A mixture of relief and irritation tore through me. I could have gleefully shot him for not announcing himself at the door.

All my anger subsided the moment I let him into the room and he gave me a rare smile. I felt myself check my new fringe before making my pistol safe and tucking it away behind my back.

He had the start of a beard which partially covered his new facial scar and he'd gelled his hair into small spikes, which suited him. His eyes sparkled in the dimly lit hotel room and he looked back to his peak: lithe, fit and typically focused.

"Sorry, did I scare you?" he said.

"A little," I replied. "My nerves aren't the best I suppose."

"I just need your passport pictures for Makris and thought the easiest thing was to collect them in person. I should have telephoned to warn you."

He wandered around my untidy room before adding, "The hair colour suits you, Lauren. It's," he fumbled for a word, "effective."

"Effective? Is that the best you can do, Rick?"

"Well, you know what I mean."

"Yes, you mean it changes my appearance sufficiently for our purposes." I pointed a playful finger. "You can compliment a girl once in a while, it won't hurt you, y'know."

His rock-solid barrier slammed down and he moved a pair of crumpled jeans to one side and sat on my bed. "Won't it?"

I gave up on any kind of confidence-boosting remark and tried to lighten the mood. I pushed my new glasses down my nose and peered over the rims. "What do you think? I thought I'd call myself Erica."

Rick pulled out a notebook and scribbled. "Erica what? And what do you do, I need some background."

He was so serious, he never let up, never gave in. I couldn't help myself. It just came out without any thought.

"Forsyth. Erica Forsyth and I am a consultant neurologist!"

He looked up from his pad, unsure if I was taking the piss, and raised an eyebrow.

"Seriously?"

I pulled back my shoulders. "Seriously."

With almost mechanical movement he continued to scribble but muttered under his breath.

"I suppose you were in the field and you were married to a consultant for a while so you could pull it off."

That was a shock.

"How the hell did you know that?"

"Hmmm? Sorry? What?"

"How did you know I was married to a consultant? Come to think of it how did you know I was even married?"

"Well, Des mentioned a few..."

"Did he now? And did he tell you anything else about me, coz as I recall in the last four months or so, I've kept very shtum about my private life?"

Rick looked as shaken as I'd seen him.

"I needed to…well things just came up in…"

He pursed his lips briefly and touched his thumb and forefinger to them. Then, he snapped himself back to his normal composed, assured self and closed his notebook with a deliberate flick of his recently manicured fingers.

His voice was clipped.

"Look, have you got the pictures?"

"No!"

"No?"

"No, I'd only just finished dying my hair, before some buffoon nearly got himself shot through my front door."

He pushed his notebook into a very nicely cut leather coat I hadn't seen before, and I thought I saw the merest hint of mirth.

"We'd better go and get them done then," he said.

"Is that a good idea?" I asked, "Going out together, I mean?"

He patted the SLP tucked neatly in the small of my back. "I think we'll be as safe as houses, Ms Forsyth."

"Don't touch what you can't afford, Mr. Fuller."
He stepped back in mock surrender.
"Madame."
I pulled on my coat, the lining felt cold against my arms and it somehow chilled the rest of me. I checked there was enough change for the photo-booth in my pocket, and, satisfied there was, I looked straight into Rick's face.
Everything I needed from life had become focused over the last weeks and at that very point another section of my existence became clear. I realised the only thing that was really vital to me was the team and finding the bastards that killed those kids in the cemetery. New identities from dodgy Greek forgers, weapons drops made by faceless ex-paratroopers, a big posh hotel in the gangster capital of Spain, all felt right. None of it seemed out of place or unusual.
I shrugged my shoulders and felt my chill subside. First we were going to Puerto Banus and then on to Gibraltar. We were to capture or kill Williamson and Goldsmith, and his two murderous offspring we knew as Susan and Stephan. Once that was achieved, we would all return to our normal everyday lives. Yeah, right. The chances of that were slim to none, but I didn't care. I didn't want to go back. I couldn't ever go back and that just didn't scare me anymore. What we had to do though, well that terrified me.
I realised I was still staring into Rick's eyes and looked at my shoes.
"God help us, Rick."
He cupped my chin with his hand and brought my face back level with his own.
"We didn't need a God, Lauren, we just needed a break."
He sat back on my bed again and pulled my file to him. He quickly flicked to a page showing an aerial photograph of a luxury home inside the old wall in Gibraltar. I had seen it myself but it had no relevance to me.
"Despite the obvious connections to Gibraltar, the file name, the tunnel blueprints, property development etc., it will still be a wild goose chase if Williamson isn't going to be there, yes?"
Rick pulled a pen from his inside pocket and made a circular motion over the picture.
"You see this?" he said. "You see the driveway, these cars here?"

I peered over at the grainy picture, unsure of what I was looking at. Rick popped the ballpoint of his pen and circled a white car on the driveway of the property.

"This car is our break, Lauren. This car is the final piece in the jigsaw. This proves that Williamson and Goldsmith operate on the Rock. Because this car is mine!"

Rick Fuller's Story:

I took Lauren to Piccadilly railway station by cab and she managed to sort a decent set of passport pictures in one of those booths just off the platforms. I had tried to compliment her on her hair, but, as usual couldn't find the words. She looked beautiful though. Her hair was russet-coloured and her new fringe stopped just above her eyes, bringing out their colour. Her pale skin was luminescent and she bristled with a new confidence which made her even more desirable. The night had cleared and the moon outshone the streetlights as we walked slowly back towards the gardens in silence. As we approached my hotel I suggested we have a drink in the bar underneath.

It was pleasant enough, especially with a beautiful woman for company and we sat in a cosy corner and settled in.

The car in the aerial photograph was a 1967 Aston Martin DB5 finished in cream with red leather interior. It was a one-off, the only one of its kind in that finish. It had been stored in the secure parking area of my building and only ever came out on special occasions. It had been my pride and joy and had been taken from me along with everything else by Stephan and his crew. Obviously someone in his organisation had taken a shine to it, and believing I was dead, didn't see a problem in driving it around the Med. Lauren toyed with her bottle of Bud.

"So how can you be so sure that the car is yours?"

"Was," I said. "Not anymore."

I knew I could never drive it again. The mere thought of that scumbag Stephan or any of the other vile murdering lot sitting in my car made me retch.

I watched Lauren take a long drink from her bottle before casually placing it back on the circular beer mat in front of her. It wasn't quite central and I adjusted it for her to make me more comfortable. She eyed me for a few seconds.

"Compulsive."

"What?"

"Obsessive compulsive disorder. You suffer from it, don't you?"

"Do I?"

"Yes, I think so. I've watched you, lining things up, putting things in order, checking and re-checking minor things. I wouldn't say you were a severe case but you certainly show some symptoms."

"I can cope."

"I'm sure you can, Rick, we all have our own idiosyncrasies. I pile all my rubbish into cupboards and pretend my house is tidy."

"That would drive me mad."

"I'll bet."

"Do you lose things that way?"

She nodded furiously and laughed. "All the time!"

It was a lovely tinkling sound, and it floated around our warm cosy corner of the bar and made me feel at home. I realised that for the first time in years I was sitting in the company of a female and felt completely at ease.

"You asked about my car, well, it's an old Aston Martin and that alone makes it quite rare, the colour is very unusual and when put together with the red interior, it makes it a one-off car. I used to love driving it. It was very special to me."

"I can imagine. My ex-husband used to have an old Triumph Stag. It was bright yellow and had a soft top; he spent more time cleaning that car than he did with me."

Lauren looked a little wistful as she mentioned her doctor ex-husband, but it passed quickly. We talked casually about my fascination with cars, clothes and gadgets, anything but our dilemma. I ordered two more bottles of beer and placed them carefully on the table. Lauren touched my hand as I did so, and watched my reaction. I tried not to flinch, I really did. In fact at that moment I wanted nothing more than her touch and her company. I felt happy to just be there in that place with Lauren. But I did flinch and I spilled a little beer on the table. She looked a little shocked at my reaction. I felt she was analysing me.

"I just wanted to see your manicure, Rick." She looked a little hurt but it was brief. "You don't like to be touched, do you?"

I looked hard at my nails. I'd had them cut and polished, and bought some decent clothes that evening. The visit to Makris loomed and I didn't want to look like my standards were slipping in front of the Greek. If he smelled weakness he charged double.

I forced myself to hold out my hand so Lauren could inspect them, fingers slightly splayed.

"I'm sorry, go ahead."

She gently took my hand and rubbed her thumb across each fingernail, pausing between each one.

Finally she looked up but didn't let go.

"When you first came onto the ward, before you were conscious, I used to sit with you and wonder where you came from and what you did. I saw then that you had nice hands and that you looked after your nails. I figured you were a businessman of some sort. Soldiers don't have manicures, do they?"

"This one does."

She let go of my hand and took a drink.

"How long have you been like this, Rick? How long is it since someone touched you and it felt good?"

I didn't know how to deal with the way the conversation was going. I hadn't confided in anyone before. Seconds ticked by and they felt like minutes. I could see Lauren wasn't going to offer me an escape route by speaking, so I just told the truth.

"I suppose it started after Cathy was murdered, and sort of crept up on me without me noticing it really. I mean, being touched by someone was the furthest thing from my mind at that time. I was a mess. I suppose it went unnoticed until later, until I came out of the other side of my grief. Des was the only person who knew where I was at that time. He was my only contact with the outside for months on end. He would tell you what I was like. I didn't wash or eat properly. I was drinking heavily too. Once I got my shit together enough to work in the outside world again, I began to notice my aversion to being touched. Then, later, came the cleaning up and straightening things, even the smallest spillage would mean cleaning the whole living space. I mean, I've always been organised and tidy, the army saw to that and I've never been 'touchy feely', but it got to the point where any physical contact was abhorrent to me. I managed a strange kind of physical relationship with Tanya, but I knew deep down that I could never love her. I don't think I could ever love anyone again. I find it hard to shake hands except with Des."

She put down her bottle, this time completely off the beer mat. I decided she was being playful rather than forgetful. She wore an impish grin.

"And how did it feel then when I held your hand?"

I felt myself smile back. "It felt good, Lauren, thank you."

Then she stood, pulled her jacket from the back of her chair and slid her arms into it with one swift movement. She pushed her hands behind her neck and released her trapped red hair from under the collar. She shook it and it fell around her shoulders.

"I think I'd better go."

"Yes," I said, and she turned and walked away without looking back.

Des Cogan's Story:

I'd been feeling pretty pissed off with myself after Rick's briefing. Even though I'd stuck by him the last ten years, I never really wanted to believe Rick's theories that Williamson was involved in the drug trade, or worse still, the murder of a fellow soldier's wife. A small part of me couldn't let go of the Regiment values. The army had been good to me and I'd always been able to rely on it. Now I wasn't so convinced and it hurt. Sure, there were plenty of bad eggs in any organisation, but I'd always looked up to Williamson. Well, now he would get the chance to explain himself, wouldn't he, and if I got the chance, it would be a very painful experience for him.

I'd taken my hair down to the wood using some cheap electric clippers from Boots. They were half the price the boy in the hairdressers across the way wanted for a cut and would do the job a few more times if needed. I had enough of a goatee to show up in my pictures and I figured that I would look sufficiently different to any grainy CCTV footage the opposition had obtained from Leeds Hospital, which as far as I was concerned were the only possible shots they had.

After digesting the file Rick had put together and then flicking through the five available channels in my shoebox of a hotel room for two hours, I decided a pint and some grub was in order.

I was about to pull on my coat when I heard Rick's voice at the door. I let him in and noticed he smelled of drink. Not pissed but he'd had one or two.

"You got your pictures done, then?" he said sitting heavily on the edge of my bed.

"I certainly have, matey."

I handed him the eight head and shoulder pictures and he glanced at them before adding,

"Ugly little Scottish fucker."

I picked up my jacket and rubbed my newly cropped head. "I'm fuckin' better looking than you, you English bastard. I can smell y've had a pint or two already. D'ya fancy another with yer old mate?"

Rick nodded slowly.

"I suppose one or two more won't hurt. I've been over to get Lauren's shots and we had a couple of bottles before I came here."

I felt a pang of envy, or was it jealousy? Whatever, I knew deep down that Lauren wasn't interested in me romantically. I also knew that it would be crazy for the three of us to be anything more than comrades in arms. When this was all over, we'd see who was left standing and take it from there, simple as.

I shook all thoughts of romance out of my bored bones and opened the door. Rick was about to step out into the hallway when I noticed it was too dimly lit. Something was wrong and the shortest of hairs stood to attention on my neck. I heard the spit of a silenced handgun first and then actually saw the two rounds slam into the door casing inches from Rick's head.

I grabbed the collar of his coat and tugged him into cover. He dropped into a crouch and drew his gun as two guys dropped in to chat. They were both straight out of a gun crime video, young black and very serious. They wore street clothes. Hoodies with sports inscriptions, pulled up over cropped heads, scarves over their faces, each with one outstretched gloved hand holding a big shiny Israeli Desert Eagle self-loading pistol. I wasn't sure if they were going to kill us or rap about us.

Now yes, the Desert Eagle is one of the most powerful handguns in the world and it makes you feel like Clint fuckin' Eastwood, but even silenced as these were, the muzzle flash is atrocious. So much so, that matey boy who had just let off two .50mm mothers into my cardboard hotel room doorway was just about blind. Tip from the wise now, never shoot one of those fuckers in the dark if you want to see for the next twenty seconds or so.

The shooter who was first through the door was squinting so much he looked like he was in a Benny Hill sketch. He shifted his weight and waved his Eagle in my general direction. I punched him square in the throat before he could get a shot away and I heard the cartilage that protected his windpipe pop and the boy make a wee whistling sound that was far from healthy. He dropped like a stone, grasping his neck. It would do him no good of course, the only thing that would save his life would be a tracheotomy and I was in no mood to perform it for him.

Player number two held his gun out at a strange angle. I'd seen it in some of the American gang movies. How the fuck you thought you could hit anything with your weapon lying on its side was beyond me. He bobbed from foot to foot aiming first at me, and then at Rick, who had his own gun trained at the boy's head.

His mate was making horrible choking sounds on the carpet near my feet and the increasingly nervous youth kept glancing down at him, unsure what to do. Now when most people are faced with an issue like I'm describing to you now, their heart rate increases and adrenaline flows through them like a river. For me, it had always been different. I felt an almost surreal calm. I suppose my nature was to sit and wait, my talents were best served on a roof in the rain with a sniper rifle, or a hole in the snow with binoculars. So when, in a grubby little hotel room, faced with this kid, who was as young as some of the African soldiers we all get so upset about by the way, you would have to forgive me for feeling a mixture of disappointment and confidence.

"Your mate's dead, son," I said, clicking the safety off my own weapon but leaving it hanging loosely by my side for the kid to see. "I don't mean that in a medical way, see. I mean it like; he'll be dead in a few minutes maybe. If he's a strong lad, he may even last half an hour. But he's dead to you, and any family he may have had. There's nothing you can do to save him so stop pissing about and do what you came here to do. Understand, sonny?"

The guy's eyes were wild and seemed uncannily white against his sweating black face. His woollen scarf was falling down and he tugged it upward nervously.

I raised my gun.

"Do you want to die here, son? Is that what you want? Because if you don't put that big stupid fuckin' gun down right now I promise you will die just as slowly as your friend here."

The guy bolted, we were off and the race was on.

He burst through the first fire doors, using his head he was so wired. I was a couple of yards behind him. We pounded down the narrow carpeted hallway past the lift doors and toward the fire escape. He looked over his shoulder directly at me, I knew what was coming. He twisted his body violently in an attempt to get a shot off. The big cumbersome Eagle and silencer slowed his movements and the round pinged off harmlessly to my right. I could have killed him there and then but I needed the kid alive. I wanted to know how he'd found us and more importantly who sent him and where they were. The green and white illuminated sign was only feet away and I was almost upon him. I stretched out my left hand. Just a few more steps and I would have him.

As he pushed at the fire escape door I was inches away and I grabbed at his clothing with my free hand and dug my pistol into his neck. We almost fell into the stairwell and the door banged shut behind us.

"Drop the fuckin' gun now!" I hissed.

I have to admit I wasn't prepared for what came next.

The split second he felt my touch he raised the Eagle to his temple and without a word, pulled the bastard trigger.

A fountain of blood erupted from the left side of his head as parts of his skull burst through his hoodie, tearing the sweatshirt material like wet paper. The massive power of the .50 soft nosed shell created a vacuum in its wake and fashioned an exit wound the size of a fist in the kid's head. Bits of bone, brain and copious amounts of claret formed a gory mural on the white wall to the left of the landing. The kid bent at the knees and slipped from my grasp. He fell forward onto the concrete steps which were to have been his escape route with a nasty crack, and even more blood poured from his head. I could smell the warm metallic liquid as it created a crimson river downward.

I took one last look at the kid. Now, with his hood and scarf pulled away from his face I got the full picture. I reckoned he was fifteen at best.

I walked swiftly back to the room and noticed that no other hotel doors had opened to see what the commotion was all about. Either the occupants were out, deaf or just too scared to look. Either way it was a good thing. As I entered my room Rick had just finished hiding the body of the other shooter in the shower room. I didn't want to look at him. I already knew he was of a similar age to the lad on the stairwell. I had seen kids fight and die his age, and younger in Africa. Now in cities all over Britain kids the same age were fighting and dying too. Life is really shit sometimes.

"He fuckin' topped himself," I heard myself say, my mouth dry. I felt a little sick; I was suffering from guilt, plain as.

Rick either didn't feel as disturbed as me or just hid it perfectly.

"We need to get the fuck out of here now."

He pissed me off with his attitude, as usual.

"I know that," I snapped. "Most of the kit is under the bed."

We cleared the room of every particle or presence of us in twenty-five minutes.

Lauren North's Story:

Rick rang.

The shit had hit the fan. Somehow Tanya's family had found Des's hotel room, or followed Rick to it, and sent a message to us that Tanya's death, together with the Moston bomb, was firmly placed on our shoulders. Having Yardies after us when we were already targeting Europe's biggest cocaine dealer was not what we needed. It would seem that the Williamson organisation's plan of propaganda and divide and conquer was still working a treat.

Also, the drink with Rick had kind of done my head in a bit and, before the call I'd spent most of the evening thinking about him.

I'd even considered ringing Jane back in Leeds, but quickly realised I could never do that.

Everything I'd known before was gone. Can you imagine that?

The emergency, and I didn't get to hear about how hairy it was 'till we'd made Spain, meant we were holed up in Rick's lock-up, freezing our bits off and pretty pissed off.

By seven-thirty in the morning we were all up and about looking pretty bleary-eyed, having washed in cold water and slept little, each of us in different vehicles. I'd chosen a van thinking I could stretch out in the back in my makeshift sleeping bag, but I was cold and the van stank really badly inside.

Rick looked smart and was getting the red Porsche ready to do the deal with Makris.

Des and I had no choice but to sit it out and wait for him to come back. I wasn't like we were going to starve; we had supplies from a nearby Spar shop and a small radio for entertainment. I felt safe enough, no one knew of Rick's lock-up and it was built like a fortress.

My secure feeling was about to take a knock.

"I'll be a few hours."

Rick checked his watch. "If you don't hear from me by 1300hrs, split the cash and weapons we have between you, and go your separate ways."

I felt myself nod, but didn't want to even dream of being alone and hunted. Des shot me a glance and a cheeky grin that made me feel a little better.

"We'll be just fine, pal," he said.

"Don't even consider leaving me alone with this mad Jock," I joked, hoping I sounded more confident than I felt.

I suppose this was the kind of moment I'd 'signed up for'.

There was a cold blast of air as the roller shutters were raised and the lock-up was filled with the noise and fumes from the Porsche as Rick rolled it out into the open air.

Within thirty seconds the doors were firmly shut again and the waiting game began.

Rick Fuller's Story:

Spiros Makris's house was half an hour or so from the city centre. It was everything a home should be. Warm and inviting, full of the noises you would associate with a large family all living together under one roof. I don't know how many rooms the house had, as I was never invited to look around, but it was substantial and I would hazard a guess that you would need a couple of million pounds to buy it.

Not that it was overwhelming in any way, small children ran around playing games. Delicious smells came from a distant kitchen and a white-haired grandmother surfed endless daytime television channels in a cosy study with the volume far too high for the rest of the household.

Despite the fact I was about to be robbed blind, I smiled as Makris sauntered toward me in the untidiest hallway I'd ever seen. I had to stop myself from hunting for a vacuum and rubber gloves.

He wore his customary faded, stained polo shirt and cheap jeans. He was wiping his hands and hairy forearms with what appeared to be an ancient tea towel.

"Richard! How good to see you, my friend. My heart is full again. Come and sit in my office."

He waved his hand around at the wrist and shrugged a very Greek shrug. "This place is a menagerie, no? How can a man do business in such a place? Come, please."

I followed him upstairs to a small office.

The room was equally untidy by anyone's standards and I marvelled the man could ever find anything. Piles of papers, pictures of bygone days simply pinned to walls. Blemishes long forgotten and bothersome dust basically pushed away with the naked palm.

He flopped in a worn armchair, opened a small drawer, removed a pack of Marlboro Red and much to my disgust, lit one and exhaled sending a bluish plume of smoke toward me. He must have noticed my obvious distaste as he quickly wafted the smoke with his hand and stubbed out the offending article.

"Sorry, Richard," he muttered. "I forget myself sometimes. I think all my visitors are Greek and smoke."

I managed a weak smile. "No problem."

Spiros settled further back into the armchair, locked his fingers together and nestled them behind his neck, revealing a damp patch under each armpit.

"So...you have the pictures and names I need?"

"Of course, Spiros."

"Good.

"And the car?"

"Outside. Do you want to have a look now?"

Spiros shook his head. "I trust you, Richard, you know that. Just as long as you have the documents so I can sell the car on legitimately if you, how you say, don't come home to roost, eh?"

I removed a wallet with all the documents I had kept since I'd collected the car from the unfortunate Jimmy at Bootle Street police station. I dropped them onto Spiro's cluttered desk.

"Everything you need is there, all genuine. The car has to be worth eighty thousand."

"It's a buyers' market Stephen, I'll be lucky to raise half of that, but you are a long term valued customer and I'm willing to make exceptions for you."

I was in no mood to argue, besides, I had nothing to bargain with. We were on our uppers with both the Williamson organisation, and what appeared to be left of Tanya's family, chasing us around Manchester, we needed to move quickly and without fuss.

I wanted to know timescales and exactly what was on offer. "What about the hardware and when can you deliver?"

Spiros became serious. "You want it conveyed to Spain, no?"

"Puerto Banus."

"Ah! The home of many gangsters."

"I suppose."

He looked at me. It was a look I'd never noticed before. I saw affection, a strange feeling; I'd never considered that Makris actually liked me.

"I will have the most excellent documents available anywhere in the world for all of you. No problems with H.M. Customs or any nosey Guardia Civil. I will also ensure you have good quality weapons, together with enough ammunition to take on Hitler himself, dropped in the back of a nice restaurant that serves the finest Beluga caviar and Bollinger. I myself have dined there when visiting my cousin in San Pedro. I avoid Banus these days, my friend, it came under the spotlight and many reporters and television people spoiled the good atmosphere. I make a point of never visiting now. It is a home for villains with no class."

He shrugged the very Greek shrug again.

"It is full of 'chavs'."

I had to suppress a smile, but I had to admit he was right.

Puerto Banus was a millionaire's playground. Just a few kilometers west of Marbella, famous for a picturesque marina filled with multi-million-dollar yachts, Puerto Banus also boasted a beach that stretched for almost a mile. The golden sands though, were not the only major attraction to this town. Neither was the three hundred euro fee for the hire of a sun bed for the day in the trendiest parts.

In 2003 Britain held a list of over two hundred known criminals wanted for questioning by UK police, sheltering in Spain. Most of the guys they were 'looking for' lived openly in and around Puerto Banus.

You could find a prick in a baseball cap, with a full sleeve of tattoos and more sovereign rings than an average car boot sale, driving a Hummer, any day of the week in Banus. It was that kind of gaff.

It was a place I hated, but a place where everyone turned a blind eye.

"You are right, Spiros, but beggars and choosers and all that."

He waved a hand knowingly.

"Twenty-four hours from now, you can collect your papers from my youngest son's café bar in Liverpool, which is where I suggest you depart from, my friend. The weapons will be in Spain twelve hours after you text my private number to say you have arrived safely."

Spiros leaned forward and placed his hand on my shoulder. I felt myself stiffen but managed to stay still.

"My dear Richard, yes, leave me the car. Rest assured, it will be here when you return. I will also be here to collect my substantial fee which I'm certain you will deliver."

I had to marvel at the man's abilities. Not just three full biometric passports in twenty-four hours, but fully automatic weapons and handguns too. No expense spared. If he'd been a woman I'd have kissed him.

We had some tea, and Spiros insisted I try his mother's kleftico, which I have to say was first class. Once fed and watered, he walked me to a double garage and handed me the keys to a battered Ford Ka. It looked like he'd been dodgem racing in it.

"Take care of my car, my friend. I had her from new, no?"

I shook his hand. Sometimes you just knew who your friends were.

I didn't hang around. I squeezed myself into the little Ford and headed for Liverpool John Lennon Airport where I paid cash for three return flights to Malaga from the EasyJet desk. No point in pussyfooting around this time. I didn't care if we were visible once we got to Spain, but I didn't trust online booking with all the technology available to Williamson and Goldsmith. The fact was, once we left the country, I wanted them to come to us. I just hoped we'd be using both parts of the ticket this time.

Des Cogan's Story:

Rick was back in good time and seemed in equally good spirits. Lauren and I had passed our temporary incarceration by packing our kit and stripping and cleaning all the weapons.

Routines had to be kept up no matter what. Lauren didn't complain and did a fair job of her tasks, asking questions only when she was stuck removing a mechanism from an MP5K.

The weapons and the hopefully valuable hard drives that would become evidence against Williamson and Goldsmith were secured in Rick's safe in the lock-up. We kept a handgun and ammunition each for the journey to John Lennon and the plan was to leave those in the Vectra until, hopefully, we all returned in one piece.

It was going to be my job to collect our new weapons and ammunition in Puerto Banus and deliver them, by sea, to Gibraltar. I always got the good jobs, eh?

On paper Rick thought it wouldn't be too hard. Then again it wasn't him who was going to have to swim the final mile or so to one of the best patrolled shores in the world whilst pulling a float with over fifty kilos of kit. It was going to be a test of my fitness and my stealth.

I was secretly looking forward to it. All this pissing around was even starting to get on my goat. The time had come for the reckoning and I was as ready as I'd ever been for the fight.

We had twenty-four hours to wait for our docs. Something I was good at but Rick was his usual caged lion the whole time. He prowled around the lock-up, checking his packing and cleaning everything in sight including the Vectra which positively gleamed. Lauren worked out, and I read the papers and drank enough tea to keep a plantation in business.

When the time came, I was confident we would all do our job in our own way.

Finally, for the patient and the intolerant alike amongst us, the night turned into a grey morning and it was time to leave our hiding place for the last time.

Rick ushered us all together. He'd dressed in a new crisp white shirt and smart trousers and looked as good as I'd seen him look in years. Lauren stood at his side, her now toned legs unusually on show in a short black skirt. With her new red hair tied back in a ponytail, her subtle make-up completed her stunning look. There was an air of self-belief in that chilly lock-up. An atmosphere of confidence brought about by the knowledge that any of us was prepared to give the ultimate sacrifice for the other.

Comrades in arms, brought together by a series of incidents no one could have anticipated.

"We all ready?" he said.

"Aye, big man."

Lauren looked at us both in turn. "Well let's fuck off then."

We all burst out laughing.

Rick Fuller's Story:

The 737-800 banked hard left on its final approach into Malaga and I felt like I'd been in a cattle truck for two hours. Screaming kids, buffoons in replica football shirts and stewardesses from the John Prescott school of charm and service, all made the in-flight experience one for me to forget.

I was considerably irritated by my lack of legroom, which in turn badly creased my new Duck and Cover Chinos. The three of us chose not to be seated together, so, on one side I was forced to listen to the inane twittering of someone called Olive, who had just bought a caravan in nearby Fuengirola where she was about to retire as soon as she could arrange the transportation of her two cats. On the other, a clinically obese bloke called Colin, who ate his way through the entire Subway menu which he'd packed for the route, explaining that 'you can't get food on these cheap flights'. Had the guy considered not pushing four thousand calories down his neck in just under an hour and a half, he might not be such a fat bastard. Add to that he spilled mayo on my Giorgio Armani shirt.

It was a good job they didn't allow firearms on aircraft.

Just because an airline advertises itself as 'budget' doesn't forgive this level of condensed offensiveness.

I will never fly in an orange plane again.

We landed with a jolt. A few of the more nervous flyers applauded the fact that we were on the ground. I managed a quick glance out over the wing to see bright sunshine, and my spirits were momentarily raised. The overall feeling of being transformed into some kind of bovine creature continued as we were herded into a 'bendy' bus and then shuffled through passport control.

All three of our new biometric documents passed their tests as the duty Guardia gave me a cursory glance and added, "Welcome to Malaga, Mr. Frasier." Ms Forsyth and Mr. McGreevy were similarly greeted.

The baggage reclaim area was awash with holidaymakers and the odd person of doubtful origin as belied the close proximity of 'Gangsters Paradise', but for all that I felt relaxed. I popped into the gents' and changed my stained Armani shirt for a short-sleeved powder blue number by Teddy Smith and by the time I met Des and Lauren at the Avis desk, I felt much better.

We hired a Jeep Grand Cherokee which had lots of space and good air-con but was a disappointing drive. In just over ninety minutes we were pulling up outside The Hotel Park Plaza Suites in Puerto Banus.

It is an excellent hotel with only forty-five double rooms and five business suites, all of which overlook the stunning harbour. Staying at the Park Plaza also gains you access to the elite beach club and keeps you firmly away from the rest of the cattle I had the unfortunate experience of flying with.

Lauren and Des were in a room together which kept down our costs but didn't seem to please Lauren much. I, of course, had a business suite which had a living room suitable for any briefings we might have.

Once I'd unpacked I found my PAYG mobile and sent the text Spiros needed to start the weapon drop. I wiped it from the phone memory, took a shower and changed into more suitable clothes for a trip to the beach bar.

Lauren North's Story:

Well at least the room had twin beds.

Sometimes I got the impression I was more 'one of the lads' than I would care to be.

Des was mildly amused, but unfazed by the outcome. I knew he had other, more pressing matters on his mind, like finding a boat to hire that he could sail to Gibraltar. He didn't even unpack, simply rooted out his PAYG phone and his pipe and tobacco, before pointing in the general direction of the beach and saying, "I'm off to the marina, and I'll catch y'later."

As for me, I was keen to check out the hotel gymnasium and Jacuzzi. Also, as The Plaza Suites had one of the most exclusive beach clubs in the Med, I figured I could start a tan.

Well, there had to be some positives to risking your neck.

I found Rick sitting in the pool bar nursing a fresh orange juice and scanning the menu. He had changed yet again and I marvelled at his collection of designer clothes. He had kept his legs covered with a pair of very lightweight linen trousers, obviously self-conscious of his scarring, and complemented them with a beautiful deep blue Ralph Lauren Polo shirt. I presumed his Ray-Bans were real, unlike my own Gucci copies.

I wore a bikini and matching kaftan from Marks and Sparks and a pair of gold sandals from Primark. To add to my lack of chic wardrobe, every woman around the pool made Elle McPherson look fat and ungainly. My old lack of self-confidence was making a spectacular comeback.

Rick looked up from the extensive à la carte lunchtime offerings and removed his sunglasses to take in what he saw.

He paused at my sandals. Finally he looked into my face and smiled, his eyes like two glittering pools a woman could fall into.

"You hungry?"

"Starving."

"You look beautiful."

I nearly fell over, until he added, "When we've eaten, I'm taking you shopping."

Des Cogan's Story:

One of the things I like about Spain is they have the common sense to allow bars to be either 'smoking' or 'non-smoking', unlike Scotland where, as usual, we had to endure Blair's cigarette police in every bloody establishment in the country; and for a year longer than the English. To me it was the bloody Poll Tax all over again.

I found a small British (for that read English) pub that allowed us lepers left in the community to indulge in our pleasure away from the burning heat of the Mediterranean sun; the kind of heat that turned the average blue-tinged Scottish skin blood-red within seconds.

It was built like a typical English pub too. It boasted a small games room, in which a quality pool table and dartboard jostled for space. I instantly realised that there just wasn't room for the two sports to be played simultaneously. Then I saw a pretty ancient poster. Darts held court on Mondays Wednesdays and Fridays. Today was obviously pool day and two very burly guys wearing more gold than Ratners, lumbered around the table being very Cockney.

The main bar was laid out as a restaurant and food was obviously the king. Attractive waitresses in traditional black and white outfits buzzed around the neat tables. The place did well and you could see why.

Despite leaning towards the new 'gastro inn' style of pub, the Midge Hall Tavern sold an excellently pint of Guinness at just under a fiver, not bad for this part of the town, believe me. The front terrace of the pub looked directly onto the marina and therefore directly onto about a billion pounds' worth of boats. The only thing that separated the pub's small patio from the water was a narrow strip of road; this was invariably blocked by equally expensive motors. By the time I was on my second pint, served by a very amiable ex-Lancashire copper-turned-landlord, and ordered the Chicken Caesar Salad (twenty-two pounds), I'd seen more Ferraris and Lamborghinis that you could shake the proverbial stick at.

I was considering how I was going to go about hiring a decent cruiser. Money wasn't an issue, neither was my qualification to sail her myself as I'd got all my credentials years ago. It was just a question of finding the right craft and someone who wasn't going to ask too many questions.

You know what people say but. Every time they go away on a break, they tell the same tale. 'It's a small world by the way, I was on ma holidays in bloody Spain and I ran into this fella I hadnae seen since I was wee'.

Well that was just the feeling I had when I heard the unmistakable voice.

"What the fuck you doin' here, doin' here, Des?"

I hadn't seen Jimmy 'Two Times' since that night over the water when we dropped 'that' package in the DLB.

I'd never really known him well and I didn't have cause to work with the guy afterward, not many did. When I'd asked some of the lads about him, long after I'd lost track of Rick, they said Jimmy had left the Regiment. Apparently his speech problems worsened and he couldn't continue. No one was that close to him, he was a loner because of his talking, like. He had a bit of a stutter and when he did speak, he said everything twice. It was like working with a fuckin' echo.

He was a good bloke though, and Rick liked to use him on ops. That was always good enough for me.

I took his hand and it was as rough and as strong as I'd remembered. He held me with a genuine smile.

"Nice to see you, man."

I waited for the repeat, but it never came.

"And great to see you, Jimmy. Fuck me! It must be ten years, mate."

"February sixth, 1996, Des."

"Wow, I wouldn't have known the exact date but, yeah, ten fuckin' years. Listen, you're looking fit y' bastard."

"I get some in, pal."

I suddenly realised that this was the longest conversation I'd ever had with Jimmy, when not talking into a radio.

"And the erm…" I pointed at my mouth like a full on *idgit*.

He looked extraordinarily pleased with himself.

"I went to a speech therapist in Doncaster, 'n she sorted me out like, I only do it now 'n again, now 'n again."

I felt a twinge of guilt. I always accepted Rick's decision to bring Jimmy in on an operation, he always did a pro job when I was involved, but I thought he was just muscle and not much more. Now, he stood in front of me, all smiles, suntan and perfect teeth.

You could tell he worked outside. Deep lines ran like a motorway network along his forehead and he obviously still liked to fight. New scar tissue sliced thin pink trace lines around his left eye.

Jimmy had given up on what hair he had and now shaved his head. The whole of his cranium sported a spectacular tattoo that snaked down the left of his neck, and disappeared down into a black vest that was struggling to contain his considerable pecs. He would never have been allowed such a noticeable tattoo in the Regiment. Any obvious mark or trait was frowned upon by the grey men.

He was still hired muscle, no question of that, but he had a brain. His eyes flicked around the patio, taking in everything and everyone in it. Back in the day, I suppose we all thought that because he couldn't join in the craic with the team and that, he was thick or antisocial or something.

We were wrong, by the way.

He pulled a stool over and sat. It felt really good to see him. I suppose I was feeling a bit edgy, and someone from the old days was a relief.

The landlord was over in a second. He obviously knew Jimmy, he was all smiles. "Pint of Bomber, Jim?"

"Please, Keith."

Keith looked at me with a new vigour. It would seem that any acquaintance of Jimmy's was a very good friend of his. He saw I was halfway down my pint.

"Another, sir?"

"Aye, why no?"

Keith retired to pull the beer and Jimmy was straight to it.

"Did you ever see Rick?"

I nearly spat my Guinness out.

"Rick who?"

Jimmy double checked his surroundings.

"You know just who I mean, Des, Rick Fuller."

I held Jimmy's eyes with mine.

Searching his gaze.

Asking the question.

The only important question.

Can I fucking trust you, pal?

He didn't wait for me to solve the puzzle.

"I resigned my post because of what they did to Rick Fuller, Des. I was at that drop, the DLB that night, back in '96. I dropped Rick off, me and Butch. Remember? You did the obs for us."

I nodded. What else could I do?

"We dropped Rick back at the DLB. He insisted that it was kept secret, and it was. Butch took it to his grave. Killed in Iraq he was. Did you hear?"

I shook my head. "No, Jimmy, I didn't."

He shrugged in matter-of-fact sort of way. "He went down in a sandstorm in a Chinook. Him and Kelly Sergeant. You remember him, Des?"

I again shook my head. I'd heard his name mentioned but that was all.

Jimmy was on a roll.

"I heard Rick was dead, killed late last year, so we're the only ones left. We never knew what he found out that night. Then his wife got the good news the day after. The Paddies claimed responsibility within hours. C'mon, Des, you must've thought somethin' was wrong?"

He leaned in close, he smelled of coconuts.

"I knew there was somethin' wrong with that job. People in power talked in front of me because they thought I was thick, or dumb. You know what I'm saying?"

I didn't react; I was waiting for the punch line.

"There's no way the PIRA had recce'd Rick's place. Fuck me; I didn't know where he lived and he liked me. They were tipped by someone inside, Des. Rick was hung out to dry by the Regiment."

Our beer came and we lapsed into silence until Keith was out of earshot.

"I knew where he lived, Jimmy. He called me straightaway. I went there just after he found Cathy. It was fucking atrocious, mate. The man went to pieces."

"Bastards."

"Yeah, I'm with you on that one."

Jimmy was like a dog with a bone. "So you never kept in touch?"

I figured the truth was easiest. Jimmy had this weird thing about reading your actions. Some thought it was creepy.

"I kept in touch for a while. The guy lost the plot, you know? Hit the bottle big time. Then, one day I went round to his bedsit and he was gone. No forwarding address, nothing."

Jimmy scratched his head but his dark eyes searched my face. "And you never saw him again?"

He looked me in the eye and did that weird thing he did. He must have recognised something. A glimmer of emotion or something, I don't know what. But he grabbed me by the wrist and almost spat out his words.

"He's fuckin' here, isn't he? You're here with him and you've come for them, haven't you?"

"Come for who, Jimmy? What the fuck are you on about?"

Jimmy looked around him once more and leaned in again. This time there was a hint of fear in his eyes, and he was not a man to scare easily.

"You're here for Charlie, Champagne Charlie Williamson."

Rick Fuller's Story:

Lauren had chosen grilled shrimps with rocket and parmesan. It arrived together with warm fresh bread and a pot of herb butter. I had sea bass in lemon and parsley, no potatoes, but a side of Greek salad.

I ordered an ice cold bottle of J-M Brocard Chablis Premier Cru 2005, to complement our food. It had a flinty almost mineral taste to it, whilst being fresh, fruity and light. The perfectly turned out waiter delivered it with a flurry. He offered me a small taste, waited, and I nodded that the wine was agreeable. He positively sloshed the freezing liquid into large fishbowl-shaped glasses rabbiting on about how good a choice I had made before retiring to leave us in peace. I was starting to enjoy myself.

Lauren did indeed look beautiful. I saw at least five or six guys risk admiring glances in her direction whilst we waited for food. Had it not been for her appalling taste in sandals, she would have had many more. I was sure of it.

We ate slowly and in almost total silence, both of us absorbing the atmosphere and the warm sunshine. It seemed a million miles from dead teenagers and poky hotels in Manchester.

I suggested Lauren change for our expedition and, although she looked a little embarrassed, I think she was looking forward to our shopping trip. She drained the last of her Chablis and disappeared to her room. I signed the bill and strolled to the cool lobby to wait for her.

All the big designer names had outlets in Puerto Banus, plus the El Corte Ingles was a good department store, so we were not short of places to shop.

The lift doors opened and Lauren stepped out. She'd opted for her FCUK T-shirt which I'd seen before and a short denim skirt. White Adidas tennis shoes completed the picture.

She raised a questioning brow.

"Better," I said, "much better."

The doorman hailed a taxi and before we knew it we were pulling up outside Emporio Armani.

I opened the glass door and ushered Lauren into the cool air-conditioned store. I waved away the stick-thin tangerine-coloured assistant who had a cold or a coke problem and set about my task.

I'd always been a Giorgio fan and went to town finding Lauren a pair of lemon beach sandals and a lovely pair of white kitten-heeled shoes for evening wear.

The assistant was a little shocked when I paid the six hundred Euros in cash. I gathered not many people ventured far away from plastic in a place like Banus.

We exited into the fierce heat of the afternoon and headed for the harbour on foot. Lauren carried her designer shopping bag and wore a massive grin. She pleaded with me not to spend any more money, so, as I knew a nice pub with a terrace on the waterfront called the Midge Hall and I fancied a cold drink whilst watching the world go by, that was the plan.

Lauren North's Story

I had to say, I was impressed. Rick made shopping so easy. Well it is very easy when you can spend four hundred and twenty pounds on two pairs of shoes and not even blink, isn't it?

I'd had a wonderful afternoon and had managed to put the reason we were in Spain behind me for a couple of hours. Suddenly that was all about to change.

Rick and I were strolling along the harbour marvelling at the fantastic array of yachts when I saw him stiffen. He was looking over at the terrace of a bar we had planned to visit.

When I followed his gaze, I could see Des was there, sitting at a table, shaded by a large Martini umbrella. He was in deep conversation with a man who looked very scary indeed.

He had a big tattoo covering his bald head and it ran down his neck and inside his top. He was very muscular. Not like a body builder, more like a professional boxer or sprinter.

He wore a pair of mirrored wraparound sunglasses which hid his eyes. Somehow I didn't feel like looking into them.

Rick stopped and let a delivery van obscure us temporarily. He flicked open his phone and dialled Des.

The conversation was brief. I heard him say something like 'are you sure?' and then close the phone.

Rick looked at me and smiled a rare smile. "Come and meet Jimmy 'Two Times' Smith," he said. "He's a good bloke from the Regiment."

From Armani to army in one fell swoop. We sauntered over to the two men.

Jimmy stood up and removed the shades to reveal eyes that were considerably more pleasant than I expected. They were chocolate brown, quick and full of life. He smiled to reveal perfect teeth that had cost more than some family cars.

"I spotted you fifty metres before the jetty there, boss. You must be getting old, getting old like."

Rick took his hand in another rare moment of physical contact and pumped it. Both men held each other's stare. Des broke the silence.

"Sit the fuck down, the lot of you. Yer makin' the place look untidy."

We sat and Jimmy turned his attention to me. He gave me an intense stare. A piercing examination that made me shift uneasily in my seat. A look that told me I wasn't one of 'them'. A look that offered me nothing yet drew on my thoughts and fears. It was as if he was reading my face itself.

Des saved me.

"This lovely creature is Lauren, Jimmy. She's part of the team. The big man would no be here if it weren't for her, isn't that right, Rick?"

"That's right, Jimmy, she knows her stuff, and a top medic. She can handle herself when the shit starts flying too."

Jimmy stopped his examination almost immediately, but I figured he'd already got the information he needed. He bowed his head in true embarrassment. He rested his hand on mine and it felt like sandpaper.

"Very sorry, ma'am, very sorry. If I didn't make you feel welcome like. Just that I'm not good around strangers."

I removed my hand from under the dense weight of his.

"No problem, Jimmy, nice to meet you."

Jimmy's dark eyes flickered in the sunshine. "So you're a medic, Lauren, a nurse no doubt, something in intensive care I'd guess and from Yorkshire?"

I'd met people like Jimmy before. They were on the spectrum. He fell short of any major learning difficulties, but carried traits of both autism and other syndromes. This was a man who could see things others couldn't. Here was Rain Man with muscles.

Rick threw his hands up faster than an Italian in a trench, his own South London accent showing through. "Fuck me, two bleedin' Yorkshires and a Jock. I'll never get a bloody drink bought for me!"

We laughed.

It was the last time we all laughed together.

Rick Fuller's Story:

An omen had come, a good luck charm. I'd always liked working with Jimmy. I used him on jobs where, if it got very physical, and I mean the times when your enemy was close enough to bleed on you, he was a big bonus.

I love Monty Python, don't you? Have you seen 'The Holy Grail?' The scene where John Cleese is the black knight and he gets all his limbs chopped off by another knight? In the end, he's just a stump left on the ground, but Cleese still won't yield and shouts at the other knight, "Come back and fight, you pansy!" or words to that effect. Well that was Jimmy 'Two Times' Smith in real life. I mean it when I say this. I have never seen a man give and take so much punishment and live.

Back in the day, everyone thought he was thick muscle, nothing more than that.

But Jimmy was much more.

He saw things we didn't. He just couldn't always tell us because of his problem.

Jimmy's talent for spotting people in a crowd was just short of creepy. His ability to read situations, almost what people were thinking, was very bizarre. The trouble had always been that he often took three days to tell you what he'd seen or worked out. Back then, to be honest, I didn't give a fuck because he could save your whole team's skin if it got to hand to hand combat. He was that good.

Now, things were like chalk and cheese for Jimmy. He could tell you there and then what he knew. He'd got some help and was doing well for himself. He'd sorted a nice little business in the harbour renting high-end powerboats. He was charging over a grand an hour and had a waiting list.

This was a very different Jimmy.

The fact was, for the last four years he'd seen Williamson drop in and out of Puerto Banus. The man shopped here, drank and ate here but lived in Gib. He'd watched him from a silent distance. After all he was just an ex-squaddie trying to scrape a living in the sun. He thought all his mates were all dead or missing anyway. God bless us all. We all needed a living wage. Jimmy's looked like it was a substantial fee too.

He had chosen to remain covert and to keep his identity and history a secret. He didn't do so just to protect himself. He had been waiting for this day. Waiting to repay Charles Williamson for his crime.

He told me that somehow he knew that this very day was coming. He also knew something we didn't back then. Back in 1996, he'd seen something we hadn't, he'd read the situation whilst we'd all missed it. Whatever it was, he'd never forgotten, and like me, never forgiven.

He truly believed that I would come and take vengeance on Williamson. When he saw Des in the Midge Hall, he wasn't surprised. To him it was the fulfilment of a dream, a vision he'd had many times.

Jimmy lounged on the plush sofa of my suite and flicked through every available channel on my TV. He settled on Mastermind, the final, 2001. He answered every question out loud, no stutter, whilst texting his girlfriend in Thailand. She didn't speak English.

We now had a fourth man. He was eerie, and very dangerous, but a very welcome addition to our menagerie.

"Did you know Butch had been killed in Iraq?" Jimmy hit the mute button. He'd beaten Magnuson. He did his weird look, the one all the lads hated back then, over the water. The one that X-rayed you.

I couldn't even start to explain. With the way my life had turned out, how would I have known about poor Butch with the way my rich but grubby existence had drawn me away from all that had been good? I knew I couldn't say the right words, so I stayed quiet. He read me, I knew he did. He gave a nod and he said, "I ran into his brother by pure accident. He was on holiday here three days after he was buried. We had a beer or two, you know, boss."

I felt bad. Like shit. He knew it. I changed the subject.

"We're off to San Pedro tonight. A little collection job. We need some hardware, if you know what I mean."

Jimmy smiled.

"Fuckin' top one, top one. I've still got the odd bit of kit myself but count me in, boss. Whatever you need, I'm in."

Lauren North's Story:

I knew it was time for Des to collect the weapons from the safe house. He was off to meet Rick. He'd showered and changed quickly and I was left in the hotel room surfing satellite TV.

I felt uneasy at what I'd witnessed. Jimmy 'Two Times,' 'good guy' whatever he was called didn't sit straight with me. In fact I was damned well suspicious of him. He was really creepy. The way he looked at people. He almost took something from you each time he spoke to you. I got the impression he did it every time he had contact with another human being. He captured something from inside you. Does that sound strange?

Well it was.

Anyway I was the new girl on the block and what could I say about an 'old boy' from the Regiment days?

I was pissed off at being left alone. I admit I was a little resentful. Once I'd flicked through all the English-speaking channels I killed the set and sat in silence for a while.

Feeling lonely for the first time in months, I opened the sliding doors which led to the balcony and sat in the warm Spanish twilight.

I could hear the sound of silver on china. It tinkled below me as the early diners devoured their fabulous evening menu at the poolside restaurant. The low mumble of voices and the occasional chorus of laughter rose up to my solitary refuge. I slid deeper into my beautiful rose-coloured armchair, feeling like the last chicken in the shop. Envy is a terrible thing.

I avoided the balcony lights and opted for the ornate oil lamp which took pride of place on the cast-iron table. It lit my small world and made me feel warm and cosy.

The sun had long since lost its battle with the horizon and darkness overcame the earth.

Taking a bottle of white from the minibar, I poured myself a large measure. It tasted fruity and calmed me. I checked my Motorola for messages but found nothing. San Pedro, where the guys had gone, was only a few miles away. I felt a sudden chill and snapped the phone shut. I looked out past the diners and onward to the fabulous harbour. The moon threw down yellow droplets of light. They shimmered on the crystal sea which rolled dark and mysterious without the sun for company. The moonlight flashed upward, iridescent against the gently swaying white hulls of million-dollar craft waiting silently for their next passage.

It was all so sweet.

Fuck this, I thought. *I'm going out.*

I took a shower but was careful not to wet my hair, then quickly dressed in my denim skirt and a pretty summer top I bought five years earlier for a holiday in Cyprus. I'd never worn it, as my husband thought it too revealing. It showed an inch of my midriff. Selecting my new kitten heels to match, I grabbed my bag and made for the door. No make-up. No perfume. No problem.

As I stepped from the lift I could hear the 'clip clop' of my new shoes on the marble tiled foyer, making me feel slightly self-conscious. The doorman must have heard me and he turned and smiled.

"Taxi, madam?"

I returned his grin and checked his name badge.

"No thank you, Louis, it's a lovely night, I'll walk."

It was indeed a warm, balmy evening and as I trotted down the steps of our hotel I felt my spirits rise. At first I enjoyed wandering around the glitzy souvenir shops along the front but soon tired of the patter and compliments from the smooth salesmen. I made myself a little promise to see the real Puerto Banus and find a nice coffee shop. With that singularly simple thought I started away from the harbour and along the cobbled streets that led me away from the tourist trap. After fifteen minutes or so of steady walking I noticed any shops that were present were actually closed and their signs no longer bothered with the English translation. Seville orange trees lined my way. They were so full of fruit that some had fallen and dotted the path. No one would pick them up to eat of course; the bitter Seville orange is only of use for making jam. That aside, they filled the warm evening air with a luscious smell that for some reason reminded me of Christmas. The bustle of the harbour was left behind and all I could hear were my own feet and the occasional barking dog.

I was close to turning back toward the hotel, disappointed that I had not managed to find the enclave I'd hoped for, when I heard the unmistakable sound of people having fun.

As I drew closer to the noise I could see that a street market was in full swing. Coloured light bulbs were strung between lamp posts and dozens of trestle tables blocked the road from any vehicles. The stalls were piled high with all manner of goods from cured meats to silver jewellery. Each stall-holder seemed to be shouting to the world that they had the best deal in town. With my very limited Spanish they could have been saying anything. The walkways between the various traders were packed with shoppers. Not a pair of Union Jack shorts in sight, I was in a locals' market. I was very much the lone tourist and glad of it.

I spent the best part of an hour wandering between the makeshift wooden shops. I even treated myself to a small silver bracelet.

As I passed a stall where a large man in a bloody apron sliced hot roast boar, my stomach told me I hadn't eaten since lunch. Two Euros bought me a huge slice of mouth-watering meat together with crusty bread and pickles.

At the north end of the market was a small square with benches and more orange trees. I parked myself there and, in the shaded moonlight, ate. Once I'd devoured half of my meal I was full and in need of that coffee I'd promised myself. I checked my mobile again for any messages from the lads but found none. I started to feel real concern. San Pedro was twenty minutes away and three hours had passed. I pushed the remnants of my meal into a nearby bin and headed east along a narrow cobbled path which boasted the sign 'Avenida Cadiz'. After a hundred and fifty meters or so, a brightly lit pavement café filled the street with the unmistakable aroma of fresh coffee.

After all the oranges trees I'd seen the last hour, I was unsurprised to find the café was named 'Cafeteria Sevilla'. The sign appeared to have been handwritten by someone without any artistic qualities. Despite the basic sign-writing the place was busy with people who, like me, had done some shopping and needed a break. I sat at an outside table where a very handsome waiter took my order. Minutes later my latte arrived steaming hot and smelling of cinnamon.

I felt my Motorola vibrate in my pocket and my spirits rose. It was a text from Des. It read *Collection complete. Where r u btw?*

I hit the reply button and started to text but was suddenly conscious of a man who had seated himself at the table to my right. He was in my peripheral vision but I was acutely aware that he was staring. I stopped pressing buttons and took a better look at the guy.

My heart lurched and I felt the palms of my hands sweat in an instant. The man was indeed staring. More than that, the piercing blue of his solitary visible eye held me for that split embarrassing second. He instantly realised my discomfort, and spoke. He brushed his white-blond hair from his face, dragging me further into his gaze. "Lovely evening," he said.

I didn't, no, couldn't reply. I felt my legs start to shake.

"You are English, I take it?" He produced a flashing smile. My throat was constricted by an invisible ligature and I remained mute. He pointed to the back of my neck, his smile broadened. "Your label," he said. "Marks and Spencer's, it's sticking out. I saw it, I'm sorry I didn't mean to embarrass you. But you are English, right?"

I fumbled with the back of my top, inwardly cursing my hurried exit from the hotel. The man's South African accent was mixed with the USA and somewhere else. It was educated, sophisticated even, yet primitive and callous all at the same time.

I fixed myself, took a breath and forced a smile back at Stephan Goldsmith.

"How observant of you, are you a detective?"

He wore a crisp white shirt that was so perfectly pressed it looked starched. His skin was tanned and he had an obvious bite scar on his cheek. Another thin white blemish led from just under his Adam's apple down over his sternum and out of sight. He tugged at the cuffs of his shirt in turn, pulling one over a solid gold Rolex and the other over an equally impressive bracelet.

"Not a detective, more of a soldier of fortune."

He nodded at my frothing cup.

"Can I get you a real drink? I know the English like to indulge."

I'd managed to stop my legs from shaking but didn't feel confident enough to lift my coffee cup. My mind was a complete whirl. My whole body was telling me to get up and run but I just knew it would be a mistake.

He persisted as I fought with my inner self.

"Xavier does a lovely margarita. It might bring some colour back to those beautiful English cheeks of yours, Lauren."

His voice cut into me. The sound of my own name had never frightened me before. In that instant I was terrified.

I instantly realised this was it. This was my personal test. How long had he followed me? Was this pure coincidence? How careless had I been? Of course, there was no way of knowing. Did the guys have similar problems? Who had really sent that text from Des's phone? I said a silent prayer.

My red hair and clear glasses, my new ID, had not fazed the man that sat five feet away from me. His smile had left his face and was replaced by an evil sneer. With the fleetness of foot a ballerina would have been proud of, he landed on the seat next to mine. My consciousness was filled with a mix of heavy cologne I couldn't name and the ferocious desire to survive what came next. He cradled my shoulders with a powerful arm. He exerted just enough pressure to make me realise I had no choice in the matter and I felt his hot sour breath in my ear.

"Hello, Sister."

Stephan held me tight with his left arm whilst he quickly searched me for any weapons with his right. He lingered briefly at my breasts and I was unable to control a shiver that went through my whole body.

I had no gun, of course, it had been left in Manchester and our delivery was still en route.

Stephan however, did have a gun and he pushed the muzzle under my right armpit.

"Now, Lauren. No tricks or funny stuff, understand? We are going to walk out of here all nice and quiet or I will shoot you here and now."

I don't know what came over me. Maybe it was all those years of abuse from my ex-husband. Maybe it was the time I'd spent with Des and Rick, their thoughts, advice and training, but I knew what Stephan wanted. He would really like me alive or I would have already been lying in a pool of my own blood in the café.

I pushed against his weight and started to bend down and reach for my heel. Stephan gripped me tighter and pressed the gun into my flesh, cutting into me.

He gritted his teeth and grabbed at my hair.

"I said no funny stuff!"

Before he could repeat himself I took my beautiful shoe from my foot and swung at his head with all the power I could muster. The heel buried itself into his cheek and I rolled to my left, kicking out with my right leg as I fell from his grip and my chair.

My foot connected with him as I hit the deck but it only succeeded in putting a few feet between us. That was enough for me. Scrambling to my bare feet, I grazed my knees on the cobbles in my haste.

Stephan had risen from his chair, his face pouring with blood. People were shouting and screaming as they saw Stephan point his gun directly at me. He couldn't miss.

"Fuckin' bitch!" he bawled.

I leapt over a table to my right, knocking cups and glasses everywhere. Hitting the ground hard, I rolled under the next and heard the explosion of gunfire as two rounds slammed into the table-top above me. There was no time to hide so, on hands and knees, I crawled out into the open, kept my head down and sprinted back the way I came, toward the market.

I had to make it to those stalls and the throng of people that had seemed so welcoming only minutes before. It was my only chance. I pumped my arms and legs. My lungs felt like they would burst. My throat was hot and dry but my vision honed in at the end of the street that would bring me to the crowds.

Stephan's heavy steps were close behind me. I could hear him but I dare not turn to see. My feet were being torn to pieces by the cobbles but I felt no pain.

Another thunderous roar came from behind me and sparks flew from the wall to my left as another bullet sliced the air but blissfully missed its target. Twenty more yards and I would be at the junction. I could smell the meat roasting and see the glint of lights.

I could almost feel Stephan's breath on my neck. He was murderously close and I knew it.

Ten yards.

Where were the cops when you needed them?

I felt his hand grip my hair and his foot kick at my ankles. My balance was lost and I crashed to the cobbles, knocking all my remaining breath from my body. He fell on me, raining blows to my head with the butt of his gun. The first strike hit me just below my left eye and sent shockwaves through my teeth and jaw. I felt blood pour from the wound and it flowed into my ear. I deflected the next with my forearm, pushed the heel of my hand into his face and made a decent connection. He seemed not to notice and tore at my hair again, holding my head against the road. I lifted my knees up in an attempt to get some leverage and push off his bull weight but he seemed superhuman. He hit me again with the SLP. This time it was the bridge of my nose that took the full force and I heard it crack under the pressure. A bright metallic taste formed at the back of my throat and I knew blood was coursing down the passageway from by ruined nose. My whole conscious was failing me and I felt drunk and sick all in the same instant.

I hadn't much left. He knew it. His blond hair was splattered with my blood as it fell over his face. He was actually laughing. He was fucking enjoying it.

He raised his hand again, the pistol gleaming in the darkness, wet and shiny from its demolition of my face. As he brought it down I lifted my right arm to block him. He thought he would just plough straight through me but I had other ideas.

His arm came down, and instead of blocking him forearm to forearm, as he expected, I went to complete the last gasp manoeuvre you would ever make in combat. I went to strip him of the pistol. He brought the weapon down with terrifying force. I withdrew my arm at the last possible moment and let the barrel of the SLP fall into the cupped fingers of my hand inches from my face. Shifting my weight to my left side to avoid the force of the blow, I forced my left arm from beneath me and slammed my forearm into the crook of his elbow.

His arm folded like paper and the SLP was inverted and pointing directly at Stephan Goldsmith's solitary visible eye.

Stephan had two choices. Let go or shoot himself.

He let go.

I rolled to my right, gripping my prize but Stephan was fast, vicious and far from discouraged. Before I could stand he had found his feet and launched a kick at me just below my left breast. The force of the blow slammed me into a shop doorway and I couldn't breathe again. Shards of pain tore at my whole body and stars filled my vision.

I lay unable to breathe or focus.

Stephan stood tall, silhouetted by the dim streetlights. He brushed back his hair, confident, callous. His voice was sickening.

"I was just going to fuck you before I shot you, Lauren. But now, I think I will have to reserve some special treatment for that fine body of yours."

Somewhere deep inside I knew I wouldn't die on that Spanish street. The sadistic piece of shit-excuse for a man, tucking in his perfectly pressed fucking shirt, was not going to get the better of me. I dragged the pistol from under my broken ribcage and somehow managed to straighten my arm. I turned the weapon in his direction, squeezed the trigger and the SLP jerked in my hand. The sheer noise in the enclosed backstreet rattled my damaged nose and teeth as the round sped toward its target.

I hit him somewhere, because he fell.

I pulled myself to my knees and vomited.

My own blood dripped and mixed with my stomach contents as I spat out the last of my meal.

I could hear Stephan groaning somewhere to my right.

Then I could hear sirens.

It was time to fuck off.

Stephan had the same idea. I heard him start to move. There was a scrabbling sound to my right and it was getting fainter by the second. The bastard was getting away. My head refused to clear but I managed to stand. God knows what I looked like, bloody broken and barefoot, I presumed, but I couldn't let Stephan escape. I fumbled in the pocket of my skirt and felt my Motorola, hit the call button more by instinct than sight, put it to my ear and staggered in the general direction of my attacker.

Des answered in an instant. "Where the fuck are you?"

I spat out a mouthful of my own blood.

"I'm on Avenida Cadiz." I forced myself to focus in the direction Stephan had lurched. "Leaving it now and heading east."

I could hardly breathe. The pain in my ribs and face was unbearable. "I'm following Stephan Goldsmith. He's hit, but moving. I'm in shit state and need some fucking help, get your Scottish ass here now."

Des was insistent.

"Stay there."

"Fuck off, Des. I'm not going to lose him now, get the guys over here and I'll ring in five with my new position."

I killed the call, wiped my own blood from the SLP, checked the magazine and clicked on the safety. I tucked it into the waistband of my skirt and staggered off in search of the man who had just come close to killing me.

Stephan was bleeding quite badly and droplets of his blood acted like the breadcrumbs of some distant Brothers Grimm tale to me. My feet were in a far worse state than I had first thought and I made a note never to sprint through cobbled streets at night barefoot.

I took careful silent steps from Cadiz and into a narrow alley barely wide enough for two people to pass each other.

I figured I'd hit Stephan in the leg as I could clearly hear his laboured gait echo further into the lane. My head banged with a hundred drums and my nose streamed with blood and soaked my top and skirt, but above it all I could hear his good leg hit the cobbles and the scrape of his injured leg being dragged behind. I followed those sounds for a full twenty silent minutes. He twisted and turned in alley after alley. I could hear him, but was careful not to get close enough to actually get a visual. The tables were turned and now it was I who wanted him in one piece.

The sirens, the market, the café were long gone and I was in almost total darkness in the tightest environment you could imagine.

Then, just as I thought he was headed for the marina, he stopped. I could hear him fumble and then the tell-tale bleep of a keypad. My breathing had returned to near normal and the sheer adrenalin that had pushed me on was dulling my pain. I listened in the silent blackness.

He was making a call.

I looked around frantically for any kind of sign or landmark so I could text the guys.

His voice was pained but clear enough.

"It's me."

Then I heard it. It was a door or gate being opened. Then, a voice, a female voice; he wasn't on the phone after all, he was at an intercom. He had found sanctuary.

His tone became muffled and unclear as if he'd entered an enclosed space, but hers was crystal. Her Dutch accent was mixed with Afrikaans.

"My God, Stephan, what happened?"

I heard the door close.

My pulse rate increased again. I waited a full five minutes in total silence. I nipped my nose to try and stem the bleeding. It seemed to help me hear too as I passed the seconds before I approached my target.

Directly in front of me stood a block of six apartments; three ground floor, three first. They were surrounded by a low wall with cast-iron railings cemented into it giving a formidable defence from any would-be burglars. A large double gate barred the way to the path leading to the building. On the left of it was a keypad. Above it was a porcelain sign with pink flowers and ornate script.

It said, 'Apt El Niño, Avenida Fredo.' It had blood on it.

Rick Fuller's Story:

We were twenty minutes from her.

Twenty minutes too long for my liking. I felt the same sickness come over me. The same as the day I lost Cathy, Des was driving, Jimmy Two-Times directing, and I was loading weapons in the back seat of a hired Lexus. It reminded me of Amsterdam and I did my best to remove that thought. Spiros had been economical with the truth when it came to the quality of the weapons order. That or the Spanish had got our kit mixed up with a set of Puerto Rican gangsters'. I had handed over a Porsche 911 for a set of weapons we could have bought in a Belgian car boot for five thousand Euros. I would have a quiet word with my Greek friend on my return. That said, despite the age of some of the kit, the armoury was more than adequate for our needs. Some was even familiar to me from my Regiment days.

We had been sold a Mac10 machine pistol. First made in the early '60s by Ingram, they were a cheap 1000 round per minute room clearer; challenging to master, but really useful. The biggest asset of the Mac10 was its noise suppressor or silencer as they call them in the movies. It was true what people said. The bolt action was louder than the round exiting the breech. The long suppressor also helped to hold the weapon with both hands and it increased accuracy. In the right hands the Mac10 could take out a full room of diners and the bad boys having cocktails next door wouldn't even spill their brandy.

They Yanks loved them, and it was the automatic weapon of choice with the street gangs of the United Sates.

At .45 calibre it made a real mess. It was two seconds of fatality in a drive-by, but a hostage taker's nightmare at close quarters.

At over sixteen rounds per second, even in the most economical hands, the extended magazine was empty and on the floor every couple of minutes.

Reassuringly ten spare mags came with the old girl and I pushed it to one side whilst I worked on the next offerings.

Two brand new, straight out the box M4 Carbines with full external sighting and M203 grenade launchers were next. Short and ideal in a car, handy again at close quarters, but at .556 calibre it had the legs to be an asset at a longer distance. The US Navy Seals used it as their preferred kit. With the launchers and what looked like a box of

NATO 40mm fragmentation grenades we had some serious fire power. I was beginning to wonder if Spiros knew something I didn't. Finally I felt a pang of reminiscence as I loaded three Browning Hi Power SLP's. The old faithful had been named the P35 by some. To me the gun was the BAP, the Browning Automatic Pistol. The Irish knew it well.

It had a thirteen round capacity. Compared to any other SLP it almost doubled your ammunition, in fact you had fourteen shots without a reload if you counted the one in the spout.

I felt ripped off with the price, but I was very comfortable with our armoury. Nothing too long range, but I had the feeling this little job would be bayonets before snipers.

I became aware that we were passing through throngs of tourists. They were having a great time and were totally unaware of what murderous thoughts were going on in our Jeep. Neon and music were on the periphery of my senses. I was concerned we were driving just a little too fast and I asked Des to take his foot off. We were no good to Lauren being hounded by the local constabulary. He snorted his displeasure.

"Why the fuck did she go out on her own without checking in?" Jimmy stared straight ahead, his tone almost absent. "The girl has done good, boss. Whatever happens now, you won't have to go looking for Charlie and his mob."

When you took the emotion out of it, Jimmy was of course, right. He instantly changed the atmosphere in the car from one of worry and anger to one of a focused team once again.

By my reckoning we had Stephan and Susan Goldsmith holed up in the same building and it was not an opportunity to be wasted. I wanted to have a little chat with them both, for very different reasons.

Lauren was in shit state, I presumed because of one or both of the Goldsmith gang. 'Shit state.' Her words. When I heard them, Des and I exchanged glances that any ignorant bastard could have read in an instant. That had been our problem the last hour. We had let it become personal and let down our guard.

Jimmy had no connection with Lauren. He was at the opposite end of that spectrum. When he heard the news he chipped in with. "She's a tough little fucker, that one, guys, mark my words."

He was right. I got on with my job and pushed rounds into magazines and together with them, Lauren's injuries from my mind.

Eventually Jimmy motioned Des to slow down and we parked alongside what looked like a town square filled with orange trees. There was plenty of litter around and the last of what appeared to be market stalls were being packed away by tired-looking traders in the street opposite.

I phoned Lauren.

"Jimmy reckons we are ten minutes by foot from you."

She sounded drowsy and as if she had the flu.

"It's all quiet. No movement as yet. How long before you get here? I'm fucked."

"We're coming for you," I said. "The second you see Des, start walking away from the plot toward him. Stay calm, Lauren. This is all good."

Jimmy had a basic map of the area and I had formulated a plan. First job was for Des to extract Lauren. Jimmy would cover the back of the building whilst I took the front. We could get the car to within a street of the plot, after that it was on foot. The good thing was, so were our quarry.

Des and Jimmy checked their Brownings over, knowing I had just done it. "I want this smooth and very relaxed, guys. Don't attract a soul. Des, you get directly to her, I'll be ten yards behind. Take her straight back to the car and give her what treatment you can. If she can drive, that's going to be her job for the next few hours."

He nodded and felt his shirt pocket for his pipe and tobacco.

"She'd better be fuckin' fine and dandy, boss, or I'm gonna have a wee disagreement with this Stephan fella myself."

Jimmy pushed his gun into his waistband. "I think you've a soft spot for this Lauren bird, Des. What do you suppose there, boss?"

Des pulled his pipe from his pocket and slowly filled the small bowl with his favourite tobacco. He then lifted his face to Jimmy's.

Des's eyes were pure blue glass, almost fish-like.

"What I think is my business, okay, big man? And if you think you're all clever now you can talk and all that, remember this. You don't know me well enough to take the fuckin' piss…okay?"

Jimmy would have murdered Des hand to hand. Jimmy knew it, Des knew it, but the wee man from Glasgow was never gonna back down.

Jimmy looked ever so slightly hurt. "Sorry, mate, I were just sayin' like, that's all."

"Well, dinnae."

Des Cogan's Story:

Jimmy had fuckin' annoyed me. It wasn't his fault like. He had no way of knowing how close we'd become, no, I'd become, to Lauren. He just saw a pretty girl and a Jock with a hard-on. He thought he was being funny, who'd he think he was? Fuckin' Billy Connolly or what? Personally in the circumstances, I wouldn't have found the Big Yin amusing. I had too much to lose.

I inched along the cobles toward where I knew Lauren would be watching the front of the plot. Our targets may have done one from the rear and be gone, but that was a serious doubt as it sounded like Stephan needed some attention to a bullet wound.

Clear skies and a near full moon had chased the last of the summer warmth from the air and, despite the narrow streets, the buildings were bathed in sapphire as the first dew of the morning glistened on the ancient stones underfoot.

Then I saw her.

Just a glimpse, but it was her. Barefoot and leaning awkwardly against a recessed gateway, her face bloodied, one eye almost closed with swelling. She saw me and tried to straighten herself. I noticed she'd done nothing to hide an SLP tucked into the waist of her miniskirt. One of her knees was damaged and I could see bloody tracks which had gravitated from the wound to her ankle and splashed around her foot as she'd walked, before drying dark on her skin as she'd waited.

I felt my temper rise. The girl was in a fucking mess. She'd had the living shit kicked out of her.

Without a trace of drama she walked steadily in my direction whilst keeping an eye over her left shoulder at the apartment. She walked straight past me and I turned in silence to follow.

Within fifteen yards we passed Rick who sauntered innocently toward the point as her relief. I saw him glance at her. He saw the blood and injuries.

I pushed all thoughts of revenge to the back of my mind. It wasn't a movie. Job first.

Once I was sure we were in the clear I caught up with her, took her arm and led her the remaining few yards to our car.

As we had been on a collection job I'd packed some field dressings and morphine in a medic bag, together with a few smaller bandages some antiseptic and some codeine.

The second she sat in the back of the Jeep, I started to work on her injuries. From the light available she had suffered a two-inch gash just below her left eye, a seriously broken nose and a few other scrapes around her forehead, elbows and knees. Her feet were bleeding and swollen. By the way she was holding herself she had a ribcage problem too. Hopefully not a break.

I dabbed the wound on her cheek with solution and taped it closed. Neither of us had spoken. Her breathing was raspy, her nose pushed horribly to the left. I did my best to keep the mood light.

"I need to sort out your nose straight away, sweetheart. Or you'll be as ugly as me before the week is out."

She coughed and nodded and I saw the tiniest smile. She knew exactly what I meant. As an experienced casualty nurse Lauren would have reset many a broken hooter in her day. It had nothing to do with aesthetics, she needed to breath. She knew how painful it would be too.

I took a syringe from my pack. "I'll give you a wee shot, babe, you won't feel a thing."

She shook her head violently and grabbed me by the wrist with surprising strength.

"No, Des! Don't do that."

I ignored her protests, I knew best.

She gripped even harder. "Please…Des…don't."

I was getting a tad fed up arguing the toss, like, when she dragged her SLP from behind her back and she stuck the fucker under my chin.

"Don't be ridiculous, Lauren! Look at the fuckin' state of ye! I'll bet you've some busted ribs too."

"I've not!"

"You don't know that."

"I fuckin' do."

"How?"

"I just do, none of your bloody business, now just set my nose and let's get moving."

It was getting stupid.

"Look, take the fuckin' gun from under ma chin. Ye no gonna shoot me. I know that, you know that."

I grabbed the pistol and put it on the seat next to her.

"I'm sorry, love, but this job is over for you. Simple as. You look like a fuckin' war zone. Once Stephan and Susan start to move, we think they'll lead us to Gibraltar and Charlie Williamson. You won't even make it through customs looking like that. You can get the next flight..."

Lauren punched me so hard that I fell backward, out of the open rear door and onto the cobbles. I sat rubbing my jaw in total disbelief. Lauren's voice was low and measured.

"I'll get into Gib the same way you will, with the weapons. I'll swim the last mile from Jimmy's boat."

She took a breath through her open mouth.

"Now fix my fucking nose."

Rick Fuller's Story:

The sun was about to make its presence felt and the birds were in full swing as Susan made her appearance at the door of the apartment. I felt the hairs on my neck do a little dance. Then I had a full on flashback of the sickening kick Stephan gave to Tanya's dead body as Susan talked on the phone feet away.

She was tanned, fit and wore a navy crop top, cream linen trousers and gold sandals. I thought I'd seen the trousers in Moschino. The shoes were definitely Jimmy Choo. Her hair was tied back in a casual ponytail and I wondered if she'd had extensions. She had large Gucci sunglasses propped on her head.

Any man could see, she was stunningly beautiful, but still had that look, the one she had the very first time I saw her at Davies's house. The one that told all around that she was mildly pissed off about something. Well this time she had plenty to be pissed about and I was going to make sure her day got even worse.

Seconds later Stephan hobbled out behind her looking pale but very much alive, and I had to grit my teeth and stop myself from slotting him there and then. That, of course, was not in the arrangement.

The new plan, and we were really on the hoof, was a simple one. Convinced that Stephan would need hospital treatment and equally sure that daddy would have contacts in Gib that could organise that on a 'no questions asked' basis, we, well I, planned to tail our two friends to the Rock by road whilst Des, Lauren, Jimmy and our weapons made the trip by boat. In the preceding couple of hours Des had fixed Lauren up and from what he'd said, she was doing okay. She looked like she'd gone ten rounds with Tyson, but she was functioning. She even said she was fit enough to make the mile or so swim to the shore to avoid the prying eyes of the British border guards so I figured she must be okay.

Banus taxis are used to ferrying beautiful women with damaged faces around the town. Old habits die hard for the Burberry tattooed twats society. They had caught a taxi to the hotel, recovered what we needed, swung by the Jeep, collected our armoury, and were at the harbour waiting for Jimmy.

I flipped open my phone and dialled.

"We have movement."

Within minutes Jimmy had dropped off his point and was on his way to his meet with Des. I was sitting in the Cherokee, thirty yards back, watching Stephan struggle to get into Susan's Lotus Elise. I had expected some support or muscle to come to their rescue, but there was none. Well, not that I could see.

The pair took the highway and headed for the most protected piece of rock in Europe.

For the first time in ten years I felt close to my goal. So close I could taste it. The one singular thing that had kept me alive was the thought that one day I would come face to face with the man responsible for the treachery that led to the murder of my wife. Now I knew I had the chance to avenge that betrayal. I would make Williamson pay for his crime. As for Goldsmith, well he would know the pain of loss. He would feel the agony of bereavement as I had.

I hit the button to open the electric roof and let in the fragrant Spanish air, pushed Jimmy's iPod into the docking station and selected shuffle. Then I sat back whilst Floyd played *Comfortably Numb*, and enjoyed the ride.

As you approach Gibraltar the scenery gets less and less picturesque. The Spanish seem to want the whole of the area to look shabby. Compare Puerto Banus with the streets surrounding the entrance to the Rock and you can see the Spanish message to the British.
Go home.

I was five cars behind Susan's Lotus. I was so confident they were headed to Gib I even allowed them out of sight for some of the journey.

The entrance to the colony is bizarre. You have thirty-five degrees of sun and British coppers in full uniform checking passports, searching vehicles and being generally suspicious of all visitors. They work out of buildings not much better than Nissan huts. On the way out it is worse. Try escaping the Rock with more than two litres of Scotch and be prepared for a very rough ride.

For all the coppers and security, they let a full IRA Active Service Unit in there back in the day, but I suppose you know what happened then.

Once you rode that gauntlet, you drove across the airport runway before crawling into town. Pretty it wasn't, it's more like Clapham than the Costas, but I wasn't there to see the sights or the apes.

The tail became more difficult as the dozens of mini-buses taking tourists up the Rock darted in and out of the traffic so I stayed well away.

Susan negotiated the narrow streets and headed toward the old army quarters. I dropped even further back. I knew exactly where she was headed. I'd seen the aerial picture of daddy's house.

I parked the Jeep, stepped into the heat and leant on what remained of a concrete wall. Most or the barracks had been demolished and JCBs lay temporarily idle waiting for the Monday morning builders to recommence the new landscape. The Lotus had disappeared through electric gates five h8undred yards ahead, to a place Susan no doubt called home. To my annoyance, an equally impressive residence was near completion next door. Now if I'd been a betting man, I'd have a pound or two on the place being Champagne Charlie Williamson's summer retreat. I'd also wager that Williamson and company had bought the prime ex-army land at a knockdown price. I checked the time. It would be twelve hours before dark and the opportunity for Des and the crew to come ashore. I slipped down in the seat of the Lexus and waited. My time would come.

Lauren North's Story:

My nose had just about stopped bleeding and the pain in my ribs had become a dull ache with the large dose of codeine-based drugs Des had made me take. I'd managed some sleep but felt like a herd of buffalo had tap-danced on my body for a laugh. The good news was that the weapons the guys had collected from San Pedro had been carefully secured onto a floatation device that looked something like a cross between a surfboard and a kayak. Des had made sure that it was totally waterproof and stowed the lot into the boat.

This was no ordinary craft either. The boat was a very beautiful Doral Algeria power cruiser that Jimmy was preparing for sea. It reminded me of the boats I'd seen at the beginning of *Miami Vice*; all white leather, chrome and muscle. It had everything you could imagine and more. Two fabulous bedrooms, one with en suite shower, hi-fi, DVD and HD plasma TV; a dining room for four guests and a captain; a cocktail bar, and all pushed through the waves as fast as you like by two powerful diesel engines. They burbled away as Jimmy entered coordinates into the state of the art navigation system and I checked what was left of my face in the bathroom mirror.

I took off my sunglasses and had a little moment.

If Jane could see me now; six strips of tape held together a cut beneath my left eye and I just knew my next dentist bill would be enormous. I had the beginnings of two fabulous black eyes and my nose? Well, Des had done his best with it.

The sun was just about to dip beneath the horizon and we were about to make way. I slipped out of the bathroom and was met in the cabin by our captain.

"Do you like to s…sail, Lauren?" asked Jimmy as he tapped away at the touch screen display.

I sat myself in a white swivel chair wide enough for two and figured the boat was made for the US market.

"I've only ever been on a ferry from Liverpool to Dublin, Jimmy. I don't think that counts."

Jimmy looked at me and I felt that shiver again. His dark eyes questioning my very existence. It was if he didn't really believe anything I said to him, or I wasn't part of his idea of an assault team. I noticed a nerve pulse under his left eye. Was he nervous? I'd never seen nerves in Des or Rick before.

I changed the subject. "What's the name of the boat, Jimmy?"

It sounded all girly and I regretted opening my mouth instantly. I really hadn't noticed a name as I'd gingerly clambered aboard but I knew the model because I'd flicked through the brochure that was right in front of me on the polished walnut drinks table. She, as I gathered they called all boats, was obviously brand new and very fucking expensive.

Des stepped in, broke my thoughts and answered my question. "Irish Eyes," he chirped with a smile that eased the mood. "Why'd you call her that, Jimmy?"

Jimmy shrugged. He still looked uncomfortable to me. Beads of sweat on his shaved head ran down his temple and neck and along the tattoo that snaked down his body. The evening air was cool. He wiped the sweat from his face before he spoke.

"You know what Shakespeare said, Des, 'What's in a name?'"

"Aye, true." Des looked at the navigation panel that was as big as my television back home in Leeds. "How long to the Gibraltar coastline then?"

Jimmy punched in the last of the information and stowed the map he'd been using. "Two hours and four minutes, Des. Spot…spot on like. Just like a plane, this baby, autopilot and everything."

He motioned to the front of the forty-seven-foot craft. "That's as soon as you let go the moorings."

Des did a mock sailor's salute and grinned at his old mate. "Aye aye, Captain Jim! Castin' off now! "

Des Cogan's Story:

We'd been at sea for about an hour. The night sky was a perfect blanket of stars as we left all ambient light on the coast. Jimmy had let the autopilot do all the work and rather than steering, had been telling old war stories to Lauren, keeping the mood light.

I hadn't heard from Rick since he landed on plot and I was feeling a little uneasy. I checked my watch again. He was forty minutes shy of his proposed contact.

Jimmy broke off from his tales of Sudanese adventures, and looked at his own watch.

"Waiting for Rick to call, Des?"

I nodded, casual but worried. "Yeah, he's late."

It was a life-changing experience for me. In all my years as a soldier, I had never been betrayed by my own.

With the speed of a cheetah Jimmy pulled a Glock from under his shirt and pointed it at me.

I'd never felt so deserted. In an instant I knew. Someone I considered a friend, someone I had fought alongside, who had shared the things only people like us could possibly share, was about to turn into a traitor. For the first time, I really knew what Rick had gone through the last ten years.

I felt sick with anger.

Jimmy, of course, read my face.

"Don't be so upset, Des. We all make mis…mistakes at our age. Were you really going to go up against Colonel Williamson with just two guys and a fuckin' nurse?"

Lauren sat to his right. He trained the gun on her. She was obviously too close for even a mere nurse and he motioned to her to sit next to me. Tight together and easy to manage, I'd have done the same. She used her arms to lift herself from the bucket seat and winced in pain as she did so. Seconds later I felt her next to me. I couldn't take my eyes from the man who was supposed to be my friend. Finally I glanced at Lauren. She looked pale in the moonlight, her swollen features exaggerated in the shadows. What was I thinking? I questioned my own judgement, bringing along an injured woman on such a dangerous job was just crazy.

Jimmy was feeling good though.

"You see this boat, Des?"

Jimmy spread his arms. Boastful, gloating.

"This boat is worth over seven hundred thousand dollars and is one of three I own. Own, Des! No fuckin' mortgage or l…loan involved here. I own them. I have two s…sailing boats too. They would fetch a million dollars each today if I wanted to sell."

He pulled himself together and aimed at me.

"Colonel Williamson gave me a chance, Des. He sent me to school to learn to talk good. He paid for that. Before, all I was good for was fighting. He gave me a chance. Look at all this!"

Lauren's voice was flat calm. "A chance to sell drugs, Jimmy?"

Jimmy moved the Glock the few inches he needed to get a perfect headshot on her. He shook his head violently, the sweat poured from him.

"Mr. Williamson and Mr. Goldsmith are Europe's only defence against drugs! They take care of the biggest dealers. They are the balance. They do what the police and MI5 can't do."

I couldn't stay quiet.

"That's what they told you, Jimmy? Did they tell you about the women and kids they killed at a graveside in Manchester? Innocents, Jimmy? I saw a kid, no more than six or seven with his fuckin' legs blown off, Jimmy. Is that the kind of people you work for now?"

He changed his stance and I looked down the barrel again, his eyes tearful, trying to focused on me. His whole body shook. I'd never seen the man look so flustered.

"Casualties of war, Des, you should know about those. We've seen enough of them. It happens in all c…conflicts. It don't matter, Des. I'm sorry, mate, but in twenty minutes we are meeting another boat. They're taking you to the 'Centre.' Rick will be there by now. Mr. Williamson wants a chat with you all."

He gave a nervous laugh and wiped his face again.

I was curious.

"The Centre?"

Jimmy nodded. Sweat dripped from his nose. "Yeah. The house where Rick was headed is just another piece of real estate the boss has ordered built. He bought the all the derelict MOD land available on Gibraltar a couple of years back, but he also bought an old secret military bunker in the Rock itself; used to be a military hospital. That's the business end of the operation. It's a fortress, Des, and it's where you are both going."

I heard the crack of two 9mm rounds and saw as they hit Jimmy square in the chest. He looked surprised until a third shot slapped his head back against the boat canopy.

Lauren flicked the safety back onto Stefan's SIG. I'd forgotten she still had it and so, obviously, had Jimmy.

"I think we need the weapons out now, mate, don't you?"

Rick Fuller's Story:

Cathy was digging the garden. The ground was still hard from the winter chill. She forced her spade into the frosted earth with her foot so it would give way and allow her to turn it, to fill it with oxygen and make it ready for the new glorious life of spring.

Two men walked casually through the garden gate.

One spoke.

"Good morning, Mrs Fuller. And where might your husband be at this moment?"

Without thought, she threw her spade in his direction, a tragic attempt at protection. She ran for the house, knowing who they were. As she reached the door the first bullets found her. Her legs gave way. She couldn't breathe. A huge weight had fallen upon her. It crushed her ribs whilst other searing pokers tore at her flesh second after second. From somewhere she found one last breath, her pale arm raised as she lay dying.

"Riiiiiiiiiick!"

"Rick?"

"Rick?"

I opened my eyes and saw Susan. She had a wide smile on her face and a Glock in mine.

She beckoned me from the Jeep. I was spread-eagled on the bonnet and searched by an unseen face. I had no weapons.

Susan opened the door of a newly washed and polished Land Cruiser and pushed me roughly inside. On my left was a real bruiser of a bloke and before the door was slammed closed I was joined by an equally steroid-induced dickhead in cheap sunglasses that sat in the personal space to my right. They didn't even bother to cuff or tie me. Confidence ruled.

A third, smaller but more sorted-looking guy drove. Susan turned in the front passenger seat to face me. She wore that same big smile that had nothing to do with her eyes.

"It's so good to see you again, Rick. You look well. You would hardly notice the scar my brother left you."

I didn't know if she was looking for a rise in me but I wasn't going to play her game. I stayed silent.

She played a big ace.

"Your friends will be joining you in a couple of hours, Rick. Won't that be nice? Jimmy has seen to that for us."

I must have shown some flicker of emotion. Jimmy? How could I have been so fuckin' stupid? She grasped it with both hands as the Cruiser turned sharp left up toward the Rock.

"Awww! Poor Rick. Your army colleagues are a constant let down for you, aren't they? First Daddy and Uncle Charlie, and now one of your very own Special Air Service boys."

The guy on my right who was doing a fair impression of The Terminator himself twisted his considerable neck to look me in the eye.

"That's coz them boys is all limp dicks, Miss Susan."

He had a Deep South American drawl. Probably ex-Marine Corps. Small bubbles of white spittle formed on his narrow lips as he shot out his words just a little too quickly for his pea brain.

My old training took over. Inside I was blazing with anger but outwardly I had to let them see they had won. Let them think that I had given up, and then maybe, just maybe, they would relax enough and I would get a chance to escape. I lowered my head and looked at my knees.

The big daft fucker was loving it. He grabbed my hair and pulled my head upright to face forward.

"Look at Miss Susan when she talkin' to you, boy."

Susan knew the drill. Obviously she'd been to the same charm school as her brother Stephan. I could see her boiling the kettle herself.

"Cody here seems to like you, Rick. Maybe I'll let him have half an hour alone with you before you have a little chat with Daddy and Charlie. They are simply aching to see you after all these years. What do you think, Rick? And I just know your little friend Lauren will be very popular with some of the boys in the Centre. Maybe you can watch them have some fun with her too?"

I still played the game.

"Look, you've got me, Susan. Why not let the others go? I'm the one you really want."

She shook her head and I even noticed the driver allow himself a wry smile. I figured everyone in the car had been through the same training manual and I was wasting my breath.

"You know that isn't going to happen, don't you, Rick? Even you with all that hatred built up inside you should understand that this is business. Just that, nothing personal."

She rested her hand on the back of the seat and I noticed a different engagement ring. She clocked me and held it up so that the rock sparkled in the ambient light.

"Nice, isn't it, Rick? It cost over one hundred thousand Euros. He's called Pablo. Italian. Very connected. All gel and designer stubble. Within the month we'll be married and it will all start again, Rick. He is my next Joel Davies, my next tame millionaire drug dealer. Within a year I will have set up the first shipment for him. Of course I will have a contact with the elusive Stern Empire. Daddy and Uncle Charlie will do me the very best rates and Pablo will be delighted. Then he'll get greedy, as they all do. He'll want bigger shipments at cheaper prices. After that, you know only too well what happens, don't you, Rick? The shipment is stolen or lost, the odd player ends up floating in the river, the right information is leaked to the right ear, and we watch the Italians go to war over drugs that never existed." She admired the stone once again and sighed heavily and theatrically before moving her had out of sight.

"Perfect," she breathed.

The Land Cruiser was revving hard as we climbed ever higher up the Rock. I noticed we passed several old entrances to the infamous wartime tunnels carved into the cliff face by different armies. Obviously the 'Centre' was one of them.

Susan hadn't finished. I always thought she liked the sound of her own voice.

"You know, Rick; I have to tell you this because it is so funny." She elongated the 'so' just like a sixth-form schoolgirl would when talking about last night's date.

I didn't think I'd ever get tired of shooting her.

She was buzzing. "All this started that day when you came round to Joel's house to look at his car or something. You had a beer, remember? I knew you were his preferred collector but never really took any notice until that day. All big dealers have one guy they rely on for all the 'wet' stuff. You were too..." she struggled for her descriptive momentarily, "too mysterious. That was it, mysterious. There was something not quite right about you. So I took your empty beer bottle and checked your DNA out. It was easy with our resources. Well, Rick, when the results came back Uncle Charlie was simply insistent that you and your friends didn't return from Holland. He thought you were dead, you see? He knew you'd be trouble one day. And he was right, wasn't he, Rick? All the mess you've caused. Well, that's all over now isn't it?"

I recalled the time when Susan had been so quick to recover my bottle. Sitting on Joel's patio, staring out at those bloody awful bushes. It answered lots of questions.

The car slowed, and by the fidgeting either side of me I gathered we'd arrived at the place Susan called the Centre.

The place was inconspicuous enough. A small parking area for six vehicles fronted a reinforced concrete arch with a solitary steel door carved straight into the Rock. It was all that announced the presence of a tunnel at all. There was no security lighting which was strange and I was marched in relative darkness to the opening. A single red light glowed dimly over the entry as Susan punched a code into the security lock. The door didn't open immediately. There was a humming sound that I gathered was lift gear bringing a car from deep within the Rock. Then the door clicked open and we were bathed in fluorescent light.

Immediately inside the old medical unit was space enough for three stretchers and ambulance crews. Decorated in World War II green hospital tiling, it gave me the creeps. You could almost hear the sailors' screams of agony reverberate off the austere ceramics. In its previous life this was the area the injured would in wait until what still looked like the original elevator car lumbered its way to the surface to take stretchers and casualties down into the depths of the Rock. It had those see-through concertina steel doors and was easily big enough to take everyone in the entrance and some. The doors looked new though and when I looked a second time so did the 1940s wall tiles.

I scanned the rest of the lobby. To the left a more modern green sign announced a fire escape and stairs.

The big Yank in the crappy shades pulled the lift door aside and grabbed me by the elbow. I was unceremoniously dumped inside and I faked a trip and fell on my arse in the corner to give him even more pleasure and confidence.

I knew I was in the shit, but I also knew I would be meeting Williamson and Goldsmith face to face.

When that time came, if they were confident that I was a 'beaten' man, they might be sloppy; they might make one small error that allowed me at them.

I was waiting for that. Ten years on.

Lauren North's Story:

We had twenty minutes to sort out a plan and our weapons before the autopilot on the powerboat delivered us to Williamson's men. Des had propped Jimmy into the captain's chair and stuck a baseball cap on his head to hide the obvious hole. If the guys coming to meet us had night sights it might just fool them long enough.

I popped another couple of co-codamol and was feeling okay apart from not being able to breathe through my nose.

Des had been unusually quiet and was working methodically unpacking weapons and searching the rest of the boat for anything useful. I knew he was working to avoid me. The disappointment of an old colleague letting the side down was giving him a hard time. I suppose it was like having a best friend shag your boyfriend but a million times worse. He'd gone all quiet.

I looked at Des and wanted to make him feel good again. I wanted to tell him, it would all be okay in the end. I had a sudden flash of Jimmy's body slapping against his own, very expensive boat.

I can't believe I'm saying this, but I actually enjoyed shooting Jimmy 'Two Times' Smith. He was a real cock.

Finally Des took a breather and I was glad of it. He stood on the deck, sweat pouring from him, his white shirt sticking to his body, showing the tight-wired muscles of his shoulders and chest; the moon highlighted the day or so growth darkening his weathered face.

"Lauren."

"Yes, Des."

"Ye did good back there, I…" His voice faltered. There was something in it I didn't recognise at first. Then, it came to me and I just knew what it was. I'd heard it in my own voice so many times over the years.

It was regret.

"It's okay, mate," I said.

He stood for a full minute, the wind in his face. He never took his eyes from me and finally he spoke.

"I'm sorry I didn't see it. Jimmy, I mean, we were, you know, I was just so certain…"

I walked from the cabin and onto the deck to join him, took him in my arms and drew him close. I felt his arms slowly react as he held me too. He was so gentle. The natural roughness of his hands, calluses gained from hard graft, felt good against my skin. I was being held by a man, a good honest man. I spoke into his ear, not wanting to lose the embrace.

"We've all been betrayed, Des. Some more than others; it's not your fault; not anyone's fault, except Jimmy himself."

He cupped my chin in his hands and looked into my face. He kissed me lightly on the corner of my mouth. The wind was blowing my hair so much it almost covered both our heads.

In that moment I forgot all of what might come.

"You're a good man, Des, a good man with a big heart, and a fair mind. You're the kind of man that could make any woman happy."

He smiled.

"Aye, but not you, Lauren, eh?"

I looked at my feet.

"No, well not in the way you're suggesting."

The sea lapped at the sides of the boat in a rhythm only it can play. I raised my head, held his face, with both palms and kissed him firmly on the mouth.

He looked shocked and I felt the start of a tear.

I started, "When this is over, Des…"

He held his fingers to my lips and shook his head.

"No. I'll have no promises Lauren.

He held me with his eyes for a few more seconds before going back to his work.

I knew exactly what he meant and he was right.

This was no time for promises.

Rick Fuller's Story:

The lift clanged to a halt. It had dropped between twenty and thirty feet. As I hadn't been cuffed or hooded I figured that I wasn't intended to survive this visit to la-la land or join a witness protection program. Fair one, I suppose.

The gate was pushed aside and we were greeted by a long well-lit corridor with more of the same '40s tiled décor. As I was marched along I could see that the doors of the adjacent rooms were ajar and each was decked out with wartime medical equipment. Doctor's offices, small wards and even an operating theatre were mapped out left and right. Everything was fifty years old but in pristine condition. All that was missing were the nurses in their starched aprons and red crosses.

Finally we reached the end of the corridor and Susan punched what looked like the same security code as before into a keypad that sat to the right of a heavy door marked 'Staff Only.'

Everything changed.

We were transported to the present. Microsoft replaced clipboard and pen, cappuccino left tea and biscuits behind. Green tiles were firmly a thing of the past and pastel colours and workstations were the order of the day. It reminded me of my one and only visit to MI5. The luxury was short-lived for me though.

I was suddenly dragged left along a short corridor. This time we waited at a door without any kind of keypad or handle. It had a security camera pointing down at us. Seconds ticked by until the door was finally opened from the inside by a man in a white coat. He reminded me of an old Nazi, all watering eyes and round gold-rimmed glasses. He didn't speak but just stood aside as I was unnecessarily dragged along yet another corridor. Carpet had disappeared again and was replaced with bare concrete floors. For the first time since entering the Centre I was aware that it was tunnelled from rock and I was deep inside a mountain.

Two players stood at the far end of the corridor close to what I supposed was an air vent. To my surprise and disgust they were smoking. Both carried MP5 machine pistols and wore the obligatory black suits that the rest of my captors seemed to favour. I noticed they were poorly cut and recalled there was a Marks and Spencer's in Gib. They were the sort of thing Des would buy for a wedding do. I mean if you are going to work for the most powerful gangsters in Europe, discover Paul Smith for God's sake.

To the pair's left was yet another metal door. One pushed it open and I was shoved into what was obviously some kind of cell. The four walls, ceiling and floor were rubberised. There was a stainless steel toilet and hand basin together with a raised cot covered in the same protective material as the floor. My heart started to race. I'd been in a similar room before and they were not good places to be. I'd collected an IRA guy from one just like it in Broadmoor Mental Hospital back in the day. He'd been on hunger strike and a dirty protest which hadn't worked, so he'd then decided he was mad. He'd spent eleven months in a rubber room before he decided he was sane again. Now I was standing in one and I wasn't keen on the interior decorations, I can tell you. They were soundproof and lightproof. Within days you would have no idea or sense of time. Solitary took on a whole new meaning.

To my dismay I was joined by Susan and Chad the big bruiser from the car. I'd taken a few kickings in my time and by the look of it I was due another.

"Take off your clothes, boy," he said. The white spittle around his mouth so prominent, you would have thought he was permanently chewing a Rennie.

I'd never taken to the Deep South accent and it grated on me.

Susan wore that grin again and motioned for me to do as I was told.

"Not shy are we, Rick?"

I got on with it, stripped bollock naked and threw my clothes into the corner for Chad to root through.

I made no attempt to cover myself and Susan had a good look as I stood in the brash light, long enough to make my flesh crawl.

Then she stared into my gaze, her flashing blue eyes devoid of any emotion.

"I just want you to know, Rick, that when the time comes, it will be me who ends your life." Her Afrikaans accent showed through. This time there was no smile, not even a fake.

I couldn't help myself.

"At least I don't have to marry you first."

Chad had a lunge at me but I just stepped aside to safety.

Susan barked at him.

"Stop that, you oaf! Bag those clothes and come with me."

She turned to me again, eyes like flames. "You'll pay for that remark, asshole."

The door was slammed shut and the lights went out.

I could hear my breathing and my heart but nothing else. I was also totally blind. I felt my way along the wall until I reached the cot, where I sat carefully. The rubber was cold against my nakedness and I felt terribly vulnerable. I touched my wedding ring. At least they hadn't taken that.

Des Cogan's Story:

All my emotions had welled up inside my chest and I hadn't been able to stop thinking about Jimmy.

The bastard.

I couldn't function. There was so much anger, hurt, regret, rejection, God only knew what was bouncing around inside me. I couldn't even put it into words myself let alone understand it.

But Lauren came to me on the deck, there in the middle of the Straits of Gibraltar, with the world falling down around us, and held me close.

It was as if an angel from heaven itself had wrapped her wings around me, emptied my heart of pain and loathing and filled it with joy and courage all in a split second.

I liked being close to her. I missed that feeling, a woman's touch, even though deep down, I knew we could never be more than what we were this very moment.

Lauren was folding a white tarpaulin sheet across the deck.

According to the Sat Nav we were ten minutes from the RV with Williamson's men. I'd removed all our kit from the floatation device and commandeered other bits of stuff from the boat. Torches, some flares, first aid kit etc would all come in handy, I hoped.

By my calculations we would be meeting another boat some five hundred meters from the coastline. Too close to start blasting away with any old kit, so we had to have a plan that was pretty quiet. I reckoned on four, maybe five guys to do the job of collecting us. It wasn't going to be easy.

I finished screwing the noise suppressor on the Mac10 and un-taped the spare magazines. Then I called Lauren over from making her hiding place on the deck.

The plan wasn't complicated, it couldn't be.

She would lie under the tarp with the Mac10 until the boat was alongside whilst I would pretend to be tied on a chair at the back of the boat in full view.

On the nod from me she would burst out, spray the offending boat and Bob was your auntie's husband.

I handed her the weapon. "You need to practice loading and unloading the mags for the next few minutes."

She nodded, "How many in each? Twenty-two?"

"Thirty, and they'll last you about a second and a half on full auto, okay?"

Another nod.

I held the weapon against my hip and gripped the suppressor with my left hand. Then I swung my body in an arc with my feet planted. "This is how I'd use it. The more stable you are the better and you need to be close. This fuckin' thing is about as accurate as a drunk pissing in the wind. Understand, babe?"

Lauren took the Mac10 and assessed it for weight and feel. Then she pushed in a magazine but removed it without sending the action forward and chambering a round. Then she removed the mag, reinserted it, dropped the action and applied the safety. With one last inspection she made sure the weapon was in fully auto mode and rested it on a nearby table.

"Feels okay to me."

I was about to complain she hadn't practiced enough when I saw the first signs of an approaching boat.

"Positions."

Rick Fuller's Story:

The door of the cell was pushed open by one of the smoking guards. It took a few moments for my eyes to adjust to the light. I studied the guard and he looked overweight to me; a pub bouncer type. His MP5 was held in his left hand, the mechanism cocked back. That meant no round in the chamber and a second or so grace. He didn't inspire confidence. It was the only good thing I saw.

Behind him was the old Nazi doctor. He had surgical gloves on his hands, and a young equally Teutonic type pushed a tray of surgical instruments in behind him.

The accent was not a surprise, but I would have bet my left bollock that they were both Jewish and real good friends of Mr. Goldsmith.

"Now, Mr. Fuller, we need to complete some medical examinations. First is the rectal probe to ensure you have not secreted any objects in that passage. Then I need to examine your teeth. Many spies have tracking devices hidden in molars these days and they must be removed."

I'd seen the film with Dustin Hoffman where the German guy tortures him with a dentist kit and this guy looked just like the fucker.

A second guard entered pushing a chair, and the bouncer type pointed his MP5 at my head.

"Do as the doc says, buddy."

The bouncer had a definite New York twang. I could just see him twenty pounds heavier, riding his 'hog' around town with a cut off denim jacket and tight black T-shirt showing of his tattoos and fat belly.

The doc motioned towards the cot. "Lie on your side facing the wall please, and lift your knees toward your chest."

I knew what was coming, I'd had several rectal exams both for medical checks and drug searches. They are mildly unpleasant and demeaning but I didn't have any choice. Better to let the guy do his job than to struggle like fuck and end up with torn tissue and a bleeding arse for your trouble.

I complied and the guy was professional about it. More than I could say for the two guards who sniggered away in the background like a pair of schoolboys.

"Sit in the chair, please."

I felt my jaws clench. I'd never liked the dentist and the thought of losing eight back teeth in this cell didn't appeal in the slightest.

The doc was removing his gloves, washing his hands in some kind of solution and preparing another pair.

Then he selected a mirror and hook from the surgical tray. He obviously sensed my displeasure.

Before I could complain the two guards pinned me to the chair and the doc's blond assistant was prising my mouth open. Any further defiance was pointless and I shouted "Okay, okay!" as best I could.

I was released and I complied as the doc scraped and tapped away at my back teeth for a few minutes.

To my surprise he straightened up and announced. "He's clean, no cavities."

As the two medical guys were cleaning up, I sat rubbing my jaw and saying a silent thank you to the British Army for regular dental checks.

I figured it was a good time to ask for food and water. I hadn't eaten in over twenty-four hours and if I had any chance of escape I needed energy.

"Any chance of some grub and some water? I feel very weak."

Guard number two, who was less overweight and around my age, was opening a clear package containing a paper suit, the kind the cops use for prisoners when they've taken their clothes for forensic examination.

He was English and I detected a Mancunian accent.

"You'll be eatin' soon mate."

He handed me the suit, together with some paper slippers, and before I could say anything else he was gone and I was in total darkness again.

I started to make final preparations. I made sure Jimmy was stable in his 'captain's' chair, I couldn't risk the fucker falling over at the wrong moment. Then I found the fridge, selected a two-litre plastic bottle of Coke, emptied it over the side and cut the nozzle off with my knife making a three-inch hole in the top. I propped the bottle up on the seat to my left making sure it didn't blow away in the wind, then sat and tucked my Beretta in the back of my jeans, both hands behind my back as if tied. For good measure, there was a fully loaded M4 Carbine at my feet if the shit really hit the fan.

The night was clear as a bell and the outline of our enemy's boat was unmistakable. It looked about the same size as our boat but less powerful. As it drew closer, I could make out three dark figures on board; one was sitting, legs dangling off the forward deck, obviously ready to board, the other two stood in the open-top cabin, one piloting.

Without warning our engines dropped to an idle and then kicked into reverse stopping The Irish Eyes directly on the spot the autopilot had plotted. We sat, the boat rocking gently in the Straits, the engines quietly idling in neutral. I prayed for some cloud cover to mask the sapphire moonlight but we weren't in luck.

I spoke in a flat calm voice, as if chatting to the un-hearing Jimmy.

"Two hundred yards to your right now, babe, no lights. I can see three targets so far. One on deck two in cabin."

"Got that."

I heard Lauren shuffle closer to the edge of the tarp and knock the safety off the Mac10. She sounded calm. I felt like a sitting duck.

I looked over at my Coke bottle to check it hadn't shifted and gripped my Beretta with my right hand. I felt sweat trickle between my shoulders and head down my spine. The wind had dropped and I could just make out the raised voices on the approaching craft.

"One hundred, Lauren, still three targets, no, wait, four, one more now on deck with what looks like an M16. You need him first, got that?"

"Got that."

It was a major gamble. How long did I wait before making the move? The Mac10 was no good over ten metres or so and Lauren had never fired one. If the guy on the deck started shouting to Jimmy twenty meters out I would have to use the M4 and that noise would alert whoever was on shore. Get any of it wrong and we were both as dead as Jimmy.

I lowered my voice.

"Fifty meters."

Lauren didn't reply.

The other craft killed its engines and the nose dipped into the water, sending spray into the air. They were twenty away. The guy with the dangling legs had stood and was holding a rope to secure the boats together.

M16 guy started to look uneasy.

"Ten meters."

The pilot turned the boat hard to starboard and hit reverse.

"Go! Go! Go!"

Lauren was up in a second and I heard the Mac10 splutter its first full magazine before I even got into the kneel. The guys on the deck had been almost cut in two. Swathes of blood and intestines splattered the deck area and were already running down the side of the craft. I pushed my Beretta into the nozzle of the Coke bottle and started to fire double taps in the direction of the two guys in the cabin. The bottle made aiming difficult but was a surprisingly good noise suppressor. Lauren had the second mag loaded, and thirty more devastating rounds tore into the cabin and the men inside.

Then silence. I hadn't even counted to ten.

I looked to my left and saw Lauren standing on the deck, the Mac10 smoking in her hand.

"Okay?"

She gave me a 'thumbs up' and then the sign for 'look'. She pointed at the cabin area. From her vantage point, she could see more than I could.

I heard some movement and a groan and gave Lauren the sign to wait and cover me. There was no time for finesse. I jumped from our

boat to theirs and swung my Beretta in an arc towards the pilot station.
One guy was propped against the bulkhead, He had a gun in his hand but he was in shit state and bleeding from his throat and guts. The plastic bottle did the trick again as I double-tapped him to the head. You'd do it for a dog, wouldn't you?

Rick Fuller's Story:

I lay on the cot beating myself up over falling asleep on the job. If one of my guys had ever done that I would have potted him there and then. Nevertheless I had done so and I couldn't change that. Although my sense of time was somewhat off kilter I had guessed that Lauren and Des would be joining the party quite soon. As much as I didn't want them captured, I figured that three heads would always be better than one. Especially if that one fell asleep every five minutes.
My ponderings were disturbed by the opening of my cell door and the sight I least wanted to see.
Stephan Goldsmith.
"Rick. You have no idea how surprised I am to see you again. You have led us a terrible dance as they say in England?"
I sat on the cot letting my eyes get used to the light again. Listening to the sound of his voice made my flesh crawl. Worse still, he looked okay. No doubt he'd had some attention to his wound and some pretty hefty painkillers. He leant against the cell wall. He wore casual trousers, jacket and an open neck shirt. They all looked Italian. His shoes let the whole thing down, though. Horrible beige slip-on square toe jobs. Spanish, probably from a market. Despite the crap shoes Stephan positively oozed confidence. He opened a pack of chewing gum and offered me one. I took it and asked.
"How did you find us?"
Stephan was his usual patronising self. That weird mix of accents that he and his sister possessed made for unusual nuances and sayings. He had the *shhh* of the Dutch, a definite African lilt; all mixed with Harvard All American boy.
"We never really lost your little crew, Rick, maybe for a while when you went off to Scotland to lick your wounds, but not for long. I have to hand it to you, I mean, the raid on Joel's house was a peach.

Only you would have had the crazy idea to try that one. I knew it was you in that hallway, just knew."

He knelt down and rested on his haunches against the wall. He looked at me quizzically.

"Why didn't you shoot me, Rick?"

I wanted to tear him limb from limb but stayed silent.

He shrugged as if my answer would have been unimportant.

"Then your little friend Lauren went and threw her hairbrush in a skip nearby, that ID'd her at the scene and we were totally convinced you were operational again."

He picked his nails absently.

"The visit to one of our estate agent properties was a mistake too. Your friend Desmond got tagged by one of Father's oldest friends. Edward Madden, he's MI5 you know? Father is building him a house in the Caymans. From then on we knew you would surface in Manchester again and you did."

He stood and I detected a wince of pain.

"Trouble was, 'old bean', it was the Moston boys who found you not us. They, of course, blame you totally for that awful carnage in the cemetery over there. Now, rather than come to our organisation for help, they sent their own little 'soljas' innit?"

He made a ridiculous rap movement with his right hand, but it came out more like a heavy metal salute. Then dismissively he added, "I believe you had a little luck and shot them."

Stephan broke into a smile and pushed his blond fringe to the side. There was an excitement to his voice, like a child on Christmas morning. "Then we found your little friend the Greek."

I felt a pang of sorrow.

Stephan chewed his gum and looked me in the eye. Beaming.

"Spiro Makris, the olive oil guy. You remember him, don't you, Rick? The fat untidy guy with the big family? He was a loyal friend to you, Rick. I can tell you that. For a man his age he could take a lot of pain. But then you know how I enjoy inflicting pain, don't you, Rick? He was so… difficult. Stubborn. You know? I had to kill one of his children before he gave you up."

He let his last comment hang as if waiting for the applause, then, brushed imaginary fluff from his lapels. His curt patronising tone excelled as he said, "My father and Colonel Williamson will see you for dinner in one hour. I hope you are well behaved in my father's company, Rick. The consequences could be terrible for your friends if you aren't. By the way, Susan is picking them up now."

He closed the door and darkness came. I was grateful for it.

I had to have a plan. All this bullshit was sticking in my throat. Des and Lauren would be here in the hour. Stephan had said so much. Susan had told me that Williamson wanted to talk to us all.

I wondered if they would be cuffed or hooded. I hadn't been, such was the arrogance of this private army. They were so self-important and sure of themselves that they might allow the three of us in this ridiculous bunker and not even bother to tie our hands.

More fool them.

Lauren North's Story:

"Can you steer a boat, hen?

As Des spoke we were clearing the enemy's craft of bodies and obvious signs of carnage. The four guys who had come to collect us on the boat called 'Susie Q' had been dumped into the sea and we used buckets of seawater to wash off most of the blood from the deck and sides.

"I've been to the lake at Southport if that helps," I replied, swilling more claret back into the ocean.

"Very fuckin' funny."

I held up my hand to Des.

"So long as I don't have to reverse it into a space I reckon I'll be okay. Why?"

Des studied the coastline with a pair of powerful binoculars found on Irish Eyes. I was grateful Susie Q hadn't been carrying the same kit or we'd be floating in the straits as cold as our adversaries.

"I reckon that's our welcome party on the jetty, you see?"

With the naked eye I couldn't.

"Nope."

I got back to my sloshing.

"Well I can, and I do." He put the binos to one side.

I put my hands on my hips.

"Anyway I don't need to drive Irish Eyes; she's got autopilot."

Des turned and gave me a grin. He was buzzing with excitement. I could see it. He loved every minute.

"You fuckin' beauty! Of course!"

He scratched his head and looked around him.

"How much extra fuel have we got between the two boats?"

"Dunno, Des, there were four jerry cans on Irish Eyes. What are you thinking?"

"We need to get all our stuff onto Susie Q and make sure Jimmy boy there still looks pretty good in his captain's chair. Then I want to move all the spare jerry cans into the cabin of Irish Eyes. Oh, and I'll need a map of the coastline."

The map was easy, both craft held them. Des jumped over to Jimmy's boat, held a chart up to the light and pushed buttons in the cabin. He cursed modern technology as he found the Sat Nav on Irish Eyes lacking in the common sense he required to make the boat arrive at the Jetty at exactly at the time he wanted it to.

It took him all of four minutes.

"Fucking thing!" he cursed as he hit 'enter' for the final time. Des was a man who found anything modern annoying.

It took us twenty minutes to move all the kit to Susie Q and all the juice to Irish Eyes. We were both sweating but I was knackered. My injuries from the fight with Stephan were tiring me faster than I'd hoped and I noticed the odd enquiring glance from Des.

I ignored them.

At last we let Jimmy's boat go on her way, her owner fixed firmly in his seat with fifty gallons of fuel for company.

Des set Susie Q a course just to the west of her. Close enough to make the guys on the jetty think we were being shadowed but far enough away for what we had in mind. We would hit the beach meters from the jetty, a minute before Jimmy reached home. I handled one of our M4 carbines and went through the drill of loading it and making it safe. Just like the Mac10, I'd never fired one and again it was important I got a feel for the thing. My shoulders ached and my breathing was laboured. To be honest, I felt like shit. I rooted for some more painkillers in my pocket and necked them before Des could see.

He was so preoccupied with sorting out his own kit, he never noticed. He loaded what looked like some kind of starting pistol, wrapped it in a plastic bag, and gave me a cheeky wink.

"Ye know, ye're no a bad kisser for an Englishwoman like."

God knows how, but with sweat pouring from every place you wouldn't want to, a broken nose, and a banging head, he made me feel all girly.

I countered in the only way I could under the circumstances.

"Fuck off and get on with it."

Des Cogan's Story:

I dropped over the side and the water felt good on my skin. The humidity of the night and the physical efforts of the last hour or so had me sweating. I felt refreshed, alert and ready for the task ahead. I held the plastic bag with the flare gun and my Beretta in my right hand as I swam gently in the direction of the jetty.

I could see a white four by four parked at the ocean's edge and two figures standing on the wooden structure looking out to sea.

To my right I could just about make out Irish Eyes burbling away on her exact heading.

The trap was set. All I needed was the prey to walk into it.

The tide was stronger than I had anticipated and I was breathing hard by the time I reached my point. With just my head protruding from the water and the moon doing her job, I could clearly see the two figures on the jetty.

There was a big muscular guy dressed in a dark suit. He held a machine pistol in his right hand and smoked with his left. The second figure was female and I had little difficulty in spotting who she was.

Susan Davies paced the wooden pier and spoke quickly into her mobile phone. The breeze didn't allow me to hear all her conversation, but she wasn't happy. I gathered it revolved around the fact that Jimmy hadn't called in and they were all feeling a little nervous.

As Irish Eyes cut a spectacular dash through the last few meters of black rolling sea, Susan ended her call. I heard the revs drop on the boat and reverse engage. The craft really did what she was supposed to do and I moved myself to a depth where my feet could find bottom and I didn't need to tread water.

Before the boat touched the jetty, the big guy jumped aboard, waving his gun around like a manic extra in some Rambo movie. I pulled the flare gun from the bag and checked the safety. This was a one shot deal. There was no margin for error.

Then the player started shouting to his boss. He'd found Jimmy and was waving for her to come aboard and look for herself.

Susan wasn't so certain. She pulled a handgun of her own and scrutinized the sea left and right. I was sure she looked directly at me but I told myself she couldn't possibly see.

Even in the cooling water I felt sweat on my brow.

Finally she joined the hulk and jumped aboard, walking across the deck toward the cabin.

I drove my feet into the sand beneath me, spreading my legs as wide as I dared for stability. Then, holding the flare-gun in both hands I made another triangle with my arms and took aim.

I'd fired flares before, but that had been straight up in the air. I knew that the cartridge would lose some height and aimed at the big guy, a head shot.

The thing went off like a cannon. It jerked in my hand and skewed off left of the target. I could see its trajectory as it fizzed through the night. For one horrible moment I thought I'd fucked up and missed. Susan turned toward the noise and light. Her face was lit by the ferocious canister. I could see the surprise in her expression, and at that moment, I knew her face, along with the many before her, would stay with me all my life.

The flare struck the edge of the canopy covering the steering gear. It tumbled into the seating area where Jimmy was strapped to his chair, and where Lauren and I had placed the spare fuel cans.

It may only have been a split second, but it felt like an age before the first of the jerry cans ignited. The guy in the suit took the full force of the first explosion. He was blown backwards, screaming in agony. His massive frame lolled backwards over the stern of the boat as he waved his arms helplessly against the all-consuming fire.

Then I saw Susan.

She looked confused by the whole scenario, as if it wasn't really happening to her. The left leg of her jeans were smouldering. She looked downward and patted them quizzically. Then, I swear she looked out to sea and, this time, straight into my eyes.

The next of the fuel cans ignited with a deep 'woomph' sound. There was a massive fireball which illuminated the night sky and framed my white shoulders in the flashing sea.

Susan's clothes and hair were instantly ablaze. Like some bizarre scarecrow set alight to rid the ocean of unwanted gulls, she stood rooted to the deck. Somehow she managed to raise her weapon in my general direction. I was in a spotlight of my own making. She even fired a couple of rounds.

I lifted my feet, allowed the dark sea to swirl around my chest and watched as she was consumed by the fire.

It was an age before she fell.

She never made a sound.

Lauren North's Story:

Des waded from the water as I dragged myself toward the four by four. We had planned on a driver, a hostage we might take, to point us in the direction of 'The Centre,' but there was none. The Cruiser was illuminated by the burning wreck that had been Irish Eyes, and stood immobile and probably useless. I was completely knackered from the effort of carrying all the kit from Suzie Q. The two carbines, three SLPs, grenades and ammunition were around the weight of a small adult and I wasn't feeling my best.

I fell to my knees the last few feet, blowing like a marathon runner at the tape. Des stood at the vehicle and gave me a worried look.

"Get some fluids inside ye, hen, before ye keel over."

He strode straight to the driver's door, looked toward the ignition and gave me a 'thumbs up'. We had keys at least, so we were in business. Susan had given us a chance.

I made it to my feet, yanked at the rear door, dumped everything on the seat and clambered into the front next to Des. I was sucking in as much air as I could and my muscles were complaining, so I did as instructed and found a water bottle and drank greedily.

I poured the last third of the bottle over my head and looked at Des who was playing with the Cruiser's Sat Nav. The chilled liquid ran down my spine and it felt fine against my steaming skin.

I heard sirens in the distance and my whole body felt suddenly alive again. Adrenaline was a marvellous friend. I scanned the horizon for tell-tale blue lights. The explosions had not gone unnoticed and we were about to have company.

Des finished tapping away at the Sat Nav.

"There you go."

He'd found exactly what he was looking for. The Cruiser was about to finish the job Irish Eyes had started and take us all the way to 'The Centre'. The previous driver of the car had saved the location we needed in the memory of the device and even named it for us. I looked Des in the eye, we were riding our luck and we knew it, but sheer desire to get to Rick and finish the job drove us on.

I tapped the dashboard.

"The wonders of modern technology, mate."

Des fired the car into life and we were on the move, headed up the Rock and away from the blazing wreckage.

I clambered over the seats and organised the weapons for our final battle.

Rick Fuller's Story:

The door of my cell opened and I shielded my eyes. Two obviously sorted-looking faces I hadn't seen before stepped in and stood against opposite walls whilst I made it to my feet. Both guys carried side arms but looked straight ahead and didn't acknowledge my existence.

Stephan made his entrance, looking a little pale.

"Colonel Williamson will see you now, Richard." He threw clothes on my cot that the doctor had previously taken from me. They had obviously been screened and my captors were happy enough to let me have them back. I took my time dressing until Stephan chimed in with, "Don't keep the boss waiting, fuck-wit."

I took the hint and followed the prick out into the corridor. He'd changed his own clothes and it stuck in my throat to admire his new Duck and Cover polo shirt.

I noticed a slight limp as he walked in front of me and the two heavies stuck close. I hoped it was fuckin' painful.

The bunker was larger than I thought and it took several minutes to arrive at my destination.

Finally, I was ushered into a fine office. Oak panels and classic furnishings held my attention. A mahogany desk was set with five matching Spanish antique chairs.

Des and Lauren were worryingly still missing, so I sat alone whilst Goldsmith and Williamson sat opposite. Both were the picture of calm only billions of dollars could attain.

The two suits stood off to my left, arms folded. Stephan took a more senior position behind his father and looked smug.

Goldsmith was how I remembered him from that night in Hereford, all CIA black suit and posh attaché case. Williamson was dressed in full army fatigues and caught me cold.

"Richard Edward Fuller."

He let each name fall from his tongue, flat, equal, with no value or worth.

The disdain in his voice was as culpable as the forced smile on his craggy face.

Years of military training took hold of me and I became aware that I'd stiffened and sat just that bit straighter in my seat. I felt like a squaddie about to be bollocked for some parade ground misdemeanour.

Williamson kept the pretence of a smile but I could see his anger behind it. Then I noticed a strange look, a look in his eyes that gave me strength. There was weakness there, I could almost taste it. Something was wrong.

"Do you remember me, Fuller?"

I didn't speak.

"I remember you well. Not a bad soldier, as I recall."

I stared straight into his face. A drinker's face if I ever saw one. Red veins drew complicated maps on his cheeks, forced to the surface by copious bottles of claret and port consumed in the officers' mess.

"You have caused a lot of trouble these past weeks, Fuller." He twisted in his chair, found a brandy decanter and glass and poured himself a generous measure.

The first gulp appeared to revive him and he strengthened some.

"Do you like our little headquarters, Fuller? You know the beauty of this place is that the MOD paid for half of the cost of the restoration believing it to be a working military museum. We actually open to the public in a month."

He gave a low chuckle which turned into a smokers cough. When he recovered from his own irony his mood changed.

"Quite frankly, this is where it ends for you, Fuller. Not just for you of course, but for your two colleagues who will be here shortly. They must pay too."

The second swig flushed his face further and he placed the glass on the table a little too heavily for a sober man.

"We thought we'd disposed of you ten years ago but the Irish missed you and took out that very pretty wife of yours."

He examined my face and his smile broadened, I felt my hackles rise.

"That's what this is all about isn't it, Fuller? That young woman?"

He shook his head in total disbelief.

"You see the problem with people like you, is you don't see the bigger picture. We have a business here worth millions of pounds a year. It stretches from Scotland to Morocco, employs close on a thousand people in sixteen countries."

He found the decanter and poured as he spoke.

"You could have been one of those fortunate people working for us. Instead you chose the scum of the earth, common drug dealers and murderers."

I couldn't help myself.

"Can't you see that you are no better? You kill, maim, torture and make money from drugs yourself. You ordered the hit on me because I saw you two at the DLB. Because you thought you might fall at the first hurdle and your little empire would tumble."

The two men looked at each other and it was obvious I'd told them something they knew nothing about.

Goldsmith spoke for the first time. He had a small voice but I could hear Susan and Stephan in it. That strange mix of accents was ever-present.

"We gave the position of your home to an informant. A man who provided us with the location of the cocaine you and your team stole. It was always going to be part of the deal."

I couldn't hide the venom in my voice.

"An informant! So it was that young kid McGovern, the one who got nicked by the RUC, the murdering fucker!"

One of the suits nervously went for his sidearm, but Williamson waved his hand at him and it was holstered immediately.

The Colonel took over the conversation.

"That 'murdering fucker' as you so callously call him, is not the young boy McGovern. He is, however, a respected member of the Northern Ireland Assembly, and a key player in the peace process." He poured yet another brandy. "He is also firmly on our payroll and will remain so for many years to come and as you won't survive this day, I see little point in indulging you with his name."

He raised his glass and another mouthful disappeared. He sneered at me.

"Do you have nine lives, Fuller? Like a cat? First the Irish missed you, and then you turn up in Amsterdam messing about in our business. Stephan here even put a gun in that foul mouth of yours and you are still here to annoy me. Sticking your nose in where it isn't wanted."

I stood up and the boys in suits both drew on me. I didn't give a fuck. I didn't care if they shot me, I needed to know that name; the name of the man who shot Cathy.

I leaned against the French-polished wooden top of the table. My face inches from Williamson's. Every sinew in me was on fire. I wanted to tear him apart.

"Give me the name and fuckin' kill me. Kill me any way you want, you bastard, I really don't care, but give me that name. I'll see the evil swine in hell and get my revenge there."

Lauren North's Story:

Des pulled the car over about twenty yards from what looked like a solitary door set into an arch of concrete. A single reddish light illuminated the entrance.

"That's the gaff," he said flatly, and slammed the gearstick forward into first. "There's no time to fuck about." He looked into my face, his hair still wet from the sea. There was a trace of a smile, "You got everything you need, babe?"

"No!" I said. "Wait! I want to know where you got the idea for the Coke bottle silencer."

He smiled, nodded and he revved the engine hard.

"Harry Bosch!"

"Who?"

"I like detective novels."

Then he let go of the clutch and with a beaming grin he shouted, "Brace yersel, Sheila," and the Cruiser lurched forward toward the metal door at full speed.

I pushed my feet hard into the foot-well as the car destroyed all in its wake.

I was still thrown forward against my seatbelt, knocking the wind out of me. The massive impact drove the metal door into its opening in a cloud of dust and debris. The engine screamed and Des forced the vehicle into reverse. The gearbox complained with a long painful howl before engaging and we flew backward from the gaping hole. One of the car's headlights had miraculously survived and through the dust and carnage I could make out a tiled entrance hall.

Des jumped from the cruiser, the sheer weight of the weapons he carried forcing him to lean into his first stride toward our target. Two SLPs and spare mags, an M4 Carbine with six fragmentation grenades for company and the trusty Mac10.

As I dropped in behind him I checked the safety of my own M4. This was the reason we came. It was always going to end this way and I'd known it for weeks.

My nose didn't hurt anymore, neither did my ribs, and if Stephan Goldsmith was inside this rock I was determined to finish what I'd started.

Rick Fuller's Story:

Williamson opened his mouth to speak but there was a dull shudder that rattled through the room and forced all three men to look toward each other in some puzzlement. Twenty seconds of silence were broken by the shock of an explosion that sounded much closer. Everyone in the room seemed frozen as the seconds ticked by. A second explosion, definitely a grenade of some kind then rocked the room, and screams cut through the sound of falling masonry from down the corridor.

The two suits sprinted toward the obvious mayhem, leaving me in the opulent company of Williamson and father and son. Then I heard automatic gunfire. Short controlled bursts of it.

My spirits rose. Des, it had to be Des and Lauren.

Goldsmith Snr. was white as a ghost.

Stephan was totally calm. He drew his own gun and produced that sick smile of his. As he strode confidently toward the open door and what was obviously a raging gun battle, he spoke; the words were to his father, but he looked me in the eye. "Keep him here. When this is over I want to kill this fucker slowly."

He turned for the exit and I took my chance.

Stephan was halfway through the door when I launched myself from my seat and drove my left shoulder into his hip. I knew he had damage around the groin area and the impact would cause him severe pain. He fell against the wall and I heard him cry out. More importantly I had gripped his wrist and held onto his gun hand with grim determination. He squeezed the trigger, sending a stray round into the ceiling, and screamed abuse at me in what I figured was Dutch. There was more movement from behind me as the two older and slower men attempted to join the fray. I smashed my elbow into Stephan's face and there was a satisfying crack as it landed. I sensed his body strength dip for a second and I made a grab for the SLP. He was a strong fucker, though, and within a breath he had fought through his pain and grabbed my own arm, causing the gun to wave wildly around the room.

There was another explosion, another grenade and more screams of agony.

This time it was very close and I heard two different reports following it. Two fighters were coming my way.

It gave me hope.

I saw panic in Stephan and he pulled the trigger again. Another wayward bullet flew harmlessly over my shoulder.

Then, amidst the chaos, somewhere behind me I heard a body fall. In that moment everything changed.

Des Cogan's Story:

I stepped into a tiled hallway that had an old-fashioned lift shaft and a staircase leading downwards into the depths of the rock. Lauren was close behind and I pointed toward the swing doors, for her to cover them. She dropped into a crouch to my left and brought up the M4 into her shoulder.

I loaded a fragmentation grenade under the barrel of my carbine, poked it downward through the concertina style gates of the lift and let it go. The car was some thirty feet below our level. Even so the ferocity of the blast surprised me. The dust was thick but I saw the drive cabling swinging loose through it, my intended task was completed. Now there was only one way in and out of the place. There is no safe way to attack a stairwell, it's marginally better going down one than fighting up in my opinion, but very marginal. We had no time to lose and I kicked open the fire door before we leapfrogged each other landing by landing, covering each other as best we could.

Ten steps or so before the bottom, the first of our enemy started their own journey upward.

Lauren had the point and the guy had no chance as she poured four rounds into his chest. He fell half in, half out of the doorway, propping it open with his immobile torso. It gave me a sight of our next battleground so I launched another grenade through the gap. The flash of the launcher forced me to close my eyes, but the explosive device was true and rattled down the corridor and I heard screams as it detonated.

I trod over the first guy's body and took a look-see. Lauren was just behind me her body pressed hard against the wall of the tiny landing, breathing hard through her mouth, her carbine covering over my head.

There was a long tiled corridor with small rooms dotted either side that looked like old military hospital treatment quarters. The grenade had torn away some of the green tiles from the walls and had also made a mess of two other guys who lay obviously dead some ten feet in front of me.

I gave Lauren a signal and she skipped past with her weapon in her shoulder. I noticed she had attached a grenade to the M4.

We started to clear each room in turn as best we could whilst keeping an eye on the locked door at the end of the corridor. Death could come from any opening at any second.

We took three rooms before the obvious happened. The end door flew open and the next wave of defenders burst into view.

This time three men in suits sprayed us with MP5s set to fully automatic. We darted left into one of the medical quarters, pinned down by the sheer volume of fire. The three men were sorted enough to fight their way about twenty feet into the corridor and get some cover in the doorways leading off. We were close to helpless in a doorway of our own as 9mm rounds bounced around us, only stopping when they found a soft surface to bury themselves.

Luckily they didn't find their targets and we started to return fire in short bursts, Lauren prone and me in the kneel. I'd hit one guy with my first shots when I heard Lauren shout "stoppage."

I was almost deaf from the fight but I could hear enough to know she was struggling to clear and reload the carbine.

The two remaining guys were laying down rounds like they had a munitions factory attached to their belts and I was forced into cover and unable to see if they were moving closer as they fired. We were in the shit and needed to split up. We needed to give them two targets to aim at.

Lauren threw her broken carbine to the floor in anger and drew her SLP. Then, in act of incredible bravery, she rolled across the open corridor to the room opposite, firing as she went.

This move prompted a hail of gunfire in her direction and I swivelled my head just in time to see her find her feet across the way and give me a 'thumbs up'.

I fumbled for another fragmentation grenade, loaded it, and aimed it on an angle at the wall opposite. It ricocheted down the tiles and there were shouts from the boys in suits to take cover.

The explosion rocked the floor as once again we stepped into the open. One guy had taken the full force of the grenade and his guts were spilled everywhere but the second was functioning just fine. Lauren double tapped him to the chest and he fell backwards against a doorframe, eyes wide and unseeing.

Rick Fuller's Story:

Stephan let out a sound I had rarely heard from a human being before. I'd heard it in the Sudan after a massacre of women and children and in Bosnia in my early days of service when ethnic cleansing was rife. It was the sound of total grief and despair. A low moan that turned into a bellowing cry, followed by hacking sobs. All his strength was gone.

I stripped the SLP from his hand with ease, stood and turned.

His father lay flat on his back; a single bullet had pierced his left eye and killed him instantly.

Williamson stood beside him, open-mouthed and unsteady on his feet. There was a lull in the fighting down the corridor. All seemed uncannily quiet.

"Richard," Williamson said, his tone hushed, calm and officer-like, a hint of weakness and pleading in his voice. "Can we?"

He held out his palms to gesture me to sit with him. I just couldn't believe his nerve. He had the fuckin' face to plead with me? "Please, let's sit down and talk."

There was a tremor in there, inside his guts, that made his voice shake. It may have taken ten years, but finally he knew how Cathy must have felt that morning when she saw the gunman at the gate; the realisation that you have no control over life and death.

I brought up the SLP and shot Colonel Charles Williamson in the head. He fell silently until he hit the carpeted floor and his last breath was forced from him.

Lauren North's Story:

We stepped over our latest casualties. Des pushed the door aside with his hand and poked the carbine through into a well-lit and plush office area. All was eerily quiet.

We moved inside and pointed our weapons at an empty space. I wiped my face of sweat and grime. There was a metallic click which made me jump and swing round towards it. Two men in white coats stepped from a door to our left with their hands up in surrender.

We hadn't planned on prisoners and I looked to Des for some guidance.

He didn't wait for me and started to bark at the two guys.

"Get on the floor now! Hands on your heads! Do it now! Do it now!"
A single shot rang out from somewhere further into the rock and
stopped him in his tracks.
We looked at each other for a couple of seconds and I felt a trickle of
sweat find its way down my back. I said a silent prayer for Rick.
"Cover these two fuckers, love," he hissed. "I'm gonna finish this."

Des Cogan's Story:

I sprinted down the carpeted corridor reloading the M4 as I went; all
idea of tactics out the window. I had a straight run with the corridor
deserted and finally I came to a panelled door. I could hear crying
behind it.
"Rick! Rick!" I shouted; the carbine trained on the opening.
I saw the handle turn and the door slowly opened. I slipped off the
safety until a very familiar voice greeted me.
"You took your time, you Scottish twat."

Rick Fuller's Story:

Des stepped into the room and glanced at the bodies of Williamson
and Goldsmith but made no comment. He found himself a seat,
tossed his carbine onto the polished desk and pulled out his dreadful
pipe.
He glanced over at me and pointed with the evil smelling instrument.
"Dinnae say a fuckin' word, pal, I've saved yer Cockney arse again
and I'm havin' a smoke."
Stephan sat blabbering in one of the fine office chairs, pleading with
me to kill him.
I raised my gun and pointed at his head. One squeeze of the trigger
and it would be all over; but I needed that name and Stephan
Goldsmith was the only man left alive that could tell me.
Then I heard the padding of feet from the corridor and Lauren
stepped into the room.
"I think we have a problem, guys."

We did indeed have a problem.
The centre had been sealed off by a British Police tactical firearms
unit. Even if we'd had the ammunition there was no way we would

have attempted to fight our way out. With no hope of escape we surrendered.

We were unceremoniously handcuffed, cautioned and dragged out into the Gibraltar night.

After four uneventful hours in police cells we were bussed to the Gib airstrip and flown by military aircraft to Farnborough.

We arrived just as daylight broke and were met on the tarmac by the men in suits.

We were separated so I can't say exactly what happened to Des and Lauren, but I figured it must have been a similar experience.

A four day MI5 de-brief is an unpleasant experience, I can tell you.

Our only plan was to remain silent and I knew the team would do just that.

On the fifth day a very plain-looking woman came to my cell holding a package. I opened it and found it contained clothing. I dressed in a terrible suit and waited for something to happen. Finally a musclebound youth escorted me into the daylight and I was driven in convoy to the City of London by silent unsmiling agents.

An hour later we stopped in Canary Wharf and I was led to a very expensive and secure office.

Once seated inside I was delighted to see my two compatriots had not come to any harm other than the same terrible clothing choices of the British Secret Service. Lauren had two lovely black eyes from her fight with Stephan but she had been given cheap sunglasses to hide her injuries.

We looked like three naughty schoolkids in the headmaster's office.

Across a massive desk sat three men.

Sir Malcolm Harris, the head of MI5, Anthony Cyril Thomson, Home Secretary and a man in dark Ray-Bans who had to be CIA.

Sir Malcolm was the first to speak.

"Richard, Desmond, Lauren, would you like some tea?"

Des chirped up. "Aye, I'll have a brew, I'm gasping."

Sir Malcolm waved at some minion who scuttled off to find a kettle.

He opened a file, peered down briefly and then turned his attention to me.

He was a classically handsome fifty-something, Harrow-educated ponce.

"Stephan Goldsmith has been a very reliable and informative witness, Richard."

He looked down his nose.

"Unlike you and your colleagues here."

He pretended to check a sheaf of papers in front of him.

"On the contrary, you have been a very bad chap these last few years, Mr. Fuller. One of a million questions I ask myself is why would a soldier of your standing work for such a low life as Joel Davies?"

He looked up and waited for a reply. When he was sure he'd get none he went on.

"We understand that you are in possession of a number of hard drives stolen from the Davies residence in what can only be described as a bloodbath?"

He removed his gold-rimmed glasses and peered at me with watery blue eyes.

"I don't suppose you would care to tell us where those particular pieces of equipment might be, Richard?"

I shuffled in my seat.

"Ask Stephan Goldsmith."

Sir Malcolm looked sheepish.

"Mr. Goldsmith hanged himself yesterday morning."

I felt a pang of pleasure.

More silence greeted our three inquisitors.

Sir Malcolm continued, his voice sounded tired, lethargic.

"Are you going to speak, Richard?"

I couldn't cope with the bollocks any longer.

"Look, sir, you know as well as I do by now, that Gerry Goldsmith Jnr, an ex-colleague of your CIA friend to your left and the 'most respected' Colonel Charles Williamson have been making millions out of drug running for years. Not only that, they have done it under the noses of the British and American Secret Service for all that time."

I crossed my legs and felt a bit more at ease.

"I'd say that a thing like that must be very embarrassing to you all. Now, if it were not for those bits of computer hardware you so desperately require, our little team here would either be floating in the Straits as dead as dodos, or locked in some high security nick awaiting trial. I presume the reason that neither of those scenarios has come about is that you are worried that the information on those drives would be a great embarrassment to Her Majesty's Government. That, or you have other plans for us."

The Home Secretary whispered into Sir Malcolm's ear and he nodded.

"Both, Richard; of course we would like to examine those drives. They are a matter of National Security and you realise how important that is to us?"

He leaned forward, elbows on desk. Here was the punchline.

"And we do have a proposition for you, Richard." He sat back in his chair and fiddled with a John Lobb tie which I liked very much. There was more than a hint of derision in his voice.

"It's a dirty little job so it should suit the three of you down to the ground. Complete it, and you will be free of any charges against you and handsomely paid."

I nearly fell off my chair when Lauren spoke.

"How much?"

Sir Malcolm raised his impressive brows.

"I beg your pardon, young lady?"

"Well, I want to know what kind of fee you have in mind. I mean, Rick's right, if you could find those drives we'd be dead meat, now you want us to do 'dirty' jobs for you. I for one don't trust a word out of your upper-class mouth." Lauren pointed at the Home Sec. "I don't trust him either, I remember when he was Health Secretary and he shafted the nurses. Said he'd give them a pay rise but never came good. I'm with Rick on this one. You're terrified that this nonsense will get out and want to buy us off. Well I don't think we need you ponces to earn a living, I think we could do that on our own."

Des gave out a low chuckle and felt for his pipe but it had been confiscated along with everything else. His broad Scottish accent cut the atmosphere in the room like a blade.

"Who is it? Who de ye want slotted?"

Sir Malcolm coughed into his hand and once again consulted the Home Sec. Finally he answered.

"O'Donnell, Patrick O'Donnell."

Des whistled through his teeth. "The First fuckin' Minister of the Northern Ireland Assembly. Fuck me, sir, and pardon my French like, but I hope you've got deep pockets."

Sir Malcolm once again turned in my direction.

"You have a vested interest in this one, Richard. Patrick O'Donnell is the man you stole the cocaine from all those years ago. It was his house you entered. I'm sure you remember how easy the job was. He even left the key, I recall."

I rubbed my face with my hands and felt nervousness in my stomach that I couldn't fathom. O'Donnell? It couldn't be, he couldn't inform on his own family could he?"

"How much? That's all that matters."

The Home Secretary spoke for the first time. "Two hundred and fifty thousand a head paid any way you want."

I was about to nod when he added.

"By the way, Fuller, O'Donnell, you're right. He was the informant, the man who shot your wife."

Game on.

End

Look out for the second novel in the Rick Fuller trilogy… THE FIRE

19174704R00198

Printed in Great Britain
by Amazon